D1432798

No Time
for an
Everyday
Woman

No Time for an Everyday Woman

Wenda
Wardell
Morrone

St. Martin's Press
New York

A THOMAS DUNNE BOOK.
An imprint of St. Martin's Press.

NO TIME FOR AN EVERYDAY WOMAN. Copyright © 1997 by Wenda
Wardell Morrone. All rights reserved. Printed in the United States
of America. No part of this book may be used or reproduced in
any manner whatsoever without written permission except in the
case of brief quotations embodied in critical articles or reviews. For
information, address St. Martin's Press, 175 Fifth Avenue, New
York, N.Y. 10010.

Design by Nancy Resnick

Library of Congress Cataloging-in-Publication Data

Morrone, Wenda Wardell.
    No time for an everyday woman / Wenda Wardell Mor-
rone.—1st ed.
        p.   cm.
    "A Thomas Dunne book."
    ISBN 0-312-15615-4
    I. Title.
    PS3563.O874973N6   1997
    813'.54—dc21   97-6270
                                                      CIP

First Edition: July 1997

10 9 8 7 6 5 4 3 2 1

No Time
for an
Everyday
Woman

Chapter One

When the phone rang late Friday afternoon, Claud Willetts let out all his breath in an enormous sigh and waved to his nephew to answer.

He felt like he'd been holding his breath all day every day that August, waiting for Barney's call at sunset. It wasn't logical. If something happened, it would happen earlier in the day; Barney's calls were basically announcements of nothing at all. But Claud had learned long ago that logic and truth weren't necessarily connected; the people who thought they were, were usually the easiest to fool.

Across the room, Stan said, "You have reached the Secret Security Forces of America. If you are calling to report a murder—"

But it wasn't Barney's voice that came into the room. "Tell your uncle it's me, Stan. I know he's there."

As if he didn't know. The Reverend Abigail Butterfield used a phone as if it was up on the last row of the balcony.

Claud held his receiver a safe distance away. "Something I can do for you, Reverend?"

"Claud, I need help. Tonight is the All-Boards Harvest Supper—"

"I always liked that idea, Reverend. At least deacons and trustees start the fall on speaking terms."

"—and Shari Finley was supposed to help out with the board members' kids, but she hasn't shown up."

"You want me to come down and do some card tricks."

"Could you? Domenica Gaylord is bringing over some spare yarn to teach the kids how to make God's eyes. But she doesn't think she can cope with the Neiderhoffer twins by herself."

He would have liked to oblige, entertaining kids being one of the more respectable things he did with cards in Merciful Valley, Montana, though Abby was obviously after his ability to maintain order.

He always denied that he had once dangled a mischief-maker from the steeple of the Bitterroot Congregational Church. But kids would look up at the narrow spire—past the peeling paint, the slats that hid the organ pipes, the cap of shingles, to the cross—and back again to Claud, a sloppily big man, the shoulders and chest of the tackle he had been twenty-five years ago still more impressive than his belly, though not by much. And—except for the Neiderhoffer twins—the kids pretty much did what they were told.

"But not tonight, Abby."

"I know about your Tuesday game, Claud. Is this a new one?"

"Who told you about my Tuesday game?" Claud rolled accusing eyes toward his nephew, arms and legs wound around his chair, his bony adolescent face as usual hovering somewhere between Lincoln and the village idiot. Stan tried to shrink.

"Don't blame Stan," Abby said, as if she was in the room watching. "Everybody knows about your Tuesday game."

Everybody knew, too, that it had begun with penny-pitch

in the high-school parking lot, a ritual Claud had starte
support another ritual he enjoyed: eating regularly. As
boys became men, went into their fathers' businesses or
started their own, the game had moved to the back right-
hand booth of Duncan's Café, downstairs.

Claud still used the back booth, but he relied now on a
game of increasingly higher stakes that moved from Tuesday
to Tuesday around the state, wherever a roomful of heavy-
enough hitters could be gathered to try their skills, comparing notes afterward with mixed pride and regret over who
had been the biggest loser to the big backcountry man with
the old Chevy truck called the Big Red Machine.

Claud nurtured his image: To be somebody a man could
brag about losing to was half the game. Not a hillbilly or a
cowboy, he would explain: a *toolie* from the Coulees—the
crosshatched hills and gullies west of Demersville where he
had grown up. Where he still lived, in the log cabin built by
his grandfather. It was even true.

"The Tuesday game is your best con job, at least that I've
heard about," Abby said with dangerous insight. "I can't
imagine how you talked people into it. Unless Senator Colman—"

"We'll leave Bandit out of this."

She ignored him. "I suppose on Fridays you fleece
tourists?"

"Always a treat to see men out of their usual zip codes,"
Claud said agreeably. "Especially when they're wearing plain
old jeans and Timberlands. It's as good as a poker game,
watching them find ways to tell each other how much money
they have: I see your Range Rover and raise you my kid's SAT
scores and my wife's breast implants."

"That's what I said, you're shopping for your next victims.
You can't toy with people's lives like that, Claud."

"Here in Merciful Valley, Reverend? Want to bet?"

Surely she would hang up. But when Abby wanted some-

3

thing, her stubbornness was biblical. "If not you, is Stan free?"

Claud took his time saying no. "If it weren't for Domenica—"

Stan tried to strike a pose suitable for a sex object and knocked over a stack of magazines.

"He'll be perfectly safe in the Parish Hall," Abby said in a tone that, in another woman, he would have called sarcastic. "Besides, she doesn't pick on teenagers."

"As if a man's age meant a lick to her."

"You have an answer for everything, don't you, Claud? Can you at least stop by Shari's cabin on your way? Check to be sure the baby's not there alone?"

The other line rang and Stan picked up. "You have reached the Secret Security Forces of America. If you are calling to report a murder—"

Hoping Abby hadn't heard, Claud said quick and loud, "I'll do that little thing, Reverend."

Montana's junior senator was the last to board the flight from Minneapolis to Billings. To Lorelei Muldoon, watching from a window seat in the front row, he seemed to bring with him the hectic energy of a campaign stop. Before she could even shift her papers and laptop from the seat beside her, he had brushed by and gone on to the coach section to ask who was from his home state.

"You understand, I owe them most of my time," he said to the cabin at large, baring his teeth in a grin.

The passengers basked in the glow. Colman could do that: make a person—a planeful of people—feel, briefly, very important. Fred Roybal Colman's coarse black hair was thick as it had been a quarter century ago, when he was a halfback at Missoula and his habit of squirting between linemen to steal yardage had won him the tag Bandit—that and his pirate's profile. A pro career was never an option (the choice then being Vietnam or law school), but the nickname stuck.

Lorelei Muldoon listened to Colman work the cabin as the plane prepared for takeoff, noting the problems of fellow travelers who were also constituents: "I'll tell my chief of staff to get right on this." (He meant it, too; she had seen him in action the previous summer.) Colman encouraged nonresidents to do business in Montana, though not to move there. Not a whisper of the real reason he was spending a week at home.

"Would you move your papers from one-B, please?"

Before Lorelei could gather herself, the first-class flight attendant repeated with a nanny's barely patient edge, "Would you please move your papers from one-B?"

"I'm sorry, it's taken."

"Excuse me?"

It had been Fred's idea that she buy both their tickets. While she rummaged in her buckskin pocketbook-cum-briefcase for the boarding passes, First Class crouched down. Perhaps she thought eye contact was persuasive.

"You see, this little boy just boarded, he's flying all by himself to Seattle to meet his daddy. We thought if he could see the cockpit—one-B is right on the aisle, and you could look after him, kids feel more comfortable that way—"

She had spent this much time and effort to look like a babysitter?

From behind, Fred Colman slid a helpful hand under First Class's elbow, easing her up to her feet. "There's a spare seat over by me, darlin'," he said, smiling down. "Park him there."

First Class didn't sound at all like a nanny as she followed Fred back, settling him two rows behind and across the aisle, the Seattle-bound boy beside him, while Lorelei watched, bewildered.

"I know you're not a native," Fred said, rumbling the way he did to Lorelei sometimes, side by side on a restaurant

5

banquette. "I wouldn't forget a constituent as pretty as you."

"Now, Senator Colman."

"What's this Senator stuff? Bandit."

"Bandit." First Class smiled. *Smile* was a mild word for it. Most people didn't have that many molars.

Sheer spite: He hadn't told her he was making a separate reservation for himself. Worse: His gaze had passed over her without a twitch of recognition.

He had warned her that he didn't want his wife to find out about this trip. Maybe that meant byzantine travel plans.

Even though, in New York, every bit of their time together had been public? Popular restaurants, theater, romantic walks—he hadn't even dodged cameras. Lorelei dug in her bag—successfully this time—for the head shot from *Sloane's Magazine* the previous week. In black and white that made the most of his hawk nose and his hair, Bandit Colman gazed with every sign of adoration at an unnamed companion.

It was a faithful likeness of the companion too, she thought with a sigh: a shock of bronze hair and a thin face, noteworthy only for the carefully painted eyes. Her father, Hank, said cameras never did her justice; they couldn't catch the way her face lit up like a kid splitting open an Oreo whenever she discovered something.

Fathers weren't always as comforting as they thought they were. Lorelei put the picture back and flipped open her laptop.

Ordinarily statistics hypnotized her: Focus on the green and white stripes of a spreadsheet, and patterns of numbers quickly loomed like the big *E* on an eye chart. Anywhere. Sitting at her swooping Formica desk, faithfully copied from *Pillow Talk*; in austere gray flannel in a client's office, trying to look taller and older than her years; pulling together data at hyperspeed to feed a speaker at a conference. On a plane. Especially on a plane.

This afternoon, though, she couldn't shut out the murmurs

and giggles behind her. Most flight attendants looked strained from long hours of unfailing cheerfulness while running their legs off; First Class's big, slow-moving blondness was a throwback. A successful one. If Fred got much more explicit, they'd have to close the curtains to the galley.

When Lorelei had worked on his campaign the previous summer, Fred had treated her like a piece of office equipment.

If he liked to indulge in offhand bedazzlement of someone like First Class, why pursue Lorelei Muldoon? Turning up at her apartment door a month ago, saying he'd been obsessed with her for a whole year and couldn't hide it one day longer. Coaxing and arguing until she agreed to go away with him.

The plane landed uneventfully. Lorelei wondered if she should stay on the plane until—where? Seattle? Could they change her ticket over the pilot's intercom? But her luggage would be here. Maybe she could get a flight back to New York. She shifted to the aisle seat and waited to join the line of passengers.

From behind, Fred Colman's hand clasped her shoulder, slipping warm and unseen up under her hair to the nape of her neck. He passed on to a farewell that made First Class color, and out the door.

Frowning, watching First Class whisper to another crewman in obvious triumph, Lorelei Muldoon let the other passengers file by. Then she set her jaw, finger-combed her hair into a bronze cloud, and got off herself.

"We must replace this chintz soon, Betty."

Olga Finaldo smoothed the love seat's blurry lavender and rose fabric with the care of hands that have not always known fine things and are mindful of them.

"Also the photographs and the bibelots. Less is more today."

"You keep telling me that." Thin, sharp-featured, with a plume of brown hair and quick, restless movements that invariably made political cartoonists draw her as a bird, Betty Colman, too, ran a hand across the love seat. "To me it still seems perfect the way it is."

Across from her, a lamp on a parchment lacquer table was reflected discreetly in crystal decanters on a silver tray. Overstuffed love seats were separated by a table of etched brass. Curtains, heavy silk moiré in a difficult shade of pink shading into mauve, dragged in folds along the floor, sashed with the intricately braided tiebacks that were one of the signatures of Bahr-Finaldo, Ltd.

Olga knew well that this condominium high up in the Watergate gave Betty Colman the satisfaction other women sought in the mirror. Change carried the anxiety of a facelift.

"Naturally. One must be skillful enough to change before the need becomes apparent to others."

"Convince me."

"All in good time, my dear." Olga stood, not gracefully but with sturdy strength, as she did everything. "I wonder how much longer we should wait for Senator Colman. The dinner won't begin for an hour, but as you have so often said, the important work is best done beforehand—"

Betty arranged a silk scarf around her shoulders with unflattering jerks. "We won't worry about Fred. Did you see that picture in *Sloane's*? He must be in New York City again. He's never been this open about his women before. He's getting worse."

"Never mind, my dear. It is the Betty Colman of Betty Colman, Inc., who matters tonight, yes? The senator was merely invited for your sake."

Sloane's had once quoted Senator Colman as saying that his wife's public relations firm didn't do any harm. It still rankled.

Appeased, Betty said, "The Hispanic Cultural Institute is my biggest client so far. You'll see, when Congress gets back here to Washington after Labor Day, I can really get to work for you."

Olga Finaldo chose her words carefully. "You have already done a great deal."

She waited for Betty to lead the way to the elevator.

Fred had told and retold Lorelei to look for the access road at the left corner of the parking lot. A good thing too, there was no one in sight to ask directions of. Hoping she was right, she picked her way down a weather-beaten road.

She had tried to prepare for the trip with videos of her favorite fifties westerns. But it was one thing to curl up on her pillowy sofa and watch Alan Ladd and John Wayne cross a bare landscape the size of her television screen. In real life, bleached grass and dirt stretched in every direction but one, where the land broke over a cliff. The sky was the intense blue of a computer screen, the sun's glare a physical weight.

At last she saw the line of corrugated metal sheds Fred had described, and Fred, hauling his plane out on the tarmac. Not easily. The plane plunged at the end of the rope. He manhandled it toward a runway, silver-dollar cuff links flashing in the sun, with a grimace of concentration that would have passed for a grin in a photograph: His chief of staff would have loved it.

Colman turned, a real grin spreading. Equally photogenic. "Well, look at you!"

"Did I get it right?" she asked. "Jean Simmons in *The Big Country*."

In the dressing-room mirror, the heavy silk shirt, wide prairie skirt, and ostrich boots had looked like a costume. She had closed her eyes when she handed over her credit card; when you paid that much for something, you ought to get behind the wheel and drive it away.

"Is that a fact." He thumped their luggage into the hold. "As long as you don't expect me to be Gregory Peck."

"Who then?"

"Right now? Bandit Colman, taking my girl home."

As though he had already forgotten First Class. It was irrationally warming.

He stretched out a hand for her laptop. "This bitty thing. Didn't I tell you I rented you a big one?"

"Then this will be the dinghy that takes me out to the yacht."

At that moment she saw, really saw, his plane.

"Fred, it's no bigger than a car. On stilts!"

"The smaller the plane, the greater the feeling of flight. You can see more, too. You'll see."

When he came to her, she expected . . . what? An embrace? Instead, he guided her up the no-skid strips on the wing and down a step into the narrow cabin. Sports-car-size seats in front, even smaller in back, with scarcely enough room in between for Fred's big square briefcase: It was as cramped and rickety on the inside as it looked from the outside. A plane of one's own represented luxury. Luxury ought not to look and feel like a kite.

"Why so, um, small?"

"So I can handle it alone." He clicked his mike. "This is seven one three niner. Over."

Barely audible. Not like the movies.

The voice over the speaker was flat and penetrating, crackling with static, just like the movies. "Welcome home, Senator. Over."

"You sound new, son. What's your name? Over."

"Jim Everard, sir. Yes, sir, Senator, what can I do for you? Over."

"Call me Bandit, for starters. Is Kit on duty or have they finally canned him? Over." Colman clicked his mike off and said, "Kit's been sitting up in that tower for so many years, he knows more about us than we know about ourselves."

So they were not yet alone.

A voice with the gravel of years of tobacco and good Scotch said, "Let me get flight twenty-two sixty-three off, Bandit, and I'll get back to you. Over."

"Jim's doing just fine, Kit. How does runway twenty-seven look, Jim? Over."

"That's a negative, uh, Bandit, the wind's gusting out of the southwest at thirty-five knots. Twenty-two sixty-three is about to take off. Give her a couple of minutes, you can follow her and loop around once you're clear of the tower. Over."

"Kit turning you into a candy-ass, Jim? This little puff wouldn't even blow up a windsock. Just point me down twenty-seven and I'm halfway home. Over."

A muffled pause. "Okay, Senator, sir, I reckon you can handle it. Do you want to file your Billings-Demersville flight plan now? Over."

"No, thanks, Jim, I'll do it from the air. Three-niner Mike over and out."

Before Lorelei could ask if it was wise to overrule a traffic controller, the engine noise swelled to a din that rocked the plane on its wheels and made speech impossible. Reassuring in a way: It sounded powerful enough to pull a much bigger plane than this one down the runway, undeterred by bucketing winds, and drag it over the cliff and into the sky.

Two hundred miles to the west, high in a lodgepole pine, a small gray alarm burred. In the clearing below, a thickset man moved unhurriedly to a larger gray unit, where a red light blinked. As he and two other men watched with the relaxed concentration of an Intensive Care Unit, the light settled to a steady pulse.

"Well?" Fenton, the taller of the other two, leaned as if he could force events into fast-forward.

Mech shrugged. "He took off. You take off, you gotta turn. First sharp turn, second, she goes. A truck, brakes are the weakness. A plane, the steering."

Fenton had watched the trucks often enough. A driver stopped for coffee or gas—either was time enough for Mech to roll under and reach up to the brake line. Somewhere along the twists in the smoky southern hills, a loosened fitting would fall off, and the driver would plow off the road. The sensor would lead them right to it. Except for the time it went over an embankment, destroying the sensor along with the truck and driver. As it would in the air.

No need for his aunt to know that Colman's death took care of a problem for Ricky Fenton, too. What she didn't know wouldn't hurt either of them.

Fenton looked back at Mech, smiling peacefully at the dials as though Colman's plane was reflected there, about to nosedive. Mech, who was like the invincible rubber ball kids used for stickball, and much the same dull red. Placid Mech, who looked up at Fenton and crunched both hands together, then opened them as slowly as a magician's to show . . . nothing at all.

Billings disappeared behind them. The plane throttled down to a drone, the air like the chop of waves under a boat. Colman pulled a thick, ungainly book out of the briefcase on the rear seat, flipped open a chart, turned knobs. The radio voice dwindled into rhythmic beeps. He let go of the wheel and settled back.

"Autopilot," he said. "We stay on this heading, I don't need to fly again till we're almost there." He let out a breath in a happy sigh, looking out and away. "Lorelei, you're looking at the northwest corner of the largest wheat field God ever made."

His face had a relaxed, faraway expression she hadn't seen before. Not for her. He might have been talking to himself.

"People think carrot cake and beet cake are gourmet stuff. Truth is, cooks invented them to save wheat flour. My granny Colman used to thicken gravy with cold mashed potatoes."

He looked at her sidelong. "You're probably too busy being a whiz kid to cook."

"Not true. Give me a phone book and I can cook anything."

"See, carrots and beets will grow anyplace you turn a spade," he went on as though he hadn't heard, "and you use the whole thing. Whereas wheat is damn wasteful to grow. *And* to harvest. Until the Civil War, Lorelei, wheat flour was like gold dust."

Had he been describing wheat fields to First Class in the galley? Maybe she already knew. Maybe this lecture was reserved for tourists.

"What did the Civil War have to do with it?"

"You know what New England soil is? Rocks and more rocks. But during the war, New England farm boys came to the banks of the Mississippi and looked across and saw a field as big as . . . Well. Soil so rich they had to shoe the oxen like horses or they sank in too deep to walk. That was the real gold rush."

Lorelei looked down with new respect at flat yellow fields rumpled by the wind.

"Where's Merciful Valley?"

"Mean you can't get geography out of a phone book?"

Colman spread his big map book open on her lap, tracing a path across the page to where the altitude changed in ripples of color. He ran his finger along the darkest brown. Down her thigh.

"There, in the middle of the mountains, just past the Continental Divide. About two and a half cainsees from here."

"Cainsees?"

"You go as far as you *cain see* . . ."

His Washington persona was sliding into something earth-

13

ier. Less familiar. She didn't know how to respond.

Apparently he was comfortable with his geography lesson. "Merciful Valley is richer than wheat fields, even. Warm and mild. French trappers more or less fell into it one winter, it kept them alive. They called it *L'heureux de la chose.*"

"Heroes?"

"Happiness." He spelled it out. "But they really meant *the best.* Settlers translated it as Merciful Valley, but to me, it's what people mean when they say 'the last best place on earth.' Lakes, rivers, hunting, fishing—it's been a summer resort for a hundred years. Mining tycoons, then cattle barons—"

"Why isn't it more famous?"

"Oh, Bogwash doesn't know about it."

"Bogwash. I suppose a bogwash is like a cainsee."

He grinned. "You could say that. Means Boston on down to Washington. The East." He made it sound like other, cruder four-letter words.

"You mean like me? New Yorkers?"

"I'm not talking about separate people, darlin'. Bogwash is bureaucracy." He drawled out the syllables with a grin that changed the subject. Politicians were good at that.

Numbers whiz kids, on the other hand, thrashed out the facts. "You mean Congress? Or agencies like EPA?"

"You don't let go, do you, darlin'? Remind me to remember that. Bogwash is all of them. The Feds." The Colman jaw jutted out even further. "Meddling bastards. Fouled their own nests, now they think they can come and mess up ours. One day I'll get mad enough to tell them about the Plummer Gang."

Before she could ask, he said, "Tom Plummer was a crooked sheriff. Vigilantes caught him and hanged him."

"Without a trial?"

"We know how to handle what needs handling without outsiders."

"You mean like the militias? Do you belong to one?"

"When you don't know what you're talking about, Lorelei, keep your mouth shut!"

The comedians who took off on Fred Colman's arrogant rasp had never felt it firsthand in a small, enclosed place. It wasn't a flashy sound bite, it was a break, right through to a rage that was obviously the real man.

She waited, small and soundless as she knew how to be, while Colman struggled to get his public face back into place.

He unclenched his jaws. "A man goes into the government to change it, Lorelei, not blow it up. Senators are the bastards who keep the other bastards in line."

"You said it would go on takeoff!"

Fenton had been circling the clearing since the red light appeared, ending each lap at the gray box.

"He don't take off normal," Mech said mildly. Explanation, not excuse. "He don't bank."

"He should have gone down an hour ago. How can it burn if he flies off his gas?"

"You think he goes all the way without turning?"

Fenton tried to predict his aunt's reaction. Failure didn't trouble Olga Finaldo, or so she claimed: Failure was merely information, unpleasant, but often more useful than success in leading one to a better plan. The only impermissible failure . . . here she would shake a hypnotizing finger . . . was one that caught the attention of those in authority, legal or illegal.

Failure wasn't so simple for her nephew. If Colman reached the Merciful Valley alive, Olga would have the upper hand again, and his summer's gamble would come to nothing.

"Maybe this is better," he brooded. "With wreckage right at the airport, they might have traced us—"

"They don't trace us, Finaldo nephew."

"I told you not to call me that!"

Neither of them bothered to look at the third man, who

was hooked to a boom box by earphones. His work was connected to the big knife at his side. Whether or not they would need it again depended not on them but on the red light.

Lorelei Muldoon concentrated on the book of maps, content to let silence fill the stuffy little plane. She could trace their route easily. Hills gathered beneath them like a rug caught underfoot, the height of each one meticulously noted on the map; winding blue lines for rivers, here and there a road.

"You ever work with your dad?"

Caught by surprise, she spilled the big book onto the floor. She pulled it back into her lap. "That's like saying a kid who knows his times tables can do Boolean algebra. I call *him* sometimes if I'm stuck. Why?"

He was taken aback. "I thought you were the best. That's what Hungerford said last year when he hired you."

"If you want multivariate or conjoint analysis, I can look at a page and tell you faster than most people. Hank wants to disprove part of the theory of relativity. How do you know about him?"

"Say what?"

"Are you investigating him?"

"I like you with your feathers ruffled." He patted her hair down as though it were fur. "It was in your file. Where do you think I found your phone number? What do you mean, trying to disprove the theory of relativity?"

She shook him off. "*Part* of it. Hank thinks Einstein took a few shortcuts he shouldn't have."

"Who pays him to do that?"

"Nobody. He teaches, works at night. It's hard to get tenure if you begin every lecture by saying, 'What you learn today will be obsolete in five years,' so it's a new college every contract."

He frowned. Fred Colman grappling with an idea bigger

than he was: It might be amusing if it didn't concern Hank Muldoon.

"Think he'll do it?"

"Probably not. People do their best science before they're thirty. Thirty-five outside."

"Then what's the point?"

"Who knows the point of pure research while it's under way? A few articles in journals you never heard of? The Nobel prize? A whole new chain of discoveries? Why the interrogation, Fred?"

"And your mother? How does she take it?"

"You mean you don't have any data on her? Maybe that's because she died when I was five. Before you ask, of cancer. Add it to my file when you get back."

He made a big show of checking his instruments. Flicked a switch up, made a minuscule adjustment in the plane's direction. Flicked it down again. So he did hear. Eventually.

"I'm sorry," he said gruffly. "Must have been lonely."

Was it? She remembered mostly nights in computer labs—nights being the only time Hank ever seemed to get access to the big machines—a TV for a baby-sitter. His screen flickering with formulae, hers with *Some Like It Hot, Gentlemen Prefer Blondes, Pillow Talk*. Knives sharp enough to cut wood for $19.95. One memorable Thanksgiving morning, *King Kong* dubbed in Spanish with English subtitles.

"I had Hank." It sounded too abrupt. She added, "I watched a lot of movies."

"That's where *The Big Country* comes from."

Along with so much else. Other girls had mothers and sisters, she had Marilyn Monroe and Doris Day. Clothes in edible colors, gloves tight at the wrist, coats looped with fur. Sumptuous offices, houses, restaurants, to wear them to, powerful men to wear them with . . .

Was that Fred's appeal? Bobbing up like James Stewart in

Vertigo? No wonder she had let him coax her into this trip.

What a comforting insight, Lorelei, a thousand feet in the air and a thousand miles from nowhere.

She said quickly, "The toughest thing was not talking about my mother. Hank coached me never to say 'cancer.' People shied away as if it were leprosy."

For some reason this took him to a raw place of his own. "Like being Spanish—Hispanic—Latino—whatever the hell today's word is. When I was a kid, it was spic, and you didn't admit to it, for yourself or your mother. One kid called me Frito Bandito. We fought every day for a whole summer."

With a shrug that was close to a shudder, he sent the chart book to the floor again. "Now they make a song and dance about my heritage. Put the damn charts back in my flight bag, will you?"

Lorelei twisted and reached back, finally hitching up on her knees. "Where do they go? You don't have an inch to spare."

"I forgot, I brought work too. Just dump the big envelope out on the seat."

And quiet as can be, out of the envelope onto the seat slid a gun. An actual, three-dimensional, Sundance Kid pistol. Heavy, with a wood grip and a long blue-black barrel.

She sat down again, holding it with awe. "*This* is what took up all the space, Fred."

"Put it back, Lorelei."

"It looks like the one Alan Ladd carried in *Shane*. I had no idea they were so heavy."

"I said put it back!" His rasp would have cut through a fire siren.

How could this man be out-of-control in love with her? with anyone?

She twisted back around, fast, and sat down again, fast. "It fell out of the envelope. I wasn't snooping."

"Never pick up a gun unless you plan to point and shoot. Never. Hear me?"

"That's a roger, Fred. Can you hear me? Turn this thing around. I want to go back."

He looked over, puzzled. "A bullet could hit one of the fuel tanks, Lorelei. Of course I was upset."

"I said, take me back, Fred. Or land at the nearest airport, that's okay too."

"You're overreacting, honey—"

"The audition's over, Fred! My father isn't important enough, I'm not bright enough, and I'm obviously not docile enough! Ask your favorite flight attendant next time! Wait till she finds out you only perform in public!"

She hadn't known what she was going to say until the words blurted out. She gasped and retreated to the window.

"You're upset about the stew, Lorelei?"

"I said, take me back!"

Colman turned her to face him, clicking his tongue at her damp lashes, blotting them with a silk calico kerchief the size of a dinner napkin. "And here I've been trying to keep my hands to myself because I could see you were upset about the plane."

"I can't imagine what gave you that idea."

"Maybe that little trick you have of closing your eyes in prayer with every wind shift."

"I didn't!"

"Didn't you." His voice fell to the rumble she could feel as well as hear. "A senator is a bastard, Lorelei, remember? That's why I wanted to get away with you someplace private. Where I won't be a senator and you won't be a number cruncher."

His eyes were brilliant, the thin, predatory line of his mouth so close she could feel her own mouth shape a response.

"Lorelei, I've never taken anybody to the cabin before. I don't even let my wife go there, you know that. It's going to be our special place."

He knotted his kerchief around her neck cowboy fashion. "There. The only thing missing."

She found that she had to swallow before she could speak. "Land this thing first—" She swallowed again. "I'll think about it on the ground."

"That won't be long. We're just the other side of this ridge."

Beneath them, slab after uncompromising slab of granite broke into deep ravines. He switched off the automatic pilot, steering with one hand, the other tracing a quivering line under his kerchief on her throat.

"Where's the landing field?"

"I use a clearing below the cabin. A local gal mows it for me."

"Mows? It's not paved?"

"If you could see the size of your eyes! Nothing to worry about, I've done it for years. Like the old barnstormers."

Rocks gave way to masses of trees. Colman pointed to a narrow straw-colored line dividing two wedges of evergreen.

"That's a firebreak. The forestry service clears it so a fire can't jump over and spread. We'll follow it home."

He shifted the nose of the plane slightly. They passed a stream no bigger than a blue line from the map. Through the trees she glimpsed a lush field.

"It's so much greener than the firebreak."

He ignored her, frowning. "We'll take a pass over the cabin first so you can see what it looks like from the air."

The engine noise rose, the plane banking so sharply Lorelei blinked. The plane jarred as if the air was suddenly solid. Colman smothered a curse and jammed a foot against a floor pedal. Shuddering, the plane's turn flattened, but only a little. With a new expression of grim concentration, Colman wrestled with a wheel that refused to move. That pointed them toward the ground.

"Right flap is frozen," Colman said calmly. "Aileron. I'll

compensate with the rudder till we land. Don't worry, they drilled us on dead-stick landings all the time during training."

How many years ago? At this altitude? Over this terrain? While the plane shuddered, Colman fought to hold it level. They teetered in dangerous jerks, lower, always lower.

Colman shouted. Lorelei could only decode the word "fire-break!" before spikes of trees filled the windows and the plane shouldered its way into the ground. The world rose up to meet her left side.

Chapter
Two

*S*ounds came back before feeling. In the silence, Lorelei replayed them one by one—the trees' hollow knocking against the plane, windows cracking, the grind of metal on metal—under them all the thud of the ground echoing like a bell after it stops ringing.

Gradually she became aware of where she was, still without feeling, a cursor bobbing from image to image. The plane's cabin was crumpled around her like the paper kite it had resembled, her door hanging like a torn scrap, splinters of unbreakable windshield on her lap, a tree limb rammed between her and Fred, the choking smell of gas—

She strained to breathe.

On second thought, no. Her left side felt as if it were on fire. But she couldn't stop. With a pain like a scab tearing, she heaved in air. Again. How could your body force you to do something that hurt so much?

The pain seemed to go down into her left arm; her watch was smashed.

She turned—at least she could turn—to Fred.

Trees pierced the cabin around him; he seemed to shelter peacefully among the branches. Lorelei gave him a little shake.

"Fred!"

His arm was flaccid. Gradually—she could only grasp one thing at a time—she saw the impossible angles of his arms and legs, saw the blotches across his shirtfront, smelled something pungent, coppery, almost as penetrating as gas.

His face was undamaged; he might have been looking back at her. But even as she watched, the fierce grin slackened.

It was so wrong that she tried to shake him, only it wasn't Fred Colman she was shaking. She touched his face, but that, too, was no longer Fred, and when she sobbed, the pain stopped her.

Yet it didn't seem that the air could be empty of him, not so soon. It was to the Fred somewhere near that Lorelei thought . . . screamed? . . . *Fred, don't go!*

She waited. For a response? She couldn't process what she was waiting for. In the silence she heard something. Distant. Unfamiliar. Alive.

Her mind crashed back into gear. Where was she? More to the point, was it the safest place she could be?

The trees were on Fred's side; on hers, the ground tipped away and the plane teetered in space, the wing ripped off.

This couldn't be Fred's field, a helicopter would be lucky to land here successfully. But it had been deliberately cleared of trees; there were stumps everywhere. This must be the yellow line she had seen from the air: the firebreak.

A firebreak protected against fire. No guarantee against grizzlies or moose or whatever was coming steadily closer.

Fred's gun leaped in front of her eyes before she had time to think *weapon*. Could she stretch into the backseat without touching Fred? Or looking at him? Or using her left arm? Unfasten seat belt. Fred's briefcase was crunched under his seat over by the door, the envelope hidden. Out of reach. If she had enough time—

The noise was distinctly closer. She looked over her shoulder. Was she safer up in the wreckage or should she forget about the gun and scramble down to hide in the trees? But the trees were bare-limbed as poles, the first branches far above her head.

A man came out of the woods at a dead run. A large man, to reach up, pluck her out through the torn door, and swing her to the ground. She could stand, in a lopsided way.

"You hurt?"

"Just my left—"

"Bleeding? Where's the pilot? How bad is he?"

She couldn't answer. She shook her head.

He jumped back to the cabin door. Back with her.

"Right. If the fuel blows, the trees go too."

He gave off urgency like an electrical charge. That, as much as his words, made her turn to flee, only to stop at the sight of a bear cub with a pack on its back.

He grinned. "Dog," he said. "His name is Blue."

Was that supposed to reassure her? Size was what intimidated, never mind species.

He grabbed a shovel from the pack and thrust a heavy steel cylinder into her hand. She looked at it blankly.

"Fire extinguisher!" he shouted, guiding her hand to the nozzle. "Do the trees as high as you can. I'll take the plane."

The fading light had an unreal quality as she struggled to comply. Her left arm flopped uselessly; without it, she couldn't even lift the canister. She propped it on one knee, bracing it with her right hand. Not steady enough. The foam fizzled onto the ground.

She dragged it closer to the trees and tried again, but she stumbled on the uneven ground—she couldn't even get her left arm up to break her fall. She lay where she fell, watching him heave shovels of pine needles away from the wreckage, clearing the ground down to dirt.

Fred was dead. Why wasn't she weeping or screaming? Shock? Fear?

Her rescuer seized the fire extinguisher, turning a strong white stream on the trees. Soon she could see the foam better than the trees. He scooped dirt onto the carcass of the plane, leaving long muddy streaks where dirt and fuel combined, then flipped up the near side of the fuselage for a final look at the engine.

Inside the plane lay Fred Colman. Already he seemed unreal: Once upon a time there was a senator with hair like a black bristle brush and a grin that could reach out and bite you. . . .

Her rescuer pulled her to her feet. "Let's have a look at you."

His scrutiny was as intense and impersonal as a spotlight. She winced as he probed a cut on her scalp she hadn't even known she had, gasped as he felt down and across her body.

"Just some cracked ribs."

"But my left arm—"

"Ribs'll do that. But they're not broken. You couldn't move with a rib through your lung."

"You're a doctor?"

"I know something about bones."

"Lucky I was in your territory."

His back was turned. He didn't answer.

The man who had burst out of the woods had given off energy like a force field. He still did, even going about the prosaic business of packing up the extinguisher and shovel. Not so tall, really, but lean as a stick of wood. Work-worn denim, scarred boots, his face unreadable under a battered black hat. Not the way a ranger would look in the movies.

"You have a two-way radio? Or you'll set up a flare? Or do you have a Jeep?"

25

He frowned at her. "We need to get a move on. It gets cold here pretty fast after dark."

She was already shivering. She looked at the plane with a purely practical longing. "I don't suppose you could bring out any luggage? A jacket?"

"I have a down bag back at camp."

Camp? Surely we're only a few miles from people? warmth? a hospital?

He slipped the pack over his own shoulders.

"Where are we going?"

"Not far."

She gave one last look back at Fred before they set off, the stranger, Lorelei, the dog Blue, crossing the firebreak into the tall pines. There was nothing under the trees but old needles, but they were ankle-deep and sucked at her boots like quicksand.

How did he know where he was headed, anyway? Striding along as though an aisle of pines were a familiar office corridor. One looked exactly like the next.

His idea of not far was clearly different from hers. If only she didn't feel as though someone had heaved a brick at her side. She gritted her teeth to go on. She thought she was, until she felt the ranger's arm propping her up. She seemed to be on her knees.

Between one red blink and the next, the light was gone. The three men waited to see if it would resume. A steady red would guide them to the crash. No light at all meant it had been destroyed.

Minutes passed. Fenton breathed out a soundless shaky sigh. "Better late than never," he said. Was his voice level? Almost. "Right. We'll pass on the word at Dead Man's Hand, Mech. Catch some dinner at the same time."

Before he could move, the tip of a knife hooked under his chin. Fenton stopped dead.

Paca, the small man at the other end of the blade, said, "All go."

He couldn't move. A knife slash meant nothing to Paca or Mech; they were tattooed with thick ropy scars, mean thin tracers, twisted stars of puncture wounds. Whereas Fenton's experience of violence was secondhand. He knew it. To jerk away, to feel the knife slide across his cheek and ear . . .

"All go," Paca said again.

Without moving his head, Fenton looked sideways to see Mech's reaction. If Mech didn't respect someone, he rolled over him like a piece of road equipment. The round face was blank.

Fenton looked down the length of the blade. As meticulously as Paca cleaned it, could it ever be traced back to him? Fenton looked from the bare-fingered leather mitt up to Paca's face, one eye half-closed as if to aim better, the diamond mounted in his eyetooth gleaming, sparse beard and ponytail. His whole head was outsized compared to his body, like a puppet's. Once seen, never forgotten.

Fenton tried to explain that without moving his jaw. It wasn't Fenton's fault. Paca had worked for Fenton's aunt in the past, hadn't he? He knew how she felt about people being noticed. Remembered.

Paca listened, his eyes so empty he looked concussed.

Fenton's eyes were drawn back to the blade. He tried again. A knife slash meant being noticed too: a trip to an emergency room. Names on papers. Questions about other knife wounds.

"Tell him, Mech," Fenton said. "Tomorrow we'll all go on a shopping trip. Batteries for his box. A new car, he gets to pick."

The lash of guttural street Spanish that followed didn't relate to what Fenton had said. But the little man hung his head. The pressure of the knife eased and disappeared.

Fenton sighed deeply and stood.

Mech didn't move. "What about the car?"

Fenton could never tell whether Mech meant his questions or asked them to point out what a pro would know without being told. Or just to make Fenton feel stupid. "You said you left it up in the north end. Past Demersville, you said."

Mech looked without apparent expression at Paca, who wilted even more. "*I?* You think *I* leave a child asleep in its mother's blood?"

"Paca, then. We'll swing by on the way, see if anybody's found them."

That seemed to be good enough. Mech nodded and began the half-hour trek out to the road.

Lorelei was muffled in something down-filled, sipping hot sweet tea from a tin mug the ranger held.

"Better?"

She took the mug, looking around. Not even a cabin: a bare spot in the forest with a fire in the middle. Across from her, from under a tangle of hair, the dog's eyes reflected the light. Behind it were rocks and the sound of running water. Trees everywhere else.

"Don't rangers rate better than this?"

"What makes you think I'm a ranger?"

Underneath the pain in her ribs, her stomach clenched in fear. *What then?* She tried to get the words out. She couldn't.

"Run through what happened. Before you crashed."

Lorelei glared at him. . . . She hoped it was a glare. "Why don't you ask how I feel? About . . . him?"

Her voice cracked. Maybe comfort wasn't such a good idea after all. She put her good hand to her neck, retracing where Fred's fingers had knotted his kerchief.

The man watched, apparently unmoved. "We'll get to that. The plane?"

"I don't know what went wrong. I've never been on a little plane like that before."

28

"Not why it crashed. Just what you saw."

"He said we were going to land. We circled. And then suddenly the plane—the engine kept switching off and on. Or maybe that's what he did to try to stop the fire—"

"Did you smell gas before or after the crash?"

"I don't remember."

"Think back. You're circling, the engine quits . . ."

She was there again, the ground heaving beside her window . . . the unimaginable boom when they hit . . .

A hand at the back of her neck held her head down until her nausea passed. When she could sit up again, he handed her another cup of tea without apology.

Squatting by the fire, he pulled a wallet out of his pack.

"That's Senator Colman's! You can't—"

But he could. His eyes didn't so much as flicker in her direction. He took out the contents piece by piece, using the edges of his fingers with a precision that was almost elegant, studying each one before putting it in a pile.

Driver's license, the picture probably resembling Fred more now than when he was alive. Senate pass, credit cards, all showing that the body back in the plane was indeed Senator Fred Roybal Colman.

He felt in a shirt pocket, pulled out the silver-dollar cuff links and studied them by the firelight before tucking them away again, along with the driver's license. Everything else went on the fire.

He pulled her pocketbook out of his pack.

Outraged, she lunged for it, forgetting her side. "You have no right—"

He was too far out of reach; she lost her balance and toppled like a tree. He eased her quickly back to a sitting position, his face puzzled. As if it hadn't occurred to him that she would defend herself. Her things.

He said awkwardly, "Best not do that again, ma'am, you might hurt yourself."

Now he mentions it. The pain was like pliers, pinching the breath out of her. She sat gasping, waiting for it to ease.

No. She sat passively because she was stiff with the same panic she had felt in the plane, listening to the approach of something unknown.

He still had her pocketbook. She could only see his hands by the fire's light, upending it, sorting its contents with the same unhurried care he had given Fred's. Passing judgment on their lives. The papers she had been working on. Her wallet, her computer call-back. What a lot of makeup she had; how spindly the tubes and bottles looked in his big-knuckled hands.

At least he didn't put any of her things on the fire; he piled them back into her pocketbook and handed it to her. She clutched it gratefully, and then felt chilled by her own gratitude. No wonder people could be easily brainwashed when they were tired and hungry and confused.

"Lorelei Muldoon. What were you doing on the plane, Muldoon?"

She had been so busy reacting that she hadn't thought ahead, she, of all people. What was at stake here? She owed Fred Colman a believable story, but God knew she couldn't concoct one on her own; until she reached his staff, the less said the better. Until she knew more about the stranger, the less said the better.

If only she felt like an analyst instead of like Janet Leigh, watching the shower curtain twitch.

She took a slow, painful breath, the counting-to-ten kind.

"I do numbers analysis."

"Which means?"

"Oh, when something's wrong with the books and the regular accountants can't spot it. I work a lot with small companies. A company of a certain size has to grow or it goes under, but they don't always know their own strengths."

"Like sharks. Eat or die."

30

"Really? I wouldn't know. And I work with politicians sometimes. They do focus groups. Sometimes they need help with the results. That's what I was going to do for Senator Colman."

"What about?"

"I don't know. The data's on the plane, I never saw it."

"No congressional I.D. here."

She fingered her hair back impatiently. "I'm not on staff. I have my own consulting firm—you saw my cards."

" 'Consultant' can mean anything. Or nothing."

Lorelei forgot to be careful. "If you're not somebody official, how can it matter who I am? Put me down as an innocent bystander, and let's go to Fred's cabin. It must be close if we flew over it. It's probably heated, and I'm sure he has a phone."

"Fred," he repeated.

"I'm on a first-name basis with all my clients! If you don't want to take me there, just get my luggage out of the plane, and I'll find it myself. Nobody even needs to know I was on the plane."

He said nothing. She counted the pulse hammering in her throat while he watched her from across the fire.

He leaned forward until she could see his eyes, unexpectedly pale beneath the dark battered hat. "You sure you wanted to tell me that, Muldoon? That nobody knows where you are except a dead man?"

Lorelei's only real asset was her hair, so thick and curly it seemed to have a life of its own. When it was freshly combed or braided, she even drew looks from men in three-piece suits and tasseled loafers; but before long the glances came from work shirts and jeans. When it was leather and painful ear jewelry, she knew she had to comb it again.

She must be at biker stage now, for him to treat her like this. Yet he had held her in his arms, twice. To get her out of the plane, again to carry her to the fire. Shouldn't that have

31

left a sense memory, some DNA tracing that would trigger kindness?

He stood. "Stay close to the fire, ma'am. Likely there are people nearby, awaiting results."

"You're not leaving me!"

"There's some stew and a pot in the pack. Blue, guard."

It was not, somehow, a good time to say, *Give me a phone book and I can cook anything.*

"You have reached the Secret Security Forces of America. If you are calling from a Touch-Tone phone, to report a murder, press one at this time."

After he hung up on Abby, Claud let Stan's spiel run. "To report a Chinese gang war, press two. To report drug smuggling—"

Barney McFaul's disembodied voice came into the room. "Give me your uncle, Sokoloff."

At the urgency in his tone, Claud brought his chair upright. But he shook his head.

Stan said, "No can do, Barney. It's Friday, remember? Claud's over at the Demersville Sheraton."

"It's an emergency. Patch me through somehow."

Stan rolled his eyes to Claud. Claud shook his head again.

"Give me a break. The hotel switchboard? You might as well call Emerson Flagg direct and read about it in the *Herald* tomorrow. Come on, you can trust me."

Claud was prepared for the extended silence. Barney McFaul didn't use words casually; he worked things out before he said them.

Stan couldn't handle it. "Hello? Testing? Calling Barney McFaul, soldier of fortune, gunman-about-town—"

A long sigh vibrated in the room. "A plane went down in the firebreak near Colman's cabin. Beech Bonanza, white with blue markings, registration 7139Mike. Registered to Fred Roybal Colman. Extensive damage to the plane, but there's enough of the right flap left to see how it was fiddled with. No fire or explosion. The pilot was killed. I.D. of Fred Roybal Colman—"

Claud stared blindly down at his desk.

"Time out! The senator himself?"

"—and I can verify that it's Colman. I've taken prints, I have his driver's license and cuff links, the silver-dollar ones, so we can confirm death even if the plane catches fire."

"You mean the plane's still smoldering 'if'? Or the best way to destroy all information 'if'?"

"Just tell your uncle. And check for a flight plan. There's also a passenger."

Claud had to stop himself from grabbing the phone. But it might be even more important now that Barney not know he was there.

"A witness! Jeez! Getting information out of you is like apprentice dentistry. How badly was *he* injured?"

"*She.* Minor injuries. Lorelei Muldoon. Lives someplace in New York." Claud wrote the address as McFaul read it out. "She says she's a consultant. Statistics, something like that."

"Do I detect a note of skepticism?"

"Not that tough to print up cards that say 'consultant.' "

Stan's voice was hushed. "You think she's the marijuana connection?"

"Theories are Claud's department, not mine."

"What else could it be? You're not suggesting that Bandit brought a girlfriend?"

"Can't tell."

"He can't tell. Give me a break. What's she like?"

"Apart from being sprayed head to foot with Colman's blood?"

This time Stan let the silence stretch. So did Claud, thinking furiously. When Barney McFaul continued, even allowing for the phone's poor voice quality, he sounded helpless.

"Say Best of Breed, if you like the breed."

"Now you're getting creative. Poodle? Cocker spaniel?"

"Something expensive."

Claud scribbled a note and shoved it across the desk. Stan said abruptly, "Listen, I forgot. Uncle Claud left me some notes. He said to ask you if you ran into Shari Finley over there today."

"She always cleans the cabin on Fridays. That's why I come in for supplies then. Why?"

"You think he tells *me* anything? Oh, and he said if there was anything out of the ordinary, to come tomorrow morning, we'd talk about it."

"We."

"We, he. Details. Anyway, this qualifies for sure. Say nine?"

"I'll be there in an hour, max."

"Waste of time, Barney. Enjoy the Muldoon woman while you have the chance."

"Try not to be more of a fool than you can help, Sokoloff." Another sigh came into the room. "I'll be there at seven."

"Are you crazy? He'll hardly be to bed by then."

"Then I'll let myself in and look around."

From the client side of Claud's big desk, his nephew looked hopefully across. "How'd I do?"

There had been an earthquake, the landscape heaved apart for all time, and Stan wanted to know how well he had talked. Surprising, the effort it took not to throw the kid down the stairs. Instead Claud looked at him, head lowered, in a way that once intimidated opposing linemen. The buffalo look, Bandit had called it. Habit now.

"I'd advise you not to sass Barney McFaul if you hope to get much older."

"I always talk that way. If I was serious, he'd have known you were here."

"In that case you were brilliant. Cut along home, and keep your mouth shut."

Stan cleared his throat self-consciously. "Actually, I thought I might head over to Dead Man's, catch Banjo Man for a set or so."

Claud snapped to baleful attention. "If you happen to be around when the sheriff drops on that hophead—shut up and listen! After what I've told you, your parents can bail you out, not me. Clear?"

"This is his last night for a while. He leaves for a gig in Denver tomorrow."

Claud made a sweeping gesture with one ham hand. Stan clattered down the stairs, tripping a few steps from the bottom and recovering with a lunge out the door.

Claud rocked the big chair back to an improbable angle. Funny what your mind did to you. He had been looking down at his desk when Barney called. He felt as though the picture was seared on the inside of his eyelids, though there was nothing memorable to see. A mug with Bandit's insignia. A doodling deck of cards to shuffle while he thought. Three unopened decks. The guest list. A handful of metal fragments dug out of him over the years.

He had been hot and swollen like this only a few times in his life, barely recognizable. Rage. He welcomed rage in others; it made them easier to maneuver. This time the weakness was his.

He topped off his mug from the bottle in the bottom right drawer of his desk. He didn't need to be told that Wild Turkey was a poor aid to thought. But when you had to shift a load of grief first, there was a lot to be said for the sting of sour mash under your nose and in your throat.

Only Barney McFaul knew for sure about Bandit's death, and he was isolated. Claud could keep a lid on for the night, at least. How best to use it?

Not tracking the flight plan, as Barney had suggested: Bandit never filed one. No. He had to find Shari Finley, the young woman Abby had talked Bandit into hiring as his long-distance odd-job man. She was the one who kept the house clean, who stocked the refrigerator and mowed the field below the cabin when he was coming home.

How would he land, knowing that the field was filled with marijuana? But why tell Shari to cut down the bait in the trap he and Claud had planned so carefully?

He dialed Shari's number. No answer. He called his own cabin. It was time to alert the toolies. The men and women who lived in trailers and sheds up and down the Coulees scratched a living in ways the law rarely discovered and even Claud sometimes had to guess at, moving through the valley like so many shadows. What they couldn't find would never be found.

He had hardly put down the receiver when the downstairs door rattled against the lock. An impatient thump became a tattoo. Claud heaved himself upright and went down.

The Reverend Abigail Butterfield stood there in her usual nonpulpit jogging suit, bright blue tonight. A foot shorter and half Claud's weight, she brushed by him and up the stairs as though he wasn't blocking the way.

Had her deacons any idea what they were getting into when they extended a call to the very new, fresh-out-of-seminary Abigail Butterfield? It was like summoning a juggernaut. From the tiny town of Bitterroot, Bitterroot Congregational had become a force up and down the valley, drawing from Demersville, the much larger town where Claud's office was, as far north as the Kinnikinnick Basin up by the Canadian border. Her Pastor's Committee sometimes told her things before the toolies told Claud.

"I didn't hear Bluebonnet."

Bluebonnet, the minister's aging Volvo station wagon, announced her wherever she went. Like the rattle of a snake.

"She quit on me. Charley Calico brought me on his Harley.

36

He's waiting outside." She offered him a paper bag. "Doughnuts left over from dinner. Dunk them in that stuff you're pretending is coffee."

"Any zucchini in them?"

She beamed like a Campbell Soup kid, rubbing her short dark hair till the cowlicks stood up. "Francine and I are working on the recipe. Well?"

He chewed and swallowed manfully. "Very tasty. You can hardly spot the zucchini."

"Not the doughnut, Claud. Have the toolies found Shari?"

Claud stretched out the mouthful as long as he could. "What makes you think I asked them?"

"Because your bump of curiosity is as big as mine. Because you like to have a hand in everything—"

"Like you. I wonder who minded our business before you came along, Reverend."

"I wonder too." Briefly her smile flashed, but she quickly sobered, studying him over her half glasses in an uncomfortable way she had. "Something's happened. Is she hurt? No, you wouldn't look like that for Shari."

"Drunk, you mean."

"Destroyed. The only person who could hurt you that much is Senator Colman, but he— That's it, isn't it? Is *he* hurt?"

"Abby, I haven't heard anything about anybody—"

"He's dead, isn't he? And you know it." Matter-of-factly, Abby bowed her head.

"You're leaping at the moon!"

"Don't interrupt." She went on in her normal conversational blare, "Almighty God, we hold before You Your child Fred Roybal Colman. We honor him in Your presence. We ask You to be with him and with us, to help him with his pain and us with ours."

Claud held in a sigh. Abby prayed with a down-to-earth intimacy that made him uncomfortable. As though the

Almighty were there with them taking turn and turnabout in the conversation, instead of (as Claud preferred) in some appropriately remote place like the top of Mount Rushmore.

He forced himself to bide his time while silence spread from Abby to fill the room.

A relief, in a way. His first chance to get outside the anger that lay in him like an old meal, and think instead about the man. What of importance in Claud's life had Bandit Colman not shared? Bandit beside him the first time he drove his now carefully restored Chevy pickup, the Big Red Machine. Bandit Colman with his crow-black head back laughing, high-fiving after a touchdown. Bandit Colman scowling over some scheme of Claud's, never interfering because they were close enough, their fathers used to say, to cast the same shadow.

Bandit Colman.

"Amen," Abby said. "I'll count on you for the eulogy, of course."

He blew his nose loudly. "If it turns out you're right, Rev, Betty Colman might have something to say about that. But I'm sure your prayer did Bandit good, wherever he is."

"Haven't I told you I can tell if you're lying when we're face-to-face? How did it happen?"

"Why don't you check with his wife?" His voice wobbled unexpectedly. He snapped to hide it.

"You haven't talked to her?" She cocked her head. "If you didn't find out from her, then . . . it happened here? No. Emerson Flagg would have a reporter there the minute he landed. Unless he flew himself."

Claud refused to meet her eye, his face as blank as a lifetime of lying had taught him, but he felt her blue gaze. And she was right, she was working out what had happened by reading his shifting expression.

"It wasn't a natural death, was it. His plane crashed. You've talked to Sheriff Neiderhoffer."

"Why would I bother Hoff in the middle of the night?"

"But if you haven't talked to him either . . ." She peered up at him. "You don't think he crashed by accident, do you, you think somebody killed him. And you want to get to them before the sheriff does. Why? So you can kill them?"

"How you can get that out of my letting Hoff get a decent night's sleep! Next thing you'll want me to call out the air patrol!"

The air patrol were volunteers, men with their own planes who fleshed out the thin lines of police and hospital emergency staff. If someone was badly burned anyplace in the state, a member of the patrol picked him up and flew him to an appropriate hospital in Houston or Seattle. If a child was lost or a plane crashed, the air patrol added their planes to the search of the highway patrol and rangers. Bandit had been a member; his fellows would be needed to bring him home.

But not just yet.

She stared at him and answered her own question. "You aren't going after them yourself. Say you're not, Claud."

Claud broke away and walked to the window. Charley Calico leaned patiently on his Harley, blowing on his hands to warm them. Whereas he, Claud Willetts, had heat to spare. Had his rage blinded him to where it pointed? But Abby had seen it clear as glass. Surprisingly, he felt no guilt. Something even eased a little.

"You know as well as I do, Rev, Orry Neiderhoffer has to ask directions up a one-way street. He's going to need help."

And now he had told her that it was all true.

"Claud, revenge destroys whoever turns to it. That's why we leave it to governments. Please. Help the sheriff if you want, but let him run this. No vigilante justice."

It took an effort to keep from shouting. "You're in over your head, Reverend. Go on home."

"You know I have to stop you, Claud." She headed for the stairs.

"Going to sic the Pastor's Committee on me?"

"In the middle of the night?" she said in a deliberate echo. "No. I'm going to stop by Shari's. Check on the baby."

"Get to her before I do, you mean."

Finding a killer couldn't be that different from finding a gullible tourist. But now he had a deadline: He had to talk to people before Abby could.

Chapter
Three

"I got no time for an everyday woman.
  Give me velvet, and spangles, and gold."

When Banjo Man raised his reedy voice in the first bars of
"Everyday Woman," the regulars at Dead Man's Hand immediately shushed the Friday night noise. The next lines carried to the back room.

"I'll take midnight champagne
  once in a while
  over everyday pie à la mode."

His backup was a drummer and a single guitar, the band-
stand a platform small enough to be lit by a single overhead
spot. Tables were packed in so tightly that in the front row,
half of Stan Sokoloff's feet were in the spotlight. The owner
didn't waste money on nonessentials.

Stan eagerly justified his privileged seat by explaining the
song to the tourists at his table.

"What I want is a now-and-then woman,
the occasional white-hot flame."

Banjo Man counted on the whispered explanations; he broke away frequently to long, complicated riffs that gave his fans plenty of time.

"I'll take a bonfire
that burns down my world
to a flashlight the rest of the time."

"Everyday Woman" was Banjo Man's signature song that summer, Stan explained; he varied the lyrics from one time to the next, depending.

The man sharing his table, old enough to know Bob Dylan by heart and find the tune derivative, was not exactly skeptical. More going-along-with-the-natives. Depending on what? he asked.

Depending on events, Stan said, hunching closer. Banjo Man wrote lyrics about what happened in Merciful Valley, a kind of musical gossip column. What kind of things? Embarrassing. Private. Like the night in June he had sung,

"There's nothing so fine as a part-time woman
who's a wife when she isn't with me.
Ever lie awake wondering
while you're on the road—"

—and the husband involved, a salesman with outside interests of his own, had lunged for Banjo Man in the middle of a down-and-dirty laugh. The woman at Stan's table gave the singer a measuring look that made her husband reflect on the distorting effect of vacations; back in New York, she would have ignored someone so artfully not-quite-clean, not-quite-shaven, not-quite-sober.

It was crowded, even for an August Friday. At the long bar in the front room, Mech commented on it while he waited for a pitcher of beer. "Something special?"

Jim Cooper, owner and principal bartender, said, "They think so. Banjo Man leaves for Denver tomorrow. He says."

"You don't sound worried."

"Won't last."

"Never does, does it, Jim?" It was the man on Mech's right. "He pulls this, what? Three, four times a year?"

Cooper was built like a walrus—all shoulders, no hips—his round bald head fringed with reddish hair as fine and straight as if he had just surfaced dripping from a dive. He ran a fair bar and didn't ask awkward questions, but he had a short temper. Behind the bar, he gave a curt nod without speaking.

"He's always back in a couple of days," Mech's neighbor explained. "My opinion, one time the sheriff will be waiting for him."

Cooper slammed the pitcher down. Beer sloshed over the edge. "Not in Dead Man's Hand!"

"Whatever you say, Coop, whatever you say."

Mech leaned back. Banjo Man's music sounded like rain on a metal roof to him. Background noise anyway; he was listening for references to a plane or a fire or a car with a body and a baby inside while he kept an eye on his empty table. But whatever Cooper's flash of temper was about, it wasn't about any of those.

When he saw Fenton come back to the table, Mech picked up his pitcher and breasted the crowd through to the back room. Farthest from the music, closest to the phone.

Ricky Fenton glanced up, shaking his head. "No answer."

Not for the first time, Fenton regretted that his aunt refused to trust an answering machine. He had to keep reminding himself that as far as she knew, Colman was *her* problem, Fenton merely her spear carrier. She didn't know Colman's death solved a major problem for him too. No reason she ever should. He was sure he could keep that from her in a recorded (rehearsed) message, but in a conversation? facing questions?

And what might Mech think if he overheard, sitting there, eyes half-closed and unreadable as a lizard's?

"What do they say at the bar?"

"*Nada.*"

"*English.* Maybe you didn't understand what you heard. He's overdue. That alone should have them talking about a search. Unless he's already called someone, been rescued."

Mech shrugged. Impossible to tell whether it was contempt or a different assessment of the risks.

Fenton said petulantly, "I hope you did a better job on the apartment."

"Control in my pocket. Want to blow it, all you got to do is dial the number and push the button. Think you can do that, Finaldo nephew?"

"I said, don't call me that."

Mech had an ugly, guttural laugh. Fenton retreated to the phone.

The phone was in an old-fashioned booth with a door, keeping conversations as private as possible even from somebody as close as your own table. That was one reason they frequented Dead Man's Hand. Fenton personally preferred bars that were more upscale, where the fact that he felt ill at ease was an assurance of quality. But Dead Man's had that phone booth, and a back entrance used so freely that Fenton and Mech could use it, too, without comment.

Every half hour Fenton tried the phone. They sat through Banjo Man's set, and the next one. Still nothing about a plane crash or a bellowing baby in an abandoned car. Gradually Fenton relaxed.

When Mech finally stood, Fenton was halfway relieved. He tried Olga one final time, then called his sister Estrella instead. Let her pass on the word that Colman was undoubtedly dead, though not in a dramatic flameout. No need to mention the girl. As good as an answering machine.

Estrella named a time for him to talk directly with Olga the following morning, and he left with Mech, in a truck this time on a street of trucks, as nearly as he could tell, unobserved.

Unobserved, unremarkable: his aunt's twin obsessions. Invisibility, she said, was what allowed failures and successes alike to go unpunished by those bigger and more powerful.

Until he arrived in Merciful Valley with Mech and Paca early in May, it hadn't occurred to Ricky Fenton that invisibility might be hard to maintain. Instead of streets filled with people, buildings latticed with fire escapes, and shops with convenient back doors, empty land rolled out until it ran into mountains. One big town and a few small ones. A big north-south road and two little ones cutting across, the one they were driving on and another at the north end. The Beargrass River, fast and swollen when they arrived in May, by August looped back and forth across the valley like a lazy landlord.

Fenton's antennae were in their own way as sensitive as a chamber of commerce. Demersville, in the center of the valley, was the largest town by far at twenty-five thousand, give or take. The few police they had watched in the valley seemed to center there; strangers, whether tourists or migrant workers, stood out.

The few towns were nothing but a couple of blocks of buildings and big, slow-moving men whose trucks and guns and dogs reminded Fenton of what he had learned to avoid in the southern hills.

Only Bitterroot, at the south end of the Valley, tucked between Cutthroat Lake and the mountains, was possible. From Gaslight Parade, the main street of carefully preserved old buildings, to the side streets of bars, celebrities mixed with tourists and locals. Townspeople were used to strangers.

After Fenton and Mech adjusted to log-framed buildings

and the fact that even the suits wore boots and jeans, they began to see telltale signs like watchful eyes and the careful exchange of Baggies in men's rooms here and there. They had found the right town.

But only for occasional visits to shop and report. Even in Bitterroot, outsiders who stayed more than a week or two would be remembered.

If they had stuck to Olga's plan, it wouldn't have mattered. A week or two was plenty of time to go back and forth across the border on the roads and off, to find out how easy or tough it would be. (Open as a sieve.) To steal a few cars and observe how well the police handled the thefts. (No progress so far, though Mech had recently become uneasy.)

When they decided to stay on for the summer, the only safe place was the woods. Sleeping bags, no power, no bathrooms: probably not that different from the burned-out buildings Mech and Paca lived in back in D.C. A world away from the Fenton condo.

Fenton watched the road unreel in the headlights, narrow, no shoulders. "You just passed the turnoff to Beargrass River Road."

"We check on the car."

"For Christ's sake, we looked on the way! What more can we do?"

"We look on the way back also."

Fenton didn't like the way Mech's hands tightened on the wheel. He subsided.

Had it been Mech's idea or his to take Olga's scheme a step further? On good days, he took full credit. Her obsession with smuggling was outdated. In California, growing marijuana had become a cottage industry, like moonshine in the South, and the forests in and around Merciful Valley were full of untenanted, unpoliced clearings. On good days, Mech was just the man who happened to have the seeds with him.

On bad days . . .

"You shouldn't have planted Colman's field."

And Olga should have told him Colman was important. And why.

"Very good land. The more sun, the bigger the sinsemilla. Where is the marijuana ripest? Colman's field. Ready any day now."

"Oh, right, Mech the farmer."

"I become one. A farmer, a good one, is always becoming."

Mech pulled off onto the gravel ruts of Coach Road, switched off the lights, and felt his way along for a mile, two. Three. But the dirty little Nova with its dangerous burden was no longer there.

It was after midnight when Betty Colman and Olga Finaldo returned to the Watergate for a final toast to a successful evening. As she unlocked the door, the phone on the parchment table burred discreetly. Barely visible in the shadows under the lamp, its message bulb blinked red. Betty made no move to answer.

"It's not going to be good news at this hour. Scarlett O'Hara had the right idea. Why think about disaster now if you can postpone it till tomorrow?"

Olga was startled into remonstrating. "But no, Betty! You must think about tomorrow today. Yesterday, even!"

An urgent tenor came into the room. "Betty, one of these times you got to be there, and we got to talk, honey. So pick it on up."

Betty snatched up the receiver. "If you're calling at this hour, you must need a favor, Claud Willetts. Calling me 'honey' is not the way to get it."

"Oh, good, I was afraid you might have gone away for the weekend, honey. I know how you feel about Washington in August."

"Did you call to say something smart, Claud? Because if so, it can wait till morning."

"No, Betty, just trying to do the polite. I really called to catch Bandit. He around somewhere?"

She forgot that Claud was only clumsy when he meant to be. "Isn't that funny, I saw Larry Hungerford tonight, and he says he doesn't know where Fred is either! Can you imagine? His own chief of staff! I'll tell you exactly what I told Larry: Call that apartment in New York! Don't pretend you don't know what I'm talking about."

"Now, don't hang up, honey! There's a rumor going around that Bandit was coming home this weekend, but he hasn't showed. It's probably nothing, but somebody else thinks they saw a light plane go down, and I've been playing ring-around-the-rosy with Bandit's answering machine and yours and Larry's all night. No luck."

Betty tried and failed to think what Claud might be angling for. She said slowly, "You're really serious, aren't you?"

"I got a gut feeling you should be here, honey—Betty. I'll call Hungerford, tell him to book the two of you in first thing tomorrow. Can you do that?"

"I suppose so." Olga put an insistent hand on her arm. "Wait a minute." Betty covered the receiver inquiringly.

"*Now* is the time to put him off till the morning!" Olga guided Betty's fingers around a healthy tumblerful of brandy. "Till *you* decide what is best for you to do."

The idea of strategy at such a time hadn't occurred to Betty, but she warmed to it. She swallowed, gave a little gasp, and swallowed again.

"Go ahead, Claud, call Larry. I can always cancel if I change my mind." She hung up before he could answer.

Olga was all apology. "But I couldn't help myself. Never commit yourself in the middle of bad news, my dear, no one has good judgment at such a time. Not that I have any idea what has upset you—"

"Oh, I suppose it will be public soon enough. If it *is* anything, I mean. Even if it isn't, once people start talking, Fred and that Muldoon woman will be in three-inch type in the *Star,* even if they turn up someplace entirely different by Monday morning."

"As I don't yet know—"

"I'm sorry. It's Fred. Or rather, his plane. Or what *might* be his plane." For some reason, when Betty said it herself, it began to sound real. "Claud Willetts—he's a friend of Fred's—he thinks Fred went to Montana this weekend. And now a plane seems to be lost and he wonders— Oh, but it's absurd. Fred's in New York, I know he is."

"Forgive my confusion, but what makes this Mr. Willetts—" since there was no *W* in Spanish, it turned into a condescending *V* on Olga's tongue—"think it was Senator Colman's plane? I remember your state from our visit in the spring. It is of commanding size. Surely there are many such planes."

"I didn't think to ask." Betty took another comforting swallow of brandy and gasped again.

"And what makes this man think Senator Colman has gone to Montana? Surely Larry Hungerford knows where his employer is."

"But he doesn't. Didn't you hear him ask me earlier? I thought he was pretending he didn't know about Fred's latest girlfriend. Like Claud, just now. Covering up for him."

"Ah, yes, Miss Muldoon. What of her? Has Mr. Willetts tried to trace your husband through her?"

"Maybe he really didn't know about her. If I know Claud, he would have twisted the knife. Well. I suppose if I'm leaving in the morning, I'd better pack. I'm glad you were here, Olga. It made it easier somehow. You've been a real friend."

"My dear Betty, surely you don't think I will let you face such a thing alone?" Olga widened her eyes in exaggerated surprise. "No, no. We will call Larry and tell him to get another ticket to this Demersville. You see? I remember the name! Naturally I want to be with you if such a thing might be true, which let us pray, still, that it is not."

"That's sweet, Olga, but I can't expect—"

"No, not another word. I must only arrange things with Estrella."

"At this time of night? She'll kill you!"

"Nonsense, my dear Betty. Doing as she is told is Estrella's job. *And* her good fortune, as she knows."

Part of Estrella Fenton's job, Olga had once explained, was to trace sofas weeks past their delivery date, to return fabric with a flaw in the center of the repeat or wallpaper on which the lilacs were insufficiently lilac. Betty had watched the two of them often enough: Estrella with a phone receiver like a permanent hearing device on one ear, Olga inevitably drawn in, directing her niece in Spanish with the passion of a Carmen, forehead deeply furrowed, shoulders hunched, arms thrown wide, her short, solid middle-aged body suddenly fluid.

This night Olga was as dramatic as ever. She hardly seemed to need the phone.

The part of Estrella's job that Olga did not explain was to arrange many of those furniture delays.

Olga had been in charge of delivery from her first days as a receptionist for Freddy Hampton Bahr, quickly passing on the work to her brothers and cousins. Just as quickly she had learned that no one questioned goods that were delayed or damaged or lost. Such inefficiencies had served her well; as she herself moved up through Hampton-Bahr, so, too, had her delivery service flourished. Occasionally trucks were hijacked; more often they were merely detoured until the black cambric beneath sofas and chairs could be loosened and to allow the addition of packages—most often plump plastic ones of cocaine, occasionally small bundles of gemstones. So far she had resisted transporting money. What happened after the delivery of the altered goods was the business of others.

A delivery service cheaper than its competitors could get business everywhere; OFC Delivery had transported more than one altered sofa to Congressional offices. Olga's problem had increasingly become that of remaining unnoticeable. The decorators and department stores she served didn't trouble her, and layers of paper separated OFC Delivery from the firm now known as Bahr-Finaldo, Ltd. The curiosity she feared was that of the various people whose small, valuable packages she transported so often. If any of them once realized all that could be accomplished with a few trucks and men, she would be forced to carry more dangerous cargo more often, someone might even take over OFC.

Then in April she had flown with Betty Colman to Merciful Valley.

Olga was no student of history, but she would have understood the farm boys–turned–soldiers whom Colman had described: the men who had looked across the Mississippi a century and a half earlier and seen a miracle. She had herself seen one that April afternoon.

Unable to drive, she nevertheless knew the value of unnumbered miles of untended border—Betty couldn't even point out to her where Montana turned into Canada. Of unnumbered miles of flat terrain that would be like a continuous highway to off-road vehicles.

Olga had slid down in her seat a little, eyes half-closed, partly to hide the black glisten of excitement she was sure must show, partly because of the vision of a new world that had flared up and consumed her. All her previous achievements had been only rehearsals.

Her graceless nephew, she now informed Estrella with

considerable force, was not going to jeapordize such a future.

Betty wandered through her living room, waiting for Olga to finish. She stopped in front of a new painting, a stark rendering of three calla lilies that made everything else in the room look a little fussy—probably Olga's intention. Olga said it was an homage to Georgia O'Keeffe. If Fred really was dead, the next painting would be the real thing.

"I regret it took more time than I expected." Olga was back to English, her poise rigidly in place.

"Oh, don't apologize," Betty said. "You know how much I enjoy listening to you and Estrella take on the world."

"And each other, I will say it for you! I fear Spanish has become the language of anger in my family. My nephew has mislaid a valuable cargo, can you imagine? Young people can be so careless." Her smile was strained. "But the client is not so valued as you, my dear Betty. Ricardo must manage for himself this time."

Three thousand miles to the northwest, Claud Willetts dangled his own receiver. He made a point of giving other people the last word. Otherwise they might be upset enough to go over a conversation and remember more than was convenient.

Unlike Claud, who had trained himself to rerun not just the words, but how they were said. What was left unsaid. Where the silences came.

He dialed Larry Hungerford, letting the phone ring until the chief of staff's answering machine cut in.

Whoever risked tampering with Bandit's plane hadn't flinched from taking on a United States senator, hadn't cared where he went down or who he took with him. That had to mean a guy whose idea of business as usual was large-scale. While Claud trolled for information, he was really listening for the chest thumping of a huge ego.

Betty, now. Her reaction had been what he expected: a petty irritation you hated to dignify with the label anger. Wasp, not elephant. But there had been something else. He replayed the conversation, unable to pin it down, but noting it in his incongruously tiny handwriting.

Was Lorelei Muldoon really a new girlfriend? He knew she had worked for Bandit the summer before, but Bandit had never once hinted that she was important enough to bring to the valley. Especially now.

Then again, if Betty knew about her . . .

Claud rolled it around for a while. More likely Lorelei Muldoon was just clutter. But she'd be valuable cheese for a trap, once he figured out when and where to spring it.

He made another note and pressed his redial button.

This time Hungerford's answering machine didn't cut in. Maybe Claud was interrupting the chief of staff at a tender moment. He grinned and let it ring until a voice from the depths of sleep said, "All right, all right."

As soon as Claud spoke, the voice became immediately and unnaturally alert. Claud grinned again.

Larry Hungerford had never quite been able to hide his resentment of Claud, of a history with Bandit that shut him out and an influence that should have been his own. On the other side of the ledger, he couldn't help but realize that Claud had to be reckoned with if—when—Hungerford ran for office himself.

Claud, reading him like a watch with the face open, treated Hungerford with a condescension just short of contempt. So far Hungerford had swallowed it and kept on smiling.

"Claud, this is amazing. I was planning to call, but I didn't want to wake you. Something came up tonight—"

"Anything I should know about?"

"No, just something Senator Colman forgot about. I wanted to check it with him."

Claud waited. Sure enough, Hungerford hurried into explanation. He had a trick of turning a statement into a question, as though offering it up for approval.

"I had him scheduled for a function at the Hispanic Cultural Institute last night? I know he knew about it, but he didn't show. It's all right, Betty covered for him. But I can't locate him. The only thing I can figure is that he's in—you know, New York? with Ms. Muldoon?"

Politically correct, even under stress.

Claud always varied what he said from one conversation to the next, so he knew the source of whatever got back to him. This time it was Barney's father who had mentioned Bandit coming home for the weekend, Stan Sokoloff who had overheard talk about a plane crash.

From Hungerford's end of the phone came a babble of shock. "My God. My God. My God." Then silence.

After what he judged a decent interval, Claud asked if he was still there.

Hungerford blurted, "It'll have to be an appointment. Thank God Governor Larsen is the right party."

Claud gave him plenty of time to realize what a fool he'd made of himself before he said, "When your wheels start to turn, boy, it's not a pretty sight. I said it was a mention."

"Claud, you wake a man in the middle of the night and expect—" Hungerford's voice cracked.

Claud waited stonily. Finally Hungerford resumed, groveling. As well he should. "I assume you've already talked to Betty? Otherwise I'd be happy to—"

"You mean, does his wife come before an employee? Strange but true. I told her you'd get her out here tomorrow. Better come yourself. She'll need somebody to run errands."

"Of coruse, absolutely. Look, what I said before, I know it sounded terrible, but it's because of what Senator Colman told me this week. I'm sure you already knew? That he was going to retire?"

"Get this, hon-yocker. Whatever Bandit gets around to telling you, I've known for a while."

Behind his big scarred desk, Claud turned this new piece of information over and over. It was bigger than he had bargained for. If Bandit had meant to retire, he would have told Claud first. No question. Well, maybe second after the Muldoon woman, if she was the reason why.

Her name surely did keep coming up. And Hungerford, like Betty, knew more about her than Claud, which must mean something, even if he didn't yet know what. Claud made a note.

On the other hand, Bandit might have announced his retirement because he was pursuing some fool tangent of his own. It wouldn't be the first time he had gone off bullheaded. Claud had a sudden vision of himself in front of the altar of the Bitterroot Congregational Church with a hand on Bandit's coffin, saying, *The thing about this man was, he was so bullheaded that . . .*

That he died.

Claud topped off his mug recklessly.

On the third hand, might Hungerford have made up the story of Bandit's retirement, knowing Bandit couldn't deny it? Had he been genuinely surprised? Or had he figured out that the more contemptible he sounded, the more apt Claud would be to believe him?

Chapter
Four

Lorelei Muldoon awoke to the smell of coffee. There was a mug on the ground near her head. She reached for it and cried out with pain: A big area of her left side seemed to be on strike for the foreseeable future. Instantly the man was there, easing her to a sitting position.

The coffee was black, unsweetened, unexpectedly weak—she could see the blue-speckled enamel through it. But it was warm.

When he held out a tin plate heaped with eggs, bacon, and hash browns, she inhaled gratefully. "I can't remember the last time I saw this much cholesterol in one place."

Back on the other side of the fire, he bolted his own food out of the pan without speaking.

Lorelei lifted her face to the sun. The air already had the apple-cider crispness of New York in October, no hint yet of the August heat to come. So the man had no small talk. He could see when she needed help, and gave it. That was what mattered. Wasn't it?

She stirred eggs and hash browns into a runny delicious mess with determined cheer. "I can't decide which is harder to believe: that the plane crashed, or that I survived. Or even that I'm here, that I won't wake up and be back in my apartment—"

"You mean with Colman? Or would he still be dead?"

Lorelei chewed in silence. Perhaps her fears hadn't been wholly due to the cold and the dark.

She tried again. "What kind of dog is Blue?"

"Bouvier." Like Fred, the man made no attempt at French pronunciation. "Means cattle herder."

"A French dog? How did you get to Montana, Blue?" Not blue, either, an indeterminate gray.

"Not French, Belgian. My dad uses Bouves to herd his cattle. Blue here is trained as a guard dog."

She looked nervously across at the eyes, grave and calm, barely visible under tangled brows. "Like a Doberman?"

"Bouves are more apt to knock people down than bite. Or scare them."

She tossed Blue a chunk of potato. The dog looked from the tidbit to the man; when he nodded, Blue lipped it up politely.

"You mean he won't take food unless you tell him he can?"

"Not from a stranger."

A stranger. So she was. And happy to remain one. She didn't want to be here long enough to be anything else.

He reached a long arm for her plate, went down the few steps to the stream, holding the clean tinware up pointedly on his return.

"Bears like easy food. Best not to teach them they can find it here. More stew in my pack when you get hungry. Blue'll let you walk that far."

It sounded like dismissal. She tried to scramble up, forgetting the pain in her side, and fell back. "Wait, wait for me!"

"You can't even sit by yourself, Muldoon. You can't keep up." He said as he had the night before, "Blue. Guard."

Suddenly Blue was in front of her, eyes almost level with her own. She tried to push him aside. "You can't leave me here again!"

"I'd let Blue be, ma'am. He likes his work."

He was already in the shelter of the trees. She watched helplessly as he moved between them and was gone. Again.

"Well." Lorelei cleared her throat. "Well, Blue, where does that leave us?"

The dog sat in front of her, ears pricked.

Lorelei's lifelong ideal might be Marilyn Monroe (no rescuer would walk away from *her*), but Doris Day was the everyday mentor who nagged her to do what she knew she had to and goaded her to try what she didn't think she could. It was Doris Day who now ordered her in a carrying singer's voice to stand. Not to try, to do it. Doris Day who had no sympathy when Lorelei fell flat on her back, scolding until she struggled back to a sitting position from which she could give a mighty shove with her good right arm and lunge, panting with pain, upright.

For the day. She'd never be able to do that twice.

The next order of business, said Doris, was a good wash at the stream purling beyond the rocks. Lorelei picked her way down the stony slope. The water was bone-chilling cold; she probably risked frostbite washing in it. She tried to finger-comb her hair back and gave up, looking around her.

The view was oddly like that from her apartment windows: looming shapes blotting out everything but the sky overhead. But instead of the muffled constant of traffic, there was a suggestive not-quite-silence. Occasional stirrings in the pine needles. Trills of birds.

Not a very big cain-see, Fred.

Fred Colman. He had been so much larger than life, and she had known him so briefly, he already seemed more like a movie character than a person. There must be others bet-

58

ter able to mourn him; but her concern now had to be Lorelei Muldoon.

Fred had done something else: pointed out the plane window at the straw-colored line of the firebreak and said, "We'll follow it home." The same firebreak, surely, where they had crashed. They had been close to his cabin, even circled it.

Last night when she thought back to the crash, horror had clamped down like a muscle spasm. This morning she could force feeling aside and run her memory like a tape. Hadn't they been on their way back toward the firebreak when the steering caught? And she and the man and dog had continued across the firebreak to this campsite. Farther away from the cabin.

What could be done could be undone. Couldn't it? The mountain man moved through the trees like a wraith, but Lorelei Muldoon had stumbled and scuffed and fallen. Surely the Hansel-and-Gretel principle applied to her path.

Lorelei slipped her pocketbook over her good shoulder, circling the clearing until dark marks in the pine needles showed even her inexperienced eyes the way they had come. One deep set of footprints where he had carried her. Beyond them, snags of silk from her shirt, skid marks, the dark splotch where she had fallen.

She set off, her left side turning her normal stride into a half stagger. Under the tall trees, sunlight dwindled quickly into shadows as misleading as twilight.

Blue was an even worse problem. He blocked her way. She stepped sideways. So did he. When with the impatience of desperation she pushed straight at him, he reluctantly gave ground, only to circle in front again and nudge her backward, one side, then the other.

Lorelei said crossly, "I do not need to be herded!"

He flattened his ears politely. But when she took another step, so did he, this time rumbling a warning deep in his throat.

"Fee fi fo fum to you too!" She was willing to push him aside with every step if she had to. She told him so, scolding. He listened, ears flattened in what she hoped was dog bafflement. Maybe even obedience.

She looked behind her to check her progress. The campsite had disappeared. Her only landmarks now were the signs of her own passage, in front, behind.

What if she got so lost that the man couldn't find her again, but nobody else could either?

She mustn't stop again, mustn't even look around. She must keep going. Keep pushing Blue aside.

There was a little more light, a little more, a tantalizing scent—perfume—of gasoline. And she was out in blazing sunlight.

Across from her was the plane, the fuselage bent in two, smeared with mud and crusts of foam, the wing from the visible side—her side—yards away. Sad wreckage of the handsome beast plunging at the end of Fred's rope the day before.

How had she survived? Why her and not Fred? Instead of Fred?

She didn't need Doris Day to tell her to save the brooding till she was back in New York. What mattered now was, was Fred's cabin to the right or left?

She sighed. Something else mattered even more. What if she had to spend this night, too, in the woods? Fred had a gun. Maybe she couldn't retrieve it, but how could she pass by without even trying?

Her side of the fuselage was way over her head, the door to the baggage compartment sagging on a single hinge. She could never reach it. Her clothes, her computer, as lost to her as if they had burned.

Fred's side had tipped down into the trees on its broken wing, his door dented in a shape that might have been his body. The lock had burst. Concentrating fiercely to keep from imagining what she might see, Lorelei pushed the door wide with a piece broken from the wing strut.

In fact, it was not so bad. The seat had jammed forward, half hiding him. The last thing he had done was turn toward her; from this side, praise God, he faced away.

The big envelope with the gun in it was wedged under his seat. If she could somehow brace herself on the broken wing, she could stretch through with her good arm . . .

She had forgotten Blue.

Apparently convinced she was about to escape, he took her ankle in his jaws. Not snarling, not even painful through her boot, just a pull down stronger than hers up. So close . . .

She screamed at him, kicking at him with her free foot. His grip shifted just long enough for her to wriggle up a step, and another, reach . . . The pain, the undeniable smells . . . She forced herself to concentrate on her right hand, groping past the metal track under the seat, feeling for the corners of the envelope, walking her fingers up far enough to grip it. . . .

Now she was only too glad to let Blue pull her back to earth. The gun thudded at her feet in a shower of papers.

Blue released her, panting contentedly.

"So you don't hold a grudge." She gave his head a weary rub to show him that she didn't either.

She pulled herself up along the wing, leaning there while she got her wind back, looking down at the gun in her hand, the big, blue-black metal barrel and wood handle, like a movie prop.

No. She needed it to be real. To be loaded. But with the safety catch on, so she didn't shoot herself by accident. If only she knew which part was the safety catch.

Don't hold it unless you need to use it and know how to, Fred had said. One out of two was the best she could do. She thrust it into her bag and hefted it. Heavy. Manageable.

Would the scattered papers tell the mountain man that she

had come this way? With a sigh, using the wing for balance, Lorelei gathered them one by one and added them, too, to her bag.

Now: left or right?

We'll follow the firebreak home.

Not enough. Could the stream at the campsite be the same thin blue line by Fred's cabin? That plus the firebreak. Another parameter and she could triangulate the cabin's location.

If she followed the firebreak to the stream, then followed the stream downhill to the lake, the cabin had to be somewhere along the route.

Looked at properly, she wasn't lost, she was two-thirds found. Tightening her fingers in the rough hair of Blue's back, she pulled herself to her feet and headed toward the stream.

Now Blue helped unwittingly. He hovered, always on the same side, trying to turn her back to what he obviously regarded as home base. That kept him on her left, painful side, where she could lean on him.

When they turned downhill along the stream, the landscape began to change, just as she had seen from the air, the screen of pines breaking away to long grasses, a scattering of wildflowers.

Not that much easier, though. Blue circled in front of her again, forcing her to fight for every step. Brambling thorny bushes tore at her clothes, her hair. The stream banks were slippery with mud. Once Blue slid awkwardly down the bank. She wiped her hands clean enough to grip his ruff and helped him scrabble back up.

There was a huddle of trees, green-leafed and lacy, where the stream broadened and deepened. Not a lake, but a good-sized pool, banked with an outcropping of stones. At least she could rest there.

She was almost at the pool before she saw the cabin. It was built of the same stone that banked the pool, with a tall chimney like a spire. If it wasn't Fred's, it was somebody's.

A telephone. A car.

Lorelei hardly felt her side as she clambered down rough rock steps to a ledge. It had been smoothed into a terrace that led from the pool across the back of the house. Farther down were more ledges, a huge garden of some kind, and then the lake.

But she didn't have to go beyond this house. She peered through the wide glass doors on the terrace. Locked, of course. The keys must be with Fred.

Could she have searched his body? No. Then forget it.

Besides, after the events of the past twenty-four hours, breaking a window didn't amount to much, even if it set off a burglar alarm.

Even if it set off a burglar alarm. Oh, dear God—there wasn't even time to frame words before she saw the narrow telltale tapes like borders on the glass of the doors. She swung her pocketbook at the nearest one like a wrecking ball.

The sky was pale and the air had that thin early morning clarity when Claud heard Barney McFaul's truck pull sedately in next to the Big Red Machine. Boots barely audible on the sidewalk, the street door opening and latching without a sound.

The office door opened just wide enough for Barney to come in. Without a greeting, he dropped a driver's license and the silver-dollar cuff links in front of Claud. He hooked a chair with his boot, slid it over in front of the desk, and slumped into it in one leathery movement.

Claud stared at the cuff links without comment before shifting his gaze to Barney.

"Want a doughnut?"

"Duncan's?"

"Abby's."

"Zucchini? I pass."

"At least take off your hat."

"It'll take that long?" Barney pitched it on the desk. His eyes were an unexpected pale gray in a face that seemed designed for brown, his mouth the straight, unrevealing line of a man with bad teeth, even though he had a set of white California chiclets when he chose to show them.

Claud had always counted on his size and bluster to intimidate. Someday he'd figure out how Barney McFaul managed to make himself felt through the moves and noises he *didn't* make. Or was he overlooked by people who didn't know him?

Claud tilted dangerously back on the curling legs of his big oak chair, his suit draping as they always did, like the cover of a bed, only showing their cost in the fine wool. "Muldoon woman still there?"

"Blue's on guard."

Perfunctory question. Just an excuse to start talking.

"I was the one who called him the Frito Bandito, your dad ever tell you that? When we were kids. Most people think it came from football. He was a skinny half-spic I bloodied up regular, till his pa threatened to sell *my* pa for breakfast money if I didn't stop. So I decided to call him names instead."

He shifted his weight. The overburdened chair protested.

"So he called me 'Gang.' Said there was too much of me for one person, even then. Only Hoff, now, left to call me that." He pressed ham hands against his belly. "Course, it was distributed differently. Nowadays it seems to be heading south without me."

"I'll warn Abby not to count on you next time she redecorates."

Briefly they shared the picture of Abby the previous spring, a determined but untrained do-it-yourselfer, burning old paint off the paneling of an upstairs bedroom and setting the parsonage ablaze. Claud had been one of the last volunteer

64

firemen on the scene but first up the stairs, slinging Abby over his shoulder, she protesting every hazardous step of the trip back down.

Memories of Bandit pulled him back. "He loaned me twenty-five bucks toward the Big Red Machine. First time I drove it was to give him a ride. He's the only one I ever let come up to my place in the Coulees. Now he's out there with the wind whistling over his bare head, while I . . .

"Reverend Butterfield should understand *that!*" He pointed a savage finger. "I owe the man, Barney. I purely owe the man."

"Along with everybody else in the valley." Barney's weight shifted impatiently. "Why do you think Dad volunteered me to watch his field for you? But his death changes it."

"Now, hold on! Last night you were willing to wait till we talked."

"Thought it over. They get the killer, they'll be getting the ones who planted the marijuana in his field."

Claud shook his head to clear it once and for all. "At least hear me out."

"Won't matter. I'm bringing the woman in this morning, turn her over to the sheriff. He can take it from there. This is just a courtesy call."

"Give me half an hour. If you won't do it for Bandit, do it for Buck."

That did it. A reference to Barney's dad always did it. Barney settled reluctantly back.

Claud leaned forward. "Little over a month ago, somebody spotted marijuana growing somewhere over in the Heroes Wilderness."

Only the signs bordering the huge federal tract of land used the official name of *L'heureux de la chose*.

Barney nodded. "One of your toolies."

Claud made as if he hadn't heard. "I passed the word to Bill Odegaard—Lew's boy? He's Forest Service. Goes through before the logging crews to check for snowy owls and yew trees. Know how big that is right now, yew-tree rustling? Who makes the market in yew trees?"

"Keep stringing this out, Willetts, I'm gone. The marijuana?"

Claud sighed. A story should be spun, not hung out to dry like a wet sheet.

"Bill found patches all through the Wilderness. On his way in to report, he swung by Bandit's cabin, not meaning anything, he says, he often does it, and there was the field, wall-to-wall plants—you know it better than I do."

"Any of the other patches wired or guarded?"

Claud shook his head.

Barney stared at nothing in an irritating way he had. "That answers some questions. Adds some too."

"How's that?"

"I told you before, the stuff in Colman's field is a pro's weed. Hybrid. It's maturing fast. The sinsemilla—the seed pods—are so big they're falling over. It makes sense that Colman's field is only part of something bigger."

"But?"

"That means outsiders. Backup money. But you get to that size operation, you find wires, guards. And they go for yuppie weed. Smooth, less smell, big price tag, high-end marketing, ship it all over. The stuff in Colman's field is an Indica hybrid."

Not for the first time, Claud wanted to ask Barney where he got his uncomfortable expertise. But it was as off-limits as his frequent, unexplained absences from his father's ranch.

"And that means?"

"Indica is skunky, strong. Afghani, some call it. It's a blue-collar weed. Tends to be grown in smaller batches close to where it's sold."

"Then why here?"

"Oh, that's easy. Federal wildernesses are naturals, Ode-

66

gaard must have told you that. Good sunlight. No lights at night—that can blow a crop. Not enough rangers to keep a decent watch. But why Indica?"

Barney shook his head and stared out again. There was time to deal and play a hand of Double Jester before he said, dangerously mild, "I give up time during threshing season for something the Forest Service knew about all along."

"You crazy? You think Bill reported something that might hurt Bandit? I told him we'd look into it and get back to him."

"Who's 'we'? You and Colman?"

"Of course I told Bandit!" Claud slammed the desk, forgetting about the mug in his hand. Bourbon flew up and spattered his suit. He brushed at it impatiently.

"That makes two fools," Barney said. "One patch, maybe the song you sang about vigilante justice made sense. But an operation this size? If you'd gone the official route, Colman would still be alive."

"Think I don't know that?" Claud suddenly felt his lack of sleep. "Friendship is a dangerous thing, Barney. It makes you soft, and then you do stupid things. Course, you wouldn't know about that."

"Colman didn't fiddle his own plane," said Barney, unheeding. "One of you must have told somebody else."

At last: curiosity. But if he found out about Shari Finley, Claud could never persuade him to delay.

"You'd think he'd have told Shari to mow the field, wouldn't you? But you say you saw her yesterday, and she didn't. I don't know who else he talked to. Me? I talked to Betty and Hungerford, but not until last night."

"And?"

"Bandit told Hungerford he might retire next year. Hungerford. Not me. Said he was coming back for good. What do you make of that?"

"I'm tactics, remember? You're strategy. Mrs. Colman?"

"She seemed her usual self. Pleased with herself, but then that's Betty all over."

"You'd know?"

"I knew her before Bandit." With a sense of escape, Claud slid again into memories. "Bandit and Betty and Hoff and me, we were all at MSU together. You wouldn't think it now, but she had the bluest eyes, I swear they glowed in the dark. There was one thing she could do . . . Well, there was more than one." He chuckled, reminiscent but not unkind. "But one she was better at than anybody I ever met before *or* since. She could spot the most important person in the room from outside the door. Still can. I don't think she even knows how she does it, something in her gut goes bong. So when she met Bandit . . . well, that was all she wrote."

"Would he quit to protect her?"

"Let me put it this way: When I asked Betty where he was, she told me to call a certain apartment in New York."

"Muldoon."

"Check. Lorelei Muldoon."

"So she *was* his mistress."

"He never told me about her. I mean that way. She met him like she said, doing some number stuff on his campaign last summer. She was the one who told him about the northern counties, the ones running against the trend? Larry Hungerford tried to brush her off, but Bandit went up and discovered some ranchers going ballistic over grain quotas. He's been riding that one ever since."

Claud fished through his notes. "Still, Betty and Hungerford both think she's his mistress. I'm not giving up on either of them, mind. I flushed them back here where we can watch them. With the two of them plus the Muldoon woman, we should get somewhere."

" 'We' again? Not me, Willetts. Sheriff Neiderhoffer can take over from here. I'll call him if you don't."

Claud was on his feet so fast his desk shifted half a foot.

In a red flash, he wanted to catch hold of Barney. Shake him. Scream, *Let somebody else get there first?*

But Barney wouldn't be moved. Claud forced himself to turn away. He prowled over to the window, gazing out at the still quiet street, rubbing his nose.

Finally he let his shoulders sag, and made his eyes rueful in defeat.

"You're right. Of course you're right. I've been wrapped so tight, I'm not thinking straight. Time to give it to the pros."

Barney reached for his hat.

Claud put up a hand. "Do me one favor, though? I don't want to go behind Bill Odegaard's back. He spotted the stuff, he should get the credit. He'll get reamed out if somebody else reports it."

"He really was the one who found the stuff?"

Claud ignored that. "He doesn't work weekends. Now, I'll do my possible to track him down, but no guarantees before Monday morning. Do you think . . . I know it's asking a lot."

Claud let the silence drag, filled, he hoped, with thoughts of the revenge he was abandoning at Barney's behest. Making Barney think it was his turn.

Claud said tentatively, "I think we can freeze the news till Monday."

"And the Muldoon woman?"

"Hey, if she wanders around after the crash for a couple of days, stranger things have happened."

"She could wander around your place."

Bandit's ex-mistress for his first-ever house guest? "Oh, right," Claud said. "Smuggle her up through Bitterroot and across Demersville. Abby'll never find out."

"I don't have provisions for two."

"I didn't think of that. Pick up whatever you need at Ottinger's, I'll sign for it." Claud tried not to babble in relief. "Give me a minute to splash some water on my face and maybe get some coffee downstairs from Duncan. Stan tells

me I'm getting too old to go around looking like I been drinking all night. Not respectable."

"And you'll tell Dad."

Buck McFaul? Not on your life. "Soon as I get that coffee."

There was a pay phone at the corner where Beargrass River
Road met Route 42, overlooked by Grady's Gas, a Laun-
dromat, and pizza take-out. Fenton felt exposed. But Dead
Man's Hand wasn't open at nine in the morning; other pay
phones all seemed to be inside stores or coffee shops. This
might be a conversation an eavesdropper would remember.

He punched up the number of his aunt's showroom. "She
there, sister?"

Estrella always gave him a clue to his aunt's mood. Giggly
five-minute sentences told him when Olga was satisfied. This
morning her voice was washed clean. She had only time to
say, "Watch yourself, little one," before Olga's harsh voice
took over.

"Have you called to tell me they are dead?"

Off-guard, he blurted, "I thought you wanted to hear
about Senator Colman."

"You didn't know he had a passenger? Thus you tell me
you have not yourself seen his plane. Truth chases lies, does
it not, my nephew?"

"Are you talking about his girlfriend? The one in New
York? She was with him?"

The undiluted acid of her anger filled and overflowed the
phone booth. "Did you take care of her apartment? Or do
you lie about that too?"

Hastily he said, "Mech wired it on the same trip he did
Colman's plane. All we have to do is push a button."

She was beyond hearing. "Since I sent you to that place, I
have had nothing but lies from you. You tell me you need
more time to check the police, and the borders, and still more

70

time, and then I find that you have gone into business for yourself, you must stay for your sinsemilla harvest. You would never have spoken so to my face!"

He bowed his head to the storm. At least she didn't know that one of the sinsemilla fields was Colman's.

At last she ran down. She said almost calmly, "How do you plan to find the plane?"

Off-balance again, he asked warily, "Why do I need to?"

"When there is no fire, people survive plane crashes."

"Not this time. It crashed in a forest, *Tía* Olga. As big as all of D.C., bigger probably."

"Difficulties exist to be overcome, my nephew."

"It's not a difficulty, it's a good thing! Even if they survived the crash, they'll starve to death before somebody finds them. It's as good as a fire."

Silence while she worked this out. "So."

From her, it was high praise. He sighed inwardly with relief.

"Then when you find the plane, there will be bodies in it."

He raised his voice in frustration. "I just told you—"

"Even now you expect me to believe you? Bring me something to prove to me that the senator and his girlfriend are dead. I think . . . yes . . . bring me the papers they have with them."

"What papers?"

"Whatever you find."

"But there could be boxes of stuff!"

"What is your question, Ricardo?"

"You want me to ship boxes of papers to Washington from here? And I'm not supposed to attract attention?"

"Not at all. I come there myself, tonight, with my good friend Mrs. Colman—"

"Then why bother? The police will give her whatever—"

"I am to await the convenience of the police?"

Silence. One of her best weapons. When she spoke it was

even worse: a cool, reflective voice. "I begin to wonder if I have sent the wrong person to this valley."

Could he say anything that would help matters? He bowed his head, resting his sweating forehead on the cool plastic of the booth wall.

Apparently satisfied that he had been humbled enough, Olga resumed, "You will also destroy the apartment."

"The girlfriend's?"

"You just push a button. Isn't that what you told me?"

He wouldn't give her the satisfaction of asking more questions, giving her another chance to squash him. He just waited until the line went dead.

Fenton was still resentful an hour later, as he sat over his third cup of coffee in a booth at Demersville's International House of Pancakes. Since his first job at OFC Delivery when he was fourteen, he had assumed he was in step to take over from Olga one day. Surely it was her intention too; why else the lectures that accompanied everything she allowed him to do? He tried to tell himself that this was more of the same. Fetch the papers, like a homework assignment. Prove yourself. Yes, teacher.

As though he had a chance of coming up with this homework. The valley was every bit as big as he had described it to Olga.

I begin to wonder if I have sent the wrong person to this valley.

Outside in the parking lot of the strip of stores that passed for a mall in this valley, Mech and Paca walked aimlessly, while Paca chose a car. Mech had always gone for cars and trucks with dents filled with dirt and rust, whose owners wouldn't report the theft promptly if at all. Fenton assumed Paca would go for a big-muscle off-roadie. But he chose a high-profile, solid-citizen car—a Sedan de Ville in an aggressive red. A new one. Olga would disapprove.

Good. Fenton clambered into the de Ville's backseat like a kid when the teacher's back is turned.

They were almost at the turnoff before he began to wonder if Olga had been forced to give him new information. Forced? Or so angry she didn't realize what she had said? Or both?

As he picked his way through the woods—Paca in front of him, Mech behind—he mulled it over.

She had said Colman's girlfriend didn't matter. That the booby trap in her apartment was only a means of getting at Colman. But even though Fenton had assured her that the senator was dead or as good as, she still wanted it blown. Another homework assignment? Or something more urgent?

Had she wrapped her urgency in insults so he wouldn't notice? So he wouldn't ask more questions?

A threat to Olga Finaldo was automatically a threat to Ricky Fenton.

Paca was the one who spotted the discreet blink of the sensor, the one triggered by the security system of Colman's cabin.

Fenton turned automatically to Mech. "Cops checking? Maybe somebody told them Colman's missing?"

Mech shrugged. "Maybe he don't die."

"What are you talking about?"

"He's in the air ninety minutes. We know the plane don't burn. Maybe he makes it to the cabin."

Paca sniggered. "For sure, it ain't the maid."

Mech scowled him into silence.

Fenton was silent too. Olga's talk about a survivor was just a stick to beat him with. For Mech to say it . . . And if there was a survivor, the threat to Olga (and Fenton) remained.

Did he want Mech and Paca to know about that threat?

One or two wounded people, amateurs. How much of a problem could they be?

He could wait a few more hours to dial the Muldoon woman's number and push the button.

Mech accepted without comment Fenton's decision to go to the cabin alone, turning to the small arsenal they had brought with them.

"To kill from a distance, you must know many things, Finaldo nephew. Where to stand, how to find where to stand." He paused.

Fenton knew the answer to this one. "I don't want bullet holes. They have to look as though they died in the plane, remember?"

Mech's face lightened in what passed for a smile. "Good. Weapons are unprofessional, always. Paca fails to remember this."

"I figure I use wreckage from the plane, a piece of wood . . ."

"Fire is good also. But if things go wrong, a man takes no chances. He uses whatever is necessary. Then he gets out." He held up a semiautomatic pistol. "You can cut a man in two with this."

Fenton nodded. Mech kicked the clip out and clapped it back in.

Paca tossed over extra clips with a half smile that almost snagged on the diamond in his eyetooth. He muttered in street Spanish.

"What did he say?"

Mech frowned. "Paca forgets himself."

"But what did he *say*?"

Carefully, so Fenton could make out each word, Paca said with relish, "At the end, they will offer you anything to live one more minute." His laugh was a high-pitched giggle.

Fenton didn't know how to respond. He said awkwardly, "If it's cops, though, I'll just watch."

Mech nodded. Paca looked contemptuous. Fenton pushed

the pistol down the back of his jeans the way Mech carried his and left.

Mech watched Fenton disappear into the trees before he turned to Paca. "You degrade yourself, little man."

Spanish lends itself to pageantry in a way that English cannot. An unflattering nickname takes on the dignity of a title; criticism deepens into a curse.

Paca hunched an uncaring shoulder. "You shouldn't have let him go alone. If it's cops, he'll tell them anything. We'll have to cut out, leave your sinsemilla."

Mech's rubber-ball body stilled.

Spanish is a language for difficult dreams, too. When Mech tended the sinsemilla he had planted throughout Heroes Wilderness, he thought of his grandfather. The old man died before Mech was born; Mech knew him only through the stories of his dried pepper of a grandmother. But when he stopped to loosen the soil around one of his plants, he felt within his hands the man who had dug in sun-drenched fields in another country, one who shared his grandson's pride in the broad blue-green leaves and vigorous seedpods of this new crop.

Mech would never give it up.

His grandmother's stories always ended in a bleak pronouncement. Unnerving to him as a child. But increasingly he found her words in his own mouth.

He said, "You are right, little man, one should expect nothing of a pig but a grunt. We will watch the Finaldo nephew use his weapon."

"You joke, man? He has the car."

"There are others."

"He's way ahead of us."

"He is an amateur," Mech said.

Paca shrugged. "He passed Mech his boomer and an AK.

He ran his thumb down the length of his knife, smoothing it into place against his thigh.

To Barney's surprise, Willetts was as good as his word. By the time the groceries were assembled, Claud was there to sign for them. He even helped carry the bags out and heave them into the truck. It made Barney feel awkward, as though he owed the big sad man something.

He fished out of his back pocket a section of wire; around it, a tiny fitting splayed open at one end. Barney flipped it to Claud. "You might want this. It's a section of the right aileron wire. That fitting's not part of the equipment. It would have passed an equipment check, but the first sharp bank, the end would spread open. Jam the aileron, keep it from closing. A miracle Colman managed that landing."

He got in and leaned out of the cab window. "I was saving it for the sheriff. Pass it on for me."

Barney slid in the clutch and pulled smoothly out, watching Claud stare in the rearview mirror.

He took the drive back at a leisurely pace. The sunlight was yellow as fresh cream, the air peeled clean. He never tired of it.

Besides, why hurry to face the Muldoon woman?

How much did he have to respect Willetts' penchant for secrecy anyway? Why not spend the weekend at Colman's cabin in comfort? Cut the phone cord so Muldoon couldn't call out.

He was still toying with the idea an hour later when he turned onto Beargrass River Road and met Blue coming the other way. Blue, built for power and not acceleration, was heading toward the truck at what was for him top speed.

Chapter Five

Lorelei Muldoon braced herself for another fight with Blue at the cabin door, but when she turned he was gone. Not so much as a growl or a waving branch to mark his passage. She felt oddly lonely as she picked her way through broken glass into the huge living room.

Her entire apartment would fit into just the part of the room where she stood. Except this ceiling was twice as high.

There was a phone on an oak chest at the far end. She dropped her pocketbook and ran.

No dial tone. She punched numbers: 911. At random. Nothing.

The lamp on the phone table worked; the power was still on. An unbroken phone cord ran all the way to the wall. Had Fred forgotten to have the service connected? Unlikely. He had promised she could work this week; there was a fax and modem somewhere, along with a rented computer.

Maybe this particular phone was malfunctioning. She found the kitchen and reached for the wall-mount beside the refrigerator. Dead as a bone.

She wanted to scream out of sheer rage—she had earned that phone call!—but who would hear?

Right. The point, Lorelei, is to get where somebody can hear. Then scream, if you still want to.

The first door she tried in the kitchen led to the basement, but the second opened to a garage and a maroon Jeep Grand Cherokee. A twisting gravel driveway must connect with a road eventually.

One set of keys was undoubtedly back at the plane with the key to the cabin, but there must be a spare. She pawed through one kitchen drawer after another.

Of course, time spent hunting car keys was time taken from walking out the door and down the road toward . . . somewhere, sometime . . . people. Then again, the burglar alarm must have gone off somewhere. If she left before the police arrived, she would short-circuit her own rescue. . . .

She forced herself to inhale, deep and shaky and slow.

Why keep running? To escape from the stranger? But she had already done that. Breaking the glass of the door had tripped an alarm, summoning the police—security— somebody! When the man returned to his camp and found her gone, he'd disappear. Like Blue.

Slowly her shivering urgency drained away, leaving behind a lumberjack hunger.

The refrigerator was empty. Their food, too, must be back at the plane. But she found a big package labeled lasagna in the freezer, and there was a microwave on a counter. She and the police could share it. She set the defrost to thirty minutes.

That left plenty of time to see what Fred had brought her here to see. Why not? For these last minutes, Fred was still alive to everyone but her. And the mountain man.

The house was built around an immense stone staircase. The concrete walls were still stamped with the wood forms, the ceiling a neck-craning distance up to rafters and a wicked-looking chandelier of interlocking antlers.

Halfway up the stairs a shaft of light lit a portrait. His mother, surely, in pale pink and pearls, but nothing could tame a profile eerily like her son's. The woman who had walked away from her own history so her son wouldn't suffer. A son who, by the time he died, had been as proudly Roybal as Colman.

The floor everywhere was the same dust-colored stone as the terrace—cool underfoot now, but how did he heat it in the winter?—scattered with big Navajo rugs in deep browns and reds. Oversize gray flannel chairs and sofas with flame-stitched blankets thrown across the backs, heavy dark oak tables and chests: What a who-cares-what-it-costs house. What a chest-thumping man's house.

She ran a hand over a carved oak table, feeling for Fred's touch beneath her own.

Fool. The last person to touch it was undoubtedly a housekeeper.

A rack in the hall held cowboy hats and an old red and black checked flannel shirt. Did the scent of Fred still cling to the fabric? It made her feel protected anyway. She let her own dirty shirt fall to the floor and wrapped his around her, like the embrace they would never have, now.

Under the hatrack was a silver-framed copy of the same picture in her pocketbook, his signature grin, her, well, identifiable hair. Above it—oh, Lord!—a mirror reflected today's Lorelei Muldoon: the hair matted and dull, the clothes torn, dirty—bloody! Like an actress in a TV shipwreck movie. Except real sweat and grime made one's skin crawl. When the police arrived, they'd think she was a vagrant.

When the police arrived. Where were they? Was the cabin so far from the nearest town or . . .

Or was the alarm not working any better than the phone?

She smoothed the security-blanket flannel of Fred's shirt. The electrical system worked—hence the microwave—the telephone didn't. Which ran the burglar alarm? Both? You had to call in if you triggered an alarm accidentally. Would the alarm work with part of the system down? One of those mechanical things she had always been happy to pay for rather than understand.

When the police tried to check back and couldn't, they'd know it was an emergency, but *she* wouldn't know they were on their way until they drove up. How far did they have to come?

She could check the microwave clock to see how much time had elapsed, but what would that tell her?

And if the alarm wasn't working?

There was still the Jeep. Or, if she couldn't find the keys, she'd hike up the road until she met somebody. It might take hours, maybe even another day. Big deal. She'd have a good meal, take the rest with her, maybe a blanket from the living room.

She was in the kitchen when she heard footsteps on the broken glass on the terrace. In the hall was a small dark man with a gun in his hand.

Claud Willetts watched Barney all the way down Cuttermill Road before he went downstairs to Duncan's Café and swung a leg over a red-topped chrome stool.

"Hey, Duncan."

Duncan was fiftyish and female, her thick iron hair pulled back in a bun. Her husband was the original Duncan. When he died, she had decided to keep the café going till Duncan-the-son was old enough to take over. But he had wandered off years earlier to find himself, so here she remained, still insisting from time to time that it was temporary. If anyone remembered her real name, they kept it to themselves.

"Hey, Claud. Coffee? With?"

As she slid a heavy white mug along the boomerang-patterned Formica counter, Stan Sokoloff coiled his legs around the next stool. She slid along a second mug.

Stan leaned forward and asked in a stage whisper, "How did the meeting with Barney go?"

Claud looked at his nephew without enthusiasm. He could remember, just, when his sister had been a giggling late night sharer of confidences. Now she was the wife of Peter Sokoloff, chairman of the Salish Federated Bank, branches in Demersville and Bitterroot, giving off condescension the way other people did sweat.

Since she considered that Claud lived one step away from disaster (meaning her own embarrassment), she had kept Stan far away from his uncle until this summer. Stan clearly thought he was living dangerously. Maybe that was what made him clumsy.

"You could have come to work on time," said Claud. "Blue stayed behind."

"I knew that. I can tell when the McFaul dogs are a mile away. That's where I like them: a mile away."

"If you didn't react, they'd leave you alone." Claud slurped coffee. "Check with the tower in Billings and find out when Bandit left, who talked to him, if they noticed anything unusual about the plane, takeoff, whatever."

"You really think they can help?"

"Time to get on record as asking. And to find out who else is."

Duncan set her idea of "with" in front of Claud with care: fried eggs over easy, hash browns, cracked-pepper bacon, elk sausage, and slabs of bread lavished with butter and jam.

"Hot plate," she warned.

"Any zucchini in this bread?"

"Not this particular one. Got some doughnuts, though. No? Your tongue hanging out, Stan?"

"He's leaving. Take your mug with you. Can't he, Dunc?"

"Ownership has its privileges, Claud."

He shoveled into his eggs. Police and rangers, air patrol and volunteers—all could search Heroes Wilderness, but the odds still were that at the end of two days, Bandit's death would still be just a rumor. A long time for someone to hide behind a story when he didn't know what facts it had to fit. The chance for mistakes multiplied. If he could spot the mistakes before Sheriff Orry Neiderhoffer knew there were any to find . . . Claud's fork bent in his hand.

Stan was back waving a scrawled memo.

"Hungerford called. The earliest they can make it is late afternoon into Billings. Then Demersville late tonight. Nine-thirty."

"Tell him you'll meet them at the airport."

"How can I? My Mustang'll never hold all three of them."

"Who's the third?" Change, any change . . .

"Some friend of Mrs. Colman's. Hungerford says she was here once before. Last spring."

"Oh, the decorator."

"You know her already?"

"They came for a weekend back in April. Bandit found out and told them to hightail it. Asked me to make sure they did."

"And now Betty has brought her back," Stan breathed. "It's like she knows he's dead."

"I called and told her he might be, remember? Did you get reservations for them at the Demersville Sheraton? No? Look, moo-hoff, if Bandit were still alive, Betty couldn't stay in the cabin. Do we know any different? Officially?"

The outside door slammed; feet took the stairs two at a time up the stairs to his office. The door rattled impatiently. Two at a time down again.

The Reverend Abigail Butterfield burst into Duncan's. She would maintain that pace all day without a noticeable pause. Bruising, to a man in his condition.

"We'll have coffee and sandwiches in the Parish Hall all day, all night if necessary," she announced. "The emergency room at Demersville General hasn't heard anything yet. Is the air patrol up?"

"For the Lord's sake, Abby, I haven't even finished my breakfast!"

Her blue gaze swept across his plate. "Leave it. You'll live longer."

"Soon as I'm through, I'll get on to Hoff. Promise."

"Get on to me about what, Gang?" A long, stringy man slipped onto the stool on Claud's other side. "Same thing Abby's been telling me about?"

Claud rolled a disillusioned gaze at Abby.

"I thought you might forget to call Sheriff Neiderhoffer."

"Anything else I need to brace for?"

She flashed the smile that made her look like a Campbell Soup kid. "Besides Buck McFaul?"

"Now, why would you complicate things with Buck, Reverend?"

"I really called to talk to Barney, I thought Barney could find Senator Colman if anybody could. But then Buck said that apparently he was at Colman's already." The glance she gave him on her way to the door was pitying. "I did warn you, Claud."

He looked over at Orry Neiderhoffer. "So we got—what?—another hour of peace before his plane lands?"

"Maybe that'll be enough, Gang. Abby says you got something I need. It could even be I've got something to put with it. Who goes first?"

Hangdog blue eyes, limp mustache, gray uniform shirt drooping over his belt, down-at-heel boots: Sheriff Orrie Neiderhoffer looked like the end of a long day instead of the beginning of one. Even half-drunk, Claud shoud be able to keep him off the scent for two days. Hoff tried so fiercely not to be outwitted that he was easily led. Claud just had to decide what line to take. Only one problem: As he got sober, it seemed to be harder to keep a lid on his rage.

He heaved himself upright. "We might as well go to the back. Have some privacy."

"And comfort. The size you're getting to be, Gang, that stool must feel like a bicycle seat."

"It's chewed-up bits of string like you that feel it."

Had the man—kid, really—been outside the cabin watching her? Adrenaline thumped in Lorelei's stomach. Relief, of course. It just felt like fear.

He stared at her without speaking.

The Raiders jacket, the reversed baseball cap and baggy jeans, seemed more like a cruising teenager than police. Or did he seem young because of the nervous way he clutched his gun? As if it made him taller. Older. Or because of his eyes, wide and moist with uncertainty? He was as scared (startled, she told herself sternly) as she was.

"It's all right, I have the right to be here." She smiled and extended a hand. A jerk of the gun waved her back. That looked official enough. Maybe he was private security.

She tried again. "I'm Lorelei Muldoon. I've done some work for your boss."

He back pedaled as though she were contaminated. *"Puta!* You don't work for my boss."

"Last summer? During the campaign?"

Someplace to the right of her painful ribs she felt cold. It wasn't fear—of course it wasn't fear!

She forced herself to continue. "I'm afraid I have sad news for you. We need the police. Where's your car? I'll explain on the way."

He breathed in a hiss.

"Did you hear me? There's a scary man out there someplace, we have to get away."

He drew himself up with pride. "I, Ricardo Fenton, am the scary man!"

"No, you are *not* the—"

His face was suddenly dramatically sly. "Was he very strong, this man, very . . ." Both hands and wild swoops of

84

the gun described a man of heroic dimensions.

The man in the woods?

Not possible.

How could she conclude that so easily?

She put the thought aside. "Can you understand me? I am a friend of Senator Colman. You work for him. I need help."

"My English is fine." His face was suddenly calm, unmistakably menacing. "I don't work for Senator Colman. I killed Senator Colman."

Someone *caused* the crash?

Fenton seemed to take her silence for fear.

"You never thought someone could take your lover and—"

She closed her eyes to shut out his crude crumpling gesture.

"But why? Did Fred do something to you?"

The gun wagged dangerously. "You don't need to know why we do anything!"

"If you'd tell me what you want—"

"Your life, *puta,*" he said softly.

Lorelei found nothing to say. Where was Blue? Where was his monosyllabic owner? On their way, maybe, if she could keep Fenton talking. It shouldn't be difficult; pretend he's a client with a problem ego.

"We will go back to the plane. We don't want one body in the plane and the other two miles away, do we?"

But if one is wearing a shirt from in the cabin . . . "What if I won't go? You'd have to shoot, and the body would have a bullet wound too, even harder to overlook—"

"*Your* body. Not *the* body, *your* body." His voice dropped to a purr that was almost sexual. "Do you know, people will do anything for another minute of life, and then another minute."

She said, fast, to get away from that chilling note of experience, "You haven't told me why you killed Fred."

In that furry voice he said, "You know, *puta.* And I think you will tell me."

"Me? You think he told his mistress important stuff? He wasn't the type."

From the kitchen came the shrill cheep of the microwave. Fenton spun and fired wildly. The shots echoed and reechoed.

So that was what it meant to see the whites of somebody's eyes. Violence must be something he had watched, not done.

And he saw that she saw it. "Enough! I'll shoot you in the kneecap! When you can't limp, I'll drag you!"

Logic was against him, but his jittery not-quite-control of the gun mattered more than logic. It wasn't until she had led him back to the terrace that she saw her pocketbook beside the broken glass door and felt an unreasonable sizzle of hope.

"My bag. I suppose you'll want it at the plane too."

Mistrustfully: "Where is it?"

She gestured vaguely, trying to look as hopeless as she had felt sixty seconds earlier. Fenton backed to it cautiously. Picked it up one-handed while the gun kept her at a safe distance. Opened it wide and waved her back a few steps before he risked a quick sideways look.

If only her paperwork hid Fred's gun. Lorelei half closed her eyes in prayer.

Oddly enough, so did he.

Why was it so easy to keep the pistol trained rock-steady on the woman, when he had never thought so hard in his life as he did at that moment, staring down at the fistful of papers? He felt a triumph so profound it was almost gratitude.

Eerily calm, he poked the woman forward with his pistol, papers clutched in his free hand. But it was too awkward. He stuffed them back in her bag and tossed it to her, conqueror to conquered.

"You carry it."

She caught it with a gasp of pain and changed it to her

other hand. Injured, then. Other injuries would fit right in.

She went ahead of him into the sunlight and up the brambly hill. Slowly, as if tired. That was okay. His mind was still in that queer hyperdrive; he could use some time to work out what to do.

On the uppermost of the papers he had grabbed was a number as familiar as his own name, as much a part of him as his name. The account number of OFC Delivery. He must know as much about OFC Delivery as Olga by now, but that sheet of figures was new to him.

The papers weren't a homework assignment, or a punishment for Ricky Fenton. They were, somehow, a threat to Olga Finaldo. How?

They had reached a strip of cleared land, pockmarked with tree stumps. The woman turned right. There was a 50 percent chance that she was pulling something. So what? It was better if she was found by the plane, but she could have strayed from it. *Had* strayed. He'd give her fifteen minutes.

Fenton was supposed to know nothing about Olga's decorating firm; the division between OFC and Bahr-Finaldo, Ltd., was supposed to be total. But he did know that Freddy Hampton Bahr had taken Olga into his business only in unwilling inches, killing himself a few weeks after making her a full partner. What was her hold over him? Had Colman found out? Or had she tried to do something similar to Colman and been discovered?

Up ahead, a scrap of metal glinted in the sun. She was actually leading him to the crash. Paca was right: anything for another minute.

No wonder Olga wanted the woman's apartment destroyed; Colman might have left stuff there too. The destruction could wait.

The papers could wait, too; Olga didn't need to know when he found them. The only number Fenton had recognized was that of OFC, but what if Estrella knew some of the others? The division between a man and his sister was not total.

There was the plane, not much bigger than a burned-out car, except that it wasn't burned at all, Mech, thank you very much. His pulse started to move in stepped-up jerks that made the gun tremble in his hand. Only a matter of seconds now. The pistol would have been mechanical, but this had to be done with his hands. A crack over the head first, give him more time—

"Hold it there."

She kept on walking.

Good. The little bit of resistance made something spark inside him.

"Don't you hear good, *puta*?"

He grabbed her bad shoulder. She gasped and lost her balance; the blow from his pistol butt was half lost in the mass of her hair. Over her head as she went down, 120 pounds of dog felled Fenton like a tree.

Duncan's back room actually led off to the right. It had been a bar when Claud bought the building and the leases; Duncan had merely punched a doorway through. There was still a hitch down from the front's linoleum to wide pine planking. The back room was dimly lit, booth backs high enough for privacy, the tables nothing more than slabs of clear-cut pine in which generations had carved their initials. (The more reckless were on the low ceiling.)

Claud had squatter's rights on the far booth on the right. He pulled a deck of cards out from under the ashtray and shuffled them while Hoff settled in across the table.

"Abby says Bandit's plane crashed."

"No, no. She just means the call I got from Barney yesterday, he thought he saw a plane go down." Careful, don't run on too much. "He was going to look into it and get back to me. He hasn't so far."

"How'd Abby get Bandit out of that?"

"Barney's camping along the Beargrass somewhere near Bandit's place. Hey, I don't blame her, I couldn't sleep last night thinking the same thing."

"Camping? During threshing season?"

"I don't ask Barney questions. You want to check it with him? Here's his number. I can't raise him. Maybe you'll have better luck."

Orry's faded blue gaze was steady. "If you're making so free with it, I reckon it won't do me any good. Bandit ever come home without telling you before?"

Claud shook his head. "That's why I don't think it's him. Check my phone records if you want to. Or call Shari Finley."

He had to mention her, or sooner or later Hoff would wonder why. And the sheriff couldn't read him the way Abby could.

Neiderhoffer leaned back. "That's just what I can't do. We found Shari's body in the middle of the night. Somebody called us, said we needed to check out an eighty-five Nova over in the strip mall."

"And she was in it?"

"But she wasn't killed there. Hardly any blood in it, and there's a pool of blood somewhere, she was damn near eviscerated. Must have been a butcher-size knife and just as sharp. Her kid's not even a year old."

Duncan, appearing with coffee refills, overheard. "What's this about Baby Lester?"

Claud looked up. "It's Lester's mom, Duncan. She's been killed."

Her expression said what he was thinking: Much of Bandit's life lay elsewhere, but Shari Finley was One of Us. Her death brought it squarely into Merciful Valley. Whatever it was.

"Does Abby know?" Claud asked the sheriff.

"I told her as soon as I found out. Abby got her the job with Bandit, remember? Even though she's Father Dick's."

"And you figure to connect Shari to Bandit?"

"Nothing in her life but that baby as far as anybody knows. The father was a summer guy. Her folks live over past Harden."

Duncan broke in. "Who's taking the baby?"

"Lynette and me for now," the sheriff said. "I tell you, Gang, what with Bandit and Shari and the car thefts—"

"Car thefts." It was one thing to play dumb and get Hoff to fill in the blanks without realizing. It was different to feel as dumb as he sounded.

A small smile lifted the bars of the sheriff's mustache. "Didn't I mention them? All summer, cars and trucks have gone missing, about one a week. Turn up after a few days, no fingerprints, no damage, running better than before. And another one's gone. One clocked more than a thousand miles, but they average two, three hundred."

"I thought you asked my help with the weird ones, Hoff."

"They left your Big Red Machine alone. I wondered if I might be looking for a toolie. But this morning the mayor's wife's Caddy went. Toolies'd know better than that."

So would everyone else in the valley. That took it back outside. Whatever it was.

Neiderhoffer sighed. "I got a bad feeling about all this, Gang. The Feds are going to come in and stomp all over us."

"If they send somebody, we'll sic Domenica on him."

Neiderhoffer permitted himself another small smile. He cranked himself out of the booth, settling the angle of his hat, but before Claud could draw a grateful breath, he slumped back down.

"Abby must have called Buck McFaul before she called me. Believe I'll wait to see what he has to say."

Claud heaved himself up in disgust to see what Hoff had seen: a pink Lincoln—the one Buck kept at the Demersville

90

airport for use in the valley—slamming into the curb in front of Duncan's.

Blue stood on Fenton's chest and bayed.

Barney McFaul bent over Muldoon, feeling under the cushioning hair. Another lump to match the one from the crash. Two knockouts in two days: not recommended.

A different shirt. Either she had broken into the hold of the plane . . . He looked up at the hole gaping in the plane's side above his head—not likely. She had needed his help to sit that morning, yet a few hours later, she had managed to get herself to Colman's cabin. She might have the cocky edge of an expensive woman, but there was something more to her.

He turned to look at Blue's quarry. Middle height, a little older than his clothes. Black liquid eyes with terrified skim-milk rims. But even scared, with Blue on his chest, he was fingering through the dead grasses for his gun.

McFaul ground his heel down. He picked up the revolver, sighted, and shot the clip into his hand.

"Beretta's overpowered for this job, wouldn't you say? Stand down, Blue."

The baying muted to an ugly mutter. Blue backed stiff-legged, one step, two, no more, jaws a slash away from Fenton's throat and face.

"What's your name?"

This time the man lay still, but he said nothing.

McFaul searched him for other weapons, ending with expert fingers tapping his rib cage.

"You could kill a man here, easy. Just reach up under far enough and grab his heart."

Waste of words, in a way: The man passed out cold.

Barney prodded him with the toe of his boot: out, but not for long. The red de Ville at the top of Beargrass River Road must have been his. Not a fighter or a stoic; he would look at Barney and tell what he knew. And then some.

By the time they had sifted truth from fiction, would the people they really wanted still be around?

If let go, on the other hand, he might lead back to them.

Barney squatted back on his heels. And if this guy told the others that he had seen two isolated people and a dog . . . They wouldn't know Willetts was available for backup.

Would Claud Willetts mind risking Muldoon if it meant catching Fred Colman's killers? Or was her safety more important?

Couldn't they manage both?

McFaul scooped up Muldoon and withdrew a few paces into the woods, easing her to the ground as gently as time allowed. He whistled to Blue. The big dog wheeled away from his prize, reluctant, a little questioning. He looked back, gnarring in his throat.

"Forget him. Take care of her. Make it stick this time."

Barney headed back down the firebreak to his truck at a ground-eating lope, wrenched open the cab door, and stretched a long arm for his phone. This time Willetts would get to dance to Barney's tune.

The phone was missing.

Nothing subtle about it: The box had been on the floor of the passenger side. It was gone.

Willetts must have taken it while McFaul had been in Ottinger's picking up supplies.

Willetts, more upset than McFaul had ever seen him and then abruptly—he could see with the clarity of hindsight—far too reasonable. Willetts, buying time until Monday.

Okay, pick up Muldoon and the man. Dump both in Willetts' lap.

The truck could make it most of the way back up the firebreak. But his ignition gave the spin of a useless battery.

Instantly McFaul dropped below windshield level. He eased the door soundlessly open and slithered out to the ground.

Willetts couldn't have cut the battery cables, and the man

lying back in the firebreak had been on the scene before Barney pulled up.

He had only been the point man, then, the heavy hitters coming up behind. They could be anywhere. They could be between him and Muldoon.

Buck McFaul was a small man who was nevertheless larger than life-size. No story about him was too tall. Had he really lost the teeth for which he was nicknamed in a brawl? Did he really chase coyotes cross-country in the dark in his Lincoln? Had he really, on a dare, taken his plane under a power line, tangling a fuel tank and shorting out half the valley? Yes. Yes. Oh, yes.

He came into Duncan's on the run, snagging a plate of doughnuts without breaking stride. Her welcome trailed him to the back room.

Behind him with enough arthritic dignity for both paced the father of Blue, grayer, even larger. The step down into the back room took a careful shifting of weight. He gave Claud and the sheriff a measuring look as if to determine whether Buck would be in one spot for a while before he collapsed as though someone had opened a sack and emptied out 140 pounds of bones.

"I never thought I'd find you here!" Buck spoke around a mouthful of doughnut. "I just came to check your whereabouts with Stan so I could light out after you."

"Where'd you think he'd be?" asked the sheriff.

Buck McFaul made a comically disapproving face and glared at what remained of his doughnut. "What the hell is in this thing? Abby said you hadn't talked to Hoff, Claud."

"About what, Buck?" the sheriff asked patiently.

Claud bent down, extending his hand to the dog. Shielding his face. "Hello, Maximum Dog."

"Rescuing my boy, what do you think?"

"Us rescue Barney," Claud said. "That'll be the day."

"Shut up or I'll shut you up, Gang. Go on, Buck."

"I been trying to raise Barney since Abby called. What I figure, the same guys that planted the marijuana jimjammed Bandit's plane."

"Camping," Hoff said sidelong to Claud, pulling the handset off his belt and flipping it open.

"We got to get to Barney before—"

A weary hand cut Buck off. The sheriff spoke into his handset, listened, said, "Right," and flipped it shut.

"Now, Buck. While we're waiting for backup, tell me about the marijuana."

"Every minute we sit here—"

"If we're too late, we're already too late. If not, the more of us the better. The marijuana."

"You mean in Bandit's field? I only know what Claud told me."

Both heads swiveled his way.

A flat-out denial was the easiest lie, but people looked for it. It usually worked better to stick to what they thought they had already figured out, veering away only where necessary. But you had to be clear about what you wanted and let the rest go.

Did they need to know about Lorelei Muldoon? Barney's phone? the piece of wire in his back pocket? He told them everything else, even the toolies' search for Shari that had ended in shifting her car to the Demersville mall and alerting the sheriff's office.

The sheriff looked over at Buck. "How much do you believe?"

Buck sucked his false teeth thoughtfully. "About Shari, for sure. He wouldn't make up something that made him look so bad."

"All I can do is turn the toolies on," Claud said defensively. "After that they're on their own."

"Which one was it?" the sheriff asked.

94

Claud made as if he hadn't heard.

"Never mind." Neiderhoffer sighed. "Nice to know there's somebody else in the valley as dumb as Elmo."

Elmo was the sheriff's wife's brother, a trooper at her pleading, easily recognizable by an Adam's apple that bobbed like a yo-yo.

"Bill Odegaard didn't find the weed, either," Buck went on.

"No, no. That was a toolie too. But I'd have thought Gang'd call out police, fire, rangers, air patrol—maybe even Boy Scouts—if something happened to Bandit. I ask myself why he hasn't."

"Wants the weekend to hisself," Buck said.

"What I figure too. Now, why?" Neiderhoffer hunched close enough for a gravelly murmur. "Claud, better me than the FBI. It's no time for freelance justice. Buck sees that, you should too."

"Quit making me out to be so twisty, Hoff. The simplest answer is always the most likely."

"Meaning?"

"Would I sit here if I knew where to go? A few miles up or down the Beargrass—we could spend days looking and never find him."

He avoided "them" just in time.

"Nice try, Claud. Ever hear of the air patrol?" asked Buck, who had headed it for years.

"They surely will find the crash if there was one," Claud agreed. "By the end of next week, say."

That stopped them. As lawman and pilot, both men had searched the endless gulches and ravines of Heroes Wilderness many times before. He watched them struggle to avoid conceding he was right.

Maximum Dog sensed Buck's frustration and rumbled a warning at Claud.

Buck perked up immediately. "Want to bet Max can't find Blue, Willetts?"

"Your old guy? You'd kill him."

"I got a good son and a good dog, but I do know which is which."

Claud shuffled cards one-handed, right against left. "Then be my guest. I'll just hold down the fort here."

His right hand appeared to be cooler under pressure. He could feel Hoff's glare. Trying to decide whether to believe him or get mad.

Stan broke the mood, coming in waving a message. He spotted Max and came to a cartoon stop, overturning a chair. Max gathered his feet under him suspiciously.

"It's okay, Max," Buck said. "It's the way you react, son—"

"I've told him a dozen times," Claud said, bored. "He'll never learn. We'll go back upstairs, Stan."

"Right now, Gang, whatever you want, I don't want," said the sheriff. "Go ahead, son."

Stan looked from Neiderhoffer's encouraging nod to his uncle's unreadable gaze.

"It's the Billings tower."

"And?"

Claud looked down at the table, his hands still. Only a fool refused to see the handwriting on the wall when his nose was pushed up against it.

"They left Billings at a little after three. Senator Colman only talked to the new kid, so they don't know much, but they're going to look for anything unusual in the fuel records and get back to us."

"They?" Neiderhoffer repeated. "*They* left at three?"

"Senator Colman and Ms. Muldoon." Stan was puzzled. "You know, Lorelei Muldoon."

Chapter Six

Lorelei could remember Fenton's face . . . she knew his name . . . she knew she was afraid of him. . . . Why?

She knew the man on the other side of the fire, too, half-turned away, pushing camping gear into a pack. She called the image up out of her aching memory. Not Fenton but the other one. Her rescuer must have come to the rescue a second time.

How could she tell who it was from where she lay?

It was the line of his neck. Not Fenton's attenuated adolescent line. But not choked with muscle like a jock's. People underestimated the importance of a man's neck. It should rise cleanly from the shoulders; there should be a swelling curve to it, and some length, and a good line cleaving into the chin, sharp enough to feel the angle under your hand. . . .

He pulled a shovel out of his pack. Fred's neck had begun to thicken a little. This man's had not.

It wasn't a shovel, it was a gun with a long barrel. Rifle? Shotgun?

Gun. Pistol. Fred's. In her pocketbook. If it was still there.

The gun leapt in the man's hands like a live thing, breaking apart, spinning, sliding back into itself with a series of oiled clicks. While he was occupied, maybe she could stretch inch by cautious inch. . . . She could feel the pistol through the side of her bag. With infinite care she withdrew it and slipped it into the pocket of her skirt.

A fearful picture suddenly came back. "He was going to kill me," she said before she could stop herself. "He said he killed Fred, and he was going to kill me."

"Good, you're conscious." Instantly he was beside her. "Can you stand?"

"Where is he? Fenton?"

"That his name? I broke his neck. Left him back beyond."

No. This time she made a conscious effort to analyze her swift reaction, slotting his statement into a grid like any other problem of probabilities. That was, after all, what she did for a living. Sometimes she had all the numbers and looked for patterns, almost like visual designs; but other times her task was to take the few numbers available and reason them into a picture.

It was with a familiar grateful certainty that she said, "You didn't kill him."

"You're telling me what I did?"

She started to shake her head, and set her teeth against the pain slamming into the back of her neck.

"I don't know what you did, that's why I asked. But you didn't kill him."

"What makes you so sure?"

Each of his actions so far had shown some overriding mission (though with no hint of what it was); a casual, purposeless death didn't fit the pattern. How would he react if she told him that?

"One of those number tricks you told me about, Muldoon?" He eased her to her feet. "A high-priced shot in the dark?"

98

The world swung and faded and finally swung into place again while he supported her.

"I don't guess! Any more than you do. Numbers make as much sense to me as your damn woodsman tricks do to you."

The long line of his mouth actually turned up. "My tricks may keep us alive. Can you walk?"

"Where? Why?"

"No time for details, Muldoon."

"I'm not moving unless you tell me where. *And* who you are."

He looked baffled. "You a slow learner, Muldoon?"

She leaned against his shoulder as if she were dizzy again. His arm tightened automatically. Thank God men always mistook weakness for surrender.

She felt for Fred's pistol in her pocket, caught hold with both hands, and rammed it—skirt and all—as hard as she could against him.

"Tell me who you are."

He looked down at the unmistakable shape of the barrel. "That real?"

"Fred's. From the plane."

"Loaded?"

"The only way I know to find out is to pull the, um, trigger."

He shook with what seemed to be genuine—silent—laughter. "Barney McFaul."

"I beg your pardon?"

"My name. Barney McFaul."

Barney McFaul had a nice face. No expression, but good lines from eyes to chin. She had been right about his chin. He looked like a man one could trust.

"That didn't hurt, did it, Barney McFaul? Where do you want us to go?"

"We're a little tight for time, Muldoon. If I'm right, your

friend Fenton is on his way back with reinforcements, and this isn't where I want to meet them."

"You let him *go?*"

"Seemed like a good idea at the time."

"I don't understand."

He sighed. "There's a spot I want to get to, Muldoon. If we make it there, and make it through the afternoon, I'll tell you whatever I can."

He shrugged into the pack and stood up under it. "Give me Colman's gun."

She stared at him unmoving. With a grudging grin, he held out the weapon she had last seen in Fenton's hand.

"Trade you for it."

"Why?"

"Don't you know when to shut up and deal? A wheel-gun doesn't have a safety, Muldoon. It's a wonder you haven't already shot your foot off. Or mine. This here one's for amateurs."

Reluctantly she made the trade. He pointed out the safety catch, making her push it on and off while he watched.

"Don't use it unless they get so close you have to. It's sloppy at any distance."

"Are we going to Fred's cabin?"

"Too much glass. Two people couldn't hold it even if they could both shoot. Same as here: Lodgepole pine aren't cover."

"Are we bait?"

Who would have thought he was capable of such a broad smile?

"Ambush. If we're lucky."

She had no trouble keeping up this time: Barney McFaul picked his way with finicky care along the edge of the fire-break. Soundless. Scowling over his shoulder when she wasn't.

He stopped and stared across the raw yellow strip while the minutes ticked before turning to Blue with a sweep of his hand. Blue slunk to his belly and wormed across, his back barely visible above the grass. He disappeared into the trees.

Barney McFaul's words seemed not so much spoken as laid quietly on the air. "Now me. If I make it, count twenty-five, then run straight across, fast as you can."

Without waiting to see if she understood, he dropped to the ground, even less visible than Blue.

Blue had been a test target?

If he made it? And if he didn't?

He did. Twenty-five seconds later, so did she.

McFaul settled her behind a thorny thicket on the slope in front of the cabin.

In that same floated voice, he said, "I'll be up twenty, twenty-five feet to the right."

"Why can't we just keep going?"

He put a palm over her mouth to shush her. "Don't want to be caught on the move."

She whispered against his hand, "Can I have Blue?"

"Can't afford to waste him."

To hell with you, Barney McFaul.

"If they want you dead so bad, keeping you alive must be worth some trouble, Muldoon. But it'll take Blue and me and a lot of luck. Hope you haven't used it all up."

For him, it was a speech. Before she could reply, man and dog were gone.

The plane crash and Fenton had both come without warning. It was different to wait for whatever . . . whoever . . . lay someplace ahead in the blameless grass and trees. Fred's cabin lay just down the hill but untouchably distant, while she and Barney McFaul—and Blue—played hide-and-seek with strangers to whom she was only prey. As quietly as she could, she moved the revolver till she could brace it without her left arm.

Again quiet words came across to her. "They're close."

Lorelei strained for a sound but heard nothing. Did that mean only a few, or any number moving as expertly as Barney McFaul?

"Stay down, Muldoon!"

Even before he got out her name there was a shallow noise, clattering, not that much louder than a computer keyboard. After the burst of rat-a-tat, a shushing like rain.

Not rain, shredded leaves. From bullets. So many bullets must mean an automatic weapon like her pistol, maybe bigger, aimed at nothing in particular. These people were willing to kill anything in the vicinity so long as Lorelei Muldoon was part of the body count.

Where's our side?

As if in answer, there was the solid sound of a gun from up ahead and an immediate shallow clatter in reply, sweeping back and forth with purpose now, like a windshield wiper.

An agonizing count of seconds before there was another solid smack.

She tried to make sense of the sounds over her head. Even if she weren't pressed flat to the ground—even when she lifted her head a cowardly inch and stared—there was nothing to see. The trees and bushes shook and rattled with death; they rained down bits of leaves. The men and the guns were hidden.

She buried her face again. It was amazing how still you could lie. Blue had better be frozen too.

Amazing, too, that people could cease to think this behavior mad. Could find a pattern in it as she could in a page of statistics.

But there *was* a pattern. Clatter, clatter from the bad guys, then the crisp solid smack of the gun she associated with Barney McFaul. The smack seemed to shift away from her, closer, away again. Did they have a weapon like McFaul's? Or was he moving?

There was a new noise, a low cough, a whistle of something overhead, a thump on the ground, and a fiery flare. What kind of weapon was that? Cough, whistle, thump, flare—this time so close that she flinched and cried out.

Immediately all the sounds converged on her. A thump directly behind her thicket, a second so close that it could have been an echo except the flare was to her left. The clatter raked the trees overhead, showering her with leaves and twigs.

The sound of Barney McFaul's gun worked quickly nearer too.

There was a new light rustling nearby. How close? In panic she fired in her turn, blindly, with no idea what the rustling might be—not Barney, not Blue, please not Blue—the kick of the shots jerking the weapon every which way.

When the clip was empty, she cowered again, straining for a further rustling. Instead she heard, dim and distant, a wail. What kind of weapon was that? The thin scream got louder. Nearer. Turned—praise God!—into an unmistakable siren.

Abruptly all other sound ceased. Now she could hear bodies lunging through the underbrush in incautious retreat, shouts too hoarse to identify.

"Mech? Paca?"

This last was repeated. Then silence.

Lorelei stayed where she was, flat against the ground, head buried in her arms. The noise of guns had been replaced at least temporarily by car and truck engines. Screeches. Sirens that came near, then throttled down to an alto vibrato. Heavy vehicle doors slamming, booted feet at a businesslike trot.

An earsplitting whistle, human this time. "Barney? You all right, boy? Blue?"

Blue heaved himself down beside her, his cold wet nose

thrust against her hand. She twisted her fingers in his ruff. Did his presence mean anything—fainthearted euphemism—had happened to McFaul? Was it safe to stand?

Above her the story continued to unfold.

"Max," came the first voice again. "Seek."

Then Barney McFaul: "I count three that may still be out here, Dad. Stay put and stay quiet."

"Right. Have you got that, Neiderhoffer?"

Another voice said, "In a minute, Buck," before dropping back to a drone that she could now identify as a radio conversation.

"Max? Where are you, boy?" came the first voice again, followed by another earsplitting whistle.

"Hold it down till we have them pinpointed, Dad."

"Barney says maybe three more, Hoff. Did you get that?" the first voice sang out, the one that must belong to McFaul Senior.

"Willetts, are you there? For Christ's sake, can't you get Dad to pipe down?"

A new light tenor said, "Shut up, Buck, or get your head blown off. If they don't do it, maybe we will."

And the already familiar one, unrepentant, "Right, right."

From the depths of her thicket, Lorelei warmed to McFaul Senior.

Beside her, Blue's ears pricked. He stood. Not hostile—how did she know that?—but gravely courteous. She turned to see his twin work his way through the brambles.

No, not his twin. This dog might be even larger. His coat was grizzled and he moved with the fragility of great age. Across her the two beasts exchanged polite sniffs and resettled on either side. Protective bookends.

There followed a period of near-silence, only the small sounds of men moving with great care through the woods. That she could hear them at all was a tribute to the power of fear. She tried to construct a picture. A planned sweep, small sounds moving in a slow wave from one side of her to the other.

Far away, at the very edge of her hearing, she heard a car engine turn over, then leap into life and surge away. Somebody cursed and began a shambling run toward the noise.

"Who was guarding the cars? Elmo?"

More people standing, moving away. The same voice, shouting: "That's a squad car! Who was last in line? Move!"

Silence no longer mattered. Several men beat back through the brambles, cursing because they couldn't take time to avoid their thorny backlash. Another car took off, its siren screaming.

"They didn't all get away!"

McFaul Senior's voice was a half squeak of triumph, no more than ten feet away.

Lorelei felt a thump of renewed fear.

There was the sound of speech, half gasp, half murmur, too low to understand.

"Who speaks Spanish? Get over here fast. He's only got but another five minutes."

People crashed her way. More cursing. The light tenor—the one Barney McFaul had addressed as Willetts—spoke.

Lorelei had heard enough street Spanish to recognize the sound of it—she could even tell that Willetts' accent was terrible—but she couldn't distinguish words. He asked several questions with increasing insistence; she couldn't hear any answers.

A rush of words in a second voice, half breathed, half spoken.

Willetts resumed his questions, but she didn't hear the other voice again.

"Well?" That was the man she now knew was Barney McFaul.

"He was blaming everything on some unprintable amateur."

"Yeah, that's what I make it too," said Barney McFaul.

Someone whistled again. Her new acquaintance barked deafeningly and struggled to stand. Footsteps beat toward her.

She rolled over on her good arm, the gun forgotten.

"Well, I never! No, don't get up."

McFaul Senior hunkered beside her, taking off his hat politely.

He had a clown's face: mouth set sideways under a shaggy gray sweep of mustache; equally bushy brows, one lowered in a scowl, the other soaring up toward what had once been his hairline, now the line between sunburn and hat-white; his nose an afterthought. His eyes were large and amazed as a child's.

"You know, you're a lucky little lady."

"She's used up more luck in the past day than most people go through in a lifetime."

Barney McFaul, his long gun resting on his shoulder, hand extended to help her up.

His father beat him to it, lifting her with small encouraging sounds as though standing up were something little ladies did only rarely and never under their own power. His son had to settle for the much more labored process of helping the aged dog to his feet. Lorelei felt a raw edge that was no longer strange, teetering between tears and laughter and nausea, not sure which would win out.

Barney looked a few steps past her.

"Your luck's holding, Muldoon."

She watched as he eased a knife out of the ground and swung it by its point. The blade must have been a foot long.

"It's all right," Buck assured her, "the owner is thoroughly dead."

"But so close!"

"No, he's a good few feet farther over. Must have heaved this when he saw he wouldn't make it."

Buck hurried into speech. Apparently little ladies ought not to be frightened. "You were Fred's friend, weren't you? He had a mighty fine eye for a lady, I surely will say that."

Lorelei met Barney's eyes over his father's head, trying not to smile. It *was* a good face. If only he had a tenth of his father's transparent gallantry.

She tried to move and stopped, wincing. Buck's scowl was horrific.

"You mean you've been hobbling around since the crash? Why didn't you get her to the hospital, Barney?"

"Before you get too friendly, Dad, let's find out who put the marijuana in Colman's field."

Buck stopped like an unwound toy. He looked at her in dismay, looked away, and excused himself to the two of them, joining a huddle of men a few feet away.

Lorelei looked after him. "He's like a child."

"In ways."

"What was that about marijuana?"

"Mean to say you didn't notice the field on the far side of Colman's cabin? The big level one he used as a landing strip?"

"Is that why we crashed? Because Fred couldn't land?"

A tall man with a heavy paunch, tree trunks of legs—a massive man altogether—came up behind Barney and answered for him. "My, no. Bandit could have put that plane down on the road if need be."

He tipped a swooping pale gray hat. "Claud Willetts, Miss Muldoon. No, the plane was tampered with."

"That's what he was bragging about, then. Fenton. Is that who—" She looked back over her shoulder.

Claud Willetts had apparently appointed himself spokesman.

"No, this one's new to Barney. You better take a look, see if you can put a name to him."

The men gave way to reveal the figure at their feet. One of

them, with the bony clumsiness of an adolescent, was wild-eyed with excitement. Suddenly in a live video game and determined not to miss a move. He looked as though he was about to ask for her autograph.

Claud Willetts jerked a head toward him. "My nephew, Stan Sokoloff. And that's Sheriff Neiderhoffer."

The other men were all in steel gray. One, older than the others, his washed-blue eyes red-rimmed with exhaustion, nodded without speaking.

At their feet, a trooper turned the dead man over on his back with gentle farmer's hands.

"I thought you weren't supposed to move him," Stan Sokoloff said.

"I told you to keep your mouth shut," his uncle snapped. "We know all we need to know about how he died. Caught in the cross fire of his own men, wouldn't you say, Hoff?"

"We'll see how it goes, Gang. If you'd come closer, Miss Muldoon."

Briefly she hung back, as though the dead man might suddenly leap to his feet brandishing his knife. But when she saw him, she forgot to be afraid.

The things that might have made the man frightening in life had become in death the costume of a child. His face was a startled mask, the brown of his eyes already flat, his jaw slack, exposing the diamond-studded tooth of which he must have been proud. His beard looked like dirty soap suds around his mouth and chin.

Without the wiry menace of life, his body looked frail, head overly large, a puppet without a puppeteer. His chest was flattened into an improbable shape. The black T-shirt didn't show blood, but for several feet behind him the pine needles looked oily with it.

Dying, he had crawled as close to her as he could; when he could no longer crawl, he had hurled his knife.

Which was harder to understand: That a stranger had used his dying strength to try to kill her? Or that none of these men seemed surprised?

"If I had seen him alive, he would have terrified me," she said. An epitaph that probably would have pleased him. "Now all I can see is how young he was. He couldn't have been much more than a teenager."

It wasn't what the men wanted to hear. It didn't matter. On impulse she bent down and closed his eyes. It didn't make him look at peace. Nothing could do that.

The tall tired man in gray nodded to one of his men, who covered the body. Another carefully took the knife from Barney by its point. Lorelei watched him try to put it into a plastic evidence bag. He settled for shrouding it in plastic wrap.

"Be particular about the handle," the sheriff said. "They say forensics can nearly always find some blood traces if there are any to be found."

Barney looked a question.

"Shari Finley," Neiderhoffer said. "Found her in the Demersville parking lot in her car early this morning."

Lorelei was interested to see that Barney McFaul immediately turned to face the big man like an adversary, elbows canted out a little, hands at a useful angle. A movie cowboy about to draw.

Still looking at him, Barney said to the sheriff, "What did you make of that section of fuel line?"

The sheriff looked from Barney back to the big man and held out a hand with a sigh. "Why am I not surprised?"

With an injured expression, the Willetts man reached into his back pocket and dropped a piece of thin tubing into the sheriff's open palm. "I was going to give it to you as soon as the subject came up."

The sheriff tipped his hat to Lorelei. "Um, I know it's hard for you, but whatever you and Barney can tell us now will help us work smarter. And the sooner we catch the rest of them, the sooner you'll be safe."

"If I could just sit down . . ."

The red cadillac was closest. The sheriff stopped her.

"Part of the crime scene, ma'am. Elmo, dust this for fingerprints and get it back to His Honor."

A patrolman most noticeable for the size of his Adam's apple dashed off with Willetts' nephew at his heels. They were about the same age. Friends, perhaps.

"If the knife checks out, you can tie Shari's death to the car thefts," Claud said. "And Bandit. So probably the marijuana is too. Figure out one, we'll have them all."

"Car thefts." Again Barney looked at Claud.

Neiderhoffer sighed. "No way to keep the Feds out now."

"I told you, Hoff, sic Domenica on them. Hoff just told me about the cars, Barney. I'll fill you in later."

Neiderhoffer ignored him, settling Lorelei on the passenger seat of a police car under Blue's watchful eye. "It'll save time to talk to you both at once, Barney, in case you saw something she missed—"

Barney propped a boot on the car's rocker panel, close enough to brush her skirt. "I don't know his name. We didn't exactly introduce ourselves."

Lorelei squinted up at him against the sun. "I've noticed you find that difficult. He told me his name was Ricardo Fenton. Ricardo, but no accent to speak of."

"What can you tell us about him?"

Lorelei propped her head on her hands. Fenton. The dark eyes, the naked need to look big. What he said, how he said it.

"At first I assumed he was a security man. That I had triggered the burglar alarm. And then—when somebody waves a gun in your face, you sort of concentrate on that."

"Nothing much to him," Barney said. "Spear carrier."

"Oh, I don't think so." She shuddered. "He meant to kill me, I know it."

"Had to screw himself up to it, I bet."

"At first. But then something changed. He was—almost absentminded about it. As though he needed to get it over with to get to something more important."

That impressed them for some reason.

"He was taking me back to the plane so my body would be there."

"Directing you? Like he knew where it was? Or did you lead him?"

"How else would he know I was at Fred's cabin? He must have come from the plane."

" 'Must have' doesn't help, ma'am. Just what you saw. Did he seem to know where you were heading?"

Facts, not analysis. She looked up at Barney McFaul. "He had a gun in my back. That's all I know."

"And he didn't mention whose orders he was following."

"He mentioned another man. A big man, he said."

"One of them is big," Barney agreed. "Strong, anyway. Had an LAW. Probably an RPG."

"Uh-huh," said the sheriff. "And what's that in civilian?"

"Bazooka. An RPG weighs upwards of twenty pounds. Their other stuff was lighter. At least one AK-47."

One of the gray-shirts came up to Neiderhoffer and murmured something. With a smothered curse, he strode to the next car and grabbed the handset to the radio.

Claud Willetts spoke quickly, too low for the sheriff to hear. "Were you the reason Bandit wanted to retire, Lorelei?"

She could feel heat from the throat of Fred's shirt to the roots of her hair. A romantic week with Fred had seemed like a private matter. To have people assume publicly that she was his mistress . . .

"He said something to the people in the tower in Billings. That's the first I heard about it."

"How long have you known him? How well?"

"Not well enough to know what someone might want to kill him for. Or me."

"Have to do better than that, Muldoon," Barney said to the air over her head.

"You'll have to allow for my lack of experience, Barney McFaul! In New York people walk for blocks at a time without getting shot at or kidnapped!"

Instantly Claud and Buck separated them, Claud with a shoulder, Buck easing her back to her feet and leading her away. When she looked back, Barney was smiling reluctantly.

"Where's the ambulance?" Buck asked the sheriff accusingly. "How long does she have to stand here?"

As if on cue, an ambulance careened around the final turn on two wheels, siren blaring and red lights rolling.

Neiderhoffer shouted at the driver, "I've already had a car wrecked! Who's going to pick up *your* pieces?"

The driver tried unsuccessfully to smother a grin. His seatmate hopped down. "My fault, Sheriff."

"Dr. Sue!"

"We've been prepping for you guys all day. I got impatient. Speaking of which, where's my patient?"

Dr. Sue Lombardy's nameplate was at a casual angle on the white jacket she wore over surgical greens. She was rangy, with the kind of tiredness that pared a person down to essentials—no makeup, thick brown hair drawn through a no-nonsense rubber band—and the kind of competence that announced itself in every understated gesture.

Lorelei was in the ambulance without even a last look at the mountain man, a.k.a. Barney McFaul. Reentering the real world with the same disorienting speed with which she had left it.

In the ambulance, Dr. Lombardy's deft fingers probed, gentle but thorough, bending Lorelei forward, asking her to breathe while she tuned the stethoscope up and down Lorelei's chest and back.

Taking all of the weight, she laid Lorelei carefully back, and then contemplated her with a level brown gaze. Comforting. You wouldn't expect anything flowery, but you could deal with a truth told by Sue Lombardy. Even if it was the same truth delivered brusquely the day before by Barney Mc-Faul: ribs that were cracked but not broken, lungs not damaged. And Sue could do nothing for her beyond painkillers.

"Doesn't make sense, does it? We used to strap ribs, but it just weakens the muscles, you'd be laid up longer. But don't try laughing any time soon."

"But it hurts—"

"Lord, yes, ribs are awful. Abby Butterfield says God made Eve out of a rib so Adam would have some idea of labor pain."

The doors closed. The ambulance lipped up over the edge of the road and drove slowly away.

Claud Willetts looked at the thicket as if he could still see Lorelei Muldoon rising from it like a Medusa, the will to live pouring off her like musk. Not at all like the placid blondes Bandit had been drawn to.

He had felt the force of her gaze briefly, before it moved past him to Barney McFaul. Bandit Colman had almost been a lucky man.

He listened to Hoff talk logistics: Where was the tow for Barney's truck, who was calling the Federal Aviation Administration, sandwiches and coffee in the Parish Hall.

"Forget all that!" Buck said. "We have to make it official. Bring Bandit home. Where's the gurney? Who let it go off with the ambulance? Claud, aren't you coming?"

"I said my good-byes last night."

The others looked at him and quickly away. They thought

he couldn't handle it. Which was true, but not for their reasons. If he saw Bandit . . . damaged . . . it might undermine his rage. Shake him apart into mere mourning. He had to save himself to figure out a new plan, now that his old one had been trashed.

"Then can I go, Claud? Can I?" Stan asked.

Claud waved him away. Stan took it as permission and followed Barney and Buck McFaul and Blue up the firebreak. Then came a few gray-shirts with a body bag. Max tried to heave himself upright; Buck ordered him ruthlessly back. He settled heavily on Claud's feet.

Barney had reacted to Lorelei Muldoon with reluctant amusement. Not anger. Not violence. Claud tucked the observation away.

Abby was at a safe distance, back at the Parish Hall.

Claud eased his numb feet out from under the dog and made his way over to Sheriff Neiderhoffer. "You lost a squad car?"

"Whoever they are, one of them's a damn good driver. He found time to swing around and force Elmo off the road. Kid thinks he's playing bumper pool."

"Stan too. Only he thinks it's a video game."

"By the time Elmo finishes his report on that squad car, he'll take it serious."

"You know, Hoff, this almost worked. If we'd been a little better prepared—"

"Whose fault is that?"

"We know they're still around, and we know they're interested in Lorelei Muldoon. There's still time to finish it ourselves. FAA, FBI, DEA, rangers—none of them can get started before tomorrow."

Hoff was too used to leaning on Claud to be anything but grateful. "You say that like a man with an idea, Gang."

"We could use her again, Hoff. Set up guards at the hospital, safe as houses. All it would take is a few words to Emerson Flagg. The Sunday *Herald*'s going to be all Bandit anyway."

"It must come in handy to have the local newspaper editor in your pocket."

Claud took that for a yes. He stretched a long arm over Hoff's shoulder and talked persuasively.

Chapter Seven

Olga Finaldo sipped coffee by herself in the living room of the Demersville Sheraton suite while she pored over the Sunday morning *Demersville Herald*. Since she dealt mainly with invoices—in the universal language of numbers—she didn't read English as easily as she spoke it. But Sunday morning she worked her way through the *Herald* from front page to last. Much bored her; some puzzled her.

One story made her sit rigidly upright.

Her hands shaking in the only sign of relief she permitted herself, she read it twice more from beginning to end.

She eased open the door to Betty Colman's bedroom to be sure the widow was not awake. Olga Finaldo went to her own bedroom and called her niece Estrella.

When she looked in again on Betty, the senator's widow still slept, her sheets muddled from a restless night. Some people mourned openly, Olga thought; others grieved with their bodies, unable either to express their feelings or be done with them. She poured herself more coffee, willing the time to pass. It was to be expected that a great opportunity would be accompanied by great risks.

The door to Betty's room creaked and Betty appeared, yawning hugely. "I don't know whether it's the time change or the altitude, I always feel so washed out the first few days here."

Instantly Olga was her smiling matter-of-fact self. "Who can blame you at such a time?" She poured coffee and handed Betty the paper. "They pay great respect to your husband."

"I should hope so. Half the good things in this state have come from the Colmans."

Olga could tell what Betty was reading by the photographs with each story. Betty was quickly done with the report of the crash. She took more time with the obituary, sitting up a little. Feeling officially a widow, perhaps.

The widow turned the page in a musing way and was transfixed. She read with care from the top of the page to the bottom. Back to the top. Through to the bottom again. Not the story that had held Olga's interest. Which one?

Fortunately Betty couldn't keep her thoughts to herself. "Governor Larsen is coming Wednesday for the memorial service."

Her voice reflected mixed feelings. Olga said cautiously, "An honor, yet you don't sound entirely pleased."

"Oh, it's only what's due, after all, but—the media are already speculating about who he's going to appoint to finish Fred's term."

"Much too soon. Barbaric!"

"Oh, not really. It's who they mention. Larry Hungerford, now—he's far too inexperienced. How many people outside Washington have even heard of him? And Claud Willetts would be ridiculous, no one trusts him. But somehow it hadn't occurred to me that *I* . . . though, of course, the widows of senators frequently . . ."

Olga had no trouble translating Betty's half sentences. Her enthusiasm came from the heart. "But of course. You are the natural choice. You know Washington well, you are well-known there—"

"Yes." Betty's sensitive tuning fork for power vibrated to a new source: her own.

"The governor will make the announcement when he arrives?"

"It doesn't say definitely, but I assume—"

"My dear Betty, forgive me, one can never assume. How often have I watched you thinking ahead of what others may do and prepare for it? The cleverness must have been born in you."

"I must not be awake yet, Olga. I haven't the slightest idea what you're talking about."

"The other people you mention: You know their weaknesses. One can easily be sure the governor also is aware of them. I see only one real problem."

Olga refolded the paper to the front page and pointed to a story below the fold, one that Betty apparently had not seen. The picture, at least, was familiar.

"Emerson, how *dare* you!" The senator's widow wrenched open the paper to read about the senator's mistress.

"That they should write about Miss Muldoon is insulting, but one could live with that. No. What matters is *what* they write. If the mistress is a heroine, what, then, is the widow? A figure of the past? Someone of small importance?"

Anger evaporating along with the daydream of power, Betty stared at Olga. "How can I stop it?"

"But, my dear Betty, it is obvious. You must demonstrate the difference between a wife and a mistress."

"You mean, at the funeral? She won't attend, I'll certainly see to that. I could do the eulogy myself, although I thought the governor—"

"Important, certainly. But days away, my dear, and to reporters, a day is a week, and a week . . ." Olga shrugged.

"You must provide a story now, before any more are written about Miss Muldoon."

Betty shifted restlessly, near the end of her attention span. Olga hurried on.

"My dear, why do you stay in a hotel like a visitor? Is his home then being kept for Miss Muldoon after her release from the hospital?"

"The cabin! You're absolutely right! Pictures of me reflecting on our years together! *Sloane's* will love it."

"But what a strategist you are!"

"Yes, but—they're taking such good care of us here." Betty looked around the suite reluctantly. Hotel staff and guests alike had treated her like minor royalty. "The cabin is so isolated."

"More so even for me than for you, Betty. Oh, yes. Perhaps you forget that I cannot drive?"

It was an irritation, one that would doubtless make complications before many more hours had passed. But it was also true that when you compelled people to do something, it was wise to help them at the same time to feel superior. Betty's petulance faded.

"And you're supposed to be the great planner! I suppose now I'll have to be your chauffeur."

"But no. I see Mr. Hungerford in that role." As Betty smiled, Olga gently enlarged this theme. "I think Larry must realize he is *your* chief of staff now. The memorial service cannot take all his time. He is well able to arrange for the transfer to *your* cabin."

While Betty happily took up the phone to give Larry Hungerford his new assignment, Olga retired to her bedroom, ostensibly to repack. It was necessary to relax her iron control, if only for a moment.

Betty Colman was almost too easy to direct; the safety precautions Olga had prepared might never have been necessary.

All the more essential to get them back, if only to destroy them.

The *Herald* was delivered to patients at Demersville General along with early morning coffee.

Lorelei Muldoon let hers wait, along with a call to her father, while she showered. She hadn't mentioned the weekend to Hank—he could pretend she didn't have a sex life, as long as he knew nothing about it—but he would need reassurance now. She would sound much more convincing when she was clean.

She stood under the water, the events of Friday and Saturday sluicing away with the dirt and blood. Her injuries were colorful this morning. Miscellaneous purple splotches, a dark swollen diagonal line left by the seat belt. But her left side, the one that hurt so much more, showed nothing. Just as Sue Lombardy had said.

Last night the idea of laughter had been unthinkable. But on this clean golden morning, cupping water to her face, working her fingers through newly clean hair, it was easy to smile.

And hard to feel the loss of Fred. Why? Already he seemed more Senator Fred Roybal Bandit Colman than Fred, larger but less real, like a movie hero a half hour after you've left the theater. By nightfall she could be back in New York, the death of Senator Colman with the police where it belonged, out of her life with as many of the unanswered questions as he had brought into it.

She twisted a towel up like a turban and contemplated her foggy image in the mirror. She looked unfamiliar without her customary eyes and mouth and hair. Drab.

There was a crisp double rap on the bathroom door. Lorelei looked around the edge.

"Good." It was Sue Lombardy. "You must be feeling better."

"A shower is better than painkillers."

There was the quick smile Lorelei remembered from the previous day. "I need to take a look at you before I go off, but I'm in no hurry. It's been a bad night." Her jacket was streaked with blood that hadn't been there the day before. Wearily she shrugged out of it, tossing it across the bed.

"Before I forget . . ." She handed Lorelei a bundle. "I thought you might want something clean to wear since all your stuff went up with the plane. Just until somebody rounds you up something better. We're about the same size."

Went up with the plane?

"Thanks." Lorelei raised her voice to be heard through the door. "That's the advantage of a female resident."

"I'll take any credit you want to give me, but surgical greens are actually unisex—"

"But a man would never think of it."

"Tell Abigail Butterfield that. She kept after the board till it was easier to hire me than to think up an excuse."

It was next to impossible to pull a comb through her hair with only one workable arm.

"I'll be out in a minute."

"No rush. I'll take your paper and some of your coffee, if you don't mind. They do a pretty good job of it."

"Be my guest."

"Besides, you want to look your best for the reporters."

"Reporters?"

"Honeybun, you not only survived a plane crash, you're part of Senator Colman's story. That's the biggest thing to happen here since I can remember. I put you off-limits last night, but you're going to be a very popular girl today."

Reporters: There was the real world with a vengeance!

The surgical greens made her look drab from head to foot. She rummaged in her bag for Fred's calico kerchief and knotted it loosely. Well, it was something. She set to work on her makeup.

There was a rustle of paper from her room. "If I hadn't gone over you myself, I wouldn't believe you got out without a burn. And how you got his body out with more guys firing at you—no wonder there's a cop outside your door."

Burns.

Got his body out?

Cop outside the door?

"Could you run that by me again?"

Another, louder rustling was the only response. Lorelei pushed open the bathroom door.

Sue Lombardy sprawled in the visitor's chair, her head tilted back, coffee spilling across her lap. It would have scalded, if she could feel it. But the ripe, purpling swelling of her neck and the sharp angle of her head made it clear that she wouldn't feel anything, ever again.

Claud rapped his folded copy of the *Herald* on the chrome door to Duncan's kitchen and pushed it open.

"Hey, Duncan."

"Hey, Claud. Coffee? With?"

"You're a lifesaver. Got any tempura?"

"At eight in the morning?" Duncan cooked what she pleased—if people stopped coming, she said, she'd retire that much sooner. Breakfast, though generous, was traditional.

But this morning she looked at Claud and relented. "You do look as though you've been through the wringer. Colman was a fine man. Fine."

"He was that."

"I'll whip up a batch just for you. It'll have to be zucchini, mind."

"When are you going to learn to say no to Abby, Duncan?"

"Remember what Bandit said last summer? That Abby was threatening to fill the collection plate with zucchini and make each of us take one in exchange for our offering?"

His face must have changed; Duncan said quickly, "You need food, not reminders."

"Just bring it to my booth."

"What good does it do to hide out when everybody knows where to look?"

"I don't mind being found, Duncan, as long as it's after ten o'clock."

"After the service starts at Bitterroot Congregational, you mean. What have you done this time?"

Claud let the door swing shut without answering. He slid into his booth with a sigh and spread his *Herald* out on the table, working his way through each story at an even pace.

He was halfway through his zucchini, melting inside a crisp batter of Duncan's devising, when two more copies hit the table. The McFauls had arrived.

Claud licked his fingers. "If you want some tempura, you'll have to get your own."

Buck snorted. "If ever I want to find you, Claud Willetts, which I rarely do, I cast around for the smell of fried fat and track it back."

It's not impossible to pick a quarrel with a man who's sitting down, but it's more difficult. Claud said without looking up, "There's a lot of me to maintain. What can I do for you gentlemen?"

Barney smiled a little in recognition of the strategem, easing his sputtering father before him into the facing seat. Once they were down, Max and Blue settled under the table, shoving Claud's feet back under him.

"Well, Barney?"

"Dad first."

Claud sighed. He tried to avoid dealing with both McFauls at once. Buck saw violence as adventure, heroes and heroines and happy endings, while Barney—maybe because he dealt with it on a regular basis—treated it like a janitor did dirt. Buck could be lulled by the kind of long fluent speculative tale Claud reveled in. Barney had to be hit with one fact after another. Not only did Claud find it hard to keep his stories straight, one frequently got in the way of the other.

But there it was: Barney had a porcupine's sensitivity about Buck. Claud had watched Barney intervene in one of his father's fights. Who with? What about? Long forgotten. But he would never forget the sight of Barney, perfectly calm but as bug-eyed as a jock under pressure, moving faster than reason.

Only Buck could get Barney back in control. Only Barney could make Buck subside, spluttering, into usefulness. A matched pair.

"Well, Buck?"

"That plane. It was in fine shape when we left with Bandit's body. Aside from the crash, I mean."

"Some aside."

"And that girl no more shot the dead man than I did. His back was tore half away."

"He was mine," Barney said.

"And why put where she is in the *Herald* for anybody to read?"

"Last time I heard, Emerson Flagg was in charge of the *Herald*."

"Just answer Dad."

"Touchy, touchy." Claud's eyes half closed with satisfaction as Buck smacked his hands on the table to leap to his feet.

Barney put a hand on his father's shoulder. "He'd rather make us mad than answer, Dad, even if it means losing a couple of teeth. Now, why is that, Willetts?"

"I'd like to see you try, Barney."

"You wouldn't see it, it would just happen."

Claud dared Barney a few seconds longer before he capitulated. "Tell me what good that plane was to us. Don't throw a fit, Buck, just tell me."

"To figure out how it was tampered with."

"We know that, Barney got the piece of wire that proves it. So what?"

"Is one of us crazy? So we can prove who did it."

"When—if—we catch up with them. But we're not looking for plane mechanics, Buck, we're looking for who *hired* them."

Buck was silent, working this out.

Barney said, "One might lead to the other."

"If they were valley people, maybe. Those weren't valley people yesterday."

"Nobody's I.D.'d the dead one?"

Claud shook his head with a certainty that spoke for the toolies as well as himself. "Nobody claims to have seen him around either. So they've got to be outsiders. Who's hiring them? The plane won't tell us that."

Barney said, "You burned the plane to take it off the table."

Claud nodded. Barney stared off into his own land, while Buck worried at it out loud. "I can't believe Orry Neiderhoffer agreed to that."

"Where does he come into it? Elmo loaded up the luggage and dismantled half the engine, and they took it all with them. Maybe they jostled some fuel loose. It went up later, after they were gone."

Barney was back. "You make it look like Muldoon is all they have to worry about, and then give them a clear shot."

Before Claud could respond, another *Herald* hit the table.

"And you're guarding her from Duncan's back booth?"

The three men looked up as a nervous one. Abby Butterfield in her weekday jogging suit was one thing. They weren't quite used to the Sunday Reverend Butterfield in velvet-banded black robes relieved only by a narrow white stock at the neck, her cowlicks slicked down into a smooth dark cap.

"Aren't you cutting it a mite fine, Abby? I make it ten o'clock already."

"Francine is singing the offertory anthem before the sermon. That gives me five minutes in hand, Claud. My present text is Psalm Fifty-seven, verse six."

At their blank expressions, she said impatiently, " 'They have digged a pit before me, into the midst whereof they are fallen themselves.' I plan to use local examples as appropriate. You have four minutes and thirty seconds to change my mind."

"Now, Abby—" Claud had a vision of the Bitterroot congregation rising as one and laying seige to Demersville Memorial Hospital.

Abby pushed up her heavy black sleeve to look pointedly at her watch.

"What exactly is it that's bothering you?"

"As if you didn't know." Her New England bray would have carried to the last row in the balcony. "Somehow you got Emerson to blame that man's death on her—for which he'll have to answer to me—and what's worse, you got him to print where to find her."

"What makes you think it was me, Abby?"

"Orry Neiderhoffer has too much red tape and too little imagination, and Emerson Flagg's idea of a front page is a review of the summer theater production plus a picture of the winner of the fourth-grade spelling contest. Or no: blue ribbon in the butter-sculpting at the County Fair."

"How do you know? Maybe you've never been here when he had a story this big."

"I've been here long enough to know he goes in terror of you. He'd never print a story about Senator Colman without showing it to you first."

"And he leaves out what I ask him to," Claud said, playing his hole card. "Like the fact that Hoff has two troopers posted outside Miss Muldoon's door."

Buck leaned back in a clown's exaggerated relief. "Why didn't you say so in the first place?"

Abby's stern expression didn't change. "This is no time for one of your schemes, Claud. Call it off while you can."

"The Lord helps those who help themselves, Reverend."

Unaccountably, the starch went out of Abby, leaving her sad and worried. "You can't do whatever wild prank occurs to you anymore, Claud. Have you forgotten? The man who always came to the rescue is dead."

"You're telling me I hid behind Bandit?"

Claud thought he spoke in a reasonable voice. He wasn't aware of standing up, wasn't aware of anything until he saw Buck leading Abby away in a swirl of black robes, and then, out the front window, her grubby Volvo pulling out, followed by the pink Lincoln.

He tried to follow and became aware of Barney's arm, clamped across his chest like a vise.

"What do you think you're doing?" He swatted it away and accidentally hit the table, which was unaccountably pulled away from the wall. Barney grinned like a toothpaste commercial.

Before Claud could do more than glower, Stan rushed in with an excitement that would have telegraphed news to a total stranger. He didn't even notice Blue.

"Didn't you get the adventure out of your system yesterday?" Claud asked irritably.

"Maybe you need a beeper, Claud," Barney said. "Then he wouldn't have to come in person for the rest of us to hear. Or a cellular phone. Got one to spare?"

"Sheriff Neiderhoffer just called from Demersville Memorial!" Stan said. "He says he's got two new bodies and the Muldoon woman is nowhere to be found."

The worn shock absorbers of the dusty van threw Ricky Fenton into the air with every bump. He giggled—there was no other word for it—he couldn't help himself, even though he knew he was losing face with Mech, staring impassively out over the wheel.

Maybe it wasn't the same for Mech; he had broken his man's neck with one clean blow. While he, Ricardo Fenton, had felt the line of her jaw under his fingers, the cords of her neck, her eyes upside down like a frog's, all her energy straining, flooding toward him, and then . . . slack.

She had been there, and then she wasn't. Because of Ricardo Fenton.

The muscles of his cheeks ached from grinning. "I didn't know what it would be like."

"You still don't."

"Just because it's different for me than it is for you. Ever think Paca might be right?"

Mech made the turnoff into Heroes Wilderness, the van bucketing on the washboard dirt road. "This was *business*. Where are the papers you went for?"

"You ran us out of there so fast, I didn't have the chance—"

"Why were the police there? Your aunt told them to expect us?"

"They probably read about it in the same newspaper she did."

"*Read about?*" Mech's huge hand came out and jerked Fenton close. "Your aunt learned where the woman would be from a *paper?*"

Put like that, it sounded terrible. "You mean, we were set up."

Fenton thought about it. It made him realize something else equally uncomfortable.

Whatever was in police hands would probably go to Colman's widow, where Olga could take what she wanted. Maybe she already had. Colman, the Muldoon woman, her apartment, the plane—all had been destroyed to erase all

128

knowledge, even awareness, of whatever was in Olga's papers. With the Muldoon woman dead, the one remaining memory was inside Ricardo Fenton's head.

The warming giddiness drained away. How much protection was it to be her nephew?

"Head back, Mech, I want to see that newspaper for myself."

Mech pulled the van in under the trees and tossed Fenton the keys. "Go yourself, Finaldo nephew."

"Wait a minute. Where're you going?"

"She's dead, isn't she? I go back to the sinsemilla."

"But you said you'd get rid of the van and the equipment too."

"Don't worry, nephew. Load up the van. I'll get it later. But it won't matter what we hide or where we run. They will find us."

Mech disappeared. Fenton returned to Grady's Gas for a paper. On his way back to camp, the cell phone rang.

He pulled over for that. Since cells couldn't be secured, Olga reserved them for situations so dire that this one had never been put to use.

Lorelei didn't remember going back inside the bathroom. There was no lock—well, how could there be? What if someone had a heart attack in the shower? The staff had to be able to get in. Self-defense wasn't in the design specs. She dug in her heels to brace the door.

As seconds ticked by with no attempt to break down the door, she dared to peer around the edge. She could see the chair where Sue Lombardy lay, its back to the door. The killer had come in from the hall, had come up behind Sue and pulled her up and over the chairback to strangle her.

Did violent death ever become so familiar that there was no wash of nausea in its wake? no sweaty weakness?

She never consciously decided what to do next. One second she was gagging over the sink, and the next her body was thinking for her at a speed she didn't know she possessed.

Without a pause for distaste or sadness—later, Sue, I promise, but first I have to make it to later—she eased the stethoscope away from the awful swelling of Sue's neck, draping it around her own, sideways, as Sue had. She put on Sue's discarded bloody jacket, repinning the nameplate halfway behind the lapel—plate visible, name obscured. Put on her own half glasses. Pulled the surgical green pants as far down over her boots as they would go.

Time for a last look in the small mirror above the bureau? Yes. Good thing: Above the professional V-necked top, jacket, and stethoscope were eyes and mouth that belonged to Sugar Kane in *Some Like It Hot*. She scrubbed her face with tissues, tore off Fred's kerchief and stuffed it in a jacket pocket.

She looked at her pocketbook with longing. But by no stretch would the most casual physician shoulder that on duty. She settled for transferring her wallet and computer beeper to her pockets.

Her eyes still gave her away: Bare of makeup, they were huge and dull with fear and shock. No good. A doctor always looked like God. She shook herself—as though fear were lint—and tried to feel like God. Then, with her own chart-clipboard like a shield in one hand, a ballpoint pen with the point out, a pathetic lance, in the other, she swung the door wide.

Outside her room in an orange kidney-shaped chair slumped a trooper.

The killer had taken more pains with him. Unlike Sue Lombardy's unnatural sprawl, he was composed as if in sleep, legs stretched out, arms crossed over a beer lover's belly, hat tipped over his eyes. If she hadn't already seen Sue, Lorelei might have walked right by. But she knew better, even as she tilted his hat up a careful inch.

His head immediately slipped toward his shoulder at a hideous angle. She shuddered and put the hat back in place as best she could.

Lorelei looked for some stairs, any stairs. She didn't want to be trapped in the car of an elevator where people had whole seconds to realize who she was . . . or who she wasn't.

Unless the killer might seek the same escape route. To meet him in a stairwell, with no other people around . . .

With barely a check, she walked on, trying to take long, confident strides, mouth pursed in a soundless whistle to keep her lips from shaking.

At the end of the hall, the wards changed to smaller rooms. Through a door she could see office chairs, a doctor's name-plate on a big oak desk. With what she hoped looked like the offhandedness of habit, she walked in and closed the door.

Did she dare lock it? Yes. If the office's legal resident arrived—she checked the name: Dr. Something Tilman—he could blame either a janitor or his own carelessness.

Lorelei circled the big desk. Three pictures in a row—one family group, the others of horses, of all things. A pile of mail centered on a newspaper, in turn centered on the blotter.

Neat, horsey, family-minded Dr. Tilman, who hadn't been in since the last mail delivery. Off for the weekend? Or due momentarily?

A picture of Fred stared back up at her. Under Dr. Tilman's mail, Lorelei Muldoon saw the Sunday *Herald* for the first time.

She shook out the paper. A grinning Senator Fred Bandit Roybal Colman, squinting into the sun, filled the top half of the page. Emerson Flagg had done him proud. She skimmed the story—full stops out on majesty, pageantry, dignity—and turned impatiently to the continued line, where a double-page spread retold the history of the generations of Colmans to readers who probably knew it already, from the original rancher to the mother whose portrait she had seen in his cabin, the profile uncannily like his own.

The next page told her how Betty Colman felt, how the governor felt, how Larry Hungerford felt, how Buck McFaul felt, how Claud Willetts felt, how the man and woman on the street felt.

They felt terrible. They recounted what they were doing at the exact moment that they heard. They wondered what they were going to do without him.

With an impatient sigh, she smacked the paper down. Only then did she see the picture of Lorelei Muldoon.

It was the photograph from *Sloane's,* from the cabin, cropped to her head and blown up to half the size of Fred's a few inches above it. Why on earth?

In thick black caps Emerson Flagg had printed: HEROINE AVENGES HER HERO'S DEATH. Eyes widening, Lorelei read how Brave Young Aide Lorelei Muldoon, having Miraculously Escaped Death, had dragged Senator Colman's body out of the burning plane (for picture see page seven). Who had Single-handedly Defended His Body against would-be thieves, killing one, still unidentified (see box for description), with Senator Colman's own pistol. Lorelei Muldoon who, having run off the other ungodly, had called the police.

No mention of Barney McFaul. Buck McFaul. Claud Willetts. Only Lorelei Muldoon, who was now to be found, said the *Herald,* resting comfortably in Demersville Memorial Hospital.

Bewildered, she turned to page seven, which showed the charred skeleton of the plane from half a dozen angles. No mention here either of anyone but Lorelei Muldoon. By separating his stories, the editor must be trying to praise the mistress without offending the wife.

She turned back to the front picture. It had never been more than an anonymous girl with a thin face and a lot of hair. With the features fuzzy from overenlargement, it could have been Lorelei Muldoon. It could have been Sue Lombardy.

Until Sue Lombardy was actually dying under the killer's hands, he would have seen only her back, the back of a woman with a lot of dark hair. Sitting in Lorelei's chair. Drinking her coffee. Reading her paper.

Chapter Eight

Stan only knew that two people had been killed and Lorelei Muldoon had disappeared; Sheriff Orry Neiderhoffer had grated out that much and hung up. Claud and Barney brushed Stan aside and made for the door to the way blocked by Larry Hungerford.

"Claud! I hoped I'd find you here."

"Make it quick or make it later, Hungerford."

"A terrible business," Hungerford said. He was on his best behavior, expression suitably grave but eyes with a suggestion of a good-natured crinkle.

Even with Abby's words echoing and reechoing in his head, Claud somehow found space to wonder how Hungerford knew. Had he been in time to hear Stan? Because if not . . . Claud swung himself around so Barney couldn't push by.

"Betty—that is, Mrs. Colman—is doing as well as can be expected. A courageous woman. She brought a friend, and that's a help, of course. Olga Finaldo, her decorator?"

"Stan met the three of you at the airport, remember? I'll stop by the Sheraton to pay my respects as soon as I can."

"Actually, that's why I'm here." Hungerford lowered his voice. "The Sheraton is so damn public. More reporters arriving on every flight, and where else can they stay? Mrs. Colman feels the need to be by herself just now. She thought that, well, now that . . ."

Even Hungerford couldn't seem to go on.

Why hadn't Claud foreseen Betty's reaction and planned for it? "Bandit took away her keys, didn't he, back in April. And now that he's dead, she wants them back? Maybe they were—"

He wanted to say, "On Bandit's body," but the words stuck. "—with him."

Since sarcasm wasn't a useful tool for a senator's chief of staff, Hungerford wasn't sensitive to it. He merely seemed relieved that the words were out without his being the one to say them.

"She says she's sure you have an extra set."

Claud swayed a little.

"It's not as though the cabin was actually the scene of the tragedy," Hungerford assured him. "The police aren't working there. I checked."

Claud felt Barney's arm clamping his chest again. "Like it or not, Willetts, the man's right. Want to thrash it out some more, I'll meet you at the hospital."

The words cleared Claud's head. The important thing to take away was that, to Hungerford, the "tragedy" was still Bandit's death, not the new ones.

Claud thrust Barney away. "Stan'll show you, Larry. In the bottom right-hand drawer of my desk, Stan. Behind the Wild Turkey."

"But I'm coming too!" Stan protested.

Hungerford ignored Stan (the underling), beaming his thanks at Claud. "And she'll look forward to talking to you—"

Barney said, "If you're staying for a kaffeeklatsch, Claud, I'm gone."

"I'm with you. Stan, do what you're told. The phone seems to be the only way we're learning anything. I want to know it when you know it."

Claud's antique truck had style, but not speed. Claud climbed up beside Barney while Blue watched from the flatbed, rumbling, ruff up.

"Barn, you're the only one of us that knows her at all. If she wasn't kidnapped, where would she go?"

"Nowhere."

"I'm serious."

"So am I. The only place in the valley she's been is Colman's cabin. Think she could find her way back there? The woman doesn't know pillar from post."

Claud drummed his fingers on the dashboard. Why hadn't it occurred to him that the cabin was her only point of reference? Turning his keys over to Hungerford like that. *Stupid* was a label that covered a lot of territory.

Twice this morning, Barney McFaul had saved Claud from his own rage. No point in letting it go to Barney's head. He looked over at the younger man, his jaw clamped over something Claud couldn't read. Anger? sadness?

"When I was in Nam," Claud said with deceptive mildness, "we tried using dogs for guard duty. The idea was to replace men, save some lives. Human ones, anyway. Makes sense, doesn't it? Know why it didn't work? The dogs did whatever their handlers did. If the man went to sleep, the dog did too. I walked right up to a shepherd once and turned a radio on in his ear. He opened an eye and yawned."

"There some point to this?"

"Just this." Claud heaved himself around to look back at Blue braced in the back, his rough hair carved into flowing mustaches by the wind.

"I watched Blue with Lorelei Muldoon. He was taking good care of your lady. Your lady." Claud raised his voice when Barney turned angrily. "Fool yourself, friend, but you don't fool me."

Barney stared back at the road with a bleak expression that didn't deceive Claud one bit. Nor was he surprised when Barney—he of the quiet skill—sent the truck viciously at a pothole, and a second, and a third.

Claud hit the ceiling with the first one. He braced himself, smiling, for the next.

By the time Claud and Barney arrived at the second floor of Demersville Memorial Hospital, the corridor was chockablock: a trooper with a roller of broad yellow DO NOT CROSS tape marking off space seemingly at random, two gurneys bearing gray body bags, lights blazing from tripods, cameras flickering, a thin-gloved trooper coating everything in sight with fine dust, followed by another thin-gloved trooper working a camera, followed in turn by a third thin-gloved trooper searching carefully. Half of the valley lawmen, all here in one room.

Barney plunged ahead, Claud followed, giving him the space villagers probably give a man about to run amok, over to where the sheriff stooped, nodding patiently at a short starchy man in a suit.

"This is a working hospital," Claud heard. "We are in the business of serving the living, not the dead."

Neiderhoffer stopped looking patient and showed underlying metal. "One of them is one of ours."

"And one of them is one of *ours*, Sheriff. This corridor is a direct route to surgery. I can give you another half an hour. after that, you'll be confined to Ms. Muldoon's room."

He set off without waiting for an answer. Not that it mattered. Deadlines could come and go if Sheriff Orry Neiderhoffer thought he might be on to something.

Claud said, "Looks like you have everything under control, Hoff."

"We're getting enough practice."

"Who was it?"

"You remember Kosetic?"

"Basketball. About ten years ago. Center."

"Right. This time it's three kids without a dad. Oldest is our Sam's age."

"And the other one was a doctor? Nurse?"

"Sue Lombardy."

Claud breathed in a low whistle. "Abby will have our heads on a plate."

"I'm putting all the blame on you. What chance keeping Feds out now?"

"Two troopers, you promised me. What happened?"

"Elmo was off in an empty room writing up his report of the squad car he totaled yesterday. I tell you, Gang, if he wasn't Lynette's brother—"

Barney thrust between them. "Muldoon?"

"Maybe you can help us, son."

Sheriff Neiderhoffer jerked a hand at the abject Elmo. Adam's apple bobbing, he disappeared into Lorelei Muldoon's room and returned with a bundle. Neiderhoffer spread the contents on an empty gurney.

"These things were in a pile in the bathroom."

These things. Barney sorted them: Lorelei's bag, the flannel shirt and her bulky skirt, heavily stained by the events of the past two days. Empty, as if the three dimensions of Lorelei Muldoon herself had been flattened into a lifeless two.

Barney didn't seem able to stop folding and refolding them.

"She was wearing good boots, too," he said. "Ostrich. Rocky Carroll's, I shouldn't wonder."

"Stands to reason," Claud agreed. "That's what Bandit wears."

138

Wore. Without warning, these deaths faded into the other one back in the shadow of the Beargrass River. For the first time something else pierced his rage, something equally terrible.

Hoff didn't seem to notice. "Now that you mention it, I remember the boots." He passed a comment on to one of his men. "We haven't found any underwear either. You happen to know what she was wearing, Barney?"

It was Claud's turn to take hold of Barney. Barney shrugged him off with disturbing ease, but it had slowed him down.

"She treated this thing—" Barney touched the big leather bag "—like a baby. I can't see her going by choice without it."

As Barney had two days before, they emptied out the bag; pens and stacks of paper tumbled together with makeup and hairbrush.

Neiderhoffer said, "Would you know if anything's missing?"

"Her wallet. Some kind of beeper." Barney watched Claud fan bottles, tubes, and wands into rows like a croupier. "Something else too."

"Credit cards?" Neiderhoffer offered.

"They'd be in the wallet," Claud said.

"Something's different." Barney's brows were a black bar of concentration. He rescued the makeup from Claud, rubbing his fingers over each one like an amulet before replacing it in the bag.

Claud and the sheriff waited. Finally Barney shook his head.

"So unless you think she'd likely walk out of the hospital wrapped in a blanket, we'd better look for a body as well as a woman." Neiderhoffer turned and gave a soft-voiced order. "And what Mr. Bureaucrat is going to say when he finds out we're taking over the whole hospital, I don't like to think."

"Yeah, you look petrified," Claud said.

"I can help search," Barney said with relief.

"All eyes and hands welcome, son."

At the far end behind police sawhorses—jammed together out of the way, unable to do their jobs, and loudly protesting—reporters who had come for routine coverage found themselves on the fringes of something much bigger, potentially career-making. Barney shouldered through them and on up the corridor. The troopers left the sawhorse barricades and followed him.

Neiderhoffer asked, "Does it strike you that he's mighty close to the edge of the safety zone?"

"He knew her twenty-four hours longer than we did, Hoff. Maybe that's all it takes."

"Getting out of the safety zone yourself, Gang?"

"Bandit isn't even in the ground! That woman must be some piece of work!"

"She didn't know Bandit from way back, Gang. No reason for her to feel what we do. Besides, if our Sandy took up with a married man as old as we are, I'd take off my badge and chase him with a shotgun."

Neiderhoffer pulled the long tails of his mustache. "Well, no, Lynette would beat me to it. Senator or no senator. Besides—" friend gave way to policeman "—there's no call for resentment. Pity, maybe."

"You don't think we're going to find her, then."

"Alive? It's about as likely as Barney running tame."

Hoff eyed Claud with something between a grudge and a plea. "I got to set up this search, Gang. But when I get back, don't you think it's time to pass on whatever you held back yesterday?"

Before Claud could reply, the sawhorses holding back the reporters fell over. Buck McFaul and another man burst into the corridor, caroming from one wall to the other, Buck clearly the aggressor, the other man, much younger and taller, fending off punishing blows to the face.

The man's real danger, though, lay in McFaul Junior seeing the fight. Claud shouted, "Where's Barney?"

"Up on the roof by now!" Neiderhoffer shouted back. "You take Buck, I'll get this one."

From the huddle of watching reporters, *Sloane's Magazine* told *The Washington Post*, "This is one time I don't mind seeing *The Times* on the front line."

"I guess he thought as long as the guy was twice his age and half his size, he could ask whatever he wanted."

Claud wrapped Buck up in a gorilla hug and pulled him away, still flailing. His teeth were missing, but *The Times* had sustained much more visible damage.

"You okay?" the sheriff asked Buck's victim.

"No, I'm not okay! Whatever you arrest him for, I'll testify!"

"Arresting him?"

"Felonious assault?" *The Times* put a hand to his nose and looked at the bloody result. "Endangering public safety? He's a menace!"

The sheriff showed amusement. "If we arrested somebody for every little mix-up, I'd need three times my payroll. Four times when Buck's around."

Buck tried to talk, fished his teeth out of his shirt pocket, slipped them back into place, and tried again. "He said something I won't repeat about Lorelei Muldoon."

"There you go," the sheriff said. "If you can't back up your play, son, maybe you'd better go back home."

"*I'd* better—"

"Make an op-ed out of it," the *Post* said without sympathy.

"Gang, I'll be looking for you later."

Claud nodded, watching Neiderhoffer murmur into his handset and set off, Buck beside him taking two steps to his one. The media pool followed, except for the dark, raw-boned reporter from *Sloane's*, who leaned against a wall in a patent attempt to look invisible.

If Buck was back from church, where was Abby?

In the excitement, she had slipped past, moving purposefully toward the heavy gray plastic bags with their sadly evocative shapes. Back in a jogging suit (navy this time), but still obviously on duty.

She unzipped the first bag gently. Her hands might have been praying: calm, undismayed, brushing Sue Lombardy's hair back, smoothing the distorted, once familiar face.

The sight shocked and saddened Claud. But it didn't mean he'd had a bad idea. The mistake had been Hoff's, entrusting a serious job to his half-wit brother-in-law. If they gave up now, the deaths would be meaningless.

They had learned so little. That Lorelei Muldoon was worth killing. (For herself? Or for something to do with Bandit?) That Bandit's death had been no accident, in case confirmation was necessary. That the intruders were still in the valley.

The *Herald*'s delivery trucks didn't take off much before 5:00 A.M. It wasn't yet noon. Was that enough time to bump information up a chain of command, send orders back, and carry them out? Or was the order giver close at hand too? Maybe even the same man as the killer?

Once the sheriff realized that Claud had more questions than answers, he'd probably get cut out of the loop. Better to play hard to get; by the time Hoff caught up with him again, they both might have new facts to trade. Claud trusted himself to make more of them than Hoff could.

But if the Feds came in . . . As outsiders, they started ten steps behind. Except for their labs back in Bogwash. Claud fingered Lorelei Muldoon's belongings. Something had caught Barney McFaul's eye. If everything was packed up and sent away, what chance would he have of figuring out what Barney had seen?

If he, Claud, took her stuff, Hoff would know it meant something and come after him. Whereas *Abby* . . .

Penitence was the line to take.

Abby was bent over the second body bag. Fleetingly he felt that Dr. Sue and Kosetic were at peace. That the living could let them go and get on to what they had to do.

When she turned and came toward him, she walked with the slip-slap steps of an old woman. It scared him.

With an honesty he hadn't intended, he blurted, "You're going to say this is my fault."

She straightened with an effort. "Oh, there's blame enough to go around. If you hadn't set that poor young woman up, if the sheriff had taken her danger seriously, if I had been more concerned with the tormented soul behind this and less about what you might do . . ."

She folded and refolded Lorelei Muldoon's clothes, as if she could reach out to Lorelei Muldoon through what she had left behind as she had reached out to Kosetic and Sue Lombardy. Her small, neat hands shook a little.

"You're going to keep on, aren't you." She looked uncertain as well as bone-weary. He hadn't seen her this way; angry or cheerful, the Reverend Abigail Butterfield always went full-tilt.

"You want me to quit just because they raised the stakes?"

"Don't."

"Answer me this, Reverend. Don't you feel the least little desire to get back at the guys who killed Shari? And Sue?"

"As if I haven't had every ugly thought you have—" It was almost a wail. She breathed in before she spoke again, her voice ragged. "You're after something. What is it?"

Claud explained his thoughts about Lorelei Muldoon's clothes. "If you'd just smuggle them out of here for me . . ."

"Yes, I'll take them." She gathered Lorelei's possessions into her arms. "But I'll keep them, too. If Barney wants to see them again, tell him to come to me."

Be careful what you ask for; you just might get it.

"I thought you said you were going to help me, Abby."

"No, I said tell me what you want." She had a ghost of a smile. "If something about Lorelei's clothes would help you set her up again, sooner or later you'd talk Orry Neiderhoffer into it. But not me."

He was so relieved to have her dander back that he didn't even protest. He stepped over to Elmo and murmured a question. The tall trooper, shock wobbling his Adam's apple, left hurriedly.

"Coast is clear," Claud said. "Are you in Bluebonnet? I'll keep you company as far as Duncan's."

"I won't give them to you, Claud."

"Did I ask?"

"In case it occurs to you, the answer is no."

At least the Bitterroot Congregational Church was easier to get at than the FBI labs at Quantico. He took a last look over his shoulder at the lights and dust and busy men that inevitably accompanied tragedy and followed her out to her car.

The reporter for *Sloane's Magazine* followed them in an unobtrusive rental sedan.

For newspapers and television, the story was always the obvious: in this case, would Lorelei Muldoon or her body be found, how soon, by whom. Those reporters had to stay at the hospital and watch the search unfold.

But *Sloane's* was a weekly. G. T. Greco rarely got to break a story. He had to find a slant with legs, one that readers would wait a week for. This time the story had reached up and bitten him on the butt, and it was an angle he specialized in.

As a reporter, Greco began with more handicaps than some. Big and bony, with a dramatic Latin face and a voice straight out of Queens, he couldn't fade into the wallpaper. He came on too strong for anyone but another New Yorker. Well, and Arabs.

He compensated by being the best at reading the background of a story.

Foreign reporting, everybody studied background. You had to, you knew you didn't know much. But domestic stories, journalists tended to make the mistake of thinking they were on familiar ground. Greco knew it wasn't so: Each story took place in an unknown country, a land of alien customs, alien rhythms and reasons.

It looked as if the customs of this particular country might *be* the story. The sheriff had been amused at the idea of an arrest for a fistfight. And Yosemite Sam had bounced up from the fight and joined in the official search, on the heels of another man who interested Greco even more, the man with the curiously vacant face.

No, not vacant. So guarded that emotion was banked, inaccessible, possibly even to himself. Greco had followed faces like that all over the world. Dreamers had them. Liars. Men who went about their business under enemy fire as casually as he, Greco, went to the corner deli. If such a man was a citizen of good standing in Merciful Valley, that had to be part of the story.

And two civilians who had talked to the sheriff as equals had just walked off with evidence.

The word *vigilante* formed itself in his mind in eight-point type.

He could always come back to the search for Lorelei Muldoon, but by that time her clothes would be gone.

Greco followed the beat-up blue Volvo a few blocks to a café. The two passengers talked briefly while he watched with a Sicilian scowl. Following kept you near the game, but it could never put you in the game.

There were a fair number of people on the street. Few cars, but people waited patiently at the single traffic light anyway—no, one jaywalker. Stared at in open shock and disapproval by everyone else in sight. Obviously a tourist.

In this country, Greco, wait for the lights.

The Volvo's passenger eased himself out and got into the red pickup parked next to it. He headed west. The woman went south.

How do you choose between strangers?

You guess. Fast.

The pickup was old but immaculate. A show piece. Easy to find again. And women were always easier to impress. Greco followed her south on Route 42.

The police and the McFauls combed the hospital from the heating/cooling plant on the roof to the emergency generator in the basement. Buck McFaul pounced with unflagging enthusiasm from one improbable hiding place to the next, but neither Lorelei Muldoon nor her body turned up. Nobody— patients, visitors, staff—remembered an unknown woman, dressed who knew how, noticeable only for her hair, wandering the halls. There was a nest of pillows and blankets by the third-floor fire door; used condoms nearby made a link to the case unlikely. Surgical greens disappeared so often, no one recommended checking supplies.

"So he took her with him," Buck said. "Or they. We're looking for a couple, or some men and a woman."

"A delivery man with a bundle," Barney said harshly, before anyone else could.

Reinterviewing began. It was Barney who finally turned up a possible witness at Admissions.

She had the Swedish fairness that made the most of a flush of excitement; a glance at Barney made her more than willing to cooperate, if she had seen how to.

"Hardly anybody visits on Sunday morning," she said with regret. "The only ones today were a mistake, even."

"Mistake?"

A man who doesn't talk much always seems like a good listener. She was more than willing to describe the visitors, but they hadn't made much of an impression. She thought one was younger and smaller than the other. There was nothing remarkable about their clothes.

"Everybody wears jeans, don't they?" she said with a sidelong look at Barney's. "But there was something. I remember thinking right away: pickers."

"Pickers? You mean for sugar beets? Maybe they were Hispanic? Something about the way they talked?"

She considered that, her head tilted at a flattering angle. "Maybe that's why I took them for pickers. They came to check on a drinking buddy cut up in a fight last night. When I showed them that no knife case had been admitted, they took off for Emergency."

Where they had never arrived.

By the time Barney reported this to Neiderhoffer, back at the murder scene, Claud and Abby were gone.

"It makes sense that Gang avoided anything resembling work," the sheriff sighed. "Did he say anything before he left?"

"Yessir," Elmo said. "He suggested that we check the morgue for an extra body. Which I did, sir. Nothing."

"So at least we're not looking for somebody who thinks like Gang Willetts."

Barney rummaged futilely on a gurney. "Ever known him to be that helpful for no good reason?"

"How's that?"

"I want to take another look at Muldoon's stuff. It was on this gurney. *Was.*"

Neiderhoffer looked from the empty gurney to his brother-in-law in fulminating silence. Elmo's Adam's apple, almost as prominent as his nose and chin, wobbled as he tried and failed to meet his chief's eyes.

Buck had found the police artist and was happily suggesting alterations Lorelei Muldoon might have made: braids, even short hair. What about a shaved part like a basketball player? Barney's discovery caught his butterfly attention.

"Those clothes're gone," he said. "Claud'll hole up, and you'll never get past the toolies."

"Try me." Barney jammed on his hat.

Buck leapt up to follow, but Barney shook his head. "Two of us won't get by them. Besides, when I meet up with Willetts, I don't want company."

The sheriff took the sketch away from his artist and sent it to Emerson Flagg. The stat room at the *Herald* printed copies by the hundreds; by afternoon, gray-clad troopers armed with copies, plus descriptions of two men, possibly migrant workers, spread in time-consuming circles out from Demersville Memorial Hospital. In a flash of inspiration, Neiderhoffer gave a stack of the photos to Buck McFaul and sent him south to pass them out to the searchers headquartered at the Parish Hall of the Bitterroot Congregational Church.

As Lorelei came down the main steps of Demersville Memorial Hospital, a Mustang careened around the corner, shaking on its springs, and lurched to a stop in the middle of a No Parking zone. The driver took the steps by twos.

Good. Something more interesting to stare at than an anonymous doctor or nurse on her break, a tweed jacket slung over her greens, hair tucked under a Stetson hat that was a little small for it. Jacket and hat courtesy of Dr. Tilman.

"Excuse me. Miss Muldoon?"

Run? Scream? Ignore?

Striving for New York indifference, she turned, prepared to deny herself.

She recognized him: the young man from the gunfight the previous day, the one who had looked at her the way she looked at Doris Day or Marilyn Monroe. Useless to pretend that she didn't know who he was.

But he mustn't tell anyone else.

At the corner, the light changed. Lorelei drew him across the street with her. "I know you, don't I? From yesterday?"

He beamed. "With my uncle. Claud Willetts. I mean, *he's* Claud Willetts. I'm Stan Sokoloff. God, what luck. They said you were missing. Wait till they find out."

No, thank you. She would brush him off when it was safe to, but for now, he could make her look like half a couple— it might not fool his uncle, but it would the killer.

Always supposing they were different people.

She set off briskly. As she seemed to tolerate his presence, Stan walked with increasing confidence—in front of her, on one side, the other, ricocheting off signs and store windows as if this were his normal way of walking. Perhaps it was.

"Can we get off the street?" she asked. "There's a killer around somewhere. I'd just as soon he didn't see me."

"I know, I talked to the sheriff." He fell obediently in beside her. "Duncan's has the best coffee, it's a few blocks away, under my uncle's office—"

"Did he have anything to do with that newspaper story? Thanks but no thanks."

His face clouded. "I don't blame you."

Something about his uncle. An opening, if she knew how to exploit it. "Anyplace more private?"

Her inner alarm clock screamed endlessly before he said, "I have a friend who's away for a while."

"A *friend's* place?"

Stan was brought up painfully short against a parking meter. Embarrassment seemed to make him even clumsier. "The thing is, I'm just home for the summer, I'm still in college. I don't have my own place."

It had come to this: Her life was at risk and her only ally was barely old enough to vote.

"So this is your girlfriend's?"

"No, no, nothing like that. It's the singer at Dead Man's

Hand. That's the best bar in Bitterroot. In the valley, most people think. His name's Banjo Man."

And being on apartment-key terms with him was probably Stan's biggest source of pride.

"How far away is it?"

"About half an hour. It would be okay. Really. Bitterroot is better than Demersville, it's full of tourists this time of year. Here, it's like one big suburb, everybody minds everybody else's business."

Comforting visions of the Brady Bunch danced in her head, but he was right. Non-Bradys would be noticed and remembered.

"Your friend left with all the tourists here?"

"He's doing a gig in Denver. Even more tourists there."

"When is he due back?"

"I don't know. He says he doesn't like to work to spec. But he only left yesterday, it's safe."

What was the alternative?

Demersville, with the brisk self-assurance of a town, broke away quickly to open fields. Stan shifted his Mustang showily up and down as they drove. Tall, thin, with the adolescent stamp of too much bone, not yet grown into his face or limbs. A lifetime younger than Ricky Fenton, who might be the same age. How deep did Stan's resentment of his uncle go?

"I need help getting out of here," she said experimentally. "Somebody to buy me a plane ticket. Would you do it? Without telling your uncle. Wait. Think about it."

The car surged forward with enthusiasm. It jerked slower again. "The thing is, everybody's seen today's paper. It's a small airport, and right now, most of the traffic is incoming. Press and television. They'd spot you even if a cop didn't."

That damn picture. And reporters probably had other, clearer ones by now.

"Maybe a car, then. Whatever, I'll need some money. Cash."

"I don't have much, but I could go to an ATM for you. Or cash a check."

"Stan." Lorelei reached for words of one syllable. "If you use a check with my name on it—or the PIN number of my ATM—people might guess that you know where I am."

His face fell further.

"What I'll do is access my computer and switch some funds to your account—you do have your own bank account? Then you withdraw the cash. It's easy to spot once they look for it, but by then I'll be gone."

The car speeded up with Stan's relief but then slowed again. "What is it?"

"There's another thing about your switching money—"

"I know," she said. "It's Sunday. You can't get at your account till tomorrow morning."

"No, no. It's not that. I have keys to the Salish—that's the bank, it's my father's bank. I work the late shift when somebody wants to go home early."

"Then what?"

"The computer you mentioned. Is it back in your apartment in New York?"

The car was crawling. "Well?"

"That's what I was on the way to tell my uncle. The New York police want to talk to you too. A bomb went off in your apartment this morning."

Chapter
Nine

When the woman in the beat-up blue station wagon pulled up in front of a church, G. T. Greco drove on past to look at the little town of Bitterroot. The street running uphill from the church bore signs for Gaslight Parade; at the top of the hill the main shopping area began, with old black gas lamps instead of streetlights. The street ran back downhill, petering into a broken track by a sheet of water with a big sign: Cutthroat Lake.

He retraced his route. He liked what he saw. The shopping area had been refurbished for tourists to a paint-by-numbers prettiness, but it was still better than a mall. A playhouse built of logs, set back from the street. An old hotel with a broad front porch and a banner announcing its restaurant, Thyme Out. The Clark Gallery, with a well-lit wintry landscape. A bakery called The Bakery. Gaylord's, a Victorian house-turned-shop. Across the street another Victorian beauty, now a bookstore, next to a rosy brick bank restored to the pioneer prosperity of golden oak, marble, and brass curlicues. Then houses all the way back down the hill to the church.

He parked a block away from the church and wandered down and around it, his camera at a sight-seeing angle. Give whoever the woman was time to settle into whatever she was doing.

The church was like a stage set too, from *Our Town* this time, small, white-framed, badly in need of paint, with a me-too parsonage next door. The name on the old-fashioned marquee told him that his luck had come through for him: The Reverend Abigail Butterfield.

A Butterfield. Here. How common a name was that?

Immediately inside the entrance were three cartons and a blue stone pot under a hand-lettered sign that read STOCK EXCHANGE. Men's clothing, women's, kids', all clean, neatly folded, though well worn. The blue stone pot was two-thirds full of coins and an occasional IOU. He pawed hastily through the women's box. Nothing resembling Lorelei Muldoon's suede skirt or her pocketbook. Too obvious anyway.

On the wall above the Stock Exchange, arrows directed him to either Sanctuary or Parish Hall. Most of the noise came from the Parish Hall. He watched from outside the doorway as a few women dragged tables and chairs, directed by the woman from the station wagon, the woman in the jogging suit.

Reverend Butterfield. And she was safely occupied.

He backed quietly. To the right, the hallway led to a few kids' rooms: finger paints, crayons, paper, smocks . . . No. In the other direction, past the Sanctuary, lay a big shabby office, obviously Reverend Butterfield's. Any of the stacks of books and papers could have covered a bundle of clothes. Could he risk shifting them? He thought he heard a squeak of rubber soles.

When Abby caught up with him, Greco was in the Sanctuary, craning his neck at an unexpectedly high ceiling and a winged balcony curving down on either side almost to a pulpit that jutted forward like the prow of a ship.

"It's a much bigger building than I expected," he said with fairly genuine admiration.

She beamed. "It was built in the late forties. Their buildings were like their marriages: so stodgy outside, you're unprepared for how generous they were inside."

He took the words in like food. Solid information came from skill and persistence, but memorable quotes were luck. Luck was infinitely more valuable.

"I'm sorry I missed the service this morning."

An intense blue gaze seemed to go right through him. "You didn't miss anything. I'm a doer, not a talker."

"You're Reverend Butterfield?"

"And you are . . ."

"G. T. Greco. My editor in chief is a Butterfield. I don't know if you—"

"Aunt Daffy? You're from *Sloane's Magazine*?"

A picture of Daffodil Butterfield Sloane—brittle, elegant, aesthetically pale—flashed through his mind. Aunt Daffy. He saved it to savor later.

"You were at the hospital? Leaning against the wall?"

He nodded. "Is all this something to do with the search for Lorelei Muldoon?"

"We keep food and coffee going and set up cots for people to nap. We haven't even cleaned up from yesterday and now we have to start up all over again."

He loped after her to the Parish Hall. "A couple of things I'm curious about, if you could spare a few minutes—"

"Have you talked to Emerson Flagg?"

"The editor of the *Demersville Herald*?" Greco tried to sound respectful. "Yes, ma'am. His briefing is fine for TV and the dailies, but since *Sloane's* is a weekly, I can't break news, I need to write about the people. Besides, if you know your aunt—" Daffy "—you know she wants *Sloane's* to have stuff nobody else gets."

"What did you have in mind?"

"Background on some of the people involved, see where it leads. There was a big guy at the hospital, ex-football type, who seemed to be on good terms with the sheriff. Where does he fit in?"

That intense blue gaze again. Greco tried to look trustworthy.

Finally she said, "Why don't you give me a hand here, Mr. . . ."

"Greco. G. T. Greco."

". . . while I think about it."

Greco obligingly set up tables and cots, humped empty coffee urns to the kitchen and full ones back to the Parish Hall. Apparently that tipped the balance. After a half hour, Reverend Butterfield beckoned him aside.

"I'll tell you who knows more than anybody else," she said. "Domenica Gaylord. She runs Gaylord's, a shop up on Main Street."

"I saw it. Beautiful old house."

"Isn't it? Her dad's office is upstairs over the shop. He's Samson de la Haye, Senator Colman's lawyer. Of course, Samson would never say anything, but Domenica usually knows whatever he knows."

She looked up at him over her glasses as mild as a cherub. Which was only fair, since she was behaving like one.

"I really appreciate what you're doing for me, Reverend Butterfield."

"The least I can do for Aunt Daffy." She was off with a friendly backhand wave.

Barney McFaul hadn't thought past getting his hands around Claud Willetts' fat throat, but when he pulled up at the building that housed Duncan's at street level, Claud Willetts' office on the floor above, the Big Red Machine was missing from its accustomed spot at the curb. Duncan hadn't seen Claud, or said she hadn't.

The office was locked and empty. If Stan was missing too, Claud must be cooking something.

Barney let himself in and looked around. He hadn't expected to find Lorelei Muldoon's belongings. He didn't, but he reclaimed his phone.

Lucky for both of them, perhaps, that Willetts had fled. Holed up, obviously, in his cabin up in the Coulees, feeling safe behind a minefield of toolies. Barney didn't think they posed a problem, but he decided to wait until dark.

It made more sense anyway to use the daylight looking for Muldoon. Not that he had any more idea of where to begin than anybody else. He found himself on Beargrass River Road, heading for Colman's cabin, just as he'd told Willetts.

Well, why not? Maybe she'd left it there, whatever it was that was missing. It might tell him where to head next.

Besides, like Muldoon with just her city wits, he had nowhere else to go.

When Hungerford came to the Demersville Sheraton with news of two new deaths and Lorelei Muldoon's disappearance, Betty Colman shrugged.

"If they'd locked her up to begin with, it wouldn't have happened," she said.

Olga Finaldo had to struggle to match Betty's lack of interest. That her nephew should fail when she herself had arranged an opportunity so foolproof . . . Ricardo-proof . . . He had much to answer for.

But his clumsiness only impeded her; the dangerous knowledge of the Muldoon woman could destroy her. The longer Lorelei Muldoon remained hidden, the more people she could tell, who would in turn have to be attended to.

Olga had to be prepared to act the instant the woman was

found. Better still, find her. In a valley of strangers, where her only tool was her nephew.

Unwinking, she watched Larry Hungerford, former high-profile chief of staff to Senator Colman, organize luggage and track down men to replace glass and repair telephones on a Sunday afternoon.

The time it took to funnel instructions to Ricardo through his sister Estrella was no longer acceptable. And it would be dangerous to ask favors of Larry Hungerford. Hungerford would be unwilling to add Olga Finaldo to his responsibilities.

Most unwilling.

The best solutions came from facing weaknesses squarely: It was a rule that had always served Olga Finaldo well.

A delicate suggestion made Betty see the value of meeting with both her lawyer and her hairdresser that afternoon as well as her minister; Samson de la Haye and Mr. Charles joined Abby on Larry Hungerford's list. He looked at Olga and closed his lips firmly over a comment he clearly longed to make.

Abby and Samson de la Haye wanted to see Betty as much as she wanted to see them, but Mr. Charles (a.k.a. Charley Calico) did not. His satellite dish picked up the Braves games, and the pennant race was tightening. By the time Larry was able to persuade him that (since he was closed Mondays as well) he couldn't leave Betty Colman to face public and press unshampooed and unback-combed for two whole days, the former high-profile chief of staff was steaming gently.

Between those efforts and the to and fro of packing, Olga slipped away unnoticed to the lobby telephone.

The drive to Mr. Charles an hour later did nothing to improve Hungerford's temper. Olga Finaldo insisted on accompanying Betty; with a madman at large, she said, she did not want to be alone.

"Mad*woman*," Betty corrected automatically, like a grammatical error. "When they catch the Muldoon woman, it will all be over."

Hungerford beat a soundless tattoo on the steering wheel with a fist, Olga had already heard him explain several times why this willful perspective was as unwise as it was untrue.

Charley Calico churned up in a fan of gravel on his motorcycle, entering his shop in boots, helmet, and gloves without a glance their way. Five minutes passed before Mr. Charles, hair slicked back into a token dun-colored ponytail, came to the door to wave Betty in.

Betty waited until Larry got out and came around to open the door. "I'm sorry Mr. Charles wouldn't take you too, dear."

"But it is not to be expected. The senator's widow, herself a senator-to-be: how different from an unknown friend."

"Larry will take you wherever you want to go in the meantime. Just as long as you're back within the hour, Larry."

Hungerford said nothing.

After a carefully weighed pause, Olga said from the backseat, "People are more than one thing, Mr. Hungerford. Betty can be difficult, but she also has unexpected insights. Perhaps there is more to Miss Muldoon than we know."

His shoulders stiffened. As clearly as if a subtitle were lettered across them, she watched the thought form: If he was now reduced to taking advice from hangers-on . . .

He took off with an overstressed screech of wheels and pulled up sharply at a corner of the main street.

"A few buildings up on the right would be better," Olga said. "The building called The Bakery. Do you think Mrs. Colman will be finished in an hour? Or will it be better to come for me first?"

Larry Hungerford had a small overbite, more obvious when he was not smiling, more obvious still when he was so angry that his esses were a little spray of saliva.

"Let's get one thing straight, Olga Finaldo. I am more than

158

willing to help Mrs. Colman. Chauffeuring you is not, and will never be, part of that help. Are you clear on that? Because if so, the door handle is right there beside you."

Olga kept her eyes wide and surprised. She drew herself up proudly and walked away from the car proudly. No one could read a subtitle from the set of *her* shoulders. Fortunately, a smile wasn't visible from the back.

Stan Sokoloff delivered Lorelei Muldoon to his friend's apartment and fled back to his uncle's office. She found herself in an apartment above a bookstore, overlooking the main street of Bitterroot. The careful restoration below reminded her of *The Big Country,* even gas lamps for streetlights. Ragtime from a piano somewhere tinkled up through the floor.

The apartment assuaged one concern: Banjo Man didn't encourage visitors. How could he? His disorder had passed beyond clutter, beyond mess, well down the road to derangement. Tape-torn poster corners were visible behind sagging madras wall hangings. The sofa bed was open, too littered to be folded up again.

She followed the narrow path remaining from living room through kitchen to bedroom. CDs in the kitchen and bathroom, used plates in the bedroom, clothes and papers in stacks everywhere.

He had even overflowed onto the fire escape, with a tatami mat, cushions, a cotton blanket, a candle in the neck of an empty Chianti bottle. One block down the hill—maybe two—she could see a broad expanse of water. Cutthroat Lake, Stan had said; if you leaned over, you could see the Beargrass Mountains where Fred Colman's cabin was.

From the back window she could see the bookstore's glass conservatory and the piano. Somebody was curled up on an old sofa, reading to a child. From the front window she could hear the contented buzz of voices from a restaurant a few doors away.

A clear view of possible intruders from either direction. A pity she no longer had Fred's gun.

A bomb had gone off in her apartment. Somebody had broken in and destroyed the place where she lived. Or had it been there all along, waiting, while she worked and slept? She shivered.

The cool limes and peaches, the squashy pillows and swooping Formica shapes. Wreckage.

Indecent to think about, when Sue Lombardy, whose humor and common sense had been as healing as her skill, lay dead. Sue's death seemed more outrageous than Fred's. His had been intended, even though the police didn't yet know why. Sue had died because of a superficial resemblance to a woman she had known less than a day. Had sacrificed a life so much harder for the world to lose than that of Lorelei Muldoon, whose heroism existed only in Emerson Flagg's headline.

A headline that in some version might have reached Hank Muldoon by now. Even if he hadn't read or heard anything (entirely possible), the New York police who had traced her to Fred Colman must also have traced her to Hank. He didn't value much besides his mathematical dispute with Albert Einstein, but one of the things on his short list was his daughter. He'd be worried, helpless, totally unpredictable. He might even be on his way to Merciful Valley.

There was a phone in the kitchen. By the time they found out where the call had come from, she'd be long gone.

G. T. Greco drove back up Gaslight Parade to park in front of the fine old house whose first floor was now Gaylord's. What had been the front porch had been converted to shop windows that—he was startled to note—could have been on Madison Avenue, a spill of intricate sweaters and silk shirts, not a vulgar price tag in sight.

160

Except for a stocky woman working her way slowly up the street, the tourists were sheltering from the hard afternoon sun on the porch of the nearby hotel. The window shopper was dressed in black linen and a broad-brimmed hat more suited to a New York summer; small wonder that Gaylord's windows caught her eye. While she concentrated on them, Greco pushed on a carved oak door with a needlework sign OPEN.

The dark of the shop was a welcome shock after the afternoon glare. Behind a big brass cash register to the right of the door, someone sat staring down at—good Lord!—knitting. Good. Middle-aged women were usually easy to approach.

He cleared his throat. When she didn't respond, he waved toward the onlooker, now looking thoughtfully at Gaylord's other window.

"Looks like you've got a serious customer."

"It's her third time by," she said without looking up. "She's just waiting for somebody."

Eye contact was interest. Lack of eye contact was lack of interest. "You must have eyes in the back of your head."

"Good peripheral vision."

His own eyes had adjusted. The shop matched the windows. One of a kind sweaters on oak tables, long linen skirts on bunkhouse hooks—except for the wall behind the knitter. It was filled by a grainy blowup of a skier, rock-firm in a racing tuck, identifiable as a woman only by the braid streaming straight out behind her. The slope looked impossibly steep. A flag in the distance had five Olympic rings.

He looked back at the shop owner. He could see her clearly now too. That same braid lay quiet against her back, nothing about her moving, in fact, except the clicking needles. But she still gave an impression he recognized from other world-class athletes: of a very large engine ticking over.

And a living, breathing example of why colorizing movies would never be successful. There must have been fifty shades of cream from the hollow of her throat to the shadows under her eyes. She was like a painting on velvet. Too much for the average living room, but you couldn't look without wanting to touch. The color of her eyes wouldn't matter much, rimmed by lashes like those.

"That's you, isn't it?"

"Once upon a time." Still she didn't look up.

"Then why isn't Gaylord a household name?"

"That was a practice run. On the next one, I popped my ACL. Anterior cruxiate ligament. Four years later I was past it."

"Tough. You think you're going through a door, and suddenly they move the wall on you."

Finally: a black-fringed look. The color of her eyes *did* matter. The same pale, barely-brown as her hair. Sherry. Dry, not cream. It was like going back out into the sun.

"We have all the snow I can handle right here," she said. "I don't mean to be rude, but I can't stop in the middle of a row or I'll never find my place again."

Greco looked at the welter of yarns in her lap.

"I see what you mean."

Plenty of time to rehearse openers while she twirled one yarn and then another, her lips in a mouthwatering pout as she counted stitches, stared at a light box where the colors of the yarns were translated into a surreal landscape, and counted some more. Once all the stuff was on a single needle, the black-fringed look swept up again, this time to stay.

He could only think of the obvious. "How many people have told you that knitting and skiing don't usually go together?"

"I got hooked when I was in the hospital with the ACL."

"Looks pretty labor-intensive."

"I just work out the pattern. Other women knit the ones

I sell." She rubbed one needle against the other in a way that reminded him of something. "You're not here to buy a sweater."

She shaped her words as though her lower lip was covered with butter and she might, if he was lucky, lick it off.

"When it's ninety outside?" He handed her his press pass. "No, thanks. I'm here about Senator Colman's death."

"Don't you want to talk to my dad? Samson de la Haye? He was Bandit's lawyer."

There was something buttery about her voice too. A very high-cholesterol lady.

"This is where his office is? But you're Domenica Gaylord. Where's Mr. Gaylord?"

"You don't want to go there."

"Promise me it has nothing to do with my story."

"What does the G. T. stand for?"

He hadn't seen her glance at his pass. The peripheral vision thing.

"You don't want to go there."

Her fingers slid along his as she handed his pass back. They smiled in mutual satisfaction.

"And why come to me, G. T. Greco?"

"Actually, Abigail Butterfield suggested it. My story will be heavy into background. She said you knew the people—"

"*Abby*. The Rev sent you to me? Not Claud Willetts?"

"Should I know who he is?"

One needle slid again along the other.

Knife-sharpening. A butcher honed his knives with that same contemplative stroke.

"Will this take a while?" she asked. "Because my apartment's behind the store. I can make coffee and we can talk there."

Some signals are the same in any country in the world.

"Why don't I just . . ."

Greco reached a long arm to the front door and flipped

the sign from OPEN to CLOSED, PLEASE COME BACK SOON. Domenica had been right about the stocky window shopper in black; she had been joined by a kid in a Raiders jacket.

Lorelei might have known that once her safety was established, Hank would zero in on the lack of logic of the past forty-eight hours.

"Think, my dear. That is, after all, what I have trained you to do. You've been there throughout, you have all the data. Where are the anomalies?"

She had tried logic successfully with Barney McFaul, once. And now? Everything inside her cried out that he would never use her as bait, but he had.

"Probability analysis doesn't work with people, Hank."

"If I refuse to accept dumbing down from my students, Lorelei, I'm hardly going to accept it from my daughter—"

"Dad, these people aren't trying to grade me, they're trying to kill me!"

She hadn't called him "Dad" since she was thirteen; maybe it would get his attention.

No.

"I'll go over the newspaper accounts and start working with what data I find," he said. "You can amend and add to it with your next call."

"If there is one." She hoped the bang of the receiver carried all the way back to New York.

The easiest windows in which Olga Finaldo could pretend interest were Gaylord's. There was a sweater as textured as matelassé, another with such brilliant flowers that she speculated about the source of the yarns. She had observed it many times: In a crisis, all senses were heightened.

How dare her nephew take so long to find her. She had cleared the time with care, but Betty's appointments would not last indefinitely. Unthinkable that Betty and Larry Hungerford should arrive before she had finished with him.

A reflection came up beside her: a slight young man in a baseball cap worn back to front and a Raiders jacket. So fidgety he cried out to be remembered. That, too, would be added to his account.

"But why come so early?" she said in Spanish. The language of anger. Also of things too easily overheard. "In a matter of moments you could have met Mrs. Colman here with me."

She took pleasure in his flinch.

"I said we'd meet at Dead Man's Hand, remember?"

"Ah, yes. The bar. I walked by it. You expected me to go inside? Olga Finaldo? She would be remembered by all. Or have you been away so long that you have forgotten how much I value who I am?"

His expression was one she had never seen. Impatience?

"If you only wanted to yell at me, you could do it on the phone."

"Can you then deliver by telephone the papers she had with her?" Olga held out an imperious hand.

Ricky Fenton looked steadily back, as unwinking as she.

"You don't have them," she said. "You were there, you killed a woman, and you couldn't manage such a simple errand—"

"You don't need them for proof. The television will tell you she is dead. And the newspapers."

"Ah, but no. They tell me that she still lives. Yes. You killed a stranger."

His reaction was puzzling. He gave a little sigh, and a nod, as if her words fit something else he already knew, also unpleasant. "Then she was a decoy."

She was too angry to register it immediately. "And then to kill one of their police: Do you guess with what urgency they hunt you?"

"If you shout like that, even in Spanish, the police will be here before long."

She stopped, shocked at her own loss of control. She turned as if to examine the sweaters in Gaylord's window. In the pause his words came back to her. "What do you mean, decoy?"

He met her eyes in the glass. "I bought a copy of the Sunday *Herald* myself, *Tía* Olga. It's all lies. The plane wasn't burned when I saw it. The girl didn't fight us off single-handed. If you'd bothered to tell me what you knew instead of just giving orders—"

"What are you saying?"

"The newspaper story was a setup. To get somebody to do exactly what you did. Why do you think there was no time to search her hospital room? The cop Mech killed was on guard outside her door."

"But she must have been there. She escaped!"

It was his turn to be taken aback. She was relieved. "Something you did not know? She is no longer at the hospital. No one knows where she is."

In silence she walked up the street with the lagging steps of a sightseer. Easy to do; her legs were shaking. Fenton followed.

"Why did you want Colman killed, *Tía* Olga?"

"You can ask, when you in your unfailing folly planted marijuana under his very nose!"

He shook his head. "You didn't know about that when you gave the order. What had he found out about OFC?"

She stopped at the bakery window, gestured as if to call his attention to a plateful of sourdough bread. "Nothing so interesting, I'm afraid. Your sister placed a deposit in Betty Colman, Inc. Mrs. Colman's public relations firm. It could be an embarrassment."

"You mean you tried to blackmail her. The way you did Freddy Hampton Bahr? He killed himself, didn't he, a couple of weeks after he made you a partner?"

"I will not discuss his private tragedies—"

"Isn't that exactly what you threatened? To discuss his private tragedies?"

His accuracy took her breath away.

"You have had too much time to daydream, my nephew."

"Did I mention that I saw the papers? Yes. In her pocketbook. You know how I knew they were the ones you wanted? By the OFC account number. So you must have blackmailed Colman with OFC funds—not cash—and made him a present of your connection to OFC. Shall I tell you why that's dangerous, *Tía* Olga?"

"I am well aware of—"

"I don't think you are." His reflection in the window bent toward hers as though he spoke soft words of love. "I haven't forgotten that you value who Olga Finaldo is. Olga Finaldo owns a decorating firm with many important customers, she is the friend of a senator's wife. She is on the board of the Hispanic Cultural Institute. How shocking if these people discovered her connection to a service that delivers so many interesting things along with its furniture."

"You threaten me?"

"Have I said so? I merely remind you who is in danger, and it isn't Ricardo Fenton. It's Olga Finaldo, who has broken the rule of my aunt. She is no longer invisible."

Where had it come from, her nephew's new strength? It had to be stopped. "You concern yourself with my dangers, Ricardo, I concern myself with yours. The marijuana, for example, and your foot soldier, both can lead the police to Ricardo Fenton."

He merely shrugged. "You going to do anything besides nag? Mrs. Colman will get here soon."

"If she interrupts, I shall explain to her that I am interviewing my new chauffeur. I have no choice, you see. Mr. Hungerford does not wish to drive me."

She permitted herself a small smile, waiting for him to ask

how she had brought that about. He only shifted restlessly.

"I'm supposed to stay with you at the hotel?"

She dragged her words, savoring his impatience. "But no. We move today to the senator's cabin, Mrs. Colman and Mr. Hungerford and I. You will rent a car openly—respectable, black—and purchase clothes for yourself. Also respectable and black. A suitable hat."

"So I can see you openly. Right. That's not the problem—"

"You still have the equipment. Resume monitoring the police. It makes sense to let them find her for you. You killed under their noses once, you can do so again. Listen also to the phone of a man named Claud Willetts. The Muldoon woman may seek his help. His number is unlisted, I will give it to you. No, not written down! A piece of my writing in your hands? Listen and remember!"

"You fear that the police might get from the nephew to the aunt? How touching."

She ignored that. "I expect to hear tomorrow that you have news of the Muldoon woman. Have I told you I am finished? Never walk away while I talk to you, Ricardo!"

But he walked on. She couldn't shout after him. She stood, legs splayed, waiting for calm to return. She straightened and went into the bakery to await Betty Colman.

Lorelei made one circuit after another from the front bow window to the rear fire escape and back again, smarting from Hank's words. He didn't understand. Then again—she was his daughter, after all, and guilt was invented for daughters—was he right?

She stared moodily out the front window.

Below her, a man in a Raiders jacket and a baseball cap walked up Gaslight Parade.

Even from this angle, she knew him. How could she not? For an endless walk yesterday, she had feared he'd be the last person in the world she saw.

Lorelei thought of Sue Lombardy, mute and swollen. She backed hurriedly into the shadows, still watching. With the fervor of prayer, she willed Stan to come back before Fenton left. Stan could follow him. Or if Stan just called, she could tell him to send the police to pick Fenton up. He could be identified by Barney McFaul. Lorelei Muldoon could stay out of it entirely.

Hands in his pockets, dawdling like a tourist, Fenton walked up the street and out of sight.

Hank had really gotten to her, hadn't he? Here she was, trying to solve the problem of Colman's murder, when (1) *her* problem was safety, (2) the only person interested in that problem was Lorelei Muldoon, and (3) the only safety lay in flight.

The data for all three conclusions were unimpeachable.

Reporters couldn't be watching all the roads. She had to buy a car. Cash, no paper trail.

And she had to do it looking like somebody other than Lorelei Muldoon.

She turned again to the charms of Banjo Man's apartment, looking at just one thing: his clothes. Jeans, short-legged enough but large at the waist. T-shirts of every description. Nothing very clean, but that didn't seemed to matter anymore.

She found a belt and, with the tip of a kitchen knife, poked an extra hole. A Hard Rock Café T-shirt tucked into the jeans, the belt cinched tight. That left her hair. She knotted Fred's kerchief as tightly as she could and surveyed the results hopefully in Banjo Man's finger-marked bathroom mirror.

Half-successful. The T-shirt and jeans had a grungy but anonymous look, but the kerchief didn't begin to disguise her hair.

Even Banjo Man must have scissors someplace, and any kind of scissors could cut hair.

It took a surprising effort to force herself to search. She had resented her hair for being so unmanageably unlike her sugary blond movie icons. But that didn't mean getting rid of it would be pain-free. She cut it without looking, in handfuls, getting a roughly even length by feel. Adding new litter to Banjo Man's floor.

Afterward she looked at herself again. A narrow face, a short unkempt brush of hair. The only good—good!—thing was that there was enough curl to make her hacking less obvious. No makeup, that had been abandoned with her pocketbook.

Not much left of Lorelei Muldoon.

Chapter
Ten

Ricky Fenton turned on the police scanner as soon as he got back to camp, but Mech would have to tap Claud Willetts' phone line. He waited, brooding.

If he found Lorelei Muldoon for Olga, killed her, rescued the papers, what guarantee did he have that Olga wouldn't turn around and do something else stupid? Why run these risks if she would have no business to pass on? He had to have some kind of guarantee, she owed him that.

When Mech returned late in the afternoon, he saw Fenton and stopped, waiting. So simply he took the initiative.

"It wasn't her," Fenton said. "We killed the wrong woman."

"A cop? The partner of the one outside the door?"

"Something like that."

"Why do you tell me?"

"There's a phone line that Olga thinks might lead to her. You have to run a tap on it."

"I don't do that no more."

"What are you talking about? It's part of the deal."

The rubber-ball body settled. "I did my part of the deal.

It's over. Now I don't do that no more."

He couldn't afford Mech to pull out, not yet. He said, "All we have to do is monitor the search and then step in when they find her. Simple."

"Simple." Mech hawked low in his throat and spat.

"So maybe it's not simple. But it's part of the deal."

"I'm a farmer now. I help you load the van, you take it to your aunt, leave me with the sinsemilla."

"It's not enough. I need the tap." Fenton studied him. "Who says the sinsemilla is yours, anyway? I've been paying all the expenses this summer."

The look in Mech's eyes took him aback. He imagined Mech slapping him, heavy as a bear's paw. Himself injured, dead even, dumped in the woods. He'd be as lost as Lorelei Muldoon. He forced himself to stare steadily back.

"How about this?" Fenton said. "After the Muldoon woman is dead, the sinsemilla is yours."

How easy it was to give away what he no longer wanted. But what an unromantic effort it was, so unlike the exhilarating, terrifying finalty of that woman's death. Even if it was the wrong woman. Would killing the right one bring that feeling back? Or was this what it was to be, like Mech, like Olga, a professional?

Mech's eyelids drooped, which meant he was at least considering it. Behind him, static on the scanner broke the silence. Mech reached out and shifted the tuner delicately, and a trooper's voice came into the clearing, running down a list of the places he had searched, in vain, for Lorelei Muldoon.

"I was hoping you were the glazier," Larry Hungerford said to Barney at the cabin door. "Either that or the telephone repairman. They promised to get here today."

"Broken window, is there?"

Barney walked past Hungerford into the cool stone-flagged hall. Luggage was piled high beside the door. Except for paths to kitchen, stairs, and living room, the floor was crowded with flower baskets.

"A door at the back, on the terrace. If you want Mrs. Colman, she's meeting with Mr. de la Haye and then Reverend Butterfield. But stay and have a beer."

Hungerford welcoming Barney McFaul, a person of no importance. Barney came warily to attention.

"Spillover from Pascoe's Funeral Home," Hungerford said, pointing to the flowers. "We're running them in shifts from there to here to the church. After the service they'll go to the hospital. You'd think if the florist can get here, the others could too. After I spent the better part of the day on the phone begging them."

"Why take the grief?"

"For the next senator? You must be joking."

Barney pushed past him to the living room. On the stone flags in front of the terrace doors, glass splinters caught the sun. He backtracked. A few splinters in the hall, a few more in the kitchen. He examined the stair treads with care, but no stray speck flickered.

Hungerford probably wasn't as talented with a broom as a telephone; it was clear that nobody had yet gone up the stairs. Anything Muldoon left had to be down here in the mess.

Hungerford followed him from room to room.

"Is this what Claud's phone call was about? After you left?"

So Willetts made Barney McFaul worth talking to. "How would you find out about a phone call and not know what it was about?"

"I was with Stan when it came." Hungerford's eyes narrowed. "Claud didn't tell you about it? The police?"

"I'm working for myself, Hungerford. What about this phone call?"

"Oh, right."

Before Hungerford could turn away, Barney clapped a friendly hand on his shoulder. Hungerford grunted and hunched awkwardly—the involuntary shrinking of a man in sudden intolerable pain.

"A shoulder blade's flat as a spade," Barney said conversationally. "Doesn't break easy. But if you work your fingers just right—"

His hand jerked. Hungerford curled a few more desperate inches.

"—you can pop a few ligaments. I'll ask you again, nice as I know how."

Barney released him with a shove that took him to his knees, on the verge of tears. "What about a phone call?"

"For God's sake . . ." Hungerford hauled himself up one-armed. "Stan took the call, I don't know what it was about. But it must have been important. Stan couldn't hide it."

Barney stared at him, wondering what to ask next. If Hungerford knew anything useful, he'd tell it, now. Before the day was over, he'd find a way of explaining to himself that he had never really been on his knees.

Barney only knew one thing to ask. "Muldoon leave anything here that you know of?"

Knowing something Barney McFaul didn't straightened Hungerford's back. He met Barney's eyes and lowered his own hastily. He led the way to the kitchen and swung open a door.

Beneath kitchen garbage was Muldoon's bloodstained silk shirt.

Barney held it, the nerves jumping in his hands. "Nothing smaller?"

"Maybe the police took something, they must have searched the place. Look, are you through? Because I have to pick up Mrs. Colman."

"Don't press your luck, Hungerford."

Back at the truck, Barney showed the shirt to Blue. Every

fifty yards back down the road he pulled up while Blue cast vainly for a scent. Bouviers weren't particularly good at tracking, but he had to pass the time somehow till it was dark enough to tackle the Coulees.

Lorelei ran for the kitchen when the phone rang. She waited for Stan's voice and broke in.

"Stan, great. When can you come over? The sooner the better."

"Lorelei! I didn't think—are you sure you should say anything?"

There was a click, a metallic sound of banjo music, and a sandy voice singing, "I got no need for an everyday woman."

"Stan, is that you? Did you put a CD on?"

"No, that's Banjo Man's machine message. Good song, isn't it?"

Two phones. The man had two phones.

"You mean we're being taped."

She didn't care what she tripped over or pushed aside.

A voice spoke over the music. "Hi. Banjo Man here. Obviously I'm doing something more interesting right now than talking to you. But leave your name, and I'll get back to you. If you're lucky."

She shivered with distaste inside Banjo Man's clothes as she upended heaps of possessions in the living room.

"Then again, maybe I won't. But hey, go for it." More tinny chords led into the beep.

"Stan, you've got to come here right away."

"If I leave early, Claud'll know and wonder why."

The message tape whirred. Stan's voice sounded stereo, once in her ear, again on the machine's speaker phone.

"Keep talking till I find the machine, Stan."

"Uh, I thought I'd bring something over later. What do you like? Fried chicken? Chinese? Pizza?"

A cook after her own heart. His voice came from the bedroom. And there was the answering machine, half-hidden under turned-back sheets. She switched it off and snatched up the receiver.

"Stan, I saw Fenton. You've got to come over. Maybe you can find him."

There was an uncomfortable pause before he said, "The thing is, after dark, my uncle will think I'm at home, but I can tell my parents I'm still searching for you."

The stubborn strength of the weak. She sighed. "If that's what's best for you. Can you bring me some hair dye, any color but mine?"

She hung up before he could argue or ask why.

The damn message bulb was blinking. She replayed the tape. There were half a dozen other messages, too many to erase without raising questions.

Make it look like a breakdown instead. Magnets. Magnets screwed up tapes. Would somebody like Banjo Man keep magnets on his refrigerator? No. And impossible to search this place for something so small.

In the kitchen was her old friend the microwave. She cooked the tape on high until it was too hot to touch, let it cool, and reinserted it in the machine. The red light still blinked insistently, but the tape now hummed with a murky resonance that made her lips buzz. That would have to do.

Once Mech accepted the bargain, he was as efficient as before. Whatever was involved in the wire tap, Mech was back at the clearing well within the time Fenton had estimated just for the trip to Demersville and back. Then he turned the shift over to Fenton, rolled up in his sleeping bag, and seemed instantly asleep.

Was Olga right, that Mech wasn't safe anymore? Still lethal, but no longer predictable, making him dangerous to Ricky Fenton?

But not to Olga Finaldo.

Lorelei Muldoon, on the other hand, was a threat to Olga Finaldo but not Ricky Fenton. All *he* had to do to be safe was to disappear—to become invisible—which Olga couldn't do anymore. A great weakness.

Did that mean his future no longer depended on hers? He had never thought that way before. Was *he* better off with Lorelei Muldoon alive or dead? With Mech alive or dead? With Olga Finaldo . . .

Cop conversations relayed from car to car; you couldn't miss them if you tried. Willetts' calls weren't laced with cop codes, but seemed to involve searchers too. Fenton listened with no particular hopes, but then suddenly there was the Muldoon woman's voice.

He closed his eyes as if that could shut out everything else.

Nothing she said made sense, until suddenly he heard his name. She was describing him. Saying she'd seen him only hours before.

How? Where? How could he not have seen her too?

Calm yourself, Ricardo Fenton, this is only business. The important thing is that you can get to her.

Good thing the cops didn't have access to Willetts' line, or they'd know where she was too.

The idea came like a spark across open wires. If the police found out where Muldoon was . . . if and where the police crossed paths with Mech . . . Right now, Ricky Fenton controlled both ifs. What if they happened at the same time?

Say, a brief delay. Enough time for Mech to kill Lorelei Muldoon before the police arrived.

Finding her was no problem. Unlike Lorelei Muldoon, Ricky Fenton had heard Banjo Man's song before.

The shadows were long and spiky before Stan's black Mustang pulled in behind the building. Lorelei watched him back out in stages, arms full of parcels, caroming off his car, tripping on the way to the door. Had he accepted the fact that walking was less predictable for him than for other people?

She had the apartment door open before he was halfway up the stairs. "Stan, Fenton was right here on the street. You've got to tell the police."

"I thought as long as I was shopping, I might as well— My God." He circled her slowly. "You must know how Clark Kent feels."

She had actually forgotten how she looked. She ran her fingers through the hair that wasn't there like a tongue over a missing tooth.

"He probably feels just fine as long as people don't recognize him. Did you hear what I said? I saw him! Fenton!"

He walked past her into the living room, sweeping papers and magazines off a big trunk. He put a bucket of fried chicken on the instant table, added two small cartons of coleslaw, a quart of milk, and a pint of ice cream. Out of a jeans jacket pocket came plastic forks and a handful of paper napkins.

"You could tell the police *you* saw him."

"What's the point? He's gone. He could be anywhere by now. It's a big valley."

Had she seriously expected Stan to charge to the rescue? No. Shelter, food, information. Not heroics.

She forced herself to sit cross-legged on the floor and accepted a plate. "How big a valley exactly?"

"Probably the size of a state where you come from."

"How many roads?"

"Just the main one, Route 42. Some smaller ones cutting across."

"I mean out of the valley."

"Oh. Four. Well, one each direction. How many do you need, anyway?"

She thought about that, eating with unnoticed speed. If there weren't many roads, the car she bought would need to go off-road.

"Where's the hair dye?"

He looked guilty. Worse: put upon. She couldn't afford that. He had the keys to his father's bank and the computers it held.

"I'll go back for the dye if it matters so much."

"I'll come with you. I don't want to be alone here anymore."

"I told you, Banjo Man just left yesterday. He won't be back for days."

Even as Stan spoke, the ground-floor door—the one to the street—clicked open and fell back shut.

They waited motionless, as if by common consent, as if it was a mistake.

The door opened again. This time something heavy scraped against the floor to hold the door open.

Lorelei recovered first. "Back window! Fire escape!"

"You're paranoid, Lorelei, you know that? He'll just think it's cool. He won't tell anybody."

She hadn't even convinced him to lower his voice.

"Stan, look at me. You weren't thinking about telling that man I was here?"

A convulsive swallow made it clear that he had been thinking just that.

Of course: Lorelei Muldoon the fugitive would give him status with Banjo Man. Stan was still in a video game. He assumed he could walk away if she were found. Or killed. He might even be right.

With the urgency of desperation, she slapped him, rocking his head from one side to the other.

"You tell him nothing!"

Stan looked shattered, but—at least for the moment—back in the real world.

"Be at your car in ten minutes." She glared one risky second longer, willing him to do as she said, before she fled to the bedroom and the back window, scooping up a cotton blanket on her way down the teetery fire escape to the conservatory roof.

She slid down the glass without a check, only pausing after she landed to let her feet and ankles find their balance. In the backseat of Stan's car, she pulled the blanket over her, transformed (hopefully) into an amorphous bundle.

It was more than ten minutes, but not much more, when Stan approached the car, calling her name.

"Here." She tried to float her voice the way Barney McFaul had.

"Banjo Man says he never went to Denver. He's been shacked up, but the husband came back early to help search for you. He thinks I've been shacking up too. I told him you were a med student."

The discarded surgical greens. "Quick thinking."

Stan's voice wobbled with laughter. "He found your hair. He thinks I've been cutting it. Kinky. I said I had to drive you home, I'd meet him at Dead Man's Hand later."

"There's something we have to do first."

"You still obsessing about that hair dye?"

"Even more important. You said you had keys to your dad's bank?"

A pause while he shifted gears. "Why?"

"I want to go in tonight."

She watched his face by the meager moonlight. Stan meets reality. Who wins?

"Why?"

"Remember this morning, when I wanted to transfer money to your account with my computer? I can use the bank's machine instead."

"You can't. There's a password."

"If I can't get the password in five minutes . . . well, ten . . . we'll leave."

He wavered. If she argued with him, she might win, but he'd change his mind just as quickly once he was away from her. She had to let the silence work, trusting that he would give in to somebody more determined.

"I don't have a flashlight," he said at last in a tired, curiously older voice.

Barney forced himself to wait until it was well and truly dark before he started up the crosscut gullies known as the Coulees, Blue a shadow at his side. There was a sketchy road, but that would be watched; he kept high and to the side of it, above the scree that broke into noisy slides at the smallest misstep.

Wherever the rocks were flat enough, there was a shed or a tattered trailer or a truck, backlit by a meager fire. Many had rags hanging somewhere near. Laundry? Awnings? Makeshift tents? A few times a toolie dog, feral as a coyote, sniffed and pointed in their direction; Blue stiffened and gnarred in his throat. Each time the dog slunk back to the fire. A lesson no doubt learned from the gray wolves that traveled these hills.

Willetts' cabin was at the top of a final steep grade that must have pushed the Big Red Machine to its limits. Barney eased his way up to the side of the cabin.

This was the real thing, not a rich man's version like Colman's. Rooms jutted out every which way, and the bark from the hundred-year-old logs came off on his hands like powder. But it was well maintained, the logs chinked, the windows triple-paned and curtained. Through a slit in the curtains he peered into a dark room. Shabby furniture, a fireplace that would have held a side of beef. But it hadn't been lit for months. The whole room looked musty.

He circled. The cabin was like Jekyll and Hyde. The north-facing side hadn't been updated at all. Cold night air whistled through open spaces between the logs and the warped frames of the plain glass windows. And here Willetts sat, slumped in an armchair, the glass in his hand tilted toward the embers of another huge fireplace. Barney watched for several minutes. Willetts stared unmoving.

Barney let himself in.

Claud looked up to see Barney poking the fire ablaze.

"I don't recall answering the door."

"Whisky must be rotting your brain."

"Maybe you forgot visitors aren't welcome here."

"Except one."

"Except one." Claud tried to look around at the big shapes of furniture in the unlit room with a newcomer's eyes. To his mother, a girl from a lean-to in the shabby hills below, this cabin had represented luxury past imagining. She would have done anything to live here. Had done: marrying a man more than twice her age and making it work.

Nothing worth a dime except for the immense rosewood grand piano.

Claud waved his glass at the chair opposite his own. "Bandit sat there time out of mind. He never made fun of it. Us."

"Laugh at what? Big house. Two living rooms."

"Two of everything. Winter and summer. My idea. Another month or so, I'll seal this side up and move over to the south side for the winter."

Barney sat on the arm of the opposite . . . Bandit's . . . chair. "What happens to the piano?"

"Bandit and I used to wheel it on through to the south side. Chatty, aren't you?"

"I want you awake."

Claud scrubbed his face with a big hand. "I just spent dinner with the merry widow and her sidekick. I deserve a good drunk. Try me again tomorrow."

"Just give me Muldoon's clothes and I'll be on my way."

"What makes you think I have them?"

"They went missing from the hospital the same time you did."

"Not guilty."

"I could pull this cabin down around your ears log by log—"

Barney's body looked taut with the effort to hold himself in check. Standing him off was too exhausting to contemplate. "Abby. Abby has them."

"Or I could call the sheriff, get him to ream out the Coulees. All those sheds and trailers, who knows what he might find?"

"Are you deaf? Abby took them. To keep them away from me. Same as you. She won't even let me look them over."

Barney stared in a distinctly untrusting way. "Where's your phone?"

Claud waggled a hand at the shadows behind the piano. "Be my guest."

Without looking away, Barney backed until he could fumble for the phone and dial.

Buck's exclamation points came into the room first, then Abby, assuring Barney in a carrying voice that this time, at least, Claud Willetts was not lying. Barney came back to the fire.

"Buck staying with Abby, is he?" Claud asked idly.

"Both of us. Too far to commute from the ranch."

"What exactly did you see in her stuff, Barney?"

"Don't know. That's why I need to go through it again."

Claud thought out loud. "And we'll never know what was in her apartment."

"How's that?"

"Stan didn't spill it? Maybe there's hope for that boy yet. Somebody set off a bomb in her apartment last night. This morning."

Something tightened around Barney's eyes. "Tell me about it."

Why should he give up information and get nothing in return? But if Barney could get to the clothes . . . "It was a cop in New York. They were trying to trace her, got onto me through Bandit's Washington office."

"What does Sheriff Neiderhoffer say?"

Claud stared into the fire, deliberately deaf. "Add the bombing to whatever you saw in her stuff, and we know that they want her for something she has, not for who she is. If you can figure out what's missing, we'll know what they're looking for. Once we advertise that we've got it, she's safe."

"Forgetting about Fenton, aren't you? She can identify him."

"So can you."

Barney didn't bother to answer. He clapped on his hat and headed toward the door. "Reckon I'll see if Stan has anything to add about that phone call. He's usually at Dead Man's Hand this time of night."

Claud tried to stir himself and gave up the effort. It would serve Stan right to run up against Barney, but he wouldn't: With Banjo Man in Denver, Stan would be safely tucked in bed.

Claud lurched over to the window. A shadow joined Barney outside the door. Man and dog were out of sight before they reached the road.

Lorelei Muldoon and Stan Sokoloff entered the bank through the rear door as quietly as householders, seen only by two incurious raccoons exploring the garbage Dumpster of the restaurant three doors up the hill. The door opened to the basement, out of sight of the oak pillars and marble floors and Victorian brass teller cages.

The basement. Where the computer lived.

While Stan nervously stood guard at the door, Lorelei switched on the power. A violinist drawing a bow across a rosin bar, a swimmer curling his toes on a starting block, a lab technician focusing her microscope: the warm-up hum of a computer to Lorelei Muldoon. Homecoming.

Green pixels filled the screen. Green made for sharp visibility, but it was hard on the eyes. Her own monitor was amber. Had been amber.

"What's your mother's name? Her date of birth? Your dad's? Any brothers or sisters?"

"My father wouldn't—"

"You'd be surprised."

He shrugged, so unconvinced that he felt safe telling her, though he had to work out his parents' birth dates.

She ran a number string, a second, a third. Three minutes later the screen lit up in a sheet of numbers. She was in.

She tapped quickly. Again. Again. If only the computer didn't chirp like a video game—or a microwave—with the completion of each demand.

"What's your account number?"

Stan swung around. "You did it?"

Dumbly he handed over his card and watched his account scroll up.

"How much do I need to buy a Jeep?" she asked. "Secondhand?"

"Fifteen thousand. Ten if you mean a Wrangler. Why?"

"If I drive out, I want something that can go cross-country, just in case."

His balance bulged before their eyes. A thousand dollars, ten thousand, twenty.

Stan looked at the screen fearfully. "They'll really never know?"

"Of course they will. But by that time, I'll be gone. It won't matter what you tell them."

He shivered involuntarily. "I've heard about you number jocks. You live and breathe this stuff, don't you? It's like a separate world."

Oh, and I want to go back. "Unfortunately, I can't sleep there. Is there an office with a sofa somewhere?"

"You mean *here?*"

Lorelei sighed. "Yes, Stan, here."

Reluctantly he led the way to an employee lounge: a coffee urn, a desk, metal chairs, a rump-sprung sofa with a mover's quilt thrown over the back. At the sight of it, exhaustion swept over her.

Would she have trouble getting him to leave? Would he see himself as the hero and try for the girl?

No. Sometime in the computer room this had stopped being a video game. Money, to a banker's son, was real.

He said, "I could bring the hair dye by later."

"I'll get something tomorrow."

"There's usually somebody here by eight, eight-thirty."

"I'll be out long before then. Seven? Before there's anybody else on the street."

He shuffled his feet. "I said I'd meet Banjo Man at Dead Man's Hand. The bar where he sings."

"So you said. Don't let me keep you."

She locked the door after him. Breathed in a sigh of fatigue, and winced. The pain was becoming more familiar than the rest of her. The tired body that felt like a stranger's, the adolescent clothes she was too old for, the unkempt hair that she would dye, somehow, somewhere, tomorrow. I promise, Doris.

For some reason the cool blond image of Doris Day was replaced by the equally cool, equally blond flight attendant bending over Fred, and his fierce responding grin.

She tried to swallow it, but a sob burst through. It hurt her ribs. *How did you find the fugitive, Officer? She was crying so loudly I heard her a block away.* She searched pockets and came up with—ah, no—Fred's bandanna.

A long time later, drawing a shaky, painful breath, she mopped her face with arms almost too heavy to lift. It was only then, her inner clock at a standstill of mourning and despair, that the events of the past days began to loom in the familiar way, shaping themselves into a pattern. An ugly one.

Fred had wanted her to come to Montana not because he had suddenly developed a taste for bronze hair, not because he loved her, but because he needed a numbers expert.

Why not consult her openly? Unless he feared it might involve someone he cared about? Or the valley he cared about? She saw again the field of what she now knew was marijuana.

Fred Colman had wanted her to work (off the record, without realizing she was being used), so that he could decide (off the record) what to do about what she found out.

Whoever it was had found out about Fred first.

Lorelei Muldoon was not, had never been, a random target. She was dangerous not because she was a witness to his death, but because someone feared she knew what *he* knew.

There must be tangible proof: On the off chance of destroying it, her entire apartment had been wrecked. A number jock who got her hands on whatever it was must be able to do a lot of damage.

There was a truth table with a vengeance.

As the crowd in Dead Man's Hand thinned, the owner, Jim Cooper, grumpily urged people into the front room with his walrus shoulders. That way the bar still felt full, and he could start cleaning up. Fenton and Mech stayed as close to the rear as they could, waiting for Banjo Man to finish. After the last set, he played on, the prodigal celebrating his return, one icy filigree breaking into another as his attention wandered, the guitar obediently anchoring him with chords.

Tonight the future seemed as simple as a child's drawing to Fenton. Either Banjo Man would lead them directly to

Lorelei Muldoon or he knew where she was. Either he and Mech would kill her tonight or they would get the musician to set up a meeting.

Either Fenton told the police about that meeting or he didn't.

It was a peaceful feeling, but it left him without much to say. He watched Mech absorb beer after beer with no visible effect beyond a mildly good-natured sleepiness.

"Maybe we should wait outside," Fenton said.

He wasn't sure Mech could still hear, let alone walk. But he rolled upright and made for the men's room.

In the back near the kitchen, a dog began frenzied barking. The bartender headed for the front door, where a man had just come in with a dog like a bear cub at his heels.

Up under his ribs, where the man had thumped them, Fenton's heart thudded. If he slid down, would he be overlooked? Or should he edge toward the back door? But the barking came from there. The bear cub headed toward the sound, blocking the exit.

The bartender had to shout to be heard. "Better get that pup of yours out of here before Sugarfoot throws a hissy!"

"Bluster."

"Huh! Maybe you forgot Sugarfoot's a Dobe?"

"Let him loose. They'll settle it."

The dog's owner sat down at a front table. Fenton craned around the heads in between. The kid already at the table was sitting petrified as the big bear cub/dog nosed up and down his jeans.

"You're probably breaking all kinds of health regulations," the kid said with nervous bravado. "You should take him back to your truck. You could even go with him."

The voice from the phone! Not what he had expected—Olga had been full of respect for this Willetts. Fenton memorized the face.

"I came especially to see you," the dog's owner said. "Calm

down and Blue will too. Stand down, Blue."

The dog reluctantly lowered himself to the floor. At the back, Fenton relaxed a little.

"I thought you might like to tell me about that phone call you took today."

On the platform in front of them, Banjo Man's doodling spun into the opening bars of "Everyday Woman." The remaining people immediately hushed and began to nod rhythmically.

> "I got no need for an everyday woman.
> Give me velvet, and spangles, and gold."

"Pipe down, will you, Barney? People are listening. So I took a phone call. I told my uncle about it."

"Tell me too."

Banjo Man's voice overwhelmed them both:

> "What I want is a medicine woman."

A new verse: Banjo Man paused for anticipation to build before continuing:

> "Cut my heart out, darlin',
> then kiss me and make me all better.
> Show me how to play doctor—"

The rest of the verse was lost as the kid lunged forward, knocking the mike away.

Fenton strained to follow what was happening. The big horrible dog, apparently deciding his command had been vacated, stalked toward the storeroom and the frenzy of the other dog. Suddenly the brute shifted and headed straight for Fenton, legs stiff, coat standing out.

Fenton made it through the back door just in time to brace

it shut before the dog's body hit. As it fell back, Fenton latched the door and ran for the van, leaving behind hideous baying, the thuds of the body against the door, and the high-pitched yipes of the imprisoned Doberman.

And Mech.

Mech stayed by the men's room door, not a muscle betraying that he knew Fenton or recognized the van engine. Just a part of the crowd watching McFaul throw the door open for the big dog to surge out.

When Barney McFaul returned, Banjo Man and Cooper were reassembling the microphone while Stan babbled apologies.

"That man," Barney said.

They looked up. They may not have intended to, but they did.

"He come here often? Alone or with somebody? Who was he?"

He looked at Banjo Man, who explained that the spotlights were in his eyes. At Stan, who wasn't going to add anything; he had already done himself enough damage. At Cooper, who scowled and shook his head, his ruff of fine reddish hair shaking. Barney stared. Cooper's scowl began to seem like something he was hiding behind. When Barney nodded and pulled out a chair, Cooper's relief was transparent.

"Sit, Cooper. Mind if we join you, Sokoloff?"

Customers were watching. Cooper lowered himself to the edge of the chair. "For a minute."

Barney gave him a friendly push farther into it and propped his boots on another chair. "That's right, put up your feet. Tough day."

Table by table, people returned to their own conversations, comparing who had seen what.

Compared to his burly belly and chest, Cooper's outstretched legs looked lanky as a teenager's. McFaul rested a hand on them. Only Cooper and a frozen Stan and Banjo Man could hear what he said.

"Some people think violence is big and noisy, Cooper. Grenades. Guns. And speaking of noise, you—get back on the stand and play."

Banjo Man obeyed hastily, if not tunefully.

"What was I saying? Oh. Violence. Myself, I've always found noise wasteful. Unnecessary. You take a man's legs, now. One hit in the right place . . ." He placed the edge of his hand across Cooper's shins.

Cooper was sweating, legs rigid. He made a strangled sound. Yet there was nothing to be seen or heard. A quiet talk between friends.

"Broken femur, maybe tibia too, depending. And you wouldn't have made a sound. That's right, put your feet down. Let me help you."

He eased off one of Cooper's boots while the manager sat hypnotized. McFaul's fingers probed through Cooper's sock at the back of his ankle. "Rip an Achilles tendon, Cooper, and it rolls up like a window shade, right up to the back of the knee. A good orthopedic man can reattach it if you get there in time, usually. I'll ask you again. Is that man a regular?"

Mech made his way out the back door. He had seen enough to understand what would happen next. In time, not much more time, the bar owner would tell whatever he knew.

Mech slid into the front seat of an unlocked sedan, not new. His fingers stroked the steering column, as knowledgeable in their way as the man he had been watching. The car came smoothly to life.

Chapter
Eleven

Claud divided lawyers into two categories: nuisances (those hired by other people) and necessary evils he was forced to hire to cope with the nuisances. Over the years, Samson de la Haye had moved back and forth between categories. Claud scowled across the desk of Samson's roomy office against a morning sun already too penetrating. He couldn't make out which Samson was this morning. He was so sincere he couldn't even speak in complete sentences.

"Spit it out, Samson," he said. "It may not have struck you, but there's a little excitement in the valley right now, I have things to do. I wouldn't even mind getting some sleep now and then, just to keep my hand in."

"That's why I want to see you. Senator Colman—tragic. Tragic. A loss for you and me personally and for all of us under the Big Sky."

Samson dressed in a way tourists would have been at home with, but he stuck out a little in the valley: suits that didn't call attention to themselves, shirts that did. Claud particularly begrudged Samson his shirts. Men of regulation size could get away with something—red stripes with a white collar this morning—that looked like tent canvas on a man Claud's size.

"Get on with it."

"Very well." De la Haye rolled a pen between his square palms, which meant he was finally about to speak. "The senator was good enough to entrust de la Haye and Rouse with his estate planning, and it was in that capacity that I met yesterday with Senator Colman's widow."

Betty hadn't lost any time.

"Naturally Mrs. Colman wanted to go over the—er—testamentary documents, the funds available to her during probate, and so on."

De la Haye put the pen down into some prearranged place, cocked his head to look at it. Shifted it infinitesimally. All without looking at Claud. "I wasn't aware that Mrs. Colman had taken up residence at the senator's cabin."

"Neiderhoffer told you about Bandit, didn't he? Since when did the domestic details get to be your business?"

"Senator Colman is—was—a special case. He was away so much, we had a larger role than we might have otherwise. That being so, de la Haye and Rouse should have been informed—"

"Next time he's killed I'll bear that in mind. If that's all—"

"No. No, it isn't."

Claud wondered how mild-mannered people got Samson to come to the point. Maybe he got hungry.

"I want to discuss the presence of—er—several people at the reading of the senator's will, which I've scheduled for Tuesday afternoon. Naturally I expect you to be present. Royal McFaul."

"Buck answering to that in public?"

"Now, the young woman. Lorelei Muldoon." Samson had the same way of wrapping his mouth around words that his daughter did, as if they were edible. He made Lorelei Muldoon sound particularly tasty. "It would be better for all concerned if she were present. You have a certain amount of—ah—influence with Sheriff Neiderhoffer. If you could encourage him to bend every effort to locate Miss Muldoon—"

"Hoff'll be glad to get that straight, Samson. He thought it was only a matter of life and death, so he naturally had the search on the back burner. Once he understands there's something legal involved, he'll really put his back into it."

"There's no need for sarcasm, Claud."

"Did you pass on that little tidbit to Betty Colman?"

"Yes. Well." De la Haye passed a remembering hand over his face. "The fact of the matter is, Mrs. Colman refuses to have any part of the reading if Miss Muldoon is present. Categorically refuses."

"She's a little combustible on the subject of Lorelei Muldoon," Claud agreed.

"We can meet without her, but it would be most unfortunate."

Claud thought of the media types bursting the seams of the Demersville Sheraton, of the headlines, of Emerson Flagg struggling to keep the story high-toned. *Unfortunate* was a fair word.

"And I'd like to handle this last matter the way Senator Colman wanted. Talk to her about it, Claud. She'll listen to you."

"Is that why you wanted to see me? That's all?" If Bandit wanted it . . . But even for Bandit, did Samson really think Claud would commit himself without a bargaining chip on the table?

Samson rolled the pen again. "As I assumed, the governor was coming for the funeral Wednesday morning. I've asked him to come earlier. Tuesday afternoon, in fact."

Claud listened so intensely he could feel the words on his skin. "You're telling me there's a bombshell in Bandit's will."

Claud waited, but Samson was too old a hand to be stampeded by silence. He continued to smile blandly. That was all Claud was going to get.

He said grudgingly, "I'll do my possible."

"I'm very grateful. I'm sure Senator Colman would be too."

"We can work out the grateful part later."

Claud hauled himself up. Samson's office was directly over Gaylord's. He wanted to get out and away before Domenica opened her shop. "Domenica around yet?"

"She said something about not opening the store today. Taking a few days off."

"Is that a fact." Another tourist would take home an irreplaceable memory, along with a weakened heart.

Claud turned his hat in his hands. He had always liked to watch Domenica's affairs, from a safe distance. They made life interesting. Somehow he couldn't do it this time. His own raw insides were making him read the same thing in other people. Another unwelcome thing he owed Bandit's killers.

"Samson, did you ever wonder why Domenica . . ."

Samson's face went rigid.

"Why does she stay on here in the valley, Samson?"

"Domenica helps whenever she's asked—on Friday night, for example, which is more than you did!" Samson stood at attention, staring past Claud's head. "To suspect her—"

"Who said anything about suspecting? I want to know if she's happy!"

"Altruism? From you?"

"I just—" If you're doing something for the first time, it stands to reason you'll bumble it. Claud headed for the stairs. "I'm going! I'm sorry!"

Samson's words peppered him all the way down the stairs. "My *daughter* has never taken advantage of anyone in the valley!"

Abby led Barney to the only place in either church or parsonage with a lock—the cabinet that held the Communion service—and left him alone.

Like many people more comfortable with action than

words, he relied on his visual memory. If something was different, given time and privacy, he would pinpoint it. Doggedly he emptied out Muldoon's leather bag for the third time.

His hands seemed to know what he did not, passing over makeup, keys, electronic gadgetry, to smooth an accordion stack of paper, folded over, crumpled by rough treatment, the unmistakable size and green stripes of a computer printout. No names. Columns of numbers that sometimes continued from one page to the next and sometimes switched to a new pattern.

Halfway through the stack, the papers shifted to white typing paper, a blockier typeface. Still numbers.

At his camp there had been no plain paper in the bag.

Not something taken away: something added.

Stan was late. In the alley behind the bank, Lorelei shivered in the early morning chill. She trotted down the gravel road to the lake, back again to the parking lot behind the restaurant, trying to look like an early morning athlete.

Eight o'clock. Eight-thirty. Nine. The street was beginning to stir. She'd be noticed soon, if she hadn't been already. She'd have to go up to the street and pretend to have a purpose there.

The black mustang jerked to a stop where the alley met the street, then inched with uncharacteristic meekness down to her.

Stan leaned across to open the door.

"What t-took you so long?"

"You're freezing! Here, take my jacket. I thought I'd make the withdrawal at the Demersville branch instead of this one. Lay a false trail."

And there was actually pride in his voice. What strange ideas people had about computers. As though a computer knew any more about geography than a vacuum cleaner.

"My uncle Claud's truck is parked up on the Parade. We have to get out of here before he spots us."

Just as quietly, he reversed back up the alley.

Claud walked far enough down Gaslight Parade to see Barney's pickup parked in front of the parsonage. He walked back up to his truck and his phone. Stan should be in the office by now; he could be in Bitterroot in half an hour. Barney might still be there. Maybe he'd let Stan have a look at the clothes.

If Samson de la Haye wanted Betty Colman out of the cabin and Lorelei Muldoon at the will reading, it wasn't hard to figure that the bombshell was a bequest. If Betty had known about it beforehand, she had more to lose than he had realized. Enough to make it worth getting rid of her rival? Exept that he seemed to remember through a whisky haze explaining to Barney McFaul why Lorelei Muldoon was just a pawn.

Lorelei Muldoon, the one time he had seen her, hair spilling down, had been terrified, filthy, powerfully alive. Poor Bandit. Lucky Bandit. Time and past time to accept that she had become more important to him than a lifelong friend. That this last inexplicable love meant something new and fine had happened to the man.

How would that sound in an elegy, with the widow sitting in the front row?

His phone light was blinking. He reached through the truck window, pushed the return button, and heard his brother-in-law's secretary, followed almost immediately by the querulous voice of Peter Sokoloff. Stan's father.

"What'd I do to rate the VIP treatment, Pete? I thought you had to keep somebody on hold or you'd lose your country club membership."

"Stan didn't come home last night, and he's not at your office. Is he with you?"

"When I was his age, I was behind a tree shooting and getting shot at. So were a lot of us. Why don't you cut the kid some slack?"

"A half hour ago Stan withdrew twenty thousand dollars from his account. Twenty thousand."

Claud straightened. "Bitterroot or Demersville branch?"

"Demersville. It was such a large sum, the teller naturally checked his account. The money was there." Peter Sokoloff's voice cracked. "Of course, they were legally bound to let him withdraw it. Unless you pay him more than his mother and I had any idea of—"

"What took you so long to call me?" Claud asked unfairly. "He could be anywhere by now!"

"They told me as soon as I got in. I called right away. The man from Dead Man's Hand you warned us about—"

"Banjo Man's out of town. You're cluttering up the line."

He closed the circuit on the senior Sokoloff's splutter to punch up his own house and tell the toolies to shift their attention from Muldoon to Stan. The flash of an incoming call interrupted him. He switched over to hear Barney's voice.

"What's in her clothes?" he asked. Catch Barney before he had time to think.

Barney chuckled. "Ask Abby. That guy Fenton was in Dead Man's last night, Willetts. Cooper says he's been there off and on all summer. Always with the same man. Built like you, it sounds like, only not as big. They both got away."

It was a measure of Claud's respect for Barney that he didn't bother to ask how. "Point men, do you think? Or the whole army?"

"We'll see when we pick them up. Cooper's working with a police artist. He may be able to I.D. them."

Claud leaned his big frame on Big Red's roof. "I wonder why he's being so helpful."

"Stan was there too," Barney said, deaf. "I tried to raise him just now at your office, but no answer. Send him up to Central, will you?"

"Was Banjo Man there too? Last night?"

"Yes. Singing that fool tune. Why?"

Because Stan has an extra twenty grand in his jeans. But Claud couldn't say it.

"By all that's holy, that's his car! Here! Right under my nose."

Claud moved with heavy, deceptive speed toward the sleek little black car three stores away.

But three stores was enough. Stan nipped through the red light across the nose of a bakery van, up and over the Parade, onto Route 42 heading north.

"That's Uncle Claud!"

Lorelei whipped around to look at the big man staring after them, swinging his weight from one foot to the other in a way that lost none of its threat as he receded.

"Hurry!"

"The Big Red Machine—his truck, I mean—couldn't catch us. Quicker just to call the sheriff. But why would he? He'll just think I'm on my way to work. Speeding because I'm late."

"And of course, he has your license number. Maybe you'd better let me out. I'll hitchhike."

"If he thinks he can run my life, just like Barney last night, I swear—"

"What about Barney McFaul?"

"He came over to Dead Man's Hand last night—that's the bar—"

"I remember. Where Banjo Man sings. What about Barney McFaul?"

"A guy named Cooper owns it. Barney came in, and he saw a guy he wanted to talk to—"

"Not Fenton?" There was a God.

"That's what he called him. So now Cooper is in a cast up to his knee, and Banjo Man and I are playing nurse."

"What did Barney do to him?"

Stan's driving hadn't changed: fast, slow, veering to right and left whenever he tried to mix driving and conversation. It was very slow as he looked at her, unnaturally somber.

"Lorelei, if Barney does catch up to you, just don't . . . don't try anything, okay?"

"But what did he *do?*"

Stan wouldn't answer. He looked even less heroic than he had last night. So did she, but she had no choice.

She hadn't given him much of one either.

"It's almost over now, Stan."

"As soon as you get out of Merciful Valley."

Should she correct him? He dribbled information like bread crumbs; the less he knew, the less he could pass on. But the less he knew, the less he could help.

"I've changed my mind about leaving."

He looked over, bewildered. She grabbed the wheel and held it straight.

"If my apartment was bombed, New York is no safer than here. I'll only be safe after I figure out who's doing this to me and why."

He drove in silence while he thought this over. At last he said—humbly, not warily; he must realize how transparent he was—"Why tell me?"

"I wish I could say it was because I owed it to you. Or because I didn't want to lie to you. But the fact is, I need your help."

He swung around a curve with a bravado that made her smile. "What can I do?"

"I had to leave all my stuff back at the hospital. Do you know where it is? Could you get it for me?"

"That's funny, Uncle Claud wants it too. Abby has it. Reverend Butterfield. I'll just give it to you instead."

"She'd give it to you but not your uncle?"

"You're right, she'll assume it's for him. Everybody always does. It's like I'm not real." The car slowed to a crawl while he brooded. She had to force herself not to worry about someone pursuing them.

The car spurted forward. Stan looked over, face alight. "I'll get Elmo to ask for them! He's a cop, she'll give them to him."

"He won't want to keep them?"

"Even I can outthink Elmo. But how do I get them to you?"

"Pick a place, I'll find it."

He bent himself into improbable contortions of thought. "The thing is, I don't know how long it'll take. Say, by tonight, latest. I have keys to Uncle Claud's office. If we wait till he's gone for the day, that's probably safest. After dinner? Say, ten?"

He described Duncan's on Cuttermill Road with Claud's office above it. "What else?"

"Can you tell me about these people? You know them. I don't."

"Like who?"

"You really will?" It was so pathetically easy to use him. "Pull off the road somewhere. I don't want to worry about being seen. Turn the car facing it out so we can get out fast if we have to."

No talk about paranoia this morning. Stan obligingly took the next right down a dirt road and made a sweeping U-turn. "Driveway. The guy who lives up there is in the movies. He's in Africa."

And Banjo Man is in Denver.

"Who do you want to know about?"

"Your uncle?"

"He grew up with Senator Colman, he would never—"

"He doesn't have to be involved in Fred's murder, Stan. There's more going on than that. He might be helping the killers and not even know it."

"Claud'd do anything to find them."

"Like setting me up? But why doesn't the sheriff stop him?"

"They're used to working together. Sort of."

"He's a deputy? A D.A.?"

"Nothing like that. Uncle Claud knows everything that goes on in the valley. Sometimes he helps the sheriff out."

"But what does he *do?*"

"Oh . . . a little of this and a little of that." Stan struggled between pride and embarrassment. "It's not so much how he gets it as how he handles it, my dad says. Claud knows the ins and outs of the tax code better than anybody in the state. Dad says half the tax work in every legislative session is to cover his loopholes."

If a man knew how numbers could be used, it would take a number jock to track him. Claud Willetts might not have planned to kill his best friend. A scheme could get out of hand in ways unimaginable at the outset.

Which must have happened, no matter who it was. Nobody sets out to kill a senator.

"And Reverend Butterfield?"

That shocked Stan just as much, but his defense of her sounded unconvincing to Lorelei: her family connections outside the valley, the Pastor's Committee to provide a network of people who could be used, perhaps without realizing it. A definite possible.

"And Buck McFaul? That sweet little jack-in-the-box?"

"He has a big ranch east of here. Wheat, some cattle."

"So Barney McFaul is a farmer," she said before she could stop herself.

"Well, partly. He used to be in one of those special forces— SEALs, Rangers, whatever. Claud thinks he still is. He goes away for weeks, months even. Then one day he's back, and he never says a word about it. Neither does Buck."

Could Barney and Buck combined keep her safe from both the killers and Claud Willetts? Tempting. But they, too, must have known about the story in the *Herald*.

Stan drummed a tattoo on the steering wheel.

"The cash I took out, that's for a car, right? Even if they can't trace it like a credit card, that much money, they'll remember you."

"I have to take that chance."

"Let me do it. I'll tell them I'm getting it for Claud and he didn't say why. He always uses cash, and it's like I said. It's like I'm his robot. They won't think twice about it."

"What will you say if the police or your uncle catch on?"

"They won't. Once I get your stuff, I'll hang out at Cooper's apartment all day. It's above Dead Man's Hand, and Dead Man's is closed Mondays. They'll never check there."

No stumbles, no hesitation. Pieces of the man he would become were falling into place at a pace hard to assimilate. The only way to thank him was to accept him as what he was struggling to be. She pulled his head down and kissed him with as much damsel-in-distress fervor as she could muster.

He swaggered back to the Mustang and shot away, chin jutting. One kiss and he was ready to slay a dragon. He reminded her of Lorelei Muldoon, wagging her tail for Fred Colman.

Now that they knew Willetts by sight, Fenton and Mech staked out his office from the shabby van, taking turns monitoring the equipment and wandering the area.

It wasn't safe. The exposure Olga had brought upon herself had made Fenton all the more sensitive to his own. The difference was that hers had been unnecessary and his was strictly business. The only way to get to Lorelei Muldoon before the police was through Willetts.

He didn't dare use the legally rented sedan that could be traced to Olga; anyway, they needed the van to house the equipment. But they had had it—how many days now? Too many. One vehicle, one location; all they could change was parking places up and down Cuttermill Road.

Willetts, the thin, clumsy kid with the big bony face, had yet to appear. A large, heavyset man had been there a few times, finally driving off with a little guy in a pink Lincoln. With another dog. Fenton debated following them but decided not to risk it.

At a changeover, Fenton said, "If this Willetts kid hasn't come in by now, he probably won't show today. But he's all we got. I'll watch till . . . say, six. You get some rest. Then you do tonight, I'll take over early tomorrow morning."

Mech nodded and left. Fenton took out rags and began polishing the surfaces of the van, inside and out. It gave him a reason to stay there for a couple of hours, and it got rid of his fingerprints. If all went as planned, this was his last chance.

Claud sat beside Buck in the big pink Lincoln, the arthritic Max relegated to the backseat. He looked down the slope at Bandit's—Betty's—cabin.

"I appreciate the company, Buck. I'm not looking forward to this. But maybe between the two of us—"

"The will-reading thing is your department, Willetts. I'm just here to talk about what the air patrol will do at the funeral."

Bandit Colman had been a member; of course the patrol would be a part of his funeral cortege.

Not in their planes; they switched to motor scooters at parades and county fairs and rodeos and high school graduations, swarming around, maintaining informal order, boots scraping the macadam to brake, grinning like Hell's Angels. Outsiders, not realizing that each scooter represented a private plane, thought they were a fine example of unspoiled Montana rednecks and took lots of pictures.

"How many people coming?"

"Everybody, pretty near. Even some from Vancouver. We've taken over a parking lot over at the airport."

Buck could ramble about the air patrol as long as he was allowed. Claud turned his mind to the question of Betty and the will reading. The paperwork of Bandit's death was as remorseless as decay, and had little to do with the hot, swollen, vulnerable feeling that seemed to be his new norm.

Of course, Stan was mixed into that now, too. Stan, who had sat in his uncle's office these past weeks, hearing every phone call, every discussion.

Whose bank balance had skyrocketed as soon as Banjo Man returned from wherever he had been.

Stan, for whom the toolies were now looking, as well as for Lorelei Muldoon. Was he still after revenge? or trying to get Stan out from under?

Stan could never have killed **Dr. Sue.** She had been killed by someone who didn't know her, who thought she was Lorelei Muldoon.

Clutching that thought, Claud forced himself to cool down. The business at hand was Betty. If Bandit had wanted her at the will reading—even just to shock her!—Claud would get her there if he had to drag her.

Claud followed Buck down the stone walk, willing Bandit to swing the big oak door wide with a welcoming slash of white. But it was his widow, her head ducking away from the sun, birdlike as ever.

"Twice in two days, Claud, my goodness. To what do we owe the honor this time?"

Betty in her glittery mood, quick to take offense.

"Buck has some stuff he needs to talk to you about. I'm just tagging along."

He followed them into the square stone hall, looking instinctively for the portrait of Elena Colman. But the wall was bare; the painting was propped against a wall like a discard.

It shook him. By the time he tuned in again, Buck and Betty were deep in procession planning.

"I suppose it's too much to expect you to use a limousine, Claud, you'll be in that truck."

"Something wrong with that?"

Olga Finaldo awaited them in the big living room, in one of the gray flannel wing chairs, barely recognizable under something flowery. "Perhaps you will do as I have done, Mr. Willetts. I have found an adequate substitute for a limousine."

Claud hadn't paid much attention to her the night before, and no wonder. She was the kind of friend some pretty women took care to have, second fiddle and knew it, from her stubby body to dark hair pulled straight back to modest jewelry at the neck of a nondescript black dress.

"How's that, Mrs. Finaldo?"

"Olga, I'm sure Larry didn't in the least mean to upset you," Betty said. "He's apologized."

"No, Betty, true words are spoken in anger. Mr. Hungerford was quite right. It is enough that he attends to your needs."

Hungerford, attending to their needs with brimming glasses of Wild Turkey, listened to the discussion without a smile, without defending himself. When the phone trilled, he left the room quickly.

Why was he still here playing barkeep and receptionist instead of back in Washington lining up his future?

Betty's hummingbird attention fluttered on. "I'd never really taken much notice of Abby before," she said. "I mean all the people she knows. Governor Larsen will speak at Fred's funeral, I suppose you know that. Abby talked to Senator Balthazar and he agreed too."

Claud snorted. "Him say something good about Bandit. That'll almost be worth hearing."

"Abby says you should speak as his—well, his oldest friend. But when I think of our differences . . ." She began to enumerate their differences.

Before Claud could bristle, Olga Finaldo played peacemaker.

"Betty, perhaps Mr. Willetts would like to walk through the cabin one last time before we make our changes. It is only proper, Mr. Willetts, that you should say here the good-bye you had no chance to say to your friend."

"You're changing the cabin? That's what this flowery stuff is?"

"Fancy you noticing, Claud. That's just a sample. Since all Fred's furniture is overscale—isn't that what you called it, Olga?—we'll be replacing it with more intimate things."

Would a slosh of bourbon make the flowery fabric beneath his glass look more intimate? "I suppose Elena's portrait doesn't fit anymore?"

Betty's laugh ran up the scale. "Why on earth would I keep a portrait of Fred's mother in my house?"

My house.

Olga said firmly, "As to that, nothing is decided. A museum, most likely."

"You mean let him get cold first, it'll look better."

Two clown spots of red sprang to Betty's cheeks. Before she could speak, Olga said smoothly, "She, too, has memories, Mr. Willetts. Why should you feel fresh pain, my dear Betty? I can escort Mr. Willetts through the cabin. Or, of course, Mr. Hungerford."

The color faded. "So thoughtful, always. If you wouldn't mind, Olga dear, since Larry's minding the phone."

Claud welcomed the opportunity to follow Betty's friend up and around the broad stairs. If Bandit's request was to have a chance, both Betty and Claud himself had to calm down.

"Feel free to look where you like," Olga said politely.

"Thank you kindly, ma'am."

They went all the way to the top of the stairs, level with the antler chandelier, up and past it to Bandit's bedroom. He paused, willing himself not to comment on the sight of Betty's clothes strewn across the bold lines of carved wood and Indian blankets. Olga stood at attention behind him. Waiting for something. Was he supposed to break down in front of her?

When he lingered at the study door on the way down, she was on him like a dog on a bone.

"You see something different? Something missing perhaps?"

So that was it: They thought Lorelei Muldoon might have taken something, and Olga was the designated floorwalker. What did it matter, if they planned to pull the place apart anyway?

Unless whatever it was, was what Barney had missed in Lorelei Muldoon's bag.

He felt six inches taller.

He waved at the computer/fax/who-knew-what on the table against the back wall, the one overlooking the lake. "That's new. Guess Bandit figured it was time to join the information superhighway."

Her eyes told him it was the wrong answer. He shrugged.

Betty and Buck had moved to the terrace. When Claud and Olga joined them, the two women glanced at each other and away.

"Did you see all you wanted, Claud?"

The calm ownership grated.

"Yes, thanks." He forced himself to add, "I hope you'll be happy here."

She and Olga exchanged another look.

"It'll be a nice retreat from Washington," Betty agreed.

"You'll keep the condo there?"

Olga said, "It depends on Betty's plans. Or rather, the plans being made for her."

"How's that?"

"The governor?" Betty reminded him. "When he's here for the funeral?"

"He will doubtless make it public then," Olga said. "That he has appointed Betty to finish her husband's term."

Immediately Buck was all over her like a cheap suit, full of congratulations.

This was Samson's bombshell? Senator Betty. It took an amazing effort not to laugh; then suddenly it took no effort at all.

Senator Betty, because her husband was dead. If she had known he planned a new life, a new will . . .

And it had nothing, blessedly nothing, to do with Stan. Now it was easy to move on to his own—Bandit's—business. He seized his opportunity with zest.

"You're at a tricky point with Governor Larsen, then." The women looked at him, Betty puzzled, her companion—now, why was that?—wary. "You want him to respect your judgment."

"If this is leading up to one of your insults, Claud Willetts—"

"No, no, honey—Betty. I'm thinking of the will reading tomorrow. If the governor is there and it turns into a big number that you're not . . ." Claud spread his hands.

"But what is this, my dear Betty?"

"Samson de la Haye wants *her* there!" The clown spots flew in Betty's cheeks again. "The Muldoon woman."

The friend's mouth popped open. She closed it carefully before she opened it again to say, "And if she is there, and the governor pays his condolences to her, and not to the senator's widow?"

Claud looked at her with respect.

Buck said soothingly, "Who's to say that Lorelei Muldoon will turn up tomorrow? If ever."

Olga said, "You are involved with the search, Mr. Mc-Faul?"

"Buck. We haven't found a trace of her."

"Because she's left the valley," said Betty. "If a woman were sheriff, Claud Willetts, she'd have the Muldoon woman in jail by now."

Before Buck could combust, Claud said, "A woman sheriff for women criminals? Sounds good to me. A woman senator would be a start. When did you talk to Larsen?"

"He hasn't actually—that is, not in so many words, but his assistant made a point of telling us he's coming a day early for the funeral. What other reason could there be?"

Larsen, with a craggy, photogenic governor's face and a mellow deep governor's voice, didn't have so many words, and those he had were written by others.

"Besides, you must have seen the *Herald* yesterday."

Claud's heart sank. Hints Larsen probably didn't know he had dropped, an editorial flight of fancy. That was all?

The screen door rattled. Barney McFaul stepped in, hat in hand.

"Sorry to bother you, ma'am. Hey, Dad. The toolies are looking for you, Claud. Gave up and got hold of me."

Toolies. Stan. Claud read disaster in Barney's unreadable face.

"Don't mind me," Betty said. "Make the cabin your head-quarters, Claud, why not?"

Barney, oblivious to insult, glanced at Claud for a go-ahead.

Claud shook his head. "Let's walk and talk."

The McFauls followed him up the slope to the road before Barney said, "Stan again, Claud. Sorry. Sullivan Motors sold him a Wrangler this morning. Fifteen thousand cash."

"I will be sold for a pup."

One thought pushed past another, none stopping long enough to make sense. If that had been getaway money, Stan might already be out of the valley; no wonder the toolies hadn't found him. More to the point: Why did he need to get away?

Lorelei Muldoon was on the run too.

Wherever that thought had come from, it made Claud's pulse jump with hope. Stan had certainly looked at her goggle-eyed at the rescue Saturday afternoon. Claud stopped, going back over the events of the last two days. Could Stan have crossed paths with her?

Little by little, hope ebbed. "Did Sullivan say if he was alone?" Claud asked.

"Far as I know. Why?"

Claud thought of Barney's helpless rage back at the hospital. At the unexpectedly cooperative Cooper. Explaining would put Stan in the same position. He said lamely, "He's been hanging around with that hophead singer. I've been expecting trouble."

"Not likely to have two different troubles at the same time, Willetts. What are you going to tell the sheriff?"

"How can I tell him that Stan—that Stan might have had something to do with—"

He tried again. "Until I know exactly what he did—"

He gave up, blowing his nose powerfully. "You got to give me time to handle this myself, Barney. You didn't hear anything, Buck, okay?"

"Hear what?" Buck asked. He swung the pink car door wide.

At the wheel of a khaki Jeep Wrangler, Lorelei retraced the route out of town. Fields on one side of the road; on the other, neat rows of Christmas trees, all sizes. She pulled off near some deep, water-filled ruts, scooped up handfuls of mud, and smeared the license plates, spattering the fenders for good measure.

She had three goals for the day: To dye her hair. To buy a sleeping bag, so she could sleep in the Jeep if necessary. To learn the geography of Merciful Valley. If she had to flee again, she wanted to know where she was going. If.

When.

She crisscrossed Merciful Valley from Demersville down past Bitterroot, with Willetts' office, the evening's meeting place, as the bull's-eye, and the rest of the valley spreading out from it.

The unpaved roads proved to be extended driveways for farms and houses in the foothills. Imposing sprawls, many of them. There was money in this valley. But, as Stan had said, only four roads led out.

Good thing a Jeep could go overland. She tested it, bucketing over a field to a small stream, where she discovered that it was possible, if miserably uncomfortable, to dye her hair Ronald McDonald red in the icy water.

As she waited damply to pull back onto the road, a mail minivan passed, followed with stagy furtiveness by an old Volvo station wagon. The mail van stopped at a clutch of mailboxes at the mouth of a dirt road. After it had passed out of sight over a hill, the Volvo stopped and made a second delivery. The driver was a woman. Shortish, dark-haired, sturdily built, in an army-green jogging suit.

Intrigued, Lorelei waited (she had all day) until mail van and Volvo were long gone before she drove back to the mailboxes to check for herself. It had to be safe. Even Fred's killers wouldn't sabotage every mailbox in the valley.

In the first box, tucked in beside catalogs from Horchow and Williams-Sonoma, bills from Visa and Ottinger's, was a foot-long zucchini. The second mailbox had a Horchow catalog, three personal letters, one bill (a hardware store), and another enormous zucchini. The third held only the zucchini.

She hefted each squash in turn. What would be Hank's opinion of this datum?

She climbed back into the Jeep. Next stop: Great Bear Outfitters.

The saleswoman made it immediately clear that a sleeping bag was a more serious purchase than Lorelei had realized. Was she planning to use it only in the summer or all year round? In a cabin? tent? out-of-doors? On an air mattress? bare ground? They thrashed their way category by category to a final selection (polyester fill; microfiber; good down to, but not below, freezing).

Lorelei turned to flashlights, shaking her head at lanterns and fog lights. Just something big and basic, plus batteries.

As she counted out bills, the woman asked, "Where will you be camping?"

"Over near Cutthroat Lake."

"Bridgewater Basin?"

"Something like that."

"You aren't having your period, are you, honey?"

Lorelei stared. The woman, sharp-eyed but friendly, looked perfectly sane.

"Lots of bears on that side of the valley—they wander out of Heroes Wilderness. They smell a woman menstruating, it's like a homing device. Brings them from fifty miles away."

The woman looked at her keenly and thumped a spray can down beside the sleeping bag. "Tell you what, I'll throw in some OC-five, gratis, free, and for nothing. Bear repellent. Bushwacker Backpack puts it out."

Lorelei examined it dubiously. Counter Assault OC-5. "What does it do?"

"Just blinds them temporarily. No permanent injury."

How reassuring. "How do you—er—apply it?"

"Well, of course, that's the catch. You have to get it right in their face, so they have to be pretty close. Effective, though. Even the rangers carry it."

Beware of Ricky Fenton and his henchman, of Claud Willetts, of women bearing zucchini . . . and bears.

At nine-thirty Monday night, Lorelei turned from Route 42 onto Cuttermill Road, driving past Duncan's to park in the alley behind the building. Feeling like a fool, she put the bear repellent in the pocket of the jacket Stan had lent her. Well, what other weapon did she have? The car jack?

She walked in the shadows to where the alley crossed a side street two stores down and edged up toward Cuttermill, hugging the building. There were still a few empty cars on the street. No people. By this time the action must be farther down in the valley, in the Bitterroot bars.

She waited a few feet behind the corner, out of sight of the street, clearing the ground around her of whatever might rattle or tip over or break. If Stan had unwittingly given away this meeting, she wanted to see any uninvited guests before they saw her.

Promptly at ten, Stan's black mustang jerked to a stop in front of his uncle's building.

He peeled himself out of the sleek black car and leaned on the roof, tapping his keys, his white T-shirt blazing in the dark. Telegraphing the fact of a meeting a lot farther than the dusty van directly across the street, visible even a block away, where Fenton watched from a nondescript sedan.

Fenton held the receiver poised to punch up 911. The central police station was only blocks away. If the police arrived just after Lorelei Muldoon, or even at the same time . . .

As soon as Lorelei stepped out on the sidewalk, it came, from the shadows across the street: the shallow clattering rat-a-tat of her nightmares.

Chapter Twelve

Lorelei dropped to the street, unsure in the first fleeting seconds whether she chose to or had to. A hasty inventory of arms, legs, breathing: all right. Stan's car must have shielded her.

Her. Not Stan.

He slumped against the front fender—sheltered now that it was too late—his T-shirt darkly blotched.

Skin prickling, hearing the next stutter of bullets in her mind, Lorelei wriggled across the sidewalk to him. He flopped willingly against her. There were wet holes on his right shoulder, high. Blood seeped quietly, steadily, over her hand. Surely that meant he was alive?

She put her mouth right next to his ear. "Stan, can you hear me?"

Stan's mouth moved. She had to lip-read as much as hear. "She wouldn't give us your stuff."

"Never mind that. You have to play dead. Make them lose interest and leave. Got it?"

". . . piece of cake."

Lorelei squeezed his hand. Comfort. Understanding. Whatever he needed. She inched up until she could peer over the hood. Across the street, the back doors of a dirty van swung in the night air.

A professional killer would have to come and check his handiwork. Wouldn't he? They? How much time did she have? She groped for Stan's keys. If she could slide into his car, pull him in after her . . .

No. Stan was a dead—scratch that, helpless—weight. She could never pull him. Even if she could push him in unnoticed, she'd have to crawl over him to the driver's seat.

She groped in her pocket for the can of bear repellent. She had been too self-conscious to read the instructions. The woman had said "close." How close was close? She smeared her bloody hands on her T-shirt and slumped against Stan as though she, too, had been hit, praying the van would pull away without putting her to the test.

Stan's blood soaked through her jacket. How long until she could assume they were safe? How long could he afford to wait?

From across the street came a scuffling sound.

A cautious killer. Not Fenton.

The barely audible scuffling came toward them, to the back of Stan's car. Damn; awkward. Bad angle.

Heavy steps. Heavy man. Stupid if Stan were killed by his own uncle.

A boot kicked her in the back, sending her sprawling. She twisted and sprayed upward at the same time, eyes shut, her other hand over her face and mouth.

There was a hoarse male scream. A heavy gun hit the sidewalk. A man blundered into the street, hands over his face, keening.

Terrible. Wonderful. In the triumph that rocketed through her, she could have moved a mountain.

But could she move Stan? She hooked his good arm around

her shoulders and urged him to his feet, staggering to balance his weight. He cried out.

"Next stop, the emergency room," she assured him.

Their attacker was almost across the street now, a thickset man, his face still buried in his hands. Why bother shooting them? He could have huffed and puffed and blown them to smithereens.

How long did the bear repellent last? How well could he see?

Stan's car was right beside them, but it was a wriggle to get into. And a stick shift. She'd have to get him to her Jeep.

"Come on, Scotty, beam me aboard," Stan said clearly.

If only I could.

The wannabe killer's gun lay abandoned on the sidewalk. Sweating under Stan's precious weight, Lorelei looked at it covetously. Was the safety catch on? Could she manage it and Stan both? She propped Stan against the building so she could stoop and pick it up. He slid bonelessly down to the sidewalk.

Don't press your luck, Lorelei. Settle for getting far, far away. She began the time-eating process of getting Stan upright again. Then heaving a step forward. Another step. How many minutes did she have? Seconds? She tried to make sense of the harsh cries behind them.

Angling the Jeep's back door open with her free hand, Lorelei pushed and shoved and hauled Stan up onto the backseat, cursing it for being so high.

He was still bleeding. They were both in T-shirts and jeans: The adolescent uniform wasn't meant to be torn into bandages. She felt feverishly in her pockets: Fred's bandanna! No doubt there was an efficient way to make a bandage. All she could do was tie it tightly around Stan's shoulder. The calico pattern disappeared wetly.

She leaped into the front seat, reversing with a haste that

made the engine shriek, jerking forward again onto the street. The van was still there. Where was the man? A braver woman would sideswipe it. She careened by at top speed, ignoring traffic lights, horn blaring.

"Tell you where hospital," said Stan quite recognizably.

"I drove around this afternoon. We'll be there before you know it."

But not before she had time to think of her next move at the speed of a cat going up a tree. When she ground to a halt in front of the emergency doors, she turned to him. "Stan, can you hear me?"

"Loud and clear, Lieutenant."

"We're at the hospital. I'm going to take you in, but I can't let anyone see me. Understand? I have to get to this Abby before anybody else does. Do you have any I.D.? Should I call your parents?"

". . . . not parents. Claud." He reeled off a phone number.

"Sure that's what you want?"

". . . . no fuss."

She opened the back door and reversed the process of hauling and shoving and pulling until Stan's weight more or less fell out onto her, blessing the seat of the Jeep for being so high.

It was a long journey to the door.

"Got the phone number?" he asked anxiously as she struggled with the stupid architectural barrier called a step.

"Numbers are my business, remember?" she panted.

They half pushed, half fell through the doors of the emergency room.

Suddenly there was a crowd of people. Strong ones who lifted Stan up on a gurney as if he were a toy. Skilled ones who had an I.V. poised instantly, who were probing the wound even as he was being wheeled away down the corridor.

She was back out the door before the bustle subsided

enough for questions. If I survive this, Dr. Sue, I'm sending a big donation.

For five minutes she turned left and right at random, before she slowed down to look for a pay phone. The phone rang for a long time. She wouldn't give odds that Stan had the number right. Finally a slow, cautious voice suggested that she try the Bitterroot Congregational Church instead. "He's visiting with Abby."

"But this is an emergency!"

After a long pause, the voice said, "You could try there."

The Congregational Church. The woman with her pocketbook.

She took precious time for thought before she got the church's number from information and dialed. A penetrating voice answered.

Trying to sound bored, Lorelei said, "I have a call for a Mr. Carl Williams. Is he there?"

"Could you mean Claud Willetts?"

"Just a minute, I'll check with my party." Lorelei put her hand half over the mouth of the receiver and garbled a believable number of syllables. "My party will speak to Mr. Willetts."

"Mr. Willetts?" She had only heard him once before, but the light tenor was unmistakable. "This is Demersville Memorial. We have a shooting case here, a Stan Sokoloff. He's asked us to notify you. Have you got that? Stan Sokoloff. Demersville Memorial."

She hung up on a spate of questions. Should she call the hospital and leave Claud's number? Surely he'd call himself.

She had told Stan she wanted to get to the woman called Abby before anyone else did. Reason told her in a clear, stern Doris Day soprano that the only excuse for not going was cowardice. Oh, to be back in a world where people used prettier words to let themselves off the hook.

* * *

Fenton trailed the khaki Jeep Wrangler all the way to the hospital. Once the kid Willetts and the Muldoon woman were settled inside, he turned back to camp. What had happened to Mech? It didn't look fatal. And the police hadn't showed.

Look on the bright side: They might be there by now.

If not, he had to erase all signs of himself from the campsite before Mech returned.

Stan was still in surgery when Claud burst through the hospital doors with Barney and Buck McFaul in his wake.

He tried to bull through to the operating room, but the combined efforts of a nurse's aide, two orderlies, and the McFauls prevailed. Finally the aide agreed to slip in and check. She returned to report that all was going as well as could be expected, no imminent danger, a couple of hours yet to go. They were taking their time to preserve maximum mobility in the shoulder, though they wouldn't know the results for some time. As a peace offering she handed them the limp bag of Stan's clothes, which Buck quickly took possession of.

"If you can go in, why can't I?" Claud demanded of the aide.

"That's his idea of a thank-you," Barney said, giving her a deliberate white smile. "Who brought the boy in?"

"They might know down in Emergency."

"You'll track us there if necessary?"

"There's no place to sit on this floor anyway," Buck said impatiently, bolting down the stairs.

Barney gave the aide another smile, making her consider going with them. But the three men were already gone.

To Claud, the immediate horror of Stan's injury was swallowed by a bigger one: The kid had gotten caught up in something dangerous and put his clumsy foot in it somehow.

220

How could Claud protect him without knowing where to throw up dust?

Either yesterday's Admissions clerk had transferred to Emergency or she had a twin. Pale blue eyes glistening, she said, "This is my first shooting. We rehearse, we all know what to do, I wouldn't want you to think—"

"Who brought him in?" Claud asked.

"That's what's so amazing! He must have walked in. They should write him up for a medical journal. The first thing we know is when he collapses right there"—she indicated a dull area on the red tile floor—"in front of our very eyes!"

"Does that sound doable to you?" Claud asked Barney.

"Anything's possible. A lot of blood with that kind of injury. He couldn't make it far."

"Maybe you heard shots?" Claud asked her.

"I'll check the parking lot," Buck said, halfway out the door.

"Maybe he drove from someplace else," Emergency said, inspired.

"Check for a dun-colored Jeep too," Claud shouted after Buck. He turned back to Emergency. "Were you the one who called me? No? Could we talk to whoever did?"

She shook back a mane of Swedish silver hair and said sullenly, "The shape he was in, he wasn't talking to anybody."

"But he could drive himself here and walk in?"

Barney moved in front of Claud before he got well warmed up. "Could we have your shift list? We'll talk to people ourselves, stop bothering you."

Before she could permit or refuse, Buck McFaul burst back through the double doors. "No Mustang in the parking lot. One Jeep, red, no bloodstains."

Before the doors could swing shut, Sheriff Orry Neiderhoffer followed him through.

Sheriff Neiderhoffer was flanked by a man in an immaculate gray suit and the patrolman Elmo, looking belligerent, his

Adam's apple bobbing. Determined to make up tonight for his goof with Lorelei's clothes the day before, Claud thought.

"Why are you checking the parking lot for Jeeps?" the sheriff asked Buck.

Buck's eyes rolled to Claud.

Claud asked, "You got a call about Stan too?"

"Too?"

"We were at Abby's. Half an hour—no, an hour now. A woman. We're trying to find out who she was. Nobody's volunteered so far."

Neiderhoffer had the soft strained voice of a man about to drop a heavy weight on someone. "We're one up on you. Our call came ahead of time. Told us to come over to Duncan's, we might be glad we did."

Claud jumped to his feet. To feel his juices running this fierce, not knowing whether to point them toward the satisfaction of revenge or the protection of his nephew . . .

"We also got calls to watch Dead Man's, the Aerie Condos, and three bars up the Kinnikinnick. And my house. Troop Number Two is having a sleep-over, they got tired of ghost stories."

A gust of . . . relief? disappointment? . . . left Claud weak at the knees.

Neiderhoffer turned to his escort. "Wait for me in the car." A jab of a nod to the McFauls. "If you folks wouldn't mind, Claud and me have a little catching up to do."

Neiderhoffer had included the gray suit in his dismissal, but the man didn't leave, instead leaning quietly back against the wall. Even in Claud's present state, that was worth a second look. *Tidy* was the word that came to mind, even in the middle of the night. Claud looked a third time in disbelief: wing-tip shoes.

"Feds finally came in, did they, Hoff? Aren't you going to introduce me?"

222

With mixed disgust and disdain, Sheriff Neiderhoffer said, "Jimmy Fineman, Claud Willetts."

"James, actually," said the neat gray man, adjusting small round wire glasses. "FBI."

A decent size and build. Under Claud's appraising eye, he flushed and straightened.

"What'd you play, Jimmy? Running back? Wide out?"

"Running back, actually."

"Who for?"

"C. W. Post, that's in—"

"Ever think about the pros?"

Fineman made a confused half gesture toward his right shoulder. "No—actually—"

"If it isn't shoulders, it's knees," Claud agreed.

"If you've finished," Neiderhoffer said in that same strained voice.

He put a hand on Claud, easing them both into orange kidney-shaped plastic chairs too small for either. Fineman continued to lean against the wall off to one side.

"I thought you and me had an agreement, Gang. Otherwise I wouldn't have gone along with you before."

"Think I know why Stan got shot? I've been trying to get my hands on him all day. But it's personal, Hoff. Nothing to do with Bandit or the others."

"I'll be the judge of that, Gang."

"After he explains it to me."

The sheriff hitched his chair closer. "Happen I'll just fasten you down right now."

"You would, wouldn't you." Leaving Stan exposed to the tender mercies of the FBI as well as his parents. "But you wouldn't use it if it didn't apply?"

Neiderhoffer gave a shrug that could mean yes or no.

Claud decided to settle for it. "Stan pulled money out of the bank this morning. Money we didn't know he had.

223

Bought a Jeep, paid cash. Where is it? I have to wonder if he got involved with Banjo Man's drugs."

"Try again, Gang."

"Hoff, you got all the pieces I do!" Claud kept swinging between hot fury at what Stan had done and an equally hot fear that the kid might die before Claud had the chance to wring his neck.

"He knew everything we were doing, Hoff, from the time we discovered the marijuana. Banjo Man must have been laughing up his sleeve—it's a wonder he didn't work up a song about it. My own blood. Might as well be my son."

"Let me make it easier for you, Gang. Banjo Man's into women, not drugs. He was planning to spend the weekend with . . . well, let's just say somebody local . . . but everybody changed their plans to search for Bandit. When the search picked up Sunday afternoon, the husband came home for a change of clothes."

"Why—"

"—would I find out about it before you? I know the man."

Claud thought about it. He had assumed women were protective coloration for Banjo Man, part of being a folk singer. Assumed, like an amateur. Something began to lighten inside him.

But Stan had undeniably bought the Jeep. Who would he put himself in danger for, if not Banjo Man? His parents? Claud himself? And when did he get clever enough to hide himself from Claud?

Before he could feel his way clear, Fineman broke in.

"We should have been brought in when the marijuana was discovered," he said severely. "Over thirty percent of the annual crop is grown on forest service land. We have a range of programs in place to deal with it, all fully cognizant of the rights of local authorities."

Claud couldn't decide whether to punish the interruption

or admire the style of it. "He sound like that all the time, Hoff?"

"So far. Go ahead, son, talk some more."

Fineman flushed and subsided.

"No? Your turn, Gang."

Claud sighed. He braced his hands on his knees and went over everything he knew, from the discovery of the marijuana to Bandit's retirement to the surprises that lay ahead in his will to whatever Barney had found in Lorelei's bag to the attack on Stan.

"Anything there you don't already know?"

"What you're thinking."

"I wouldn't mind knowing myself." Claud sighed again. "It's like I'm watching two pictures that don't fit together. On the one hand, they know us. How we live, who works for who. They must have known Shari Finley was Bandit's handyman. Handywoman. They knew that Bandit was coming, where he landed. But if they knew anything about Stan, they'd know he's harmless."

He paused. Sometimes it was easiest to lie with a question. "Why go after him unless they were trying to get at me? Right in front of my office?"

"That's the other picture?"

"I don't know. The other picture is all big stuff. Tinkering with a plane half a state away, bombing an apartment on the other side of the country. Even . . ." He looked at Fineman, effaced against the wall. "Even back in Bogwash, that's big. And marijuana . . ."

Claud stared at his knees for so long that the sheriff stirred on his chair, but he waited.

"It's two different things too. The scale of it, and the fact that it's a hybrid: Barney says that makes it pros. But it's blue-collar stuff, he says, not yuppie. That's generally local. Who'd do that?"

"You mean, besides you?"

"Have I ever—*ever*—had anything to do with drugs?"

"Sit back down, Gang."

"I don't think so!"

"Could there be more to Larry Hungerford than we think?"

Claud sat reluctantly. "You could make a case on paper. You need an open seat and money to run a campaign. Now there's a seat, and a crop of marijuana would buy a lot of ads. But Hungerford is so . . ." Claud made a frustrated backhand swipe at the air. "All hat and no cattle."

"I hear Betty Colman is going to be our next senator anyway. Maybe that's behind it."

"She's for sure trying to look the part. If you need a laugh, Hoff, go watch Hungerford and that flunky of hers make entourage noises. But you've known her as long as I have. Pawn, sure, all her life. Queen? It'd be easier to picture Hungerford, but he wouldn't do it for anybody but himself."

Neiderhoffer studied the red tiles of the floor. "The name I keep coming back to is Muldoon."

"That's why you sent Barney outside? Maybe you're forgetting somebody tried to kill her."

"And failed. Or maybe she got greedy."

Claud sighed. "Tell you one thing I *am* sure of, Hoff, we're short of time. They don't seem to care who they kill anymore."

Before the sheriff could respond, Elmo stuck his head around the door. "Is it okay if the McFauls leave?"

Claud beat the sheriff through the doors to see Barney's truck about to gun out to the street. He was barely in time to block its way. For a sickening moment he looked through the windshield at Barney's face and thought he wouldn't stop. Couldn't. At the last possible second he stood on the brakes with a jerk that threw his father to the windshield and Blue off his feet.

Claud swung over to the door. "Going somewhere, Barney?"

Barney had that bug-eyed look. "Stan's been with Muldoon."

Buck sat beside Barney, shattered and still.

"What makes you think that?"

"Blue. Last night at Dead Man's he wouldn't let Stan alone, nosing him—"

"I've told him a hundred times, if he just didn't—"

"It wasn't Stan, it was his clothes. When I tossed them in back just now, Blue went ballistic. Well, they wouldn't bother him unless Stan was in them. So I looked."

He held out the bandanna, stiff with blood.

Claud and Hoff both reached for it, but Barney held it high and away.

"That damn song Banjo Man was singing—he must have meant Muldoon. Her and the two of them—" The truck's motor raced. "Leave go the door, Claud."

"Banjo Man'll be at Dead Man's Hand. You can't get at him till later anyway."

"They're closed Mondays. He'll be at his apartment."

"What if he doesn't want to tell you anything?" Neiderhoffer spoke for the first time.

"I reckon he will."

"Like Jim Cooper?"

Barney paused, but only briefly. "His fingers matter more to him than they do to me. Move out of the way, Sheriff."

"I can't rightly do that, son, till I know you won't be committing mayhem in my jurisdiction."

The truck rocked on the shocks as Barney raced the motor again.

"I have no plans to kill the man!"

"Mood you're in, he could be dead before you had time to draw a cool breath."

Buck McFaul found his tongue. "What am I, a potted

plant? All Banjo Man has to do is answer a few questions. Go, son."

The engine roared. The truck lunged forward, swerved through the gates, and careened in a wide swing to the south.

Claud, Elmo, and Fineman frowned at Neiderhoffer.

Fineman got in first. "You're letting them go?"

"You don't like the idea?"

"Sheriff, this is beyond the line. First, throughout this man's entire interview"—Fineman flipped a palm toward Claud—"you treated him like a member of your force. Letting him decide when and how much to tell you about his nephew?"

Neiderhoffer smiled dourly. "Back in Bogwash, Jimmy, you can probably whistle up all the men you want. Here in Merciful Valley, we're thin on the ground. I have to make use of everybody, the ones I get paid to order around and the ones I ask and thank kindly. No smart remarks from you about vigilantes, Gang."

"Vigilante? He's a member of a militia?"

"No, and I'm not Oliver Stone, either!"

"Shut up, Gang."

"If he thinks I'm going to put up with a Bogwash lunkhead—"

"Don't give me that buffalo look. He's an *official* lunkhead, you have to put up with him. Like you've been putting up with me all these years."

Neiderhoffer turned to the FBI agent. "This here's Senator Colman's best friend. Crucial to the investigation. Any further questions?"

"And the one who just left? An admittedly violent man, and you're letting him question a witness?"

"Happens I know something you don't, Jimmy." Neiderhoffer nodded toward the hospital's third floor. "Banjo Man and Jim Cooper are up there for the night."

"Jim Cooper is the man with the cast on his foot?" Fineman asked. "The one who's being so helpful?"

The sheriff nodded. "Helpfulness courtesy of Barney Mc-Faul. We figure if we keep Banjo Man here where Barney can't get at him, he might be grateful enough to help too."

Claud gave a shout of laughter. "You mean the McFauls will have gone all the way down to Bitterroot and back to cool off."

When he had time to think, he roared all over again. Bad news for Barney wasn't bad news for Claud. So Stan had been aiding and abetting Lorelei Muldoon after all. Not Banjo Man. Not the ungodly.

Not Stan the master criminal, just Stan the clumsy nephew, trying to run the maze in a video game.

And Banjo Man was right here, ready to question.

"And McFaul's expertise regarding marijuana?" Fineman asked.

Claud chuckled. "Check with your boss, Jimmy. Or DEA, or ATF. He's in your computer somewhere."

Hoff clapped Fineman on his weak shoulder. Fineman winced. "If you want to get up to speed on the people here, Jimmy, there's a woman down in Bitterroot who could give you some background, Domenica Gaylord—"

Claud opened his mouth to tell the sheriff somebody had got there first, but then unaccountably he decided it was none of his business.

Since the police scanner was back with Mech in the van across from Willetts' office, Fenton couldn't know the results of his 911 call. But it was time he cleared out of the camp anyway. He sorted quickly through the gear for anything that could identify him. Little more than clothes. He spread his jacket flat and piled it with the jeans and T-shirts, tying the arms together in a rough pack.

There was a chill of metal against his neck. "Leaving, Finaldo nephew?"

229

An eternity ago, Paca had put his knife there, and Fenton had thought of the blood and shuddered. Now his first thought was irritation: Couldn't the cops in this place get anything right? Valuable information, of course, if—finally fear kicked in—he got the chance to use it.

"She's dead, what do we have to hide from?" he asked as coolly as he could. Where was his own gun? Across the clearing. He had to maneuver Mech over that way.

He turned, eyes suddenly watering. Mech's face was lopsidedly swollen, his stare a single malevolent slit, the other eye buried. He tilted his head to keep Fenton in focus.

"Jesus, man! What happened?"

"*She* did this to me." Mech's voice was muffled, like a bad cold. A spray. Mace, something. "Why you don't ask me if she lives?"

Fenton moistened his lips. "Does she? Live?"

"Oh, yes. She even dragged the other one—Willetts?—away. A minute, two, before the cops came."

"Cops?" Fenton tried to sound shocked.

The muzzle of Mech's gun jammed tighter into Fenton's chin. "You called them, didn't you, Finaldo nephew? I kill her, they kill me."

The pressure was so hard he could feel the muscles in Mech's hand tighten. His eyes wanted to wince shut, but he forced them open. "What you really mean is, you screwed up," he said. Hoarse. But the gun accounted for that. "What are you going to do about it?"

The single glittering eye was unreadable. Unaccountably, the pressure against his neck eased. Mech lowered the gun to hang at his side. He took a step back. "Our business is finished. All yours now."

"But you can't—"

"Ask yourself why I can, Finaldo nephew."

Fenton backed in the direction of his own gun. "But where will you stay?"

230

"So you can look for me?" Mech spat bloodily. From the heap of possessions he fished out a sleeping bag. "The rest is yours, nephew."

"You mean the van? And the stuff in it?"

"All the pretty machines, nephew. The guns. All yours."

Almost there now. "And the marijuana—"

Mech strode across the clearing and jerked Fenton by his shirtfront, putting his hatchet face close. "It is mine. What I do with it is mine."

"Everything except Colman's field. You leave that one alone."

"*Especially* Colman's field." Mech threw him to the ground. "You and your aunt, Finaldo, you want the sow and the piglets and the sausage machine."

He dropped his gun without looking to see where it fell, groped in a pocket for the van's keys, held them up for Fenton to see, and dropped them too.

"They're watching that field, it's too dangerous. To all of us—"

"To you, nephew, if I find you there." The big rubbery-tough man disappeared into the trees, his oversize shit-kickers making no sound.

Fenton stayed where he was, grateful, for the moment, to be alive. To be the one with all the guns. That mattered, if he and Mech crossed paths again. And when he found the Muldoon woman, who could identify him as the man who had bragged of killing Senator Colman.

What a child he had been.

The church doors weren't locked. Lorelei slipped in and stood at the entrance to the Sanctuary, calm and dimly lit as the forest floor, until her eyes adjusted to the dark, noticing first the soaring balcony and only then the small figure kneeling at the altar. Lorelei recognized her immediately. Shortish, sturdily built, in an army-green jogging suit.

She went back outside to wait. Half an hour? An hour? The heavy doors shifted, the small figure came out.

Before she thought, Lorelei blurted, "You're the woman with all the zucchini!"

The woman looked at her with relief, warmth even. But not surprise. "I'm Abby Butterfield, yes. And you're Lorelei Muldoon, the woman with all the hair. Without the hair, it looks like."

She took an unhurried step forward.

Lorelei retreated, groping for her can of bear repellent. "Stay where you are!"

Abby looked at the bear repellent with interest. "It's not that I'm particularly brave, but I think my glasses would protect me from the worst of that stuff. Did you use it on the guy who tried to kill you? You probably saved Stan's life. Did you recognize the killer?"

Lorelei plucked at the bloody stiffness of her . . . Stan's . . . jacket, her other hand on the OC-5. "You knew I was there?"

"All that blood. Stan's? Or were you hurt too?"

Lorelei shook her head.

The minister led the way surefootedly through the dark to the parsonage. "What you want now is your clothes."

Lorelei was glad she was walking behind, so she didn't have to worry about her expression. She said cautiously, "I suppose you think that's vain of me, with Stan . . ."

"No, no. Barney looked through your stuff today and found something. He warned me to keep it safe."

Barney . . .

They went through to the back of the house, the kitchen. Abby pulled down a lamp over a round oak table and lit it. The flickering kerosene light spread through the room. In the soft light, the minister's eyes were a stab of blue.

"Now explain to me why I should turn what he found over to you."

A day wasn't enough to form scar tissue over her newfound

humiliation. But she needed to hear what it sounded like to somebody else. Not Barney. It might as well be the small round woman across the table.

But where, after all, did it begin?

She reached back to the familiar icons of her childhood. "Do you remember the character Marilyn Monroe played in *Some Like It Hot*? Sugar Kane?"

"Of course. We both went to Bryn Mawr."

Lorelei stared at her. She stared back over her glasses, unblinking, looking like a Campbell Soup kid. Lorelei struggled on.

"The Tony Curtis character pretends to be rich so she'll fall in love with him, remember? Fred Colman did the opposite— he *was* rich—he pretended to be in love. With me. And I believed him. Me, little Miss Logic."

Lorelei started to run her fingers through her hair and settled for rubbing her head.

"I doubt that he did it just to amuse himself, Lorelei, he wasn't that kind of man."

"I don't think he did either. I think his reason is in my bag."

Abby narrowed her eyes briefly before she nodded. From behind the garbage disposal under the sink, she pulled Lorelei's pocketbook.

"Be my guest."

Lorelei dumped out the contents on the oak table, pushing aside everything but a thick swatch of papers. The green and white striped printout, and folded inside, the other, plain white sheets. Fred's, which she had gathered up when they fell out of the plane. Here and there were notations in his cramped handwriting.

"This is Fred's writing. This is why . . ."

Abby blew out the kerosene lamp and turned on a strong overhead light. Lorelei spread out the sheets.

Abby watched as Lorelei withdrew into another world.

She looked like a homeless person: the carrot-red hair

curled in unkempt bunches, T-shirt and jacket stiff with blood. But this was unmistakably the real Lorelei Muldoon, face grave as a priestess, ablaze with intelligence. Her thin, well-cared-for hands smoothed the papers, fingered through them quickly, more slowly, sorting. Single sheets shifted from one pile to another, back again.

The tarot reader of today, Abby thought. I place the cards for love and hate and power over, under, beside you; I read danger, life and death.

Once Lorelei surfaced with the blind stare of a swimmer. Abby, guessing correctly, gave her a legal pad and a fat stack of pencils. Lorelei dived back in.

Chapter
Thirteen

The blue truck pulled slowly into the parsonage drive behind the khaki Jeep. The two men in the cab sat woodenly, dull with disappointment, but the dog in the back knew better; he leaped over the side, bounding toward the house and through a rear window.

Barney and Buck were slow to catch on. By the time they reached the parsonage kitchen, Blue's big body was curved around Lorelei Muldoon in an improbable wriggle of delight. He sat back, panting.

Did Barney McFaul give a shout of laughter? Lorelei thought she heard one. He swooped her up and around before letting her slide to the ground through his arms. Only then did he look at her hair.

The hair that wasn't there. She covered her head with her hands. He pulled them down, shushing her, holding her tight against his shoulder, his face still split by a white grin.

She shook so hard he must have felt it; he slid a hand inside her jacket, down inside her jeans, open palm against her stomach. A pulse inside her knocked against his palm like a gong. Without thinking, she lifted her face to him.

Buck cleared his throat. "Does Claud know she's here?"

"Let's see what she finds first. This is not censorship," Abby added, raising her voice, "but I think it's time for Lorelei to tell us what she's found."

Lorelei laughed, and broke away. When they had all found seats at the big oak table (Blue draped equally across Barney's feet and her own), she said apologetically, "It won't sound like much, but I think it's what Fred found. There's a pattern of biweekly deposits to Betty's firm, with one exception—in June a payment went to their joint account instead."

June, just before Senator Colman began his relentless pursuit of Lorelei Muldoon. "I think it was done by mistake."

Buck McFaul sat upright, toes hooked on a chair rung like a school kid, an exaggerated squint of concentration. "How can that be worth killing somebody?"

"I can't tell from this, not without a computer. The codes are in numbers. I only know those two accounts because of Fred's notes. He doesn't say where the deposits came from. My own guess is that they were cash." She pointed. "That's probably the bank's code for cash."

"Because?" Abby's eyes were blazing.

"If the deposits could have been traced easily, Fred wouldn't have needed me."

Buck said, "I still don't see it. Lobbyists give money all the time."

"But openly. If Fred never knew about these deposits, he wouldn't report them. No taxes would be paid. It could look like bribery. Tax evasion. A senator is a public person, it's a kind of blackmail."

Barney McFaul leaned back, not troubling to follow, just watching. Without his even touching her, she seemed to be basking in his body heat. Her voice shook a little as she went on.

"But then why deposits to Betty's firm? There might be an entirely different explanation. Fred didn't get any further than the deposits. At least from what I see."

"And with a computer?" Abby asked.

"We'd just have to see. I could bring my dad in on it too." Lorelei jingled her hands restlessly in her jacket pockets. "I've been afraid of drawing attention to him. But one computer to another, it's harder to trace."

Abby looked from Lorelei to Buck to Barney. "It's time to bring Claud and the sheriff in."

Lorelei hesitated. "I don't know how well you know Claud Willetts—"

"You can't shock me, if that's what you mean."

"From what Stan said, his uncle seems the most likely person to work this."

Abby shook her head so vigorously her cowlick shook. "Claud would never hurt Fred Colman. Never. Senator Colman was the only person he's ever really cared about. That's why he's behaving so badly."

"You may believe that. I can't."

"You're not thinking clearly, Lorelei. You need reinforcements. Maybe you're the only one who could have figured this out—"

"No, no. It's not even my area, particularly. Fred Colman only picked me because I was young and seducible. I'd do the work and not ask questions."

This kind of mention of Colman apparently didn't disturb Barney. He rubbed Lorelei's back gently, his mouth curving when she couldn't hide a shiver.

"What I figured," he said.

"Of all of us, Claud is most apt to understand what you've found," Abby said. "He's also the best one to convince the sheriff to find you a computer."

I could handle that part myself. Lorelei pulled her hands out of her jacket pockets before Abby could read her mind and spot Stan's keys there.

* * *

If Abby had been able to talk to Sheriff Neiderhoffer directly, Fenton wouldn't have overheard. But when the message was relayed over Elmo's radio in the car outside the hospital, "Abby" became "Reverend Butterfield," and Fenton overheard every staticky word.

Ministers had to be listed in the phone book. She was.

Claud followed Sheriff Neiderhoffer and Agent Fineman up the steps of Abby's porch.

"How's Shari Finley's baby, Sheriff?" Abby asked.

"The twins were kicking up a little. Duncan took him, at least till after the funeral."

Abby bustled behind them to the kitchen.

"Hungry? I have zucchini muffins, terrible if I do say so, zucchini bread, not so bad. Anything else you want out of zucchini, I'll be happy to try. Omelet?"

Fineman, seeing no takers and obviously afraid of looking foolish, asked, "Why everything with zucchini, Reverend Butterfield?"

Abby grinned. "I can't figure out what else to do with it."

She flicked on lights to show terraces down her back slope pendulous with vegetables: zucchini, cucumbers, the blaze of tomatoes.

"Francine cans the tomatoes and pickles the cucumbers, but the zucchini always seem to get away from us. This afternoon I even filled up the back of Bluebonnet and made some deliveries."

She described what Lorelei had watched earlier. Claud and the McFauls and the sheriff rocked with laughter. After a pause, Fineman joined in.

Abby had warned Claud about the change in Lorelei Muldoon's appearance—overwarned, in his opinion. Her hair looked as though she'd backed into a lawn mower, and instead of her silk and suede, she wore an old sweatshirt that read IF GOD IS DEAD, WHO PUSHES UP THE NEXT KLEENEX? But life still poured off her, leaning there against Barney as if he were the opposite magnetic pole.

"So," Claud said. "We meet again, Lorelei Muldoon."

He wouldn't have thought she could get closer to Barney, but she did.

"I only agreed to see you because Barney and Abby are here."

"I reckon Abby's is neutral territory. She says you've got something."

"Excuse me for interrupting, Gang, but do you mind if Jimmy and me go first?" the sheriff asked.

It was a reminder, not a request. Salish Federated Bank might have the biggest computer in the valley and Peter Sokoloff might be its chairman, but he had entrusted his keys to the sheriff, not his brother-in-law. Neiderhoffer wasn't yet convinced to hand them over.

They took Lorelei's description of the shooting apart shred by shred and then knit them back together while Claud teetered his chair back and listened. Was she giving them anything useful? A medium-sized thickset man whose face she hadn't seen clearly, whose only words had been hoarse screams. A gun she could only describe by the sound. All filtered through terror.

He was waiting for the part that came next.

As she began the walk through Bandit's bank records, Buck and Barney stood. "Heard it once," said Barney. "We'll take the watch."

Neiderhoffer was lost before she had gone two sentences, but Fineman's focus tightened, on Lorelei Muldoon as well as on what she said. Claud thought it was a good thing Barney had left the room.

So Bandit had only wanted her talent all along.

Had it really been revenge burning Claud all this time? Or the dread that even before his life ended, Bandit had been moving out from under their friendship?

Whereas Bandit had merely charged off bullheaded, as usual. No awful discoveries to be feared or covered up for either Bandit or Stan. With what Lorelei Muldoon was giving them, surely Hoff and the Feds between them could get to the bottom of this, while he, Claud Willetts, went home and worked on his eulogy. Logically speaking.

But the thought of it brought something like heartburn to the back of his throat. Maybe revenge didn't have much to do with logic.

The sheriff said, "Why can't you tell us who made the deposits?"

Fineman answered for her. "Deposits less than ten thousand dollars wouldn't be routinely flagged. It's a strong indication they were cash, however."

Lorelei nodded. "And this may just be a part of the scheme, whatever it is. We can't track it any further without a computer."

Fineman said, "Hungerford was his chief of staff. Senator Colman probably said he was retiring so Hungerford wouldn't question it when he started going over all his accounts. We should start there."

"Bandit may have figured that was the quickest way to get the story out," the sheriff argued. "Bait a trap and see who jumps."

Ignoring them, Claud said to Lorelei, "You used this trick to get money to Stan, didn't you? Then he withdrew it and gave it to you. Oh, don't look so startled. It was more than ten thousand, remember?"

Before she had a chance to answer, Barney cat-footed back to take a protective chair behind her.

Abby said, "Lorelei says this method is easy to check on, Claud. I plan to see that your accounts are monitored on a regular basis. Do you hear?"

"Why, Reverend Butterfield, what an unworthy thought."

Fineman cleared his throat impatiently. "Sheriff Neiderhoffer, I'll take charge of these now. I'll fax them back to Washington. We may have some answers tomorrow."

The sheriff looked unhappy but at a loss. Claud put an oar in. "You mean the case stays in Washington, Jimmy? Or do the answers come back for Hoff here to use?"

"Bank fraud? Washington? Federal jurisdiction, Mr. Willetts."

"With or without the papers?"

"Don't listen to Claud, Sheriff," Abby said. "They can solve it much faster than we can. The sooner this is back in Washington and everybody knows it, the sooner Lorelei will be safe."

"When she's already halfway there, Rev? If she was good enough for Bandit, she's good enough for me."

Buck tried to pat Abby, but she pushed his hand away, fluffing up like a pigeon. "Stay out of this, Claud. Do you really want to keep working, Lorelei?"

Lorelei rubbed her cockscomb of hair apologetically. "I'm sort of into it now, Abby."

Neiderhoffer looked at Fineman. He flipped a ring of keys on the table. "Claud, Peter says the back door key is the Molson."

Fineman said, "Then I'll work with Ms. Muldoon while you concentrate on the search for the perpetrators."

Barney came soundlessly to attention, his hands poised at hip level.

The sheriff said quickly, "I need you to ride shotgun, Jimmy. We left Elmo back at the station to make room for Claud, remember?"

"But if Ms. Muldoon is on the right track, Sheriff—"

"I don't think so." Eyes on Barney, Neiderhoffer hauled Fineman up with a shoulder grip that made the younger man flinch.

He shook it off, twitching his jacket back into place. "Very well, Sheriff, we'll do it your way. For tonight. If Ms. Muldoon doesn't get any results, I'll take charge of the material tomorrow."

"Could he do that, Hoff? Take Bandit's papers right out from under our noses?"

"You people have no idea of the rules of evidence, do you? Or the jurisdiction of the federal government? I've offered to work with Ms. Muldoon—"

Neiderhoffer harrumphed, a long sinus rattle that was his idea of a tactful interruption. "Papers? I don't see any papers, do you, Gang? I'm just dropping off some keys for Abby."

"Only till morning," Abby said. "After that they go to the FBI."

"Sheriff, this is so far outside the bounds of acceptable practice—"

"You're outnumbered, Jimmy."

He clasped Fineman's shoulder again, maintaining his grip until they were well down the front walk. His words drifted back. "Let me tell you a story about a man named Cooper."

The white church was dark. Fenton headed for the small house beside it, with a porch almost as big as itself, the same wood frame as the church, the same need—obvious even by moonlight—for paint.

There was a tan Jeep in the driveway, sandwiched between a battered station wagon, a pickup, and a police car. He drove on a few blocks and parked.

He brushed through bushes as quietly as he could, peering in the windows. Living and dining rooms were unlit. He worked with care back to a kitchen that stretched across the whole width of the house. Here was the messiness of use. A round oak table spread with papers, surrounded by people.

One by one he identified them. The sheriff. A gray suit with government stamped all over him. A short, sturdily built woman. The big man he had seen going in and out of Claud

Willetts' office. He didn't recognize a short mustached guy who bounced like a kid's toy, or the other woman, the scruffy one.

Yes, he did. Walking through the papers like a teacher: It had to be Lorelei Muldoon.

He looked away, waiting for his night sight to come back. Where was the guy with the dog?

Coming through the door into the kitchen. How close could he get without being smelled by the dog?

Not very.

The big man had a light tenor Fenton had to strain to hear. After the cop and the gray suit left, Fenton inched closer.

"I know what Bandit did and how he did it better than anybody," he said. "If Lorelei finds something, I'm most apt to know what it means. But there's no need for you to come, Abby."

A nasal voice carried easily through the window. "Aren't you forgetting? The sheriff left the keys with *me*. Besides, if Lorelei finds something, who guarantees that the information reaches the sheriff? You?"

The big man hunched an indifferent shoulder. "If we're going to chitchat, we might as well have given the stuff to Fineman."

When they stood up to leave, Fenton retreated to the van.

Lorelei wasn't trying to access the bank's records this time; the bank computer was merely her conduit to the machines in other banks and the information they held. When it winked to life, she tapped energetically. "I'll key into Hank. My dad. We can work from both ends."

A stream of numbers began to fill the screen. It looked like another stream tried to interrupt, but Lorelei kept typing ruthlessly.

"My dad," Lorelei said briefly. "We haven't talked since

Sunday. But the personal stuff will have to wait."

Claud straddled a chair behind her. Barney dragged in the old sofa for Buck and Abby before he and Blue set out on patrol.

"Is Betty's firm big?"

"More like a vanity operation, I always thought, didn't you, Abby?" Claud said. "Why?"

"Some pretty impressive money moves in and out of her account." More screens scrolled.

She paused. Paper rattled off the printer. Claud leaned forward tensely, even though the sheets meant nothing to him.

Lorelei said, "I've checked Fred's account backward and forward. The June deposit is the only break in the pattern, for either him or Betty's firm."

"That's what this is? Stuff we already had?"

She shook her head. "This is every other deposit made within a half hour of ours, at the same bank branches. Background. The man we're looking for might have been doing business for himself at the same time. I'll cross-check anything else I find against this list."

"For a lady with only one night to work, you spend a lot of time on details."

"It's all details. Put enough of them together, and you have coincidences, then similarities, then patterns—that's my specialty. But it starts with details."

Claud had assumed the computer would be a shortcut. Instead, it was more like an electronic version of Hoff's plodding. What had he expected? Intuition like his own, only at light speed?

He had to admit she was trying, working the keys as fast as a restless man could drum his fingers on a table, oblivious to the patrols Claud and Barney made in turn, to Buck dozing on the sofa and Abby perched beside him, rigid with disapproval. One screen of numbers folded into another. Forward, back; slow, fast. Slow again. The chopped red hair, the

244

borrowed sweatshirt—nothing mattered except her mind-link with the machine. She was as tunnel-visioned as Barney. Different tunnel, that was all.

By the combined light of the dim gas streetlights and the moon, Fenton watched the little group walk up the hill to a restored brick building. Salish National Bank.

Lorelei Muldoon plus the papers plus a bank to work from. And the police knew about all three. Was there anything to be salvaged?

Whatever happened, he had to know. He turned on the police scanner and tried to make himself comfortable.

It was nearly dawn before Claud saw a change. Computer screens flashed by so fast they cheeped like mechanical birds. An inset bloomed to fill the screen; before he could even bring it into focus, another replaced it, and another. Lorelei Muldoon looked like a kid who had just raided a candy store. She stretched over to the printer and paper streamed out onto the floor.

"What've you got?" His voice woke Buck and brought him and Abby over. Barney, one hip on the table, faced the door and paid no attention.

"A couple of things." The effort over, she looked as flaccid as old celery, barely able to talk through her yawns. She circled numbers in red. "First: Every time one of these deposits was made to Betty's firm, another account number shows a transaction within minutes. Different branches from one time to the next, but on each date, deposits were made to both. It holds true all the way back to April. *And* on the date that a deposit was made to their joint account."

"He made a mistake. We've got him."

"That would be too easy. I said the other account also gets *deposits*. Also cash."

"Who is it? Anybody we know?"

"So far I've only got the initials HCI. Maybe they mean more to you than they do to me."

Claud slumped. "That'd be too easy too. HCI stands for the Hispanic Cultural Institute. Hungerford scheduled Bandit for a dinner there Friday night. Betty went in his place."

"Could it be a client of hers?" She yawned again. "That would explain the rest of it."

"Which is?"

"The deposits aren't the only links between Betty Colman, Inc., and HCI. They're so interwoven, if I didn't know who owned it, I'd say it was a dummy. And lots of money moves offshore. Dad's tracking that. He has a bigger machine."

She drew red lines that meant nothing to Claud. "Offshore banks can be as hard to access as the Pentagon. Or the IRS. There are password-breaking programs to throw number strings, but only places like university labs have mainframes with enough memory to run them."

Betty serving as a front for somebody. Without even knowing it? He rolled that around and liked it. What didn't fit was the Hispanic Cultural Institute.

"Could the man we're hunting be bribing somebody at the Hispanic Cultural Institute too? Or blackmailing?"

"Possible. I'll spend more time in that account."

"If you locate the bribe, we can lean on them. Can you get that by morning?"

"No way to predict. I may just find more places to look. Like now. It may take half an hour or half a day to get in."

His disgust must have showed. She said, "It *will* get faster. The more you learn, the more you know where to look. What kind of mistakes to look for."

Claud straightened with a creak. "So you don't even know how much more time you need?"

"Stop bullying, Claud." Abby spoke for the first time. "She's done enough to show that this began in Washington. We should send it back there. How can we trace offshore banks? Besides, Lorelei needs rest. She has a big day tomorrow."

At their stares, she said, "For the reading of Senator Colman's will. Don't say you don't know about it, Claud. His lawyer wants you to be there, Lorelei."

If ever there was a woman without a grain of tact . . . "How would you know about it?" Claud asked to divert the flow. "The nefarious Pastor's Committee?"

"Don't make mysteries out of nothing, Claud. I'm supposed to be there too, but I'll be up in the Kinnikinnick Basin. Shari Finley's funeral."

"But what does Fred's will have to do with me?"

Either Lorelei's sleepy bewilderment was real, or she was a good actress.

Abby was relentless. "It's not for us to say, Lorelei. It's something we owe the dead."

Lorelei looked reluctantly impressed, but when she ran her fingers through her hair, she stopped short, her thoughts as clear to Claud as glass. Tonight the Ronald McDonald hair and bloodstained jeans didn't matter. But to face Colman's people . . .

He looked at Abby's jogging suit. Lorelei was going to balk, and Abby wouldn't have a clue why.

"I've already talked to Charley Calico," Abby said. "He has the closest beauty parlor, farther up the Parade. He's a deacon, he'll do me a favor. You can go on to Gaylord's afterward. Domenica said she'd get out some stuff."

So Domenica was already on her own again? Or had Abby barged in?

Lorelei rubbed her cropped hair with a hungry look. "A haircut and some clothes doesn't mean I'm promising anything."

Claud looked to see how Barney was taking it. His eyes were bleak, but the bleakness peeled back to a look so naked, Claud had to avert his eyes and clear his throat.

Maybe that was what made him say harshly, "Reverend, you're meddling again."

Buck bobbed up. "Isn't that cute. Condemning the woman for what you did yourself."

"Yeah, I wondered how long you could stay quiet before you bust a gut."

Out of the corner of his eye Claud watched for Barney. He might not even have heard, hunched on the table edge, as though his arms and legs were no longer working according to plan.

Lorelei put a protective arm—protecting Barney!—around his shoulders, rocking him like a child.

"Setting Lorelei up like a fish in a barrel!" Buck said. "You brought this down on us, Claud Willetts."

Something broke inside. Claud stood up with a heave that threw the printer on the floor. "I did *not* kill Sue Lombardy! I did *not* kill Bobby Kosetic! You are *not* going to make them my fault!"

"Who else is treating this like a poker game?"

"Are you saying I think Bandit's death is a game?"

Abby pushed between them. Buck talked as though she wasn't there. "I'm saying you're about to find out what it's like to bluff without Bandit around to back your play."

In a voice that would have carried to the last row of the balcony, Abby said, "Buck, go back to the parsonage. Now."

Without waiting to see if he left, she put a hand on Claud's arm.

Claud flung it off. "Why shut him up, Rev? You agree with him all along the line."

"Claud, I'm good at getting things done, wouldn't you say?"

"You and that—"

"I know, the Pastor's Committee. But sometimes I miss things that are more important."

What was she after? She didn't have that conniving innocent stare. Her voice was unexpectedly soft.

"I'm trying to apologize, Claud. I've had it backward. Most of us have. Bandit didn't come to your rescue."

Claud had to squeeze out the words. "The man was there every time—"

"No. *You* were there for *him*. You were the most genuine—the *only* genuine thing in his life, Claud. If he was our David, you were his Jonathan. The only person in his life that he trusted. That he loved."

Claud swung away to the door, away from all of them. Was this what it was to grieve? To think you were in control when suddenly the pavement broke into lava underneath?

How did you find your way back?

Abby put the comforting hand back on his arm.

He jerked away again. "Stop praying over me! When I need to be prayed over, I'll ask for it."

He stumbled out into the graying dark.

First came the little guy who reminded Fenton of a kid's toy. Shortly thereafter, the sloppily big man came out with the small, dark-haired woman, the one Fenton had decided was the minister, running after him. The big guy brushed her away, but she kept on coming. Had to be the minister. She was still hassling him when they passed from Fenton's line of sight.

That left Lorelei Muldoon, still working, with only the guy and the dog to guard her. She must be on the track of something.

If he crashed the party now, maybe he'd never learn the details of what his aunt had been doing. And he needed them, if not to use here, then somewhere else. He wouldn't have any trouble getting the Muldoon woman to tell whatever she knew.

"But I'm no further on," Lorelei said to Barney with a sigh after the door closed behind Abby.

"Want to talk about it?"

How to be tactful? "Other people's ideas tend to get in my way."

"But I don't have any."

She looked at him dubiously. "All we really have to work with is this HCI thing. I can track its contributors to see if there's a pattern to them, but it could take weeks. An FBI team could be much faster."

"So that's a dead end. What else?"

"Hank's working on the offshore stuff. There's nothing else really except to blue-sky it. Look at stuff like everyday expenses. Sweep through different kinds of common transactions for HCI. Do the same for Betty's firm, see if they link up anywhere."

Screens began to roll by again as she zigged and zagged, comparing stationery supplies and phone records, furniture deliveries . . . She was hopscotching so fast and the connection was so unexpected, she almost missed it: a sofa (bgdy. leather, 84″, bun feet), delivered to Betty's office by a delivery service with the sign-off letters OFC. She spun back to the previous month at the Hispanic Cultural Institute. Another sofa, same delivery service.

As she scrolled through expense records of HCI contributors, OFC popped up like letters on an eye chart.

She tracked furniture deliveries back to the manufacturers, combed their files, and moved on to department stores.

"You got something."

"Something. A private delivery service of medium-heavy stuff. Furniture, fabric, hardware. For decorators and department stores, some cleaners. Why would Fred trace the records of a delivery service?"

"It's just in the Washington area?"

"As far south as Florida. Not much north of D.C., at least so far. Some Maryland. Why?"

"A delivery service between Florida and Washington. A lot of people might be interested."

"You mean like Jimmy Fineman?"

"He'd be one of them. What else can you find out about it?"

"I'm tracing accounts payable." Numbers briefly compressed to a single line, then sprayed out to fill the screen.

"Delivery sheets don't give billing addresses?"

"But not who owns it. OFC looks like a dummy corporation."

The screen shrank back to a single line. Lorelei stared at it. Barney could only read the slump of her shoulders. "Something's wrong."

"Actually, it's probably very right. But off-limits. OFC's records end up offshore too."

"Hank's department."

"Hank's department," she agreed with a yawn, sending her data across the country in a clatter of type.

"Tell him later." Barney ran his thumb delicately from the nape of her neck down her spine. She leaped to face him, eyes wild.

"Ah, Muldoon." He pulled her into his arms and soothed her, but almost immediately his hands moved down her body, knowing and sure.

Whereas she was all uncertainty. Lorelei Muldoon no longer had her heavy silks and heavy hair; who was the woman who had scrabbled into being in her place? Who felt this man's touch like heat? Who had known him only days? Was this like the eerie bond between hostage and terrorist?

And yet . . . how many times in those days had her body taken over for her mind? If she had stopped to think when Dr. Sue was killed, or when Stan was shot . . . Maybe this was such a time.

Maybe not.

"Not now, Barney." She put her hands over his where they cupped her breasts. "Not here."

"You know what Buck says?" He dragged his hands under

hers as though she were guiding his delicate, inflaming touch. His face was serene. "He says you never really feel at ease in a room till you've made love in it."

Her mouth felt swollen. "You made that up."

"Just cleaned it up a little. That's why the bathtubs back at the ranch are king-size. And you should see the size of the kitchen table."

He had rescued her twice. He had made her feel afraid, and he had made her feel safe. It had never occurred to her that he could make her laugh, but now she giggled helplessly. She put her head back and felt his mouth follow the laughter down her throat. It seemed to free her to feel any number of things.

Chapter Fourteen

Lorelei had every intention of turning her paperwork over to the sheriff and his FBI colleague first thing Tuesday morning. But when Abby woke her with a cup of steaming coffee, she announced that they were already overdue at Mr. Charles. The temptation to look civilized first thing instead was overwhelming. And Hank was working; no time would be lost.

When she met Mr. Charles, she thought she might still be asleep and dreaming. Charley Calico looked like a carpenter, an unassuming man in a T-shirt and jeans and motorcycle boots—and a tool belt, with scissors and comb and pistol-grip hairdryer thrust through like screwdrivers and drill. And carpenters had ponytails as often as hairdressers.

But it was definitely a hairdresser who snapped a cape around Lorelei like a toreador and tugged at her hair with disapproval, moved to a different angle—tripping over Barney in the process—and tugged again.

"I can see why you're here. Something special you want? Or just the best I can do?"

"Get rid of the color. And give it some kind of shape. Flattering is too much to hope."

"Oh, I wouldn't say that." He tugged again in the measuring way of hairdressers the world over. Hair is a stuff like fabric or yarn; features are merely clay blobs that have to be accommodated. "If it were longer, it would curl?"

"In a frizzy sort of way." She met Abby's eyes in the mirror. "How's Stan?" Was that only last night?

"Conscious off and on. Not as uncomfortable as he will be."

"No great loss," Barney said.

"You're wrong." She looked determinedly past him at Abby. "He barely knew me and he risked his life for me. When can I see him?"

"I don't think his parents would welcome you just now."

Charley stepped back onto Barney's foot. "The only way to get rid of the color is to bleach it, you know that? Then I'll take it back to a brown with red highlights. I'll have to go shorter to even it up."

"Little Orphan Annie," Barney suggested.

Charley scowled. "Why don't you try out my new Harley, Barney." He tossed over the keys. "It's that new aluminum body. Faster. Harder to control."

"Not today."

"That's not fair, Charley. The other night up at Claud's, you told me I could," Abby said.

"I said they were harder to handle, Reverend—"

"Besides, I forgot something. Do you want me to walk back?"

Charley sighed and surrendered. From his front window they watched Abby pull on his Darth Vader helmet; on her it looked more like an old-fashioned diving helmet. She kicked the starter and bucked across the parking lot onto Gaslight Parade.

Charley turned an unhappy back and set his hair dryer on the counter out of his way while he painted Lorelei's hair with chalky peroxide. When it stood in stiff gray peaks and he wound the timer, Abby still had not returned.

Barney watched the pale gritty paste metamorphose into an Elvis pompadour, black and moist and sticky. He couldn't look away.

Lorelei watched him in the mirror, troubled. He was as familiar—and as strange—as the woman she now faced in the mirror. The bruised-looking, heavy lids, the long line of his mouth, curled at one end. His hands, crossed along the back of the chair he straddled.

His hands . . .

What was he, a one-night stand? Barney met her eyes in the mirror. An added, heavy pulse began along her veins. Much, much more than a one-night stand. But what place could he possibly have in the world she was returning to?

There was a ping. She turned to the timer in relief.

It still ticked. Ricky Fenton stood in the doorway. The Raiders jacket, the hat. The gun.

She had seen them all before.

But not nervous this time, his face set, eyes empty, gun rock-steady.

Blue stepped forward on stiff legs, rumbling. The gun dipped and came swiftly back up.

"Are you familiar with the Ruger? It fires a full clip in thirty seconds, I'm told. I think I can do the dog and get back to you before you reach me."

"Blue," Barney said quietly.

Blue subsided, arguing deep in his throat, his front feet still dug in pigeon-toed.

Fenton smiled broadly at Lorelei. "So this is what has become of you, *puta*. Charming."

"You're too late," she said quickly. "We found the papers, they're with the FBI now."

"Is that a fact. Then why did you keep working after the sheriff left last night?"

Fenton kicked her chair, spinning her to face him. Without pause for thought, she hid her face. She had played the coward last time; he wouldn't be surprised.

"We just took the opportunity for a little privacy." Barney's voice was hoarse with strain. "You know what I mean. Besides, why pick on her? I can I.D. you too."

"But you can't tell me about the papers." He prodded Lorelei with the gun barrel. "Time to go, *puta.*"

"You can't mean like this." She sought Fenton's eyes in the mirror, shocked and urgent. She pointed to her sticky hair. "It only needs to stay on a few more minutes—look, there's the timer. If the bleach stays on too long, my hair will turn white. It'll break off."

Over Fenton's shoulder was Barney's reflection, tight with disapproval.

Block it out.

She poured every ounce of her concentration on Fenton. Willing him to hear nothing but her terrified, wheedling voice.

"How can it matter if I rinse it out?" She leaned so far toward his reflection, she threatened the balance of her chair—she had to grab the counter to steady it. She pointed to Charley Calico. "He could rinse it for me, it would only take a few minutes."

Let him look at her hair, at Charley—anyplace but at her right hand, closing over the butt of the hair dryer. Invisibly, delicately, she felt for the switch.

Fenton shook himself. He slid his glance briefly to the men behind her. "She begs very well, doesn't she? Colman teach her that?"

There was another ping. This time no one bothered with the timer.

Abby's voice carried from the front door. "It's not that hard to handle, Charley."

Fenton would have to turn to look. Have to.

256

"There's this one thing, though—"

He backed a step. Glanced quickly over his shoulder.

Lorelei caught up the hair dryer. When he turned back, she switched it on full in his face. Even as he recoiled from the blast of heat and noise, she dropped to the floor.

Fenton's gun stitched up a mirrored wall and across the ceiling in an eerie chime of breaking glass.

Blue launched himself at Fenton half a step ahead of Barney. Both were snagged in the trailing hair-dryer cord and fell back, caught in the shower of glass.

Fenton retreated a step, two, trying to steady and aim his gun, but where first?

From the back of the room, Charley hurled the bowl with the remaining peroxide at Fenton's face. He ducked. It sailed over his shoulder, only flecking his face in passing.

Behind him as he straightened, the Reverend Abigail Butterfield broke a zucchini the size of a baseball bat over his head.

Fenton shook his head, more bewildered than stunned. Shook his head again, turned, flinging Abby aside, and fled.

The Harley was in front, keys still in the lock, motor idling. Fenton barely took time to shove his pistol in his belt before he was on it and away.

Blue was first through the doorway, spraying glass as he lunged after the bike. The rest of them could only watch the motorcycle fade noisily into the morning.

Charley sighed. "What was that one little thing, Reverend?"

"I thought the idle was a little rich," she said, pained. "I left it on so Barney could listen to it too."

Barney's throat was so tight his voice had no timbre. "If he's the guy doing the cars, Charley, in a few days we'll find your bike running smooth as silk."

By the time a sink could be cleared of splinters, Lorelei's

hair was white and flossy, her scalp peeling like the third day after a bad sunburn. In front of a wedge of mirror, Charley cupped snowy edges in his hands.

"I'm sorry. It's the best I can do."

"I like it," Abby said. "It reminds me of Doris Day."

Lorelei met Abby's eyes in the mirror. She studied her image—grim, huge-eyed, her skull a clean curve of platinum. Did Doris Day have a dark side?

She asked Barney, "How did he know I was here?"

"He knew where you were last night too," Barney said. "Our phones aren't secure. Are we done here? Because we'll head back to the parsonage. Abby, you're on your way up the Kinnikinnick? Stop by the sheriff's and tell him to meet us there."

"He'll be at the will reading this afternoon," Abby said.

"Not till then?" Lorelei asked. "But I thought—"

"The will reading is out. We're going back to the parsonage and stay under lock and key."

"Oh, no," Lorelei said. "I'm going. Somebody will be scared to death when I walk in, and I intend to see who."

"Abby'll back me up," Barney said. "Abby?"

"Abby's the one who wants me to go, remember?"

Barney caught her shoulder as if he didn't trust words to convince her.

Lorelei didn't bother with them either. She whipped the can of OC-5 out, thumb on the top poised for use.

His anger faded into reluctant amusement the way it had when she challenged him with Fred's gun.

"You'd do it, wouldn't you."

"In a heartbeat."

He grinned with a sheer male voltage that made her feel like Jell-O. "Then I guess we better get you a new dress."

Domenica Gaylord startled Lorelei: the waist-length braid, the tawny eyes, the eyelashes, the electric leanness. A heroine out of film noir, one of the gorgeous, whiplash-tough women who made up their own rules and suffered the consequences. Only the nineties update didn't appear to be suffering at all. A tall, lanky man rested an understandably possessive arm on her shoulder.

"My, my," Barney said. His stance squared subtly, hands hovering at his hips in the suggestive way Lorelei had seen before. "Who's the lucky man, Domenica?"

Lorelei looked beyond them to silk shirts and pants and one-of-a-kind sweaters. She was in Abby's hand-me-downs. And it was safe to use her credit cards again. She squeezed by Barney.

Domenica shifted out from under Greco's arm, lover-turned-shopkeeper in one lithe movement. "I set out some things, but Abby said you had red hair."

"That was this morning. Well, earlier this morning."

Behind them, Barney said, "You were at the hospital."

"At the other end of the corridor with the rest of the pack. G. T. Greco, journalist. I'm impressed. I'm paid to notice, but you were busy at the time."

"Where'd you run into Domenica?"

"Reverend Butterfield sent me here."

"Abby!"

"That's exactly the way Domenica said it. Interesting. My editor is Abby's aunt. I guess that's why she gave me an inside tip."

"Is that a fact."

Greco raised his voice. "Ms. Muldoon, how does it feel to be the last woman in Bandit Colman's life?"

"No, you don't, Greco."

"Hey, would you rather have somebody you don't even know? The valley's full of us."

Lorelei looked back at them nervously, two aggressive silhouettes against the harsh sun of the street.

Behind them, on the other side of the street, was a bookstore with a bow window on the second floor.

She whirled to Domenica. "Were you open Sunday afternoon? Did you see a guy—"

She could describe Fenton quickly by now.

Domenica, looking from a bright green dress to Lorelei's hair with distaste, nodded.

"Was he with anybody?"

Domenica had moved on to a burnt-orange chenille shift and didn't seem to hear. "Nothing I picked out goes with platinum. Do you have anything in mind? Black?"

"No. Mourning is Betty Colman's department. I want to look—" she consulted the still straight candle flame of her anger "—invulnerable. Did he meet anybody?"

"In the summer I do clothes, Lorelei. In the winter I ski. And all year round I mind my own business. People think platinum hair goes with anything, but it's tricky."

"But we're talking about the man who killed Fred Colman!"

"I don't know you. What if I know the killer? Or his friends?"

Disconsolate, Lorelei assembled shirts, sweaters, linen pants, by the big brass register. Beside it, a half-knit sweater dangled yarns, the pattern on the light box beside it.

"You're making one yourself?"

"I work out the patterns, women in the valley knit them. Something Abby set up. But I can't seem to get the kinks out of this one."

Lorelei's professional interest stirred. "You could graph it on a computer."

"It's not that simple. Knitting takes fewer stitches per inch across than up and down, so patterns that look good on a graph come out as wide as a fun-house mirror."

She held up for Lorelei's approval a shaft of silk that fell like the folds of a statue.

Even at that moment, Lorelei could see herself in the dress. A moonlit color, now gray as gunmetal, now silver, now almost green. Like her hair. Unreal. Threatening.

She shook off the image with an effort. "If you talk to the sheriff, Domenica, I'll work up a computer program for your sweater."

"I told you, it can't be done."

"Trust me. I can do it."

The cool, heavily fringed eyes measured her. Behind them was something hard, bright . . . Lorelei surprised herself with the word . . . lonely.

Domenica's gaze traveled on to Greco.

"I'll think about it," she said without conviction.

Lorelei caught Barney's arm. "Barney, Domenica saw Fenton Sunday afternoon. And who he met."

Greco pulled himself upright, eyes gleaming. "Is that important? Because I—"

His voice died. Turning, Lorelei intercepted a look from Domenica so highly charged with sexual promise and threat that her own words caught in her throat. She had tried the same thing with Fenton at Charley Calico's. With Domenica's firepower, he would have rolled over and played dead.

Still, Greco had seen whatever Domenica Gaylord had seen. He wouldn't be in her shop forever.

Fortunately, Lorelei and Barney were in perfect agreement about the will reading: She wanted to make an entrance, and Barney thought it was safest to be last. With Buck preceding her up the stairs and Barney vigilant behind her, Lorelei reached the big sunny office on the floor above Gaylord's, pausing in the doorway to see and be seen.

She might as well have been invisible.

Just inside the door, Claud Willetts, his face seamed with exhaustion, his eyes sunken, was talking to the sheriff. After a cursory glance at her, he went on dully, "It has an impromptu smell. Maybe Fenton and his boss aren't on the same page anymore."

He had to be talking about the incident at Mr. Charles. But she wasn't sure he had even registered who she was. At least Sheriff Neiderhoffer reacted, straightening and clearing his throat noisily at this new version of Lorelei Muldoon.

"Maybe Miss Muldoon could help us," he said. "If you wouldn't mind—"

Lorelei wouldn't mind, but before she could respond, Claud said brusquely, "Later. Barney has you a pew there in a corner." Lorelei shrugged and turned to the back, where Barney stood behind a chair well back in the shadows of the front window curtains.

Not a movement from the two chairs directly in front of Samson de la Haye's desk. The widow sat in one of them, head to foot in dull, matte black: unadorned suede pumps, opaque stockings, gloves halfway up her arms despite the August heat. Unnoticed behind her, a shorter, sturdier woman, her own drab black subtly suggesting lady-in-waiting rather than mourner.

Seen up close, Betty Colman didn't look like a wronged wife or a mourning wife, but she didn't look like the wicked queen, either: none of the major passions. Perhaps not even clever. Would she jump through someone else's hoops without even knowing it?

Around her and the man next to her milled several earnest young men, including Larry Hungerford. So they must be aides, and the other focus of attention must be Governor Donald Larsen. Lorelei had heard Claud's pungent opinion of him, but she thought he looked every inch a governor: a big man with once fair Swedish hair now blazing white, a face of crags and furrows. In ten years he would look forbidding.

Betty Colman was as oblivious to his entourage as she was

to the latecomer at the door, her light voice easily overriding other conversations.

"Olga has fallen in love with Montana, Don. Let me tell him, dear. She might actually set up a branch of her firm here. She thinks a lot of us could use her talents."

The friend's black eyes flickered. "I am convinced there is money to be made in Merciful Valley. But I must get a sense of the resources of the community."

Lorelei knew that tone: serious, dispassionate. Whoever Betty's friend was, she was a businesswoman.

"She means builders or painters or whatever," Betty said. "Olga might have to bring some of her own people from Washington."

So much for scaring someone to death.

No, that wasn't quite right. While the governor rumbled a response, Betty gave her a swift basilisk stare that said, Upstart. Pretender. She looked puzzled too, clearly also thinking, Skinny. Plain. Cheap hair. But good dress.

"Cut the cackle and get to the horses, Samson," Claud Willetts said roughly. He and the sheriff had settled behind the others, blocking off Lorelei's view of anything but their own broad backs. She shifted her chair.

The lawyer looked at him with distaste, but his gaze softened. Claud must still look ravaged.

"Very well, Claud. You may not be aware, any of you, that Senator Colman made a new will roughly two weeks ago."

Everyone except Lorelei had a comment, but Claud was loudest. "Wasn't that the time you said you'd been invited to be a judge at the Yellowstone County Fair?"

De la Haye's smile made deep lines in his cheeks, a very masculine version of his daughter's. "I was in Washington."

Betty had stiffened. "I never saw you. Did you, Larry?"

Behind her, Hungerford was motionless. The man wouldn't even move his head until he knew whether to shake or nod.

De la Haye nodded. "I regret that, but it was what he

wanted. We met in a local restaurant. The will was witnessed by the owner and another customer, a Senator Duecker from—is it Iowa?"

"Ohio," Hungerford said.

Two weeks ago, Lorelei thought from her invisible chair. After Fred had finally convinced her to come to Montana.

The heavy parchment rustled; before Samson could begin, Claud Willetts said harshly, "Spare us the boilerplate. Just tell us what has to be told so we can get out of here."

"Let the man speak, Willetts," the governor said.

"Do you really think he'd use boilerplate?" the lawyer asked as if the governor hadn't spoken. "The first paragraphs, of course—of sound mind and so on—I'll skip them." He raised his head to survey the room. "I assure you this is a legal document. It's in Senator Colman's words, but it is perfectly legal."

The papers rustled this time in silence.

" 'To the state of Montana, my condominium in the Watergate, to be established as a permanent senatorial residence, together with a trust to maintain it, and an urgent plea that my fellow members of Congress do the same damn thing. Why should the taxpayers raise our salaries to underwrite the Washington real estate merry-go-round?' "

Vintage Fred Colman, even in Samson de la Haye's voice. There was a murmur halfway between amusement and *Hear, hear!*

" 'To the Bitterroot Congregational Church, a match to the amount of the annual giving for as long as Abigail Butterfield serves as minister, to be spent under her direction.

" 'To Claud Willetts, a trust that will pay him annually the equivalent of the best year's income he ever had, plus ten percent, plus adjustment for inflation. Samson will see that there aren't any loopholes. Let that be enough, old friend.

" 'To Orrin Neiderhoffer, a college education for however many kids you and Lynette end up with.' "

Fred's wealth had been part of his glamour, not dollar sums and what they could do. It was sobering to hear a list of bequests that would have stripped many estates, and he hadn't even come to Betty.

" 'To Royal McFaul, my cuff-link collection.' "

Buck's ears turned red. He tried a snort that turned into a sniff and pulled out a young flag of a handkerchief.

" 'To Lawrence Hungerford, twenty-five thousand dollars to be used in a campaign for any state office. You have to walk before you can run, Larry.' "

Bequest by bequest, Fred Colman had become a palpable presence in the room. Lorelei felt . . . Before she could pinpoint what she felt, the dry voice continued,

" 'To Lorelei Muldoon—' "

Even though every face was turned to de la Haye, she felt at last the combined weight of their attention.

" 'To Lorelei Muldoon, my cabin on Cutthroat Lake with all its surrounding land.' "

Before she could cover her face—before conversations could spring up—Barney McFaul was across the room and down the stairs. Fast, silent, final.

Before she could say to him, *I wasn't Fred Colman's mistress.* He didn't love me any more than I did him. Before she could say, It doesn't make any more sense to me than it does to you, or Why didn't he leave the cabin, too, to Claud?

The murmur refused to hush. De la Haye spoke over it. "The next paragraph had to be boilerplate, so I'll just explain it. Senator Colman wanted the bequest I've just read to stand irregardless of the customary policy regarding survival. That is, if the order of his and Ms. Muldoon's deaths could not be determined, he nevertheless wanted the cabin to pass to Ms. Muldoon's father, Henry Muldoon, and the bequest is so framed.

" 'To my wife, Betty—' "

Betty. What must she think of this public acknowledgment? If you could acknowledge something that wasn't true.

" '—in memory of her many years at my side, besides the pension and insurance policies in her name, a trust sufficient to provide an income that matches her own income in today's dollars. After her death, the trust will revert to the estate.

" 'The remainder of the estate will be held in trust, to purchase and preserve land throughout Merciful Valley wherever the land, or waters, or animals are threatened.' "

De la Haye paused. "The rest sets up the terms of the various trusts. Royal McFaul, Claud Willetts, and I are appointed trustees, and after their . . . our . . . deaths, trustees to be named by the governor."

He dropped the thick sheets on his desk and looked up. It was the signal for the men to rise and gather there.

Betty Colman sat unmoving, staring stonily ahead, burning spots of color in each cheek that didn't quite match her makeup. The plump woman in black offered Betty a handkerchief, talking in low tones, a soothing hand stroking her arm. Fred hadn't been ungenerous; she would still have as much money as she needed. She was still the widow of a senator. But that's all she was.

It was indecent to watch. But with Barney gone, Lorelei was afraid to leave. She could only stay out of Betty's way until someone remembered her. She walked over to the window and watched idly as a black sedan joined the string on the street below. The driver leaned out and looked up impatiently.

Even in sunglasses and a black cap, Ricky Fenton was unmistakable.

Now that she needed it, the sheltering flame of her anger thinned into smoke and disappeared.

Surely he hadn't recognized her. How many men would know what the black sludge of peroxide turns into? The logic didn't seem to stop her from shaking. Her body, way ahead of her mind again.

266

From the shelter of the curtains, she looked again.

Unmistakably Fenton. She could even see a spray of hot red spots like cigarette burns on one cheek from Charley Calico's peroxide.

Who was he waiting for? Did whoever it was know what he did apart from his day job?

If she screamed it out right now, would she drive Fenton's boss out into the open? But what could she prove?

Let the sheriff decide. He was with Claud Willetts, while Betty pinned down the governor on the other side of the room.

When Samson had finished, Claud went over to the desk.

"Why in hell didn't you tell me about the cabin?" Claud asked.

"The proper authorities were notified."

"Then Hoff—"

"And the governor. The proper authorities, as I said."

"He give you any explanation?"

"I didn't ask."

Because Lorelei Muldoon was his mistress? Because he knew he was putting her in danger? Or merely to keep it out of Betty Colman's hands . . .

"Are you wondering why he didn't leave it to you, Claud?"

"That *and* a trust? I look that greedy?"

The trust . . . Bandit, reaching beyond death to do a last thing for Claud Willetts, the biggest one of all.

Had he sounded like his normal combative self to Samson? How long could he keep it up? Memories threatened to push out of him like a geyser.

He turned to Neiderhoffer. All that was left now. "I'm coming apart at the seams, Hoff."

"You mean the cabin? I guess you have to leave a mistress something, but why not keep that in the valley? Give her jewelry?"

Of course, Hoff had Lynette and his thriving tribe of Neiderhoffers; the loss wasn't the same for him.

And of course, if Hoff thought the cabin was a mistress's reward, it was most certainly nothing of the kind. Guilt? Had he had an inkling of the danger, and that he had forced her to share it?

Lorelei Muldoon clutched at the sheriff's arm.

"Sheriff, I have to talk to you," she said urgently. "There's something I've just found out—"

"Don't worry, Abby already told me," he said. "She stopped in on her way up the Kinnikinnick—"

"Not that!"

"An interesting document, Mr. Willetts. He was an original, your friend. Betty's husband."

Claud wheeled, glad to let off steam in temper. "He knew what he wanted and went after it. *And* he knew how to hold it. I doubt his will can be overturned, if that's what you're wondering."

"As to that, I know nothing. I come to you on quite another matter. I have discussed the painting of the Señora Colman with Betty. She feels it should be displayed at the funeral. And you are the most appropriate person to take charge of it afterward."

"Mighty good of her, and I'm honored to do so," Claud said. And meant with all his heart.

Which didn't mean he was fooled. Betty's name might be invoked, but this was Olga Finaldo's tender offer. Why?

In place of the welcome vision of Elena opposite his desk watching over him slid another image, as smooth as if it had always been there.

"I thought it was going to a museum. Someplace like the Hispanic Cultural Institute."

This time he had herded his ducks and aimed straight. Her smile froze. Thick white lids came down to cover her eyes.

Olga. Not Betty, not Hungerford. And he had gotten to her

before the computer. But who would blackmail a decorator?

If only Hoff wasn't standing there with Muldoon, bulging with questions that would expose how little Claud really knew.

Hastily Claud said, "Have you met Lorelei Muldoon? Lorelei, this is Olga Finaldo, a friend of Betty's."

"Olga Finaldo," Lorelei Muldoon said. She repeated the name slowly, like a dreamer. "You're involved with the Hispanic Cultural Institute?"

Olga's smile at Muldoon was as stiff as the one she'd turned on Claud. Maybe it was the only one she had and he was giving her too much credit.

"I am a supporter, yes. So many in the Latin community yearn for proper recognition of our heritage." Olga turned to Claud, which meant turning her back on Lorelei Muldoon. "It is settled, then?"

"You bring in the painting for the funeral tomorrow, I'll take over from there."

From behind her, Lorelei Muldoon asked, "Did you come out with Betty from Washington, Olga Finaldo?"

The thick lids came down again, but not soon enough. Claud could have sworn he saw wheels turning. What had Muldoon said?

Before Olga could respond, Betty plunged forward, her cheeks still hot.

"Have you come to discuss your new property, Miss Muldoon?" She dragged the sibilants in a rush of saliva. "You can talk to me face-to-face, you don't have to go behind my back to Claud. Just tell me when you want us to move out."

"Please, don't even think about it." Lorelei Muldoon still stared at Olga. "I'm sure Abby won't mind if I stay on with her."

"Oh, I wouldn't want to put you out, Miss Muldoon. We'll leave today."

"Wouldn't you prefer to stay until after, well—"

"But what a perfect time for you to move in, Miss Muldoon. You were talking about tomorrow morning, weren't you? While the rest of us are otherwise occupied?" Betty threw the words: "At my husband's funeral."

Claud pushed Lorelei behind him. "Muldoon, for the love of Mike—"

Betty went right around him. "Have you noticed me calling you 'Miss Muldoon,' Miss Muldoon? Why don't you call me by *my* name? *That* at least still belongs to me. Let me hear you say it. Mrs. Fred Colman."

The storm broke. Olga Finaldo eased Betty away, murmuring something soothing. Seizing his chance, Claud grabbed Lorelei Muldoon by the shoulder and headed for the door.

There was another storm on the landing. Claud was just in time to see Buck McFaul bob to his feet and launch himself—apparently not for the first time—at a lanky man with a mop of black hair and a tape recorder.

Claud got him in a bear hug. "Okay, Buck, what is it this time?"

"He listened to the whole thing! He's been taping it!"

Claud shifted to Buck's adversary. "Well?"

"You're better off with me than somebody you don't know."

"I know you?"

"G. T. Greco. I work for Abby's aunt. Daffodil Butterfield Sloane, *Sloane's Magazine*. I was across the hall at Domenica's place, I couldn't help knowing what was going on—"

"So you're the one." Still gripping Buck, Claud leaned forward to stare into eyes not far below his own. "Three days, is it now? Four?"

"Leave go of me, Gang, I'm like to kill him!"

"No. No, you're not. Like the man says, some fool reporter's bound to hound us. Come on, Lorelei."

"Lorelei?" The microphone of the tape recorder reached behind him. "Remember me from Gaylord's this morning? Did you know about your legacy then?"

Claud had the recorder in his hands before Greco knew he was after it, relishing as always the surprise when someone discovered how fast a big man could be.

"I don't think so."

"But you just said—"

"I didn't say we'd answer. Where's Domenica? If you're a good boy, I won't mention how you tried to use her. Buck, you go ahead of us, check out the street. One sniper attack per day is my quota."

There was a black-and-white in front of the parsonage, in front of Barney's truck. Barney stood on the porch, his pack and his father's bag at his feet. He looked at Lorelei and away.

Claud recognized the look: like a man missing a skin. Good, bad; it all hurt. It was easy to spot because Claud felt the same way himself. And for the same reason; it hadn't occurred to him that Barney would be hit as hard by the will as Claud himself.

"We can't stay here, Dad."

"There could be a hundred reasons for leaving Lorelei the cabin," Buck said. "Look how he gave me his cuff links, out of pure friendship. Maybe he knew *Mr.* Muldoon. Or it could be a business arrangement—well, not business exactly . . ."

Lorelei Muldoon looked at Barney sadly. But absently too, as if he were already a long way away, getting farther by the second.

"We can't leave Lorelei here with no one to protect her," Buck said triumphantly.

"Don't look at me," Claud said. "I haven't even started my eulogy."

"It's all taken care of." Barney jerked his head at the black-and-white. "That's why Elmo's here."

"We can't go back home," Buck said. "Not before Bandit's funeral. We probably can't even find a room. The press sewed them up days ago."

Again Barney looked at Lorelei Muldoon and away. Claud wasn't sure she knew. The haunted eyes turned to Claud.

"You got room to spare, Willetts."

Buck's eyes were bright as a bird's. "Unless you figure to set up a game with the governor. Never mind Bandit's will."

Claud looked from one McFaul to the other.

Why had it ever mattered who saw his cabin? What was there about it—or the Coulees, come to that—that would surprise anyone who knew him?

"Suit yourself. You can help me move the piano. But don't expect company, I still got that speech to write."

Lorelei Muldoon watched the stately red pickup drive past the police car and on up Gaslight Parade, followed by Barney's blue one and Buck's pink Lincoln. The trooper with the Adam's apple paced importantly up and down.

On Fred's plane, each time she reached out to him, he had withdrawn with unflattering speed. Had looked—with hindsight, she could label it—guilty.

When she saw Fenton dressed as a chauffeur, her first instinct had been to warn whomever he worked for, not to assume that his boss had been there in Samson de la Haye's office. Even when she matched Olga Finaldo's initials to OFC Delivery, Lorelei had found it hard to picture the short, sedate woman as a coconspirator. Would anyone else believe it? Abby, for example? The sheriff would believe Abby.

As the afternoon wore on, Elmo retreated to his car. It was dusk by the time Reverend Butterfield turned up her front walk. She stopped briefly to talk to him before coming up to meet Lorelei on the porch.

"Sorry I'm so late. Bluebonnet died on me. I had to leave her up at Grady's."

"That's why you look as though you had a rough after-noon. Long walk home."

"No, it's just a few blocks. Up where Beargrass River Road meets Route 42. It was the funeral."

Abby led the way through to the kitchen, tossing her hat onto a chair and retousling her hair with a grateful sigh. "I always have trouble with civilian clothes."

Lorelei had to agree—Abby's funeral attire was a fitted wool suit over a T-shirt, oxfords and ankle socks, gloves, a straw hat with a veil—but it seemed tactless to say so. "What made it so hard?"

"Shari's parents didn't come. They don't want her body sent back to Harden. Senator Colman's death has had so much attention, no one notices this tragedy in the shadows."

"Because of the baby?"

"They refuse to admit that they have a grandchild."

"What will happen to him?"

Abby brightened a little. "That's the one good to come out of it. Duncan's going to keep him. She says she doubts she'll get a grandchild any other way. Now she'll have somebody to pass the restaurant on to."

Lorelei felt tongue-tied—one more person looking away from that tragedy in the shadows—and yet her next step required Abby's help.

Before she could work out what to say, Abby shook her-self briskly, like a wet dog. "And Barney's not here, so I as-sume he can't accept Senator Colman's bequest to you."

"You knew about it?"

"I thought he'd do something for you. And I thought he'd try to keep his most important possessions out of Betty's hands. And through her, Olga Finaldo. If he'd lived, he'd probably have changed his will, once you solved the mys-tery."

"You *knew* about Olga?"

"Then it is her? I didn't *know*. I've wondered ever since I met her." Abby sliced two doorstops of bread and handed one to Lorelei. She mumbled through it, "She seems so *implacable*. Strong enough to do anything and sleep afterward. I take it you've found a direct connection?"

"Now that I know who it is, I'll log on to Hank. Working from both ends—"

" 'Log on to' means get on the computer?"

"I thought I'd go in again tonight."

"And you want me to get the keys from the sheriff again? Or are those Stan's keys you're jingling? His dad has been turning the hospital upside down."

Lorelei took her hands out of her pockets. Abby held out an imperious hand. Reluctantly Lorelei dropped the keys into it.

"We'll talk to the sheriff tomorrow afternoon, right after the funeral."

"After the funeral! A whole other day! I thought you were in a rush to get everything to the police."

"Now that we know who to watch, it won't be a problem. Olga's not going to run away, she's going to have her hands full with Betty."

"Abby, Olga could erase everything by tomorrow."

"Why? She hasn't done it so far."

"Because she thought she could erase me instead, and she didn't know how much I knew. But I think I gave myself away today."

Abby's gaze was very blue. "We will not humiliate Betty Colman further by arresting her closest friend on the eve of her husband's funeral."

Lorelei sighed. Olga Finaldo didn't have a monopoly on implacability.

Computer illiterates didn't know what they didn't know. They might realize they were uninformed about CD-ROM and bytes and DOS, but they rarely understood that they were as ignorant of a computer's limits as of its abilities. Abby equated a computer's memory with a person's, where events left traces, forgetfulness could be prodded. Information in a computer was more like something written on water that would settle again, empty and still.

Olga Finaldo could be up in Fred's study this very minute, using the computer he had rented for Lorelei to shift assets offshore.

The computer in Fred's study.

She looked with regret at the kitchen. For a few hours she had been warm and safe. The norm, once, long ago, last week. Now it was a luxury that felt like fat on her bones. It was hard to walk away from.

Chapter
Fifteen

Wise to the ways of Macy's Thanksgiving Day parades and
Christmas gridlock, Lorelei Muldoon drove up to Grady's
Gas at the crack of dawn that August Wednesday. The
trooper Elmo, his Adam's apple visible in her rearview mirror, trailed her all the way to the turnoff to Beargrass River
Road, waited while she parked the Jeep beside Bluebonnet,
and kept pace with her as she walked back to Abby's. But
then, as she had hoped, he apparently assumed that without
wheels, she was helpless. He drove past her and on to the
church.

By the time the morning chill burned away, the people of
Merciful Valley, plus tourists, reporters, and cameramen, had
lined the shoulders of Route 42 from Demersville to Bitterroot for the final journey of Fred Bandit Roybal Colman. The
only ones missing (besides Lorelei Muldoon) were members
of the Pastor's Committee, back in the Parish Hall setting up
for the post-funeral gathering, and baby-sitters.

Just after ten o'clock, Claud Willetts, at the wheel of the
Big Red Machine, left Pascoe's Funeral Home in Demersville,

en route to the Bitterroot Congregational Church thirty miles to the south. Behind him, leading the air patrol in a phalanx of motor scooters, was Buck McFaul. In the sidecar beside Buck, his dignity perfectly suited to the occasion, sat huge, graying Maximum Dog.

Next came a wrecker with a flatbed bearing the senator's coffin and a lone kilted man playing the bagpipes, then a string of sober dignitaries' sedans, Charley Calico on his Harley (the old one), a fire truck (Bandit Colman had been an honorary volunteer), and floats bearing Bitterroot Scout Troop No. #2 (he had been an Eagle Scout) and the Demersville high school band, playing a wavering rendition of Tchaikovwsky's "March Slav."

On the national news that night the film footage rolled with a voice-over that skated the edge of mocking the small-town solemnity, but that morning, except for the occasional tourist describing it into his video cam, people watched in silence, the cortege lengthening as watchers jumped into cars and trucks and fell into line behind the band. By the time they reached Bitterroot, "March Slav" sounded very much like the bagpipes.

Under Duncan's supervision, the Pastor's Committee had been in the Parish Hall since early morning, passing Baby Lester Finley from arm to arm while they set up tables. Casseroles took turns in the warming ovens. They would be served up piping hot at the last minute, but rolls and salads were already on display. Over on the dessert table, cakes and pies and pecan tassies were flanked by a coffee urn and an enormous bowl of punch.

The Pastor's Committee swore that nothing contained zucchini.

By the time Reverend Butterfield gave a final nod of approval and went to the Sanctuary, Gaslight Parade and all its side streets were choked with more cars than the single traffic light could regulate. People parked wherever their forward

277

progress stopped. The church filled and crammed and over-flowed.

Nobody took a second look at the smallish young man in the white shirt and sober black pants and chauffeur's hat moving against the flow. Ricky Fenton zigzagged through parked cars away from the church, stopping at random, bending as if tying a shoe. Each time he moved on, air hissed gently from tires behind him. When he thought he'd done enough, he drove back to Grady's Gas and parked.

When Lorelei walked back to Grady's and pulled out, she had the road to herself. Not that it mattered. As the widow's friend-in-chief, Olga Finaldo had a big role at the funeral; her chauffeur must even now be trapped in traffic.

The khaki Wrangler turned off on Beargrass River Road, the only route to Colman's cabin. Just as Olga had predicted. Fenton checked to be sure she wasn't followed before he drove back to Bitterroot. He parked at the agreed-upon place—up by the highway, at the edge of the traffic—and walked back to the church. Since it was never locked, Olga had been able to take him inside the previous night and point out the side room for family and special guests. From its second row, one could easily see the left-hand door to the sanctuary. Fenton now opened this door a few inches to a gust of "Amazing Grace" in a determined middle-aged soprano voice and walked back to the car to wait.

"I spend two years doing research on trade practices. Bandit Colman looks over my position papers, finds a camera, and drawls, 'Are our boys going to die for fuel for Japanese factories?' and suddenly it's a headline. *His* headline. He knew where the cameras were, and he could slap a reporter down in a sound bite."

Claud thought Senator Balthazar was having trouble bringing himself to say what Montana's remaining senator was duty-bound to say about the man he had called a showboat too many times to count.

"Tell the truth, I was mad as hell every time he pulled it. But without Bandit Colman, the stories wouldn't have been written, the questions wouldn't have been raised. Between us, we did a damn fine job. I don't know how I'm going to manage without him."

Balthazar gave way to Governor Larsen, who said ponderously all the things about Senator Fred Bandit Roybal Colman that everybody present knew already but that still had to be said to make the service official.

Farewells to a career, not a man. Abby was right. There had been no love lost among these men. They hadn't really known him.

Claud walked up the aisle to Bandit's coffin in front of the altar and looked out, aboil with the need to make these people see the man he had known. Not sure how to do it.

He looked down at the elegantly plain black box, the portrait of Elena in pride of place beside it, suddenly not sure he could get out any words at all.

He cleared his throat. Nothing to do but start and see.

Tentatively, then with increasing confidence, he described nicknaming Fred Colman the Frito Bandito, Bandit responding by picking a fight every time he heard it. "I like to think I got tired of beating him up, but truth to tell, I thought he might get good enough to win in a year or two. It just got easier to be on the same side.

"That was Bandit. He knew what he wanted, and he had to have it. His way. He lived like that . . ."

Claud looked out over pews largely filled with strangers. Olga Finaldo bent forward for a whispered word to Betty and excused her way out of the pew, a handkerchief pressed to her mouth. It couldn't be the heat—he knew the transparent,

279

sweaty look of heat prostration; Olga's skin was thick and clear. Bathroom, of course.

". . . he died like that."

One eye on Olga's vacant place, he talked about the purchase of the Big Red Machine, the first proud trip with Bandit at his side. He spun it out, moved on to another story, and another, all the while waiting for Olga to come back, until, to his horror, he found himself describing another farewell, one he had never intended to share.

"He drove me to the plane when I left for Vietnam. Neither of us expected me back. Well, look at me: talk about targets. Course, even then I knew a thing or two about hiding behind somebody else."

Still no Olga. Claud tried to catch Barney's eye, but he was staring up as if committing the ceiling to memory.

How could he get out from under this story?

He couldn't warn Barney once he was back in the pew; the sheriff, Buck McFaul, and Senator Balthazar would be between them.

Fast, that's how.

"We were trying to find a way to say what we felt but keep our testosterone intact—if you've ever been twenty and male, you know what I'm talking about. Finally Bandit swatted me on the shoulder and said, 'See ya, fella.' And he walked away without looking back."

Did that cover it? Whatever else was left could lie between him and Bandit forever. Claud put one slab of a hand on the lid of the coffin, as if the wood were the man. As if he could reach through the wood to the man.

"See ya, fella."

In the silence, he walked to the family pew. Past it. Down the center aisle and out of the church.

Lorelei wondered if the terrace door in Fred's . . . her . . . cabin had been repaired since her first break-in. She was prepared to break it again. If she triggered the burglar alarm and summoned the police? And they came? This *was* her property.

The massive oak door was unlocked.

No brooding about Fred today. She headed directly for his study.

She seated herself, looking out over the terrace, down the open field to the lake. The plants she now knew were marijuana were still there, taller than many men, with fluted leaves of greenish blue almost like palm fronds. Even on this windless day, they rippled as if to mark someone's passage. Surely they no longer served a purpose. She would ask the sheriff to have them destroyed.

She sounded like an owner. Not at all Fred's intention. Abby was right; he would have changed his will once this was settled.

He was nothing if not thorough: computer, fax, modem, printer, were all up and talking to each other. Suddenly she could picture Hank Muldoon sitting where she sat, with this equipment and more, tapping away, looking up occasionally at something waving greenly in the sun.

She keyed Hank's call number. Type added itself to her screen at breakneck speed. She broke in, asking Hank if he had saved everything she had sent; the information they had now might be only as important as the files they kept of it. Before Hank could do more than the equivalent of an indignant nod, she broke in again to tell him what she planned.

A pause, followed by a burst of asterisks. Hank's computer laughter. Then from opposite ends of the country the Muldoons set out to pull down Olga Finaldo's financial house of cards.

Olga Finaldo picked her way sedately through the parked cars, fanning herself with the program from the memorial service. She entered the car without speaking.

She looked as she had from Fenton's earliest memories: unsparingly neat hair, plain dress over a plain body, yet somehow swollen with life. Even now, when the months of waiting and longer years, probably, of wishing—the subtle plans, thoughts, failures, and attempts to regroup—had come down to this final, brutal cut-and-run . . . even now, Olga Finaldo looked no different.

"They doing their big hero proud?"

"Later, perhaps, we may talk of heroes."

His hands tightened on the wheel. He drove in silence down the narrow gravel road. Past the windfall without a pause. Even knowing the van was hidden there, he could barely make it out himself. And he had been even more careful setting up the big gun in Colman's field. Still unharvested. Mech must have decided to leave it alone after all.

At the final turn before Colman's cabin, she stopped him. "You tell me it will take you fifteen minutes to position yourself in the field below the terrace."

"More, if you can give it to me. You never know about angles."

"As you know from your vast experience of angles."

He slid the clip of his gun out and smacked it back without speaking.

Apparently satisfied that she had slapped him down, she patted his shoulder. "The purpose of this meeting is not merely to dispose of Miss Muldoon, remember. First I must learn what she knows, and can prove, and has told others. What can be salvaged. Then I will walk to the glass and nod. Then you will shoot."

Had it once occurred to Olga that she, too, would be in front of the glass? No. She assumed—he had allowed her to assume—that Ricky Fenton had been cowed into obedience.

She wouldn't have the last assumption much longer; Lorelei Muldoon would hardly spill her guts without mentioning his kidnap attempt the previous morning.

"What if she doesn't talk?"

"I will call you in. You will convince her."

"I still think we should make it look like an accident."

"The time for such artistry passed long ago." She patted his shoulder again. "Your time will come, my nephew. But you must be guided by me now."

My nephew.

He opened the car door for her. Contemptuous, grasping, fiercely energetic, and . . . his aunt.

"*Tía* Olga, if you had to decide again . . ."

"Well?"

"Would you do this all over?"

Her eyes popped wide. "Rarely in life is one given such an opportunity, you foolish boy. It would be criminal to waste it."

He watched as she picked her way down the final yards of the gravel road to the cabin, getting smaller and smaller. She opened the door and disappeared.

In the passage between the Sanctuary and the Parish Hall, Claud pushed open the door labeled Ladies. Empty. No quiver to the water in the toilet tank. A dry sink.

Outside the church door, Elmo leaned against a black-and-white in deep conversation with another trooper.

Claud shouted over, "Is Lorelei Muldoon still at Abby's?"

Elmo shook his head. "She left a good hour ago."

"And you didn't follow her."

Elmo waved at the frozen stampede of empty vehicles, the Big Red Machine in the middle of the herd. "Nobody else could either."

If he had time, he'd smack the kid. He searched for words to describe the unmemorable Olga Finaldo. Gave up. "Anyone come out this door in the past fifteen minutes?"

"Half a dozen people. It's a hot day, Claud."

Buck McFaul's motor scooter was the closest one. From the sidecar and Barney's truck, Maximum Dog and Blue hurled profanities, but Blue wouldn't actually attack in Buck's behalf, and Claud shoved the sidecar out of range with a boot before Max could seriously catch hold of him.

It was harder to fit onto the scooter than it was to hot-wire it.

"Get your boss on the horn," he shouted back to Elmo. "Tell him about Muldoon."

The only way to wedge his foot on the gas pedal was to stick his knee out at an angle that whacked every car he passed. Sputtering like a lawn mower, he threaded his way through the maze of cars, up and over onto Route 42.

"Do I interrupt you, Miss Muldoon?"

Lorelei jerked her hands off the keyboard and swiveled.

Olga Finaldo's sturdy legs were planted on the sun-warmed stone of the stairs outside the study door. Short, prosaic: hardly the dragon lady of Lorelei's imagination. How long had she been watching?

Lorelei said numbly, "Aren't you supposed to be at the funeral?"

"I am indisposed. My driver is even now taking me back to the hotel."

Olga took a step into the room. Two. "Are you catching up on your work, Miss Muldoon?"

Lorelei spun back and punched exit. She yanked the modem cord out of its socket. Between the two, Hank should understand a shriek for help. Call somebody, Hank. Call anybody. Call everybody.

Why didn't Olga have a gun pointing at her? Or was that Fenton's department? Fenton, her driver. Was he putting the car away? How much time did that take?

"Are you doing something you don't want me to see, Miss Muldoon? Perhaps you will tell me about it."

Where was the OC-5? In her pocketbook by the door. By Olga.

Lorelei licked dry lips. "You'll find out soon enough."

"Then we are agreed that you will tell me. But can we not talk in a more comfortable place? Tell me what you think of the changes Mrs. Colman has made in the living room."

It was a chance to dart for her pocketbook.

Olga Finaldo seemed amused. "But of course, bring your papers, Miss Muldoon. They are the purpose of our meeting, are they not?"

She ushered Lorelei down the stairs and into the living room like a hostess.

It was like pulling down screens to work on several programs at once: Where was Fenton? What was Hank doing?

How could she get away from them?

The wing chairs were in front of the glass terrace doors. An inset on Lorelei's mind-screen noted sadly that Fred's iron will had met its match in flowery chintz.

Olga settled into one chair and gestured to the other; only then did she prompt, "Now let us discuss your efforts, Miss Muldoon."

Why was Olga so firmly in charge?

Because manipulating people was her business; of course she could keep Lorelei off-balance. Whereas Lorelei Muldoon's business was numbers.

"What does the C of OFC stand for, Olga Finaldo? Company? Corporation?"

Briefly Olga was rigid. She resettled herself deliberately. "I don't understand you, Miss Muldoon. However, in the interests of courtesy, please continue."

Wordlessly Lorelei held out the printout of hers and Hank's work-in-progress.

Olga's eyebrows twitched as if at rudeness, but Lorelei was not fooled. The hand taking the papers was as icily damp as her own.

"You have two companies, don't you? Everybody knows about Bahr-Finaldo, but how many people know you also own OFC? Why so secretive about a delivery service, Olga? Because that's where your real profits are? I can even make some guesses about what you deliver."

Olga turned the sheets with a show of indifference. Lorelei took the opportunity to grope in her bag for the can of bear repellent.

As Olga began to comprehend what she read, pretense burned away. She turned faster. Flipped back and forth as quickly as Lorelei could have. It was a relief, in a way. Lorelei hadn't known how much of Olga's expertise had been hired.

Olga's body seemed to thicken and pull down hard into itself like a spring. "These cannot be the papers Senator Colman carried."

Lorelei shook her head.

Olga's voice sank to a whisper. "What have you done?"

"The only link I could find between OFC and Bahr-Finaldo was through the Hispanic Cultural Institute. Until this spring. For some reason, in April you began to funnel a stream of money through Betty Colman, Inc. By now you're so intertwined, only an expert would see that Betty Colman, Inc., may not even know how it's being used. That's where I come in."

"Don't tell me what I know, tell me what I ask."

"I figured that before I could gather proof, you could move everything offshore. So I decided to do something you couldn't stop."

Even now she was careful to keep Hank out of it. "I've been doing what you did to Betty, only on a larger scale. All this morning, you've been making deposits to every member of Congress, every spouse, every campaign committee. Fifty thousand each. It has a nice round sound, don't you think? Some through OFC, some through Bahr-Finaldo, some through the Hispanic Cultural Institute."

What would happen when the sheer size of it sank in?

"It was about eighty percent complete when you arrived.

Can you cover them all? I can't vouch for every beneficiary, but with hundreds involved, I'm sure some will be upset enough to investigate. If not, I've been faxing duplicates to the *Washington Post*."

Olga Finaldo's rage came into the room like a live thing. She was as much at its mercy as Lorelei. Long seconds passed before she gave a convulsive shudder and dragged herself up from her chair and across to the terrace doors. She stared out and down.

"So. It is over."

"Yes."

Olga nodded. "Then let us be calm at last." She waved toward the lush green field below. "Come, share a last look at this so beautiful country with me, Miss Muldoon."

Lorelei did so, weak-kneed with relief, marveling at Olga's self-possession. Except for her head, nodding on as if of its volition as Olga said again, "It is over at last."

A sandy tenor cut through the room.

"To the floor, Lorelei!"

Without thinking, Lorelei threw herself down. Bullets shattered the glass door at heart level above her.

When the pallbearers gathered at the altar, Claud Willetts was still absent. Abby asked Barney McFaul to take his place.

"Where did he go?" Barney asked. "Spare me Dad's theory about being overcome by his own words."

"Olga Finaldo left during the service. You couldn't see her, she was in the pew behind. Claud must have gone after her."

In his insinuating way, G. T. Greco was somehow at hand. "Lorelei Muldoon's Wrangler isn't in your driveway, Reverend Butterfield."

Barney threw back his head and screamed until the cords of his throat stood out like rope. He didn't know then or ever if he did it aloud or inside his head.

Greco watched with interest. "And somebody let air out

a lot of car tires. Nobody's going to move for a while."

"You telling me this for a reason?" Barney asked.

Greco dangled keys. "Domenica's. Up behind her store—away from this mess."

Barney grabbed for them, but Greco backed away too fast. "I'm coming too."

"I could take them."

"In front of all these people? You're wasting time."

Barney snatched the keys. "Then keep up."

He was out of the church and up Gaslight Parade at a ground-eating run, Blue at his heels, Greco a panting third. Sure enough, Domenica's army-surplus jeep was free and clear behind Gaylord's. Blue surged over the open back. Greco caught hold as the jeep came back past him and pulled himself aboard.

Barney drove on the sidewalk of the Parade, clearing flower pots, mailboxes, and a bench like underbrush. What he did wasn't as impressive as the tearaway speed with which he did it.

Greco clutched the roll bar. "Where'd you learn to drive like this?"

"You don't want to know."

A shortcut over a convenient lawn brought the jeep within sight of two troopers listening intently to Domenica Gaylord. She pointed furiously after them.

Elmo shouted, "Hold it right there!"

Greco looked through the jeep's open back, over Blue's pricked ears. Barney didn't bother. Elmo would be on the horn, alerting police throughout the valley to look out for Domenica Gaylord's jeep. Elmo loved to use the horn.

Olga Finaldo frowned at Claud as though he were a bad smell. As though she hadn't heard the gunfire, as though she wasn't standing in a field of shattered glass. Olga but not Olga: This was a swollen stranger packed into her skin, try-

ing to remember who Olga Finaldo was and how she be-
haved. The immensity of the effort made her move like a
wind-up toy.

"Mr. Willetts. Senator Colman's disreputable friend."

"And you're Betty's disreputable friend, it looks like,"
Claud said.

"You dare!"

Claud was afraid to break eye contact, but he could see the
vague shape of Lorelei Muldoon. He jerked a thumb toward
the front door. He had to buy her time to get there.

"You're mixed up in Bandit's death, aren't you? Why'd you
do it, Olga? How could Fred Colman be a threat to a decorator?"

"That's only a cover, Claud." Lorelei lifted her head. She
hadn't moved. "Most of her money comes from smuggling.
Drugs, Olga? Or just drug money?"

"You lie! Bahr-Finaldo is a fine firm."

"Stop lecturing and take a hike, Lorelei!"

"I should have blackmailed you, Mr. Willetts, not Betty
Colman. You have so much to be ashamed of."

Suddenly her rigid control fractured into a stream of shrill
Spanish. She was summoning her nephew.

Nephew?

Holding her eyes, Claud walked toward her, cool as if they
faced each other across a dance floor. "Honey, I'm unblack-
mailable. What could you say that people don't believe already?"

He ducked. Grabbed Lorelei Muldoon and shoved her behind him. "What did you get Betty for? Sucking up beyond
the call of duty?"

Olga had forgotten about Lorelei. "Mrs. Colman would
have been shocked to learn how much of the money of Betty
Colman, Inc., found its way to the Caribbean and Colom-
bia. Oh, yes. As times change, what shocks people changes,
but there is always something one must hide."

Another break into that shriek of Spanish. A thin kid bobbed up onto the terrace and picked his way over the glass and inside.

"You! Claud, he's the one who killed Fred. The one who bragged about it."

He didn't look dangerous enough to justify the loathing in Lorelei's voice, except for the automatic pistol he gripped by the clip. His sallow cheeks were flushed, but he gave no other sign of having heard her.

"I suppose you've been waiting in the field all morning," Lorelei said bitterly to Fenton. "I was so stupid, I thought it was the wind."

"There's only room for one hero in this room, Lorelei. Git!"

Wind? Claud risked a look at the field. Halfway down the slope to Cutthroat Lake, a swath of plants wide enough to drive a tank through had been cut down.

So this of all days was the one chosen to harvest the marijuana.

Not by this kid, though. Not dressed for it. He must have fetched Olga from the funeral.

He swung his attention back to Fenton and his aunt. Their rapid-fire conversation made no sense.

"Time out!" He suddenly outyelled both of them. "He thinks he shot *me* Monday night?"

He had shaken her briefly. "You speak Spanish, Mr. Willetts?"

"*I'm* Claud Willetts, kid. Tell him, Olga. Who did he think he was after?"

Another flood of Latin invective. Fenton muttered back sullenly. But the pistol was rock-steady; he wasn't as cowed as Olga seemed to think he was, if Claud was any judge. And he had to be. The fault line between the two of them was all he had to work with.

"Is he the one who killed Dr. Sue by mistake too?" he asked

before Olga could simmer down. "Is that why he didn't take out Muldoon yesterday, up at Charley Calico's? Another mistake?"

"But what is this, my nephew? Plans of your own? Again?"

Gotcha. If he could ratchet the tension up one more notch . . . He thought of the half-harvested marijuana and crossed mental fingers. "Why don't you call in the other guy, Olga? The one out there in the field?"

The whole swollen force of her anger poured over her nephew. "Your soldier lives?"

Squealing like a pig in a python, she cast about for a weapon. She came up with the fireplace shovel and swung at him. "Fool, fool above fools, prince of fools! Deal with him if you die for it. I will manage these."

As Fenton shied back from the wicked arc of the shovel, Claud lunged for the gun. Bullets spat uncertainly from him, beyond to Lorelei. Back again.

At least he was luckier than Stan. No, he wasn't.

Arteries were the problem with leg wounds, in which case his foot would be sopping wet in seconds, and he'd be dead seconds later. But with his meat, the odds were against it.

He tried to topple between Olga and Lorelei, but Olga circled him and went on inexorably like the tank she resembled. He couldn't tell if Lorelei had been hit or was hypnotized by the sight of Olga bearing down on her, swinging the shovel in vicious chops, shrieking at Fenton. "If you are afraid to shoot him, burn him! Set fire to the field!"

Out of the corner of his eye, Claud saw Fenton leap off the stone ledge of the terrace. "Olga, listen to me!"

She was too far gone to hear. The shovel whistled by his head and bit into Lorelei's arm with a thud that echoed in his ears, hooked, held. Pulled free with a rush of blood.

The nephew then. "Stick to guns, Fenton!" Claud shouted after him. "Forget about a fire!"

"So." Suddenly Olga was still. She stared at him. "Something matters to you after all, Mr. Willetts?"

At least he had succeeded in deflecting her from Lorelei. "Olga, there aren't enough people in this valley to fight a fire once it's well away."

But he could see her take it in as weakness, not fact. People like her always thought they knew best. Whereas sometimes they were merely crazy.

"Have you ever seen a fire out of control? Call him back while you can."

"Perhaps it can move faster than you and Ms. Muldoon. A brilliant accident."

"And how'll you get away? You think I just patted your car on the hood when I passed by? You got a spare distributor wire?"

He felt his back pocket as though the wire was really there, nostrils flared for the first hint of smoke.

Instead there was the sound of plants crashing. It could have been a fight. It could have been the beginning of a fire.

"You pros," he said desperately. "You always make the same mistake."

There it was, the first thin smell, sharper than the smoke of a good cigar. A dog barking, too, loud and deep as a piece of highway equipment warming up. Olga had to turn to check it out—had to. Claud dived for the nearest chunky leg.

A cough, a sledgehammer thud. Olga jerked upward like a stubby little tree uprooted, hovered for a heartbeat—two— before she collapsed onto the stone floor. There was a dark, fallen-away spot the size of a coffee mug in her middle. A pool spread underneath her with startling speed. For the first time since he had seen her, she looked relaxed.

So this was what revenge came down to: watching a woman who had already lost everything die without even a hand to hold.

The barking must mean Blue—and Barney—had arrived. They could take care of Lorelei and call the police and the fire brigade. Claud hitched himself over to Olga. Her hand was already clammy, but the wheels still turned behind her eyes.

She said with a mighty effort, "What is this mistake I make?"

"You took everything too serious." He bent down to whisper. "Life's a game, Olga. A big, juicy, barroom brawl of a game. Right up to the last minute."

She stared at him with outrage. And stared.

Chapter
Sixteen

Charley Calico, his hair in a well-managed mane, was the deacon in charge of regular coffee. He was on his way to the kitchen for a refill when he glanced out and saw smoke in the direction of Cutthroat Lake. Urn clattering to the floor, he headed back toward the Parish Hall at a dead run.

"Fire!"

Valley people fell silent, hoping against hope for a joke. But when Charley ran in, he was already midway through a mental transformation to the chief of the Merciful Valley Volunteer Fire Department. Every able-bodied man knew the drill: drop what he was doing and head for the smoke. Before tourists and media had time to react, coffee cups came to rest on every available surface; ties loosened; coats hit the floor. Bodies jostled for position in the doorways. They were gone.

Only to halt at the car-choked roads.

"Everybody to their cars!" roared Charley Calico. "Move them and let us out!"

"Can't be done!" Elmo knew his lines by heart. He waved his arms up, down, around. "Take a look."

Up and down the narrow streets, one driver after another was discovering flat tires. In the logistical nightmare, Neiderhoffer was in no mood to hear about Domenica's Jeep.

He was making this clear to Elmo at the top of his lungs when a motor scooter putt-putted up the sidewalk beside him. Buck McFaul was driving, Doc Tilman riding pillion. Scooters lined up Indian file behind him.

"We'll stop at the firehouse for our gear and follow the smoke!"

Charley Calico gunned up on his old Harley. He shouted, "Double up, everybody! We'll call you with a location, Hoff, and hope you've got the pumper clear by then. The rest of you, after me. As many summer people as we can take."

When they chugged up the gravel road to Colman's cabin, they found Lorelei Muldoon leaning against Domenica's Jeep, one arm tied in a sling of bloodstained white cloth that had recently been on Barney McFaul's back. Blue stood in front of her, hackles up.

"Where's Barney?" Buck shouted from a safe distance.

She waved toward the cabin with her good arm. Shovels in hand, the volunteers trotted on around her as Barney and Greco, with Claud hanging on their shoulders, staggered out of the cabin and up the hill. More of Barney's shirt was knotted around Claud's right leg.

"Shouldn't they be using the fireman's carry, Charley?" Claud complained through gritted teeth.

"That must be for smaller mammals," Greco gasped. "There's a body back in the cabin. Somebody better get it before the fire does."

Charley Calico quickly took charge. "Barney, call off your dog so Doc Tilman can tend to Lorelei and Claud. I'll leave the other body to you. Everybody else: down the hill!"

Claud's wound was bleeding with sullen slowness. Doc Tilman gave him only a cursory glance before turning to

Lorelei. With exquisite care, he eased her arm out of the sling and onto an inflatable cast. The bleeding quickened anyway.

"What gave you the idea of using a condom for a tourniquet, Barney?"

"Is it holding?"

"It'll do till I set the stitches."

"You're in luck, Lorelei," Claud said. "Doc Tilman is as finicky as a watchmaker. Only doctor on the planet with legible handwriting."

"Dr. Tilman!" she said, like somebody wakened from a dream. "I borrowed your hat and your jacket."

He didn't look up. "I'll add it to my bill. I'm giving you a shot, Lorelei, but I can't wait till it kicks in to start."

"She's in shock anyway, Doc," Claud said.

"If you've taken up medicine, Willetts, maybe I won't need to treat you at all. Take that dog away while I work, Barney, he makes me nervous."

"Blue'll do what he's told."

"You might as well go, Barney," Claud said. "Somebody has to call an ambulance. Fetch the other body. Not to mention the fire. At this stage, the more people, the better chance of stopping it. You know that as well as I do."

Barney had shaped his body around Lorelei's in an embrace that held her injured arm immovable. "Greco's strong enough to dial a phone. And carry what's left of that little woman."

He didn't care. Barney honestly didn't care what happened except for Lorelei. If the fire was tearing out to the road right now, he'd throw Lorelei into Domenica's Jeep and take off without a look back.

Claud, on the other hand, had a few things left to arrange. And his mind didn't seem exactly familiar; even though his thoughts were racing, they seemed to be floating at the top of his head.

"Good idea, Barn," he said peaceably. "You wanted to be in the middle of the story, Greco, here's your chance."

"But I don't—"

"You can dial 911, can't you? And fetch and carry?"

With a dramatic scowl of distaste, the rangy reporter set off down the slope.

Lorelei's eyes were sleepy. That was the shock; Claud knew the signs. She winced a little with each stitch, but with a delayed reaction, as though it was happening far away to somebody else.

She said drowsily to Barney, "I don't seem to be able to do anything without you coming to the rescue."

"Shouldn't have needed me this time. Of all the hare-brained stunts—did Willetts put you up to it?"

Lorelei shook her head. "What choice did I have? I was the one who knew what she was doing, and I was the only one with the tools to stop her."

Claud seized the opening. "I was a little preoccupied when you were talking about Olga inside. Mind running through it for me again?"

The sleepy gaze turned to him. "Why don't I wait for the sheriff? Tell you all at once?"

"I'd rather hear it while that reporter's occupied. Leaves me free to ask questions."

She looked up at Barney for guidance. He shrugged. "Keep your mind off the doc."

Her words came in long sighing breaths, as though she relinquished the responsibility for each detail as she told it. The delivery service that had delivered drugs as well as furniture. The profits that had been funneled through Betty Colman's firm.

Claud listened, watching the progress of the blaze behind her. It was balked at one end by Cutthroat Lake; on either side of the field, shadowy figures dug hasty trenches between it and the trees and brush, herding the fire straight up the slope toward them. Only Bandit's cabin barred the way. There was still as much sound as fury: narrow tongues of dull, shallow red rather than the swollen harvest gold of a fire that has taken hold and is on the move. Against its glare, Greco was a black ant, toiling up the hill toward them with his awkward burden.

Lorelei stopped with a gasp as Dr. Tilman ripped off Barney's makeshift tourniquet and blood began reworking down her numb arm. He eased it back into the sling.

"I still want you to go to the hospital for X rays, see if there's a break. Your turn, Willetts."

"Just slap on a butterfly or two till—"

Tilman snorted. "As if that would hold." Before Claud could stop him, he slashed through the pant leg of Claud's best Armani suit.

"Have a heart, Doc—"

"You didn't tell me it was a bullet wound. Where's the exit?" Little as he was, he spun Claud halfway around. "Then you have at least one bullet in there."

"That's why it can wait—"

"Lie down. I said, lie down, Claud Willetts."

Claud compromised by sliding to a sitting position, propped against the Jeep. Blue stirred beside him, mumbled, shifted to make room. Apparently he wasn't in shock; Tillman's probing felt as if he were stirring the bone.

"I should have asked Greco to bring back Bandit's Wild Turkey. Yours, excuse me, Lorelei. You'd have spared it for a good cause, wouldn't you?"

"Just breathe deep," Barney said.

"How's that?"

"Why do you think the fire's so slow to catch? The field's full of ripe weed. Very expensive smoke, it should blunt the edges for you."

No wonder he felt light-headed.

"Shall I go on?" Lorelei asked politely.

"Later," Claud said, trying to keep it from being a grunt. "Don't want *him* to hear."

Him being Greco, a few steps away. Barney went to meet him; together they laid Olga Finaldo's body down.

Sitting, he was too close to the still angry face. "A little farther away, if you don't mind."

They grinned and shifted her to the other side of the road.

"I called the police," Greco said. "The sheriff'll be here any minute."

Now that he mentioned it, Claud could hear a dull, far-off whine.

"But the ambulance will be a while. The hospital says it's at the north end of the valley. Some kids locked their babysitter out of the house, climbed out an attic window, and dared each other to jump off the roof. I thought he said the name was Neiderhoffer, but that can't be right—"

"Oh, yes it can."

"And your dad is up on the terrace with another body, Barney."

"Male? Female?" Claud asked.

"Male. Not much bigger than this one."

Claud and Lorelei exchanged glances. "Fenton."

When Barney turned to leave, Lorelei clutched at him with her good arm. "You're not leaving me!"

"You're safe now, Muldoon."

"I'm not in condition to guard anybody," Claud said. "And Greco's on his way back to the fire, aren't you, Greco?"

"No guards needed." Barney jerked his head toward Olga. "You said she was in charge, didn't you? If there's anybody left, they're pros. She's dead, the job's over. On your feet, Greco. Claud's right, this stage of a fire, the more hands, the better."

Greco stumbled along behind him, but he was still in earshot when the whine switched to a scream and a black-

and-white made the final turn to the cabin.

"Let me handle this, Lorelei."

"I can't take the responsibility for not telling the sheriff," Lorelei said.

"They won't blame *you*, honey."

She looked down at him, big-eyed, weary. Troubled, not stubborn.

"You're safe, Barney says so," Claud argued. "Olga's dead. The less we have to make public, the less embarrassment for Betty Colman. I don't know if that matters much to you—"

Guilt was always a great persuader. "Abby said something like that too. But I'm afraid after what I did this morning, there's no way to keep it from getting public. Five hundred fax machines . . ."

He had to try. When the sheriff swung into position behind Domenica's Jeep, Claud spoke up before Lorelei could say anything. "Hoff, the twins through with that ambulance yet? Lorelei here is about to fade out on us."

"It just left Demersville Memorial. Say, another half hour."

"They busted up much?"

The sheriff scowled. "They broke an arm each. Sullivan broke his wrist too. Seems to think that puts him one up."

Before Claud could come up with another diversion, Doc Tilman found whatever he had been digging for. Claud's attention shrank abruptly to his right leg.

By the time the doctor finally wrapped him up and left him alone, Lorelei was almost done with her lecture, Hoff breathing through his nose in an effort to concentrate, Jimmy Fineman bursting out with indignation every paragraph or so.

Interesting, how she never mentioned her father's part in it.

This time through, her explanation sounded obvious. He'd have got there sooner or later.

No. Lying to other people was one thing; was he going to start lying to himself? This scheme was as far beyond his petty chiseling as . . . as Abby had said days ago.

Claud watched the fire nibble at the edges of the terrace and stretch witches' fingers toward the cabin. "Give me a hand here, Hoff. I'm tired of looking at your belt buckle."

Together Neiderhoffer and Fineman heaved Claud to his feet. He flopped back against the hood of the sheriff's car; the others naturally arranged themselves in a semicircle facing him. Away from the cabin.

The sheriff said to Lorelei, "It's like quicksand. Each step makes sense when you tell me, but as soon as you go on to the next one, the first one closes up behind me."

"Look at it from the other end," Lorelei said. "As soon as Olga decided to move to the valley, she began involving Betty. Sort of pre-blackmail. To fall back on if she got into trouble."

"The thing I can't understand is why." Hoff pulled the bars of his mustache in weary frustration.

"Why do it at all?" Claud asked. "Or why pick on Merciful Valley?"

"Both."

"The second one's obvious. She thought we were easy meat," Claud said.

"More than that, don't you think?" Lorelei said deferentially. "You live here, maybe you don't see it, but when I was driving around Monday, it seemed to me that with a four-wheel drive, you could go anywhere. You wouldn't need a road. Or a border crossing. Olga was a smuggler, she'd know about borders."

"I wonder why she left Washington," Claud said, his gaze steady down the hill. Only a few more minutes . . . "She'd been operating under Jimmy's nose for years."

"Maybe she was a shark." Lorelei explained, "A business that's not quite small and not quite big has to grow or die. Like a shark, Barney said once. Maybe she couldn't get any bigger in Washington without attracting attention."

The sheriff gave Lorelei a tired look. "But why did you come here this morning? Why not just tell us?"

"By the time you could get at her records officially, she could close her accounts, change the records electronically, move everything offshore. So I thought, if Washington was full of angry people looking for her money, she couldn't cover her tracks fast enough. I used her own method. I had OFC contribute to every member of Congress. Plus spouses. Plus campaign funds."

Fineman said, "This is the most outrageous—"

"Don't get all hot and bothered, Jimmy," Claud said. "You'll never prove a thing."

"Mr. Willetts, you greatly underestimate the skills of—"

The sheriff put a detaining hand on Fineman's arm. "Why not, Gang?"

"The papers were in the cabin. Notice I say, *were.*"

They turned to see what he had been watching. With a howl, Fineman took off down the slope.

But Claud's timing was good. A roaring ball of red engulfed the cabin and reared up above it, hungry for more. There was no more. The floors held briefly, then collapsed in on each other with an almost animal sound. By the time Fineman got there, just the concrete stairs remained, thrust upward through the flames like the carcass of somebody burned at the stake.

So many evenings spent on the big chairs in front of Bandit's fire, so many arguments, so much whisky. Everything but Elena's portrait gone in a shower of sparks.

The grimy men throwing up dirt in front of the cabin kept Fineman from going closer. He protested; somebody stuck a shovel in his hand and pointed. He started digging, gray suit and all.

Claud forced himself to watch it all. The last thing he could do.

No, not quite the last.

"It's so close, Claud," Lorelei said. "Are we safe? Shouldn't we move farther away?"

"No, this is the last hurrah, wouldn't you say, Hoff? See how they're throwing up dirt in front of the cabin? What's left of it. That means they think they can stop it there. Starve it. It won't get up here to us."

As the fire's noise lessened, a rumble was audible behind them. Claud turned to see a truck making the last turn. The Scout troop's float, loaded with Bitterroot Scout Troop No. 2. The road wasn't wide enough for both the truck and Hoff's black-and-white; it geared down, the engine roaring a protest against the transmission, and made its own road on by, swung back onto the gravel, pushed a few feet closer to the tangle of motor scooters, and stopped. Scouts spilled squealing off the sides.

"Get Charley pronto," Claud said to Hoff. "And keep an eye peeled for Abby. This is her kind of stunt."

The sheriff summoned Charley with the bullhorn. "I don't think Abby can get here. Bluebonnet's sick. Saw it parked up at Grady's."

Claud looked beyond him and sighed. "Not anymore."

Abby's shabby blue station wagon came into view. It bucked around the final turn in fits and starts and jerked to a stop.

Abby bounced out, beaming, conferred briefly with a smoke-blackened Charley Calico, and took over the bullhorn.

Abigail Butterfield plus a bullhorn: They probably heard her in Denver.

"Mr. C. says you're to head for the woods on either side! Clear away the undergrowth, that'll keep the fire from spreading. One hour's work goes toward your community service badge!"

He couldn't walk over to Abby, he had to wait for her curiosity to bring her to him. He didn't think it would take long.

He watched the Scouts energetically hacking at the brambles and alders while Abby talked briefly to Lorelei, longer to the sheriff. Then it was his turn.

"They shouldn't set back regrowth more than half a dozen years, Abby." Claud wagged his head at the Scouts. "Decided to move the funeral meats here, did you?"

"Not me. Whoever set the fire." She waved at the road, which had begun to resemble a parking lot: Charley's Harley plus the motor scooters, abandoned every which way; Domenica's Jeep; Hoff's black-and-white; the Scout float. Farther away, the black sedan that had been Olga's, and Bluebonnet, back by the turn.

"Besides, coffee and sandwiches are always welcome. Here, Duncan, let me give you a hand."

"Domenica's got it."

Claud had to admit they were perfectly safe; except for the lingering acrid smoke, the fire was mostly embers. They propped the coffee urn more or less stably on the trunk of Hoff's car. Soon the smell of coffee competed with the smoke, and the firefighters began to straggle up toward the road.

Samson was right. Domenica always pitched in, whether it was entertaining the kids for Abby or here, serenely stacking up paper cups and pouring coffee while Duncan slapped meat loaf and ham between thick slabs of bread. She probably even filled a cup for Greco.

Maybe she didn't recognize him; one sweaty, smudged, slump-shouldered volunteer looked pretty much like the next.

Not to Blue. He sorted out Barney and nudged him toward Domenica's Jeep, where Lorelei leaned back limply in the passenger seat. Claud thought of his first sight of her, the magnificent tangled hair and heavy silk clothes. Now she had Doris Day platinum, shorter than the top of a dandelion. In the skinny jeans she looked about fourteen.

Barney swung himself under the roll bar to the driver's seat. Claud hitched himself along the hood of Hoff's car to where he could launch his weight, one-legged, over to the Jeep's open back.

"You surely earned your inheritance today, Lorelei. Too bad you won't get to claim it."

She looked at the rubble of the cabin and back to them. "And my apartment in New York. Not to mention my files, all my clothes—" She tried to shrug and winced instead. She gave a watery chuckle.

Too close to hysteria for Claud's comfort. He said quickly, "I don't know about your stuff in New York, but Bandit had every kind of insurance known to man. You can rebuild."

Barney's smile was white in his blackened face. "Makes it yours. Not his."

She sighed. "Maybe it's better just to abandon it. Barney, you know I can't—"

Her voice dropped to a bedroom-soft murmur that a polite man would have ignored. Claud listened shamelessly.

"You know I could never come and live here."

"Of course you couldn't."

"But, Barney, you could never live in New York."

His mouth curved. "Make up your mind, Muldoon. Afraid I won't let you go or afraid I will?"

She looked at him uncertainly. He shook her gently, not with anger, with the frustration of a man for whom words were the last resort. Finally he seemed to find satisfactory ones.

"Muldoon, I got no need for an everyday woman."

Claud knew what he meant, but did she? When had she had a chance to hear Banjo Man's song?

"And you got no need for an everyday man."

She had heard it someplace; the expression that took over her face made Claud think of fraternity-house sofas and backseats of cars, couplings too urgent for a civilized time and place. No, not fourteen.

Barney McFaul gave his rare, body-shaking laugh. "You

look like somebody just handed you a bowl of whipped cream, Muldoon."

"No, no. Champagne. Champagne at midnight!"

"Couple of months, you'll need to come back here to get the cabin started up again."

"You'll bring the champagne?"

Barney wrapped himself around Lorelei Muldoon, stirring up enough hormones to make her forget any amount of pain. "I *am* the champagne, Muldoon."

Even Claud had to shift and look away. Which was the only reason he spotted the other eavesdropper, whose extra large grin identified him at once as Greco.

Greco nodded toward the two bodies laid out neatly beside the road.

"I know the woman is Olga Finaldo," he said. "The other one—the one you called Fenton—who's he?"

"Her nephew, if I can trust my Spanish."

Greco looked from one body to the other. "So she was killed by her own nephew? Why?"

"A family feud, maybe? And Bandit got in the way somehow. I suppose we'll never really know."

"Senator Colman, killed by his wife's best friend." Greco all but smacked his lips. This wasn't idle gossip to him, he was taking notes for a story. Dream on, buster. "I wonder if it'll affect her bid to become senator."

"Watch your language! A senator's wife, best friend of a decorator? By tonight, they'll be just nodding acquaintances, wouldn't you say, Hoff?"

The sheriff cleared his throat noncommittally.

"But she won't be able to stay in Washington, not with Bandit giving away the condo right out from under her. My guess is she'll decide to make herself useful to the governor, what do you think?"

"And he won't understand until it's too late!"

Claud didn't know whose voice that was, but he didn't care; the story was turning into local gossip. No use to Greco or *Sloane's*.

"But then who'll be senator?" Greco asked. "You, Mr. Willetts?"

"Dad," Barney said.

Barney and Lorelei, the business between them settled, were tuning back in again.

"Is that a fact," Claud said.

Royal (Buck) McFaul, a senator. He liked it. The little man with the big pink car and the big gray dog up against all of Bogwash . . . Claud could find it in his heart to pity Congress.

"When did that happen?" Greco asked. He was patting his shirtfront. For pencil and paper? Did he have a recorder on him?

"The governor asked him this morning. At the service."

"Before any of this came out?" Claud shook his head in admiration. "Sometimes lucky is better than smart."

"Tell the governor to make you a commissioner on the tax review board instead." It was Lorelei Muldoon, snug in the crook of Barney's arm.

Claud turned toward her along with everybody else. She shrank back, startled, at the attention.

"Now, there's an idea," Neiderhoffer said. "If the biggest fox was in the henhouse, maybe he'd spot any other fox coming or going. If Larsen offered, would you take it?"

"Sounds too much like work to me."

"You don't have much choice, do you?" Lorelei asked.

Claud looked sharply at her. What was she talking about? It was so clear to her that she assumed he saw it too.

"What exactly do you mean, Lorelei?" Abby asked.

She looked over at Claud, as if for permission. He shrugged. He couldn't find a loophole until he identified the problem.

"Fred's bequest was ten percent above your best year, wasn't it? Everybody says you're a wizard at hiding income to avoid taxes. But any money you hid can't be used as a basis for the bequest, can it?"

It sounded even worse out loud. "You've been breathing too much of that smoke, Lorelei."

"So if you want to refile past returns with minimum penalties, you'd better be on the review board, don't you think?"

A grin ran around the scattered group like a rumor.

Neiderhoffer pulled urgently at the ends of his mustache. "I don't know as Governor Larsen is subtle enough to think of that for himself. Do you, Abby?"

"I'll find a way to bring it up." Her voice, like the sheriff's, trembled over laughter.

This was a higher price than Claud was ready to pay for keeping the conversation local.

And it didn't even work. Greco was hovering over the bodies again, and now he had everyone's attention.

"Mr. Willetts here says the senator was just an innocent bystander in a family feud," Greco said to Lorelei. "You were here too. Was that your impression?"

Lorelei looked over at Claud, shrugged, and winced. "Barney—"

"We won't wait any longer, Muldoon."

Gently but surely over the gravel ruts, the Jeep took Lorelei out of range.

"Is that what you thought?"

Claud said, louder than he needed to, "You're determined to write that story, aren't you, Greco?"

"Better me than someone you don't—"

This time Claud pitched his voice to carry to the coffee urn. "Is that why you listened in on us yesterday, at Samson's office?"

Domenica Gaylord pivoted. Her gaze on Greco became very intent.

"That was just—"

"Why didn't you just set up a wiretap in the room? Or did you do that too?"

Over the reporter's shoulder Claud watched Domenica stalk down the road toward him, a walking anatomy lesson, one perfect hip bunching while the other lengthened, then the first one stretching . . .

Maybe the smoke really was getting to him.

She touched down behind Greco like a tornado, grabbing at his shirt before he realized she was there, and came up with a miniature recorder.

Greco's effort to speak calmly hurt Claud just to watch. "What do you think you're doing?"

She fished out the tiny cassette, clawed at it, and loops of tape showered them like confetti. "What does it look like?"

"Domenica, that was not a good idea." The loose-limbed Greco looked as if he would fly apart at the joints. "Sicilians have had generations of genetic programming for revenge."

"If you're as clever as you think you are, mister, you'll get out of here before I think of something else. Like your manuscript. Is it in the Jeep? Back at my place?"

"Damn it, Domenica, I never tried to hide that I was a reporter. Why get pissed—excuse me, Reverend—about it now?"

"You used me. You used my dad. You stole my Jeep. All to make a story out of my friends—"

"What you mean is, I'm doing my job. Despite your charms."

Eyes alight, Domenica launched herself. An even match: Greco's arms were longer, but Domenica was faster and probably stronger. Claud leaned himself across Abby to keep her from interfering.

Greco broke free and bolted. He yanked Charley Calico's Harley upright, gave it a mighty kick, and was gone.

Domenica leaped up into the cab of the Scout float. There

was no room to turn, but she didn't hesitate. She backed at top speed, gravel spewing up like water. Firefighters scattered. She spun the truck in a two-wheeled U-turn and took off again facing forward.

Part of him regretted making such shameless use of Domenica, but much more of him sighed with the satisfaction. That really was the last thing.

See ya, fella.

Claud watched them around the turn.

"If I was still allowed to be a betting man, Reverend, I'd give you two to one on Domenica. Four to one that story will never appear."

"Why does that matter so much, Claud?"

Abby's blue gaze was like a drill.

"As though you haven't been trying to squash it too."

She shook her head. "Only to keep Lorelei safe. And then only until after the funeral. But you—you seem to think you can hide it forever."

"Light-headed from loss of blood, no doubt," he said pathetically. "Like poor Lorelei. If I could ask you to take *me* along to Demersville Memorial—"

"Bluebonnet died. You saw her."

"You never know, give it a whirl."

Abby stared at him suspiciously before darting down the road.

He said to the sheriff, "When the ambulance comes, Hoff, you can use it to take those two to the morgue."

Neiderhoffer looked as tired as if a dead Olga Finaldo represented a problem instead of a solution. "They'll bring us right up to capacity, Gang. At least we know who these two are. They won't be with us long."

"Maybe whoever comes to claim them will know who the other one is, the one with the diamond tooth."

"Knowing is one thing. Admitting to it is a different thing."

Claud nodded. "Turn Jimmy loose on it. That'll keep it back there in Washington."

Hoff and Elmo combined to ease Claud into Bluebonnet's passenger seat. Pushed all the way back, his legs weren't too jammed.

Give credit where credit was due; Abby waited a good mile before the inquisition resumed. "Now, Claud. Tell me why you're doing what you're doing."

He had known this would be the price for his ride to the hospital. "It didn't occur to you that I'm trying to protect Bandit's good name?"

"If you're using him to hide behind, you must be feeling better than I thought."

Was he? The feeling of Bandit as part of himself, the other half of his inner conversations—that was gone. There probably wasn't room for more than one friend like that in a lifetime. The man himself had passed over the horizon and out of sight.

"Maybe I'm just toying with people's lives again."

"Claud, Lorelei sent her dad everything she found. If you don't give me a straight answer, I'll get a copy and send it to Greco. And Agent Fineman."

"You wouldn't."

Abby sighed. "No, I wouldn't. But I'll think of something you'll dislike just as much."

When Abby was set on something, her stubbornness was biblical.

"You first, then. What you said about Bandit and me? That night in the bank?"

"That you were the only person he cared about?"

"Why say it just then? You're fighting tooth and nail, and then you turn and pour a boat of butter over me—"

"That was when it hit me, in the bank. That the only one of us who could stop you was *you*. Once you started thinking about how much you had cared about each other, you wouldn't have any more room for revenge."

"How can you say that, when you just saw me sic Domenica on—"

Abby ignored that. "Your turn."

Bluebonnet came out of the last stand of pines into sunlight. It was still early afternoon. The valley unrolled in front of them. Claud could see all the way across to his beloved Coulees and the mountains above them, purple with the distance. He looked back at Abby, her body braced in the effort to listen.

People would believe anything of him, he had said to Olga Finaldo. Even, occasionally, the truth?

He could always blame it on all the smoke he had inhaled.

"Remember what Bandit said in his will? About saving Merciful Valley if it was threatened?" Claud cleared his throat loudly. "Abby, I break out in a sweat when I think how close Olga Finaldo came to making this work. And Lorelei says she wasn't even that big a crook. Think I want somebody else to hear about what she did? Somebody with real firepower?"

Abby's forehead puckered in her effort to understand. "You're appointing yourself vigilante for the valley, is that it?"

"Say, godfather."

"Lots of people come here, Claud. They bring their worst as well as their best. You won't be able to stop that."

"Here in Merciful Valley, Reverend? Want to bet?"